MW00353634

Advance Praise

"Consistently the best of the annual award volumes in the genre – and this year is the most boundless, reaping "national flash fiction days" across the globe and across time, from small historical fictions to an Akutagawa classic to experiments with every form. A who's who of authors, presses, and journals, Best Small Fictions is the one book you should buy in the genre this year if you could buy only one."
  - Robert Shapard, co-editor *Flash Fiction International*

"This is an excellent selection of flash fiction from expert practitioners at the top of their game. The works selected here demonstrate the power of this extremely short form, each tiny piece of text leaving an imprint on the reader much bigger than its original size. At times they appear to work together with the others, forming a single constellation of beauty and stillness."
  - David Gaffney, author of *All the Places I've Ever Lived* and *Sawn-Off Tales*

"Brilliant, incendiary, incandescent, these tiny stories capture worlds both intimate and universal. Give this book to anyone who says flash fiction doesn't go deep. This newest volume of Best Small Fictions demonstrates once and for all that flash fiction writers are the Ginger Rogers of the literary world, accomplishing all that novelists and short story writers do, only backwards and in high heels."
  - Kathy Fish, author of *Wild Life: Collected Works*

"An outstanding collection. From a newly translated piece by Akatugawa, to my mind one of the greatest story writers of all time, to current favorites like Carmen Machado and Jacob Appel and many others I needed to know and now do this book has remarkable range. And is proof, if we needed it, that the more compact the force, the more powerful the blow."
  - Peter Orner, author of *MaggieBrown & Others*

The Best Small Fictions

2019

Nathan Leslie | Series Editor

Rilla Askew | Guest Editor

Michelle Elvy | Assistant Editor

SONDER PRESS

Sonder Press
New York
www.thesonderpress.com

© 2019 Nathan Leslie
All rights of this collected work are reserved. No portion of this collected work, in part or in whole, may be used or reproduced in any manner without the explicit permission of the publisher, Sonder Press, excepting brief quotations used within critical articles or reviews.

All rights of the individual works published herein are reserved and copyrighted by thier respective authors. Credit for the original prublication of each story appears alongside them. No individual work may be used or reproduced without the excplicit permission of the author, or of the agencies, writers, and publishers listed below.

ISBN 978-0-9997501-5-5

First U.S. Edition 2019
Printed in the USA

"On the Train to Stavanger" by Lydia Davis. Copyright © 2018 by Lydia Davis. First appeared in *F(r)iction #11*. Reprinted with the permission of Lydia Davis and Denise Shannon Literary Agency, Inc.

"Why Brother Stayed Away" by Ann Beattie. Copyright © Ann Beattie 2018.

"My Mother is a Fish" is from the book *Days of Awe* by A.M. Homes. Copyright © 2018 by A.M. Homes. Published by arrangement with Viking, a division of Penguin Random House LLC.

"The Forgotten Story" first appeared in *Five Points*, Vol, I, No, 3, December, 2016; *Fine, Fine, Fine, Fine* (McSweeney's, 2016); *The Collected Stories of Diane Williams* (Soho Press, 2018). Reprinted by permissions of Diane Williams.

Best Small Fictions Founding Series Editor: Tara Lynn Masih.

Cover Design by Chad Miller
Distribution via Ingram

The Best Small Fictions 2019

2019

UNCORRECTED PAGE PROOFS

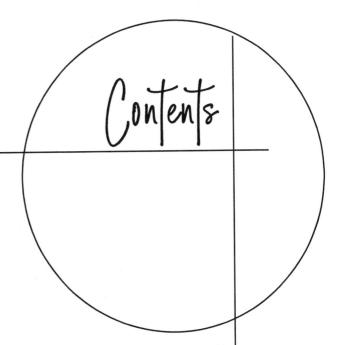

Contents

Spotlighted Journals

Nathan Leslie

An Introduction

YOU HOLD *BEST SMALL Fictions* 2019 in your hands, dear reader—but what, exactly, are these small fictions, and why are they the best? It is difficult, if not impossible, to offer accurate generalities about small fictions. One might say they are short, very short—yes, this is (mostly) true. One might say they offer a focused singularity rarely presented in a short story, novella or novel—also (mostly) true. One might say small fictions bring a poetic attention to language not necessarily present in longer forms. Yes, perhaps. But beyond these fairly obvious insights I cannot stand with two feet on the ground and say, "Here, this is a perfect, shining example of what we like to call good small fiction." The most precise way, perhaps, to characterize small fictions is to say that they defy thumb-nail categorization. Diversity of form, content and approach are essential traits of the best small fictions.

Thus: *Best Small Fictions* 2019.

Within these pages each work encapsulates a character, a voice, an image. This year, as in previous years of the series, we see new writers alongside experienced writers. I have especially noticed that authors who have not necessarily focused on small fictions before are now dabbling the form. I, for one, find this refreshing and exciting. It is not the case that small fictions are just now having a "moment"; this interest in small fictions transcends trendy dilettantism. Because small fictions are, in a sense, liberated from the shackles of a full narrative, they get at a certain kind of "truth" that short stories cannot. The almost post-narrative quality of small fictions offers something short stories, for instance, cannot; they crystalize something about our world—and something exceptional in the resourceful writerly imagination.

In this latest iteration of *Best Small Fictions*, the diversity of voices represents an expanded internationalism. *Best Small Fictions* 2019 catalogues small fictions not just from the United States but also, notably, from all over the world: Africa, Central America, South America, the Caribbean,

Canada, Europe, the Middle-East, Asia and New Zealand, as well as from the Pacific Rim islands.

In a word: *Best Small Fictions* 2019 is extensive. This is a hefty anthology. Its heft indicates, we believe, the current expansive quality of the small fictions universe. Small fictions are not composed by a small community; small fictions are composed by the writing world at large. The 2019 *Best Small Fictions* anthology is the most comprehensive annual anthology. This mirrors reality: with so many outstanding writers taking up their small fictions pens, the writing world is experiencing a small fictions enlargement.

A further change in the series, necessitated by its expanded view, is the removal of lists of semi-finalists and finalists. As *Best Small Fictions* experienced a change in leadership and a team overhaul (with the exception of the senior general advisory board), we decided to offer inclusion in the anthology to a greater number of authors. We have officially moved away from the paradigm of a limited number of "winning" stories included each year to an anthology model that more generally represents the wealth of great work being published. It is an important distinction worth noting.

Even so, we were not able to include more than a small percentage of the terrific small fictions published this year. There are many deserving authors whose work was not accepted for the 2019 anthology. With reading in the thousands, we simply had to choose a representation of the form and pack it into these pages.

Another expansion in this volume: *Best Small Fictions* 2019 features a super-sized spotlight section, with five literary journals and ten stories. The journals were chosen by the editing team; the stories were chosen by Guest Editor Rilla Askew, whose selections represent the pinnacle of what small fictions can achieve. As for the spotlighted journals—*AFREADA, Cha: An Asian Literary Journal, Conjunctions, matchbook and New Flash Fiction Review*—they were selected because of the exceptional work published in their pages in 2018.

A note about nominations and selections, about fairness and transparency. House policy is that no author/editor serving on the editorial boards or involved with nominating or advising in any capacity may have work published within the pages of *Best Small Fictions*. Works from the pages of literary journals edited by board members and advisors, however, were considered for this year's anthology. Nominations came from editors and agents, as well as consulting editors, general advisory board members, senior general advisory board members and the assistant editor and series editor (yours truly). For the selection of works, the series editor and assistant editor were responsible, with guidance by the general advisory board and consulting editors. Rilla Askew, the 2019 guest editor, selected the spotlighted works after going through the stories with a fine-toothed comb.

A huge thank you goes out to the general advisory board and the senior advisory board, specifically to Jen Michalski, Charles Rammelkamp, Jenny Drummey, Tyrese Coleman and Ryan

Ridge. I would also like to thank editorial rock star, Robert Shapard (from *BSF*'s senior advisory board), for both digital guidance and tips at key moments in the process. We also count ourselves as very lucky to have had two interns— Gisele Gehre Bomfim and Kevin Gray—who frequently went above and beyond the call of duty. I would also like to take a moment thank *BSF* founding editor Tara Masih, who sought me out and believed in me from the outset. Thank you, also, to Sherrie Flick, who offered some very helpful advice along the way. To everyone who has had a hand in supporting the 2019 volume: we could not have done it without you.

I must also profusely thank Michelle Elvy, who was a stalwart assistant editor from day one, who provided not only needed assistance, but also guidance and counsel. She stuck by me from the beginning, when she was even perhaps unsure of my vision for *Best Small Fictions*. Michelle has some serious street cred as an editor in her own right and her experience lent a stabilizing force to this year's anthology.

Finally, I would like to thank Rilla Askew—what a pleasure to work with such a tremendous writer. Even during our transition in the early months, when the series was in the midst of changing publishers and publishing models, Rilla was unfazed. Her reading was prompt, thorough and insightful. I could not have asked for a better, more responsive guest editor than Rilla Askew.

As for me, reading and considering work for *Best Small Fictions* 2019 has been a delight. Though I have co-edited other anthologies and edited fiction for a number of literary magazines, *Best Small Fictions* is my first genre-specific anthology of this magnitude. There have been blips and bumps along the way; mistakes were made—how could they not be? But the outcome speaks for itself, and I'm excited to share this book with you.

Dear reader, we believe you will have much to revel in within these pages. This year's *Best Small Fictions* represents one hundred and forty six of the very best stories published from ninety-three different literary journals, presses and magazines. It's a jam-packed supersized variety pack. I hope you will enjoy reading it as much as I have enjoyed putting it together.

Nathan Leslie
Series Editor, *Best Small Fictions*
Spring, 2019

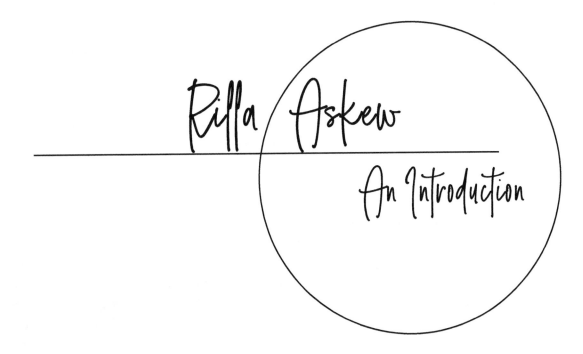

Rilla Askew

An Introduction

THESE MICROBURSTS OF FICTION seem acutely expressive of our compressed, Twitter-driven age. They distill story to its essence. They eschew many of the traditional tools of fiction. There may be no dialogue, or only dialogue; setting is implied, not rendered; characterization arises through voice alone, or flat narrative, or clever elision. Description is minimal. And as for action, there may be none. They are dystopian, magical, fablelike: hellish fairy tales, reimagined histories, speculative futures. They are almost uniformly dark, often violent, frequently transgressive. They stretch form. They disguise themselves as something other than story. They tell again and again of displacement, urgency, bad fathers, bad mothers, violence against girls and women, violence within all of us. Cumulatively they paint a troubling portrait of our age, and, for all their fabulism, an accurate one. And yet...

And yet.

These small fictions do what good fiction has always done: render the human heart in conflict with itself, as Faulkner long ago said, and most certainly the human heart in conflict with others. We have yearning here, and disgust, love and hatred, greed and envy, indeed all the seven deadly sins, and a few unspeakable others. We even sense, in some of these tales, glimpses of redemption.

In choosing ten stories to spotlight at the beginning of this excellent collection I've relied most on story. These ten stayed with me (as did many others, which are included in the feast-in- small-bites that comprises the body of this book), and achieved, at first reading, what *story* does: gave me a sense of revelation, layers of meaning beneath the words, the wonder, hunger, and powerlessness of being human, and an abiding notion that, after this moment, nothing will ever be the same. I've sought also to give a sampling of the multiplicity of styles, forms, voices, cultures, realities in the collection as a whole. The intrepid series editor, Nathan

Leslie, and his tireless assistant editor, Michelle Elvy, have drawn from literary sources around the world. I've tried to touch on a few of the recurring themes I gleaned as I read: dispossession, immigration, cultural and sexual violence, lost loves, lost lives, end-of-the-world anarchy.

Thus, Hiwat Adilow gives us the full life of an abused everywoman, with powerful vocal resonance, layer upon layer of prevarication, and an acute punch at the end—all miraculously contained in one brief paragraph. Dionne Irving Bremyer renders the vast sensory-rich story of island immigrants in a cold American landscape through the particularities of one shop girl's work life. Time travel and lost love marry in R. M. Cooper's delightful hermit-crab-disguised fiction (to repurpose Brenda Miller's and Suzanne Paolo's term), "Emergency Instructions." We see a borderland world we recognize and yet hope never to witness in Elisa Lunda-Ady's hauntingly beautiful, brutal rendering of the Aztec god Huitzilopochtli's demands in "Ninas del Fuego." A 21st century existentialist hell arises in Kristine Ong Muslim's "The Malingerers," and yet we recognize this place too: a photo booth that "tunnels all the way down," reflecting only the self to the blind and narcissistic self—an apt eternity for our self-absorbed, selfie-obsessed age.

Portraits of human pain—to my mind, a specifically male outsider type of pain—and grief, and torment, are exquisitely rendered in Christopher Gonzalez's "Dress Yourself" and Keith Woodruff's "Dog as Battlefield." The voices here are lyrical and ruthless, the narratives arc beautifully, succinctly, as the best stories do, and at the last line deliver a gut punch, leaving behind an aftermath of disturbance and sorrow. The same with Carmen Maria Machado's "Mary When You Follow Her," wherein, in a glorious one-sentence voice-driven deluge, Machado gives us Time and Place, Before and After, what women fear, long for, endure, and resist, and an indictment of the unacknowledged shame, worldwide, of multitudes of missing and murdered women. Michael Martone uses form and voice and exquisitely distilled history to cause us to see again, see for the first time, an America we thought we knew, an age of invention and discovery when the American Midwest was the epitome of the nation's notion of itself, and most Americans still thought they were the good guys.

By a narratively perfect alphabetical accident, Rewa Zeinati's powerful "What We Will Tell" ends the spotlighted section: her voice is prophetic and achingly real; she illuminates what has been done and will be done, our relentlessly selfish past and increasingly hopeless future, every war zone, every dying planet, every murdered mother/child/landscape, how we surrender to helplessness, justify our actions and inactions, how we'll mourn our lost world and explain ourselves to our children's children's children.

...and what, after all, *will* we tell them?

Rilla Askew
Guest Editor, *Best Small Fictions*
Spring, 2019

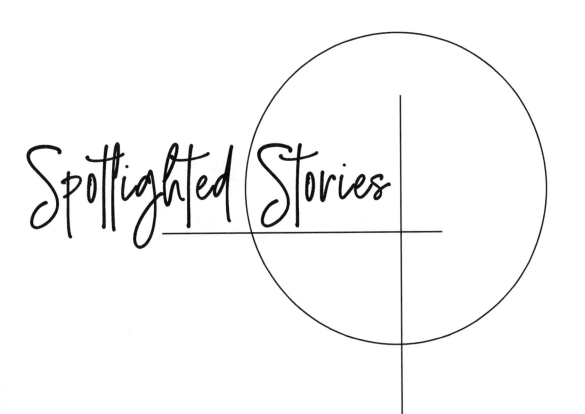

Spotlighted Stories

and when i couldn't leave i lied

From Brunel International Poetry Prize (2018)

Hiwot Adilow

I'M OKAY I'M FINE i promise it's just a little bruise from a clumsy bump i ran into a door i fell i jumped in front of his hand it was my fault i did it to myself i looked him in the eye and he got scared of me i'm fine there's nothing wrong i'm safe and sound you hear him breathing behind me that means he's not mad what do you mean i sound sad this is just the tempo fresh love takes i'm a little restless that's the only reason i run some nights i knock on your door because i miss you not cause i'm scared who told you that who said i was barefoot in the black night fleeing like a wench you know that's just gossip i'd tell you if anything went wrong if there was anything to flinch about i'd flinch bitch i'm just cold that's the only reason i'm jumping you know we had to turn the heat off just to save a lil somethin to eat it's all money problems and that's what everyone here is worried about not just me why you so concerned about my man and me when you been in the house all weekend tellin me you fine you haven't moved in days callin me sick at least i have somebody to lay by me someone to say sorry when it hurts too much you just achin on your own judgin me i told you nothin's wrong that's just love and besides you don't know nothin bout that been by yourself your whole damn life wouldn't know the difference between a hickey and a hit mark i didn't mean to get mean with you it's just my feelings hurt i can't stand you lookin at me with those damp and wondersome eyes look like you been crying what you so sad about not like anybody hit you

---

Hiwot Adilow is co-winner of the 2018 Brunel International African Poetry Prize and author of the chapbook *In The House of My Father* (Two Sylvias Press, 2018). Her second chapbook, *Prodigal*

Daughter, will be published by Akashic Books as part of the New Generation African Poets series, edited by Kwame Dawes and Chris Abani. Hiwot's poems appear in *Callaloo, Vinyl,* and *The Breakbeat Poets Vol. 2: Black Girl Magic* (Haymarket Books, 2018). She received her BA from the University of Wisconsin-Madison as a member of the First Wave Hip Hop and Urban Arts Learning Community.

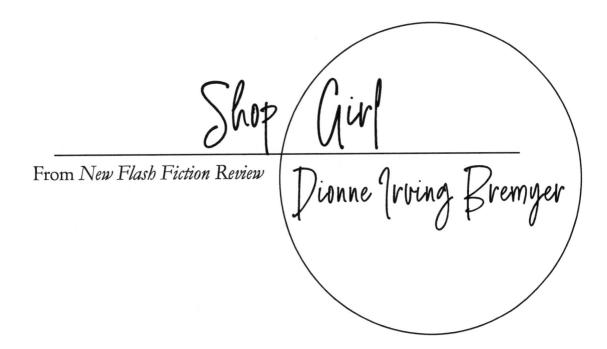

Shop Girl

From *New Flash Fiction Review*

Dionne Irving Bremyer

YOU WILL SPEND YOUR entire life selling — but this is the first time. So small, you barely reach the counter. You are given a stool. You are told if you work hard, there will be a reward. You are taught to make change. You are taught to make smiles at the customers. You are taught to cut yam, to chop pig feet, to take hot patties from the hotter oven. The burns and scrapes and cuts will last through adulthood, will last beyond death. Injury will always remind you of what it means to work.

And: *"We're gone help our people, help them right / Oh, Lord, help us tonight! / Cast away that evil spell / Throw some water in the well / And smile!"*

On Saturday morning, the shop is clotted with people from the Island, all there to buy oxtail, and pig feet, to take packages of tripe, leaking, wrapped in heavy butcher paper — and to argue and laugh, and laugh and argue. They'll lean toward bags of otaheiti apples, or chocho, or tins of Milo. If only you could inhale the coming future in which these foods will become fashionable, in which this education in butchery, in food and flavor, will twenty and more years later help you appear hip and cultured — exotic, even — to lighter-skinned friends in particular. You can't now know, but you will be the lonely one who understands how blood thickens stew, how marrow complicates flavor, how the perfect pepper in the bin needs to be found. Forget this work? No. Never. This work defines you, contains you. Allows you. But much later, your friends somehow think you spent your early years traveling — not, in fact, in the back room of a small shop inside a strip mall, listening to the high musical Bajans remind you that *Coward dog keep whole bone.* Listening to the Trinis insist, *better belly buss than good food waste.* And the Jamaicans, the Jamaicans, measuring out mutton with their eyes, asking, *Just a toops more fi make mi belly na cry fi hunga.* Floors always need sweeping, candies kept clean, not to eat. You dust shelves stocked with things you cannot imagine your friends at school eating: Guava jelly, tamarind paste, cock soup. There's always, always a cricket match on the small portable television, and everyone complaining about the gassed bananas and eating gizzada and bun and processed cheese that comes in a tin. How can you explain this, any of it? Your history with food, with work, the way they are fastened together? The way that you love and hate the shop equally?

Your parents don't understand the shame of Monday morning. Don't know what it means to have fish scales on your pink Keds, or what it means that your hair smells like brown stew chicken, or that your sandwich is corned beef and salad cream between two thick slices of hard dough bread, or that a boy tells you it looks like mashed brains so you look down and chew and chew and chew. You won't know for years that it tasted like home and empire.

And: *"Dancin' to the reggae rhythm / Oh, island in the sun"*

On Saturday you will hear – over and over again – It's so good to have the whole family here. Working. Over and over again – all day – you will hear it, thinking of other girls your age in ballet classes. Sleeping in. Shopping with their mothers. Settling into Saturday morning cartoons. And Bowls of Captain Crunch. You sweep floors, cut dasheen, and try to read when you can, waiting for the book to be snatched from your hands. *This shop is your story, your inheritance.* Over and over again – as you haul ten-pound bags of basmati, stack tins of coconut milk. *I'm glad you are doing it. Just like the Chinese. We need to be more like them.* You will remember *Oliver Twist*, which you read between snatches, and the workhouse and Fagin. And you can't imagine why someone won't come and save you, too. But you remember that these are your real parents, that these Saturdays are your real life. That this world and everything beyond it is yours, and not yours. You will always associate work with the coppery smell of animal blood and saw dust and blades that cut fish.

And: *"Miss lady whey Sonny bite yuh / Right deh, right deh, right deh"*

If you could, you'd squint and look into the future. Tell the customers – so much in love with your work, with your working – that the Chinese and everyone but them will own their Island one day. Hurt them. If you could, you would look down, fold your arms, suck your teeth, and tell them that you won't remember them fondly. You can't know if they will remember you with fondness either – or perhaps at all. You – the little girl, swinging with effortless precision, wielding that machete– the magic of it all. You close your eyes and the rest of you becomes the machete too. Cutting through their dreams, as they lie in bed, their bellies full. Will they remember the sound of the blade cutting meat, cutting bone, before it thuds home of the butcher's block? Will they remember who did the selling? Or will they only remember buying?

You will just remember the work.

Dionne Irving Bremyer is originally from Toronto, Ontario. Her work has appeared in *Boulevard Magazine*, *LitHub*, *Missouri Review*, and *New Delta Review*, among others. Her essay "Treading Water" was a notable essay in *Best American Essays 2017*, and she recently co-edited the collection *Breastfeeding & Culture: Discourses and Representations*. She has also received fellowships from the Voices of Our Nation Arts Foundation and Sewanee Writers' Conference. She is an associate professor at the University of West Georgia. She lives outside of Atlanta with her husband and son.

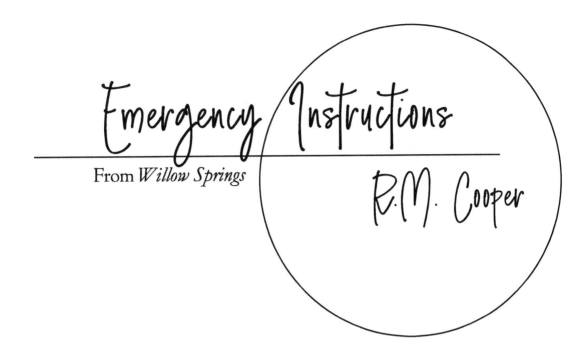

Emergency Instructions

From *Willow Springs*

R.M. Cooper

I. REMEMBER: YOU WILL NEVER convince them why you did it.

    A. Everyone believes hypotheticals about time machines righting wrongs.

        i. E.g. You should find/kill baby Hitler (you aren't a baby-killer) or snuff the match that started the Chicago fire (it's probably in the common interest that Chicago is no longer made of balsa wood).

        ii. There are things you don't have the stomach for, and there are things that happen for a reason, and history is filled with both of them.

    B. Everyone wants/believes in time travel.

        i. In a recent survey asking, *What future technology are you most looking forward to?* 85% answered C.) *Time Travel*.

            I. Second was B.) *Cure for Disease* (9%).

            2. A.) *Flying Cars* and D.) *Space Travel* combined for less than 6%.

        ii. Time travel in application only works once.

            I. Not once per machine. Not once per person. *Once*, per keeping space/time from folding into itself like an existence-crushing origami swan (discounting multiple realities).

            2. This is problematic (see I. - A & B).

II. Set the date to 4:13 PM, May 4, 1977, and leave it.

III. Don't get lost in the novelty.

    A. In addition to everyone else on a ball field, you will see Benny Jennings in left field (dead, car accident, '83), Floyd Gilmore at shortstop (dead, throat cancer, '12) and your brother-in-law Connor pitching (not speaking, Christmas, '97).

        i. The moment will change if you try and warn Benny or Floyd about their

death(s). Ditto for Connor (who was a prick before and after '97; if it wasn't the chocolate pudding, it would've been something else).

    ii. If you change anything, you might miss Tess.

  B. Don't *do* anything.

    i. Don't bury a 2029 quarter in the dirt for the sake of scientific masturbation.

    ii. Don't try to talk to your past-self and cause a paradox-aneurism in nine-year-old you.

    iii. Mathematics says nothing about the divergence of reality(ies).

  C. Act like you've been here before. (You have.)

IV. Observe.

  A. After finding your clothes in the luggage compartment:

    i. Move quickly.

      1. It's a five minute jog between the garage and ballpark.

      2. This will leave you twenty-five minutes at the park to catch Tess.

    ii. Find somewhere secluded with a view behind first.

      1. Tess will emerge from the home dugout to argue with Connor on the mound. (Five minutes later, the game will be called for rain.)

      2. From behind first, you'll have a good view of yourself at third.

    iii. Stay out of sight: The game was called once when a homeless man pissed over the right field fence, and Joey White was skittish ever since. (Your hanging about might draw attention.)

  B. Do's and Don'ts:

    i. Don't focus on Connor and Tess's argument. (Expect screaming and a few tears.)

    ii. Don't think about Tess in terms of the past/future. (Forget the night you spent together on the hood of your Ford; forget the day beneath the elms; forget your child staring up at you with her eyes; forget the months of Tess at the hospital; forget the tests; forget words like tumor(s), aggressive, genetic, inoperable; forget the sound of ventilators pumping air in and out of her; forget the way she felt in the end, already so weak that you couldn't feel when they turned off the machine.)

    iii. You only have twenty minutes; you can't have her again.

  C. Remember to look beyond Tess and Connor arguing. Focus on (young) you standing at third. Look at your furrowed brow. Look at the way you smack your glove impatiently. Listen to the edge in your voice when you yell, "Common, let's move this along." Watch the relief on your face when Connor and Tess go quiet. Watch your smile when Connor's kid sister leaves the mound. Watch the way you bend your knees and squint, anticipating the next pitch. Memorize that moment, the game, the pitch, you chasing a foul ball behind third. Remember how time once passed as if that girl in the dugout didn't mean a thing in the world to you.

R. M. Cooper's writing has appeared in dozens of publications, including *Baltimore Review, Best American Experimental Writing, Denver Quarterly, Fugue, Normal School, Redivider, Willow Springs,* and *Wisconsin Review* and has received awards and recognition from UC Berkeley and *American Short Fiction.* Cooper lives in the Colorado Front Range and is the managing editor of *Sequestrum.*

Dress Yourself

From *Split Lip Magazine*

Christopher Gonzalez

WATCH OUT FOR SHIRTS with horizontal stripes, Abuelita says, because you're too fat and it looks bad. Best to choose shirts with more slimming patterns. Vertical lines. Solid blacks, nothing lighter than gray. This shirt is O.K., she says, draping it over her ironing board, because the vertical lines pop out. They're brighter, so you should be fine. But how can you believe her? You've worn this shirt at least, what, forty-seven times now? You know how the fabric struggles to contain your body. You adjust and readjust yourself while wearing it, about eighty tugs and tucks an hour, but the vertical lines always wiggle and slant as they groove over your shoulders and slope down your back, the right and left-side patterns meeting at the base of a wide V. You've spotted this in tagged photos of yourself online, avoiding the comments every time just in case. Still, it's one of the better shirts you own.

And these, Abuelita says, moving onto your pants, these are so cheap. Look. She stretches them out and tries to match up the legs, but they are uneven. The seam should go here, she says, now holding them by the seat. Look. You lean forward to identify the seam, but all you see are wrinkles. Then she folds back one pant leg like a purse flap, exposing the crotch; what should be tan is disintegrating into a papier-mâché white. She rubs the faded fabric between two fingers and scratches at it with a chipped nail. One false move and they will rip. This wouldn't be the first time. Most of the pants you've owned have eventually split down the inseam, the gap widening to reveal the polka-dot print of your worn-out boxers.

You are frowning now, and when Abuelita raises her head to face you, her smile is limp. You feel ten again—short and stout and terrified. Back then, she dragged you into all the major department stores—J. C. Penney, Macy's, Kohl's, Sears—and would thrust shirts, pants, sweaters, bags of underwear, and bundles of socks into your arms. She forced you into fitting rooms and made you try on every item, sending you back in to triple check that the XXL graphic t-shirt didn't fall past your knees, like a frock. She tugged on the waistband of your husky jeans, inserting two fingers into the opening between your pelvis and the fabric. You never told her how much you hated the clothes, because she paid for every item. When she swiped the store credit card, her eyes warmed, and for a moment, in between leaving the store and slipping into the backseat of her car, you felt O.K. with pretending.

Now, she continues ironing and shaking her head. When you buy this bad material, she says, the pants fit too loose, right? She's pinching around her waist to demonstrate. I know, I know, she says, it's hard. You have to pay rent and buy groceries, pero, Papito, you need nice clothes, too.

Yes, you pay for rent and groceries, a monthly MetroCard, the Internet service you rely on to keep sane, and you hand over at least sixty bucks a week to Seamless for meals that leave your stomach and heart empty. You wish money were the issue. But no matter if you spend ten or thirty or seventy-five dollars on a single pair of pants, nothing will change. At the end of any given day, you will stand in the corner of your bedroom, your knees buckling as you peel the material from your swollen, sweaty legs. You will turn them inside out, raise them to your nose, and sniff the seat. You will pray that your irritated hemorrhoids have not leaked, have not left behind the ripe, coppery smell of blood and stool.

Finished with her ironing, Abuelita takes your chin in her loose-skinned hand. You will look so nice tomorrow, she says. So handsome. You say, Thank you. You say, I love you. You wait for her to leave the room. Once you hear the final creak of her footsteps going down the stairs, you slide off the bed and begin dressing yourself. The collar is still warm. The creases down your pant legs are impeccable. And yet, maybe Abuelita has a point: it's time for something new.

You drive to the nearest Walmart, alone. Once in the men's section, you pull collared shirts from round garment racks and reach into denim-packed shelves. You double-check each tag for a correct size. But the clothes you like and could maybe imagine yourself wearing weren't tailored for your build; your hands shake as you return every item. An hour of back-and-forth pacing passes. Your breathing thins. Eventually, you rush into an open fitting room with an assembled shirt-and-khakis combination. The process is tiring: buttoning and unbuttoning the shirt, stretching the pants over your legs, holding in your breath while fussing with the zipper. Finally, you stand fully dressed and sticky with sweat. Your eyes are shut. This is the part where you should face yourself in the mirror. You know this, it's so routine. But your eyes remain clamped. If you catch sight of your body spilling out of clothes too small or drowning in large, excess fabric, you will scream. You will, you will. You can feel it, waiting to rupture at the back of your throat. So: you undress yourself, with your eyes still closed, because even if the clothes look nice on you, even if you don't look half bad, how could you ever trust yourself to see the good?

Christopher Gonzalez serves as a fiction editor at *Barrelhouse* and a contributing editor at *Split Lip*. His stories appear or are forthcoming in a number of journals, including *Wasafiri*, *Third Point Press*, *Cosmonauts Avenue*, *Pithead Chapel*, and *The Acentos Review*. He was the recipient of the 2015 Ann E. Imbrie Prize for Excellence in Fiction Writing from Vassar College. Cleveland-raised, he now lives and writes in Brooklyn, NY and spends most of his free time on Twitter: @livesinpages. You can also find him online at www.chris-gonzalez.com. He's currently working on a collection of stories.

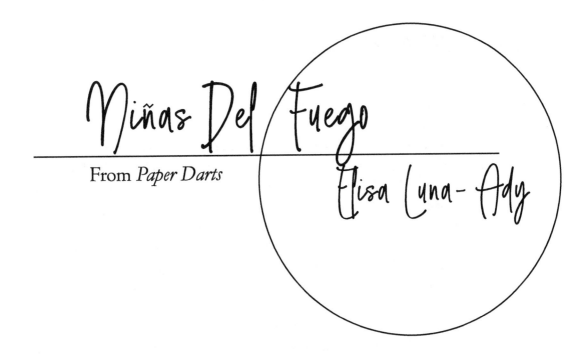

Niñas Del Fuego

From *Paper Darts*

Elisa Luna-Ady

MY SISTER AMMA USED to say the borderlands is the place brown girls go to die when they have no reason left to live. They give themselves up to the fence like a burnt offering, body crumpled at its teeth, and await capture. I read somewhere that some animals will commit suicide—suffocate themselves or stop eating altogether—to escape captivity. I think it's like that.

Eso, allá, es la boca del infierno, she'd say, pointing to the border fence in the far distance.

The mouth of hell. Then she'd go back to braiding my hair.

Once, when I was a girl, I watched a riot cop take Amma into his arms during a confrontation at the fence. She'd thrown a rock that landed and, in a fury, he abandoned his tear gas canister and scooped her up. She—older and wilier than me, black hair loosened down her back in a show of feminine maturity, in a dirty T-shirt with the sleeves slashed off—began to thrash like a wild fish. The crowd gathering went silent at the sound of her shrieks, everybody's voice but my own stilling.

Amma had a howl like la llorona. Everyone was always saying she'd end up walking the blackest body of water in our village for eternity after she died, forever lamenting the lost.

Whenever she wept, it felt like a seismic shift.

The riot cop tightened his grip and her keening grew in volume. It was like watching el carnicero through a window in the slaughterhouse. Despite the obvious suffering of the animal, we could not look away.

I, the younger sister, lurched forward as if in flight, our eyes meeting briefly, and thought: This is where I go to die. But Amma was the most clever in our village, and she slipped through the cop's arms just as suddenly as she'd been caught in them. She scuttled back into the crowd, cackling, skinny mosquito-bitten legs pounding asphalt, until she was once again environed by sweaty brown bodies.

I could see that this irritated the cop, but before my equilibrium settled, the crowd was roaring again and a rum bottle had found its way into my small bird hands. I looked down at it, confused, as the crush of bodies crawled closer.

"¡Tíralo! ¡Tíralo! ¡P'arriba!" the crowd chanted.

And, standing in the dying gold of a streetlamp that had beguiled an eclipse of moths, I launched the bottle into the air without another thought. It swung forward, landed, and burst into flames. The cop dropped to the floor, his body a long line of red.

La boca del infierno, I thought to myself as the crowd lifted me into the air. I sat suspended, watching the heat gorge.

This was all before the borderlands had a real name.

Tonight, the heart of Huitzilopochtli is burning and my sister Amma is dead.

Center city is teeming with riot cops. It's evening, half sunset, and the few mesquite trees left are lit up like a row of ugly candles. Our people clutch their saints close, send a silent prayer to the god of war that tonight might favor the nationless, and then we set fire to a gutted pig's head. It's ritual to watch the smoke rise and dissipate before a riot.

Two rail-thin boys to my left—Micho and Chalchi, I realize—lower their gas masks and take turns lugging dirty jugs of milk behind our makeshift barricade in preparation. A gnarled woman manning a kiosk to our right offers us free refreshments: a pack of Marlboros, matches, elotes asados, clean rags. Street vendors don't stop selling for storms, much less riots.

"Here is where los clandestinos wait to die, eh, Cipri?" Chalchi says in my direction, half his mouth curling as he slides a pack of cigarettes into his pocket. He's always poking fun at me for being a pessimist.

I ignore this and lower my mask.

"Ain't nobody dying tonight, carnal," Micho says. "No one 'cept a few pigs."

A chorus of snorting rises up in response to this, taunting, that quickly dissolves into laughter at the sight of hundreds of riot cops assembled along the border fence before us. Their helmets belie the revulsion held between each piece of their black armor. I know with certainty that they hate us. Behind them, thirty-seven paint-splattered shirts are displayed along the fence's barbed wire—one for each girl stolen in the last month.

My eyes find the fifth shirt down, a sleeveless white.

When I wonder why I fight, I remember each girl's face: upturned to the sun like lost pennies, bodies sterilized then charred, each limb a blackened river. Hundreds of immigrant girls lifted from their beds with none but the moon as witness. I remember their names and I do not weep. I remind myself: There is no flesh my fingers will not find and tear. No place exists beyond the distance my arm can throw, beyond the place my flame will eat.

I remind myself: There is no flesh my fingers will not find and tear.

Chalchi lets out a long whistle and the crowd of gas-masked rioters begins to clap and stomp at once. Their chanting rises up, tides my throat, and permeates the air as a bleeding song.

"¡P'arriba! ¡P'arriba! ¡P'arriba!"

My eyes find the girl closest to me and then I am hoisting her onto my shoulders. I recognize her by the long red curls—Lupe, the little thing I rescued just last week, right before they could sterilize her. She's tiny but fierce. Someone places a bottle in her hand and the chanting grows in volume.

"¡Tíralo! ¡Tíralo! ¡Tíralo!"

In Huitzilopochtli, it is tradition to let a small girl throw the first bottle. We call them niñas del fuego. They are our strongest and most vulnerable.

Lupe pulls her arm back, her round, vernal face determined, and hurls the bottle at the cops. It lands, then bursts.

Elisa Luna-Ady is a Mexican-American poet and writer from southern California. Her work has previously appeared or is forthcoming in wildness, The Blueshift Journal, Paper Darts, and elsewhere. She's a designated California Arts Scholar, a Scholastic Art & Writing Awards National Silver Medalist, a two-time *Pushcart Prize* nominee, a *Best New Poets* nominee, and a *Best of the Net* nominee.

Mary When You Follow Her

From *Virginia Quarterly Review*

Carmen Maria Machado

IN THE AUTUMN OF Maria's eighteenth year, the year that her beloved father—amateur coin collector, retired autoworker, lapsed Catholic—died silently of liver cancer three weeks after his diagnosis, and the autumn her favorite dog killed her favorite cat on the brown, crisped grass of their front lawn, and the cold came so early that the apples on the trees froze and fell like stones dropped from heaven, and the fifth local Dominican teenager in as many months disappeared while walking home from her minimum-wage, dead-end job, leaving behind a kid sister and an unfinished journal and a bedroom in her mother's house she'd never made enough to leave—deepening the community's collective paroxysm of anxiety, which made them yell at their daughters and give out abstruse and nonsensical advice about how to avoid being a victim and boosted the sales of pepper spray and Saint Anthony pendants, and also prompted no action from the police, who said that the girls were likely runaways—the same autumn she finally figured out how to give herself an orgasm, right after the summer when she broke up with her boyfriend of two years, Ira, who had for their entire relationship been attempting to make her come with the grim resolve of a pioneer woman churning butter and failing 100 percent of the time, and she got herself one of those minimum-wage, dead-end jobs because she was saving for a bus ticket to Chicago, and she was finally hired at Phil's Outlet, where she folded cheap T-shirts and shelved overstock home goods and learned quickly to evade Phil's hands (which always seemed to brush against her body when the two of them passed each other in the bowels of the store), which is also the same autumn that Maria had started taking a shortcut home at night—in spite of her mother's warnings—through the unlit parking lot of the bankrupt, half-gutted strip mall where she'd once bought her coppery quinceañera dress with its magnificent, animal flounce, and listened to the leaves rasping over the pavement and watched an owl dismember a mouse in the shadows and then slipped her Walk-man's headphones over her ears even though her mother had warned her that music would conceal an attacker's approaching footsteps, and felt her ponytail bouncing against the back of her neck even though her mother had warned her that a ponytail was little more than a handle for rapists, and felt thrilled to her trembling core much in the same way she felt when her orgasms ebbed away, and after she had gone to a party held in a foreclosed house and drank deeply of syrupy, mysterious liquids in paper cups and talked about the missing girls with Dolores and Perdita, whose own parents had forbidden them to walk alone or go out at night, and after her mother's shitty station wagon broke down twenty miles away from home when she'd been on an errand to refill her brother's asthma medication and she had to hitchhike back in the passenger seat of an 18-wheeler while chatting manically to fill the dangerous silence, and after she went home with a coworker who sort of looked like Ira and smelled a bit like him too (because even though Ira'd been bad at sex and kissing and so many other things besides, she'd found his presence comforting and stable and missed him a little), and after that coworker turned out to have a foot fetish and wanted to rub his erect dick all over Maria's boots and Maria let him because she didn't know what would happen if she didn't, and after she tried to clean the faux leather with fallen leaves in that unlit parking lot of the bankrupt, half-gutted strip mall and while hunched over her project heard the sound of someone walking toward her with exquisite patience and so she didn't look back but bolted like a deer and in her socks, leaving her boots (her favorite pair!) behind, and after Perdita showed up at her front door on a Sunday morning because Dolores had gone missing, too, and they'd searched and searched and eventually found Dolores's keys in a ditch next to the road next to the elementary school but never anything else, and after Phil handed her a paycheck with his other hand shoved deeply into his pocket and didn't let go right away when she tried to take the envelope, and after Maria told him to go fuck himself and he shoved her against the OSHA poster and called her a bitch and told her he'd let her keep her job under one condition, and after she ran home through the unlit parking lot of the bankrupt, half-gutted strip mall and looked up as she ran hoping to see a cathedral of stars but instead just saw a terrible darkness, and after she snapped at her mother that she was fine and collapsed in her bedroom wheezing and crying and then overturned her father's old cigar box and counted her money, but months before a white girl from a rich neighborhood also disappeared and suddenly her pale, thin-lipped face was fluttering like a flag of surrender on every telephone pole and the police were combing through the snarled streets in full force and Maria's mother said that she wished Maria was around to see them finally doing their jobs, and before the town was buried under four feet of snow, which no one could deny gave them a strange sense of relief, a sense that time's terrible, ticking advancement had been stilled for a spell, and before a snowplow operator accidentally uncovered the shallow graves and their bodies near the unlit parking lot of the bankrupt, half-gutted strip mall, and before they arrested the high school chemistry teacher and the community demanded answers, and before they learned that they would never, ever get them, Maria left a note for her mother on the fridge telling her that she loved her and was sorry and missed her already, that Papa was watching out for her and she'd be all right and she'd write when she got there, and as she sat on the bus to Chicago, her backpack in her lap and her rosary coiled in her coat pocket and the windows smeared with someone else's face grease, she imagined that the missing girls were all living in the city in brick row houses on a single block, a well-lit block with gardens and parks and cafés and a sidewalk, where they all laughed and made art and dated and dined and fucked and danced and aged and married and had children, and at night told stories to each other about the last, long-ago time they'd truly been afraid.

Carmen Maria Machado's debut story collection, *Her Body and Other Parties*, was a finalist for the National Book Award, the Kirkus Prize, LA Times Book Prize Art Seidenbaum Award, the World Fantasy Award, the Dylan Thomas Prize, the PEN/Robert W. Bingham Prize, and the winner of the Bard Fiction Prize, a Lambda Literary Award, the Brooklyn Public Library Literature Prize, a Shirley Jackson Award, and the National Book Critics Circle's John Leonard Prize. Her essays, fiction, and criticism have appeared in the *New Yorker*, the *New York Times*, *Granta*, *Harper's Bazaar*, *Tin House*, *McSweeney's*, *Vogue*, *Best American Science Fiction & Fantasy*, and elsewhere.

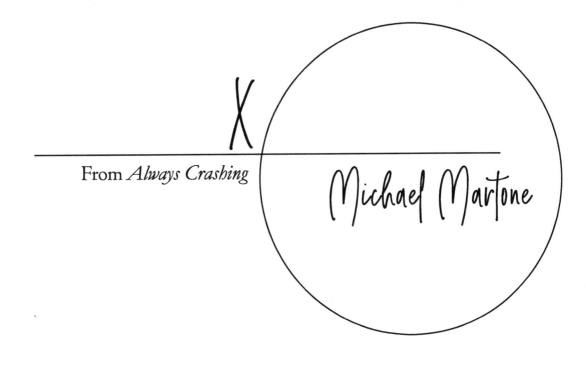

From *Always Crashing*

Michael Martone

IN 1913, GIDEON SUNDBACK, working as head designer for the Fastener Manufacturing and Machine Company in Meadville, Pennsylvania, invented the modern zipper. The name "zipper," however, was trademarked by B.F. Goodrich Company, which coined the term when it added the fastener to its rubber galoshes in 1923. Seven years before that, Art Smith, The Bird Boy of Fort Wayne, stitched this advertising message onto the clear blue skies over Fort Bliss in El Paso, Texas. In 1916, the Fastener Manufacturing and Machine Company, having changed its name to Talon, was now aggressively marketing the device, commissioned our skywriter to cryptically affix this tattoo over larger cities—especially those with military installations, armories, and quartermaster depots. Talon's thinking was (what with the war raging in Europe and with the America's intervention there seeming inevitable) the expeditionary forces would need new modern efficient closures for their kits and caboodle. Art Smith designed the display himself having been mesmerized by the new, yet unnamed "zipper" zipper now installed over his heart on a slash pocket of his double-breasted leather flying jacket for safe storing of his folded oilcloth maps. He pulled at the pull tab, running the slider up and down, admiring the sound of the contraption—its controlled tear, its rasp and ratchet—knitting and unknotting, a miracle, each tooth fitting into its diastema, a suture, laced fingers. He worried the design like a prayer and sewed up the sky in smoke.

X

X

X

X

Art Smith, The Bird Boy of Fort Wayne, was also known as The Crash Kid. There had been many crashes leading up to this afternoon spent knotting up the sky over El Paso. Not that he felt in any way in any peril that day. The aeronautics were relatively benign—the lazy figure 8 with the smoke extinguished through the radii of the wide banking turns. And his airplane that day the reliable Curtis JN-3 an infinitely more stable platform than his homebuilt spit and baling wire Pushers. They had, more often than not, stuttered and stalled and slammed into the corn-stubbled ground or a canopy of unforgiving trees, a litany of being let down. He'd come to after a crash, the smoldering bamboo and balsa just beginning to catch and burn, and see his personal catastrophes—the gashes, the slick lacerations, the protruding tibia or fibula, looking to him, in shock, like the control sticks of his splintered aircraft. Ha! It would be something if the skin came equipped with such cunning little fasteners, slide the slice right up. A part of him wanted desperately to fly in the impending war, take off into the leading edge of experimental flight. Dogfights! Immelmanns! Tailslides! Hammerheads! But the fix was already in. The shattering and re-settings of his legs and arms, his back, his fingers, his toes in all those crashes would wash him out of the Air Service when the time came. His feet would be unable to reach the pedals on the "Tommy" trainer. His arthritic hands would be unable to grasp the throttle on the Avro. But, in 1916, another war was knocking on the door—the Mexican Revolution across the border. In his landing approaches, he would swing out and around effortlessly through that alien airspace, banking over Juarez as the Revolution was entering its final phases below. And here he was on the border advertising new fangled notions for notions in an unraveling world.

It hadn't been that long, a little over a year, that his companion in the celebrated aerial elopement and marriage, the love of his life, Aimee Cour, had left him in California and returned to the Midwest. Now, here on this extreme border, still smarting from that crash, he sought solace on the outer edges of what had been his known world. This was Art Smith's, The Bird Boy's, migration to mitigate those nagging injuries. He thought of his assignment here as a kind of banishment, forty days of wandering alone in the wilderness, the desert—the deserted desert itself and the wide deserted sky that seemed even wider than usual, endlessly cloudless, ever expanding, empty even of empty. After his daily skywriting, introducing to the quartermasters of Fort Bliss below the modern mechanism of closure, Art Smith would set a course along the international boundary, expending the last of his calligraphic fuel, tracing the sovereign demarcation, making visible, in his mind, an "us" and a "them," hoping to purse up all those feelings that constantly percolated within him. Oh, but even as he drew the drawstrings closed, irrational geography, he knew. He wasn't fooling himself. He knew he was not of one place or the other but constantly between, in between the between. Heaven and Hell. America and Mexico. Day and Night. Flying and Falling. He left in his wake, always, a stuttering and impermanent imaginary geometry, a porous border made up of tenuous threads of fleeting gossamer, the gauziest of insubstantial clouds.

X—X—X—X

Eighty miles due west from El Paso, Art Smith, The Bird Boy of Fort Wayne, flew along the border to Columbus, New Mexico. It was March 19th. Ten days before, Pancho Villa and the remnants of his failing Army of the North had crossed the border, raiding Columbus, burning the train station and other buildings, killing seventeen Americans. Now, Columbus would become the rallying point for the Army's 1st Aero Squadron, eight JN-2s and eleven pilots, as they kicked off the Punitive Expedition in support of General Pershing's force of 6,600 already deep into Mexico searching for Villa. The planes, unarmed and underpowered for the high desert, were ordered to rendezvous with the ground forces in Casas Grandes 90 miles south into Mexico. Art Smith in his skywriting "Jenny," circled, watching as the Army's airplanes lumbered into the air, too late in the day, into the gathering dusty darkness. They would be gone a year, looking for Villa and his raiders. Smith by then would be long gone, back up north, would hear of the spectacular failures of the airplanes and airmen—the wooden propellers delaminating in the dry heat, the crash landings in shifting sand, the radiator explosions spewing blood red water into the open cockpits. In Chihuahua City, Lt. Drague would be fired upon by four Mexican policemen with Winchester rifles, the first recorded attack on a U.S military plane. But all of this would be forgotten. All of it eclipsed. The War in Europe would intervene in this intervention, calling Pershing and his troops over there instead. The Mexican Revolution would end in amnesty for Villa and his men. Villa himself would be assassinated years later driving home in his Dodge touring car to the hacienda in Canutillo by a pumpkinseed seller shouting "Viva Villa!" But all of that was from a different country, the undiscovered country of the Future. The next morning in Columbus, New Mexico, after the 1st Aero Squadron had disappeared into old Mexico, Art Smith headed back along the invisible border to El Paso, landing at Fort Bliss to share the news of the Expedition's incursion. Along the way he closed the door behind him, so to speak, posting something like a fence wire warning along the way, a patriotic gesture, he believed

then, adorned with a few menacing Xs, barbing the line in the sky. They were, he hoped, of such scale, such majesty, he imagined, no one would ever want to cross this way again, now or in that unknown future.

Michael Martone's new books are *Brooding*, essays, and *The Moon Over Wapakoneta: Fictions And Science Fictions From Indiana and Beyond*. He lives in Tuscaloosa and teaches in the university there.

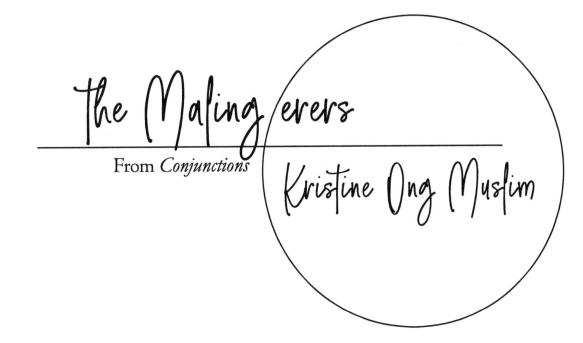

The Malingerers

From *Conjunctions*

Kristine Ong Muslim

8:00 P.M. IN THIS perpetual night shift, and we talk again to the person inside the photo booth, you know, that one photo booth that tunnels all the way down—or up, depending on where you are—to that familiar place where all afterlife and underworld mythologies owe their artifice, the predictability of salvation they purport to deliver.

The compact booth holds everyone's smallness. It cuts through everyone's lifelong delusions of uniqueness and individuality. Because: what if the endgame comes down to this—*just* this, being an underworld that hosts everyone in the afterlife. An underworld that is staffed by legion—*for we are many*—legion of inanimate objects everyone had taken for granted in life. And because we have been taken for granted, the long, long elastic arc of the moral universe must right itself and end up appointing us—who have grown proficient in the universal language of pain and denial—sole arbiters of everyone's fate. Then we take the closest possible form that makes it easier for us to measure everyone.

"Open your non-eyes away from the light, Sean," we say, our finger, our manifestation of a human finger, poised on the camera button. "Say cheese." Then Sean, like most of the ones before him, finally got his last picture taken while fuck-you-all-ing us as we processed his naturalized form on glossy photo paper, an economical two-dimensional entropy-compliant archival method.

One can think of it this way:

There's this shallow lake in the forest. You are standing before this shallow lake. You insist on having your head, as well as your gaze, be fixed in such a way that you only get to see the reflection of the forest on the water surface. Someone keeps telling you that it was all right to move your head, to look at other directions, to see beyond the woods, to see the clearing where thorny wild shrubs grow in abundance. But you maintain that there is just no way for you to move your head, no way to shift the direction of your gaze. So, you see only what's reflected on the water surface: branches, tops of some trees, birds on some of the branches, strip of sky that may be blood red during sunset, the occasional moon at night when it is bright enough to produce a visible image on the reflective surface of the still water. This, this reflection and all its possible finite variations are your only pictures of the world. You believe that each reflection already represents the entirety of the forest. And because this is a lake, it won't last forever. It won't be long before the water in the shallow lake completely evaporates. Someday, it will be just dried-up muck, no longer a reflective surface. All you will have left will be the memory of the reflection that you mistakenly believe serves as accurate representation of the forest. And what is memory but an organic construct whose integrity gets eaten away by time.

Or maybe this way:

Once a day, you knock on every door of every house along the street that cuts across an area once considered to be the bad part of town. You knock because all the doorbells on all the front doors are no longer working. They have stopped working for years. You don't expect anyone to answer the door. Yellow door, red door, royal blue door, black door—doesn't matter what color of door, because all doors and all colors signify the same thing: nobody is ever home. Nobody has been home for years. There are no more people in this part of the world. Not even in the fields beyond where people had been told long ago to use only for burying their dead. You knock on the door, knowing that no one will answer, because this is how it is when you are alone and you live forever: you keep knocking. Once a day, you knock on every door of every house along the street that cuts across an area once considered to be the bad part of town. You keep knocking, knowing that no one will answer the door—and most especially because no one will answer the door.

Somewhere in the complex, a photo booth operator's voice can be heard calling out the names of absentee supervisors—Moloch, Beelzebub, Moab, Baalin, Ashtaroth, Satanas. Must be another hard case putting up quite a resistance, which is understandable, even expected, considering the dissonance ingrained among those who have spent their lives believing in the existence and nature of the sacred place and then only getting what we have to offer in the end: a picture taken inside a custom-built photo booth.

Somewhere in the complex, a photo booth operator says, "No, ma'am. There's no boat, no ferryman, no coin for the boatman, no water. No river fucking Styx and Lethe. This is it. This is all there is to it. But I can play Rachmaninoff's *Isle of the Dead* for you, if that will make you feel better. Now please step inside the booth."

Night after night after night.

Kristine Ong Muslim is the author of nine books, including the short fiction collections *Age of Blight* (Unnamed Press, 2016), *Butterfly Dream* (Snuggly Books, 2016), and *The Drone Outside*

(Eibonvale Press, 2017), as well as editor of two anthologies—the *British Fantasy Award-winning People of Colo(u)r Destroy Science Fiction* (with Nalo Hopkinson et al.) and *Sigwa: Climate Fiction Anthology* from the Philippines (with Paolo Enrico Melendez). Her short stories have appeared in *The Cincinnati Review, Tin House,* and *World Literature Today.* She grew up and continues to live in a rural town in southern Philippines.

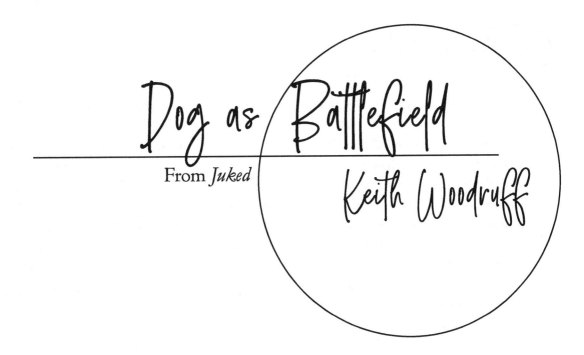

Dog as Battlefield

From *Juked*

Keith Woodruff

IS THIS THE HEART attack I wish for with every eyelash? Dad Thing jumpfalls up from the table, potato, beer and chops blowing from his face hole. Then I see what he sees. My dog Pete is begging for snackers at the sliding glass door that looks down on our table. His right side has been shaved clean down to that piglet pink skin, and someone has carved *Leesh your FUCKING dog* with black marker. Dad Thing rants around the room, speculating which neighbor would trespass him this way. They all hate him so good luck with that. *"Idiots! They fucking spelled leash wrong."* Dad Thing has that scowly, permanent sorehead look on his face like he just can't wait for the next fight. And here it is. He drags all of the air out of the room as he storms off to the kitchen for a marker.

We live in the country on a dirt road, woods everywhere. Every half-mile or so a house appears. Because it's remote, people from J-town come here to dump dogs they don't want anymore. Dad Thing has shot every one that found me. They are starving he says. They will get knocked up with puppies we can't afford to feed he says. We have to put them out of their misery he says. I say he just likes to shoot dogs. But he spared this one. Who knows.

Dad Thing clomps back into the room. He drops down beside Pete, bites the marker cap off and starts scratching *it's called freedom fuck you* beneath the *Leesh* comment. He is grunting, biting down harder on the marker cap and getting pissed because it's news to him that dog skin is hard to write on. The marker makes the air smell like medicine. I stroke Pete's head and look into his sad human eyes, hoping he reads my face as saying I'm sorry. Dad Thing finishes, and shoos Pete out the door. *"Get lost dipshit, go tell whoever what I said."* Pete stands there, confused, but finally slinks away when Dad Thing chucks his beer can. Pete's a drifter. He comes and goes, but I say he's mine.

I call my stepfather Dad Thing after Swamp Thing—from the comics—and the first time I tried to kill him it backfired. It was his bar night, and while he was hosing off in the shower, I packed cigarette loads into his Camels. But here comes the curve. Instead, he says *"Come on, get in the truck."* My balls shrink when he picks his smokes off the table. It's two days into deer season, which means the deer are on the move, and he wants to cruise 131 looking for fresh road kill. We're going along, Donna Fargo's Funny Face on the radio, when he takes the smokes out of his pocket. I have my hand on the door, bracing to jump out when the Bic sparks and Holy Shit. The bang is so loud inside the truck air raid sirens go off in my ears. Like I planned, he loses control of the truck. Like I didn't plan, I am with him, slap-grabbing the dash for a hold as we weave in and out of the ditch, nearly on our side at one point, until we smash through an exit sign and stop hard. First I feel the hot piss filling my pants, then it's Dad Thing's elbow deep in my eye socket.

The next morning, Pete's back with more sass on his side. Dad Thing loses his shit, runs to the closet, pulls his old silver clippers out of a box, and gets busy buzzing the fur off Pete's other side. *"Hold him still bonehead,"* yells Dad Thing. Pete's skin is specked with blood where the clippers have nicked him.

As Grandpa would say, my turtle left its shell. I am climbing to the loft of our old-as-hell barn. Usually I come here to be with my *Hustlers*—the ones I find ditched on the roadside when I am hitching. I take a seat on a hay bale and poke the tip of my 410 through a knothole toward the house. It's 1975, summer in the country, where every day we put things out of their misery.

Keith Woodruff has a Master's in poetry from Purdue University. He lives in Akron, Ohio. His poetry and flash fiction have appeared in *Poetry East*, *Quarter After Eight*, *Salamander*, *The Journal*, *Wigleaf* and is forthcoming in *RHINO*. His prose poem "Summer" appeared in the Best Small Fictions 2017 anthology, and his flash fiction "Elegy" received a 2018 *Pushcart Prize*.

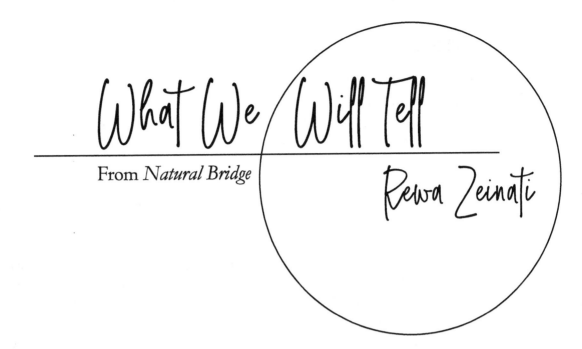

What We Will Tell

From *Natural Bridge*

Rewa Zeinati

WE'LL TELL THEM WE tried. We told stories and wrote poems and were sometimes ignored. We filled the classrooms with manifestos and sex. We filled the classrooms with questions. We'll tell them we rode buses from the villages all the way to the city and back. We burned candles in church and then we burned down the church. We'll tell them we did not all want to believe in the holy stories that we were fed. That we had needles pushed into our uterus and breast. How even once was enough. We'll tell them we did not mean to keep the ones in power in power. We'll tell them about power outages. The leaving of water. The shifting sun and all the wrong colors. We'll tell them there was war here once and then again there was war. We'll tell them we ate too much and spent too much and considered the street beggar with the drugged child on her chest invisible. We'll tell them how we became invisible. How we told on each other. How we stayed up some nights because we did not believe the moon would ever come back. We'll tell them we believed in the muscle of the moon and the ebb and flow of lies. We will tell them we lied. Stole from each other. Never forgave forgiveness. We'll tell them how we hated food. Processed it. Threw it up. And /sometimes/ we ate it. We'll tell them there was once a word and that word was [home] but we did not know what it meant so we left it behind to burn. We watched it on the news and remembered its light. Its infinite forest where trees were and weren't. Where the scent of *yasmeen* reminded us of the hands of our mothers and the leaving of grass. We'll tell them about grass. And how we were forced instead to learn the language of concrete and billboards and deserts /and the absence of birds./ We'll tell them about birds and the thick song of departure stuck in our throat. How these birds took us from one country to another. We'll tell them about countries. And how we needed papers to visit. We'll try to explain permission. [We will try to explain permission.] And how sometimes we got it and sometimes we didn't. We will say we did not all deserve the passage. We'll tell them how we pulled off our

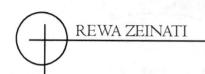

limbs and folded our bones and drowned them in the red womb of water to get there. We'll explain water. How it came down in threads from the thick blue attic and how it spread as a river. We will try to explain river. And we will fail.

Rewa Zeinati is the founding editor of *Sukoon,* and the author of *Bullets & Orchids* and *Nietzsche's Camel Must Die.* Her poems, essays, interviews and translations are published in *Prairie Schooner, Guernica, Bird's Thumb, Natural Bridge Journal, Quiddity, Mizna, The Common, Fen Magazine, Common Boundary: Stories of Immigration, Making Mirrors: Writing/Righting by Refugees, Poetry Daily,* among other journals and anthologies. With an MFA from the University of Missouri-St. Louis, Rewa is a creative copywriter and university instructor of creative & academic writing.

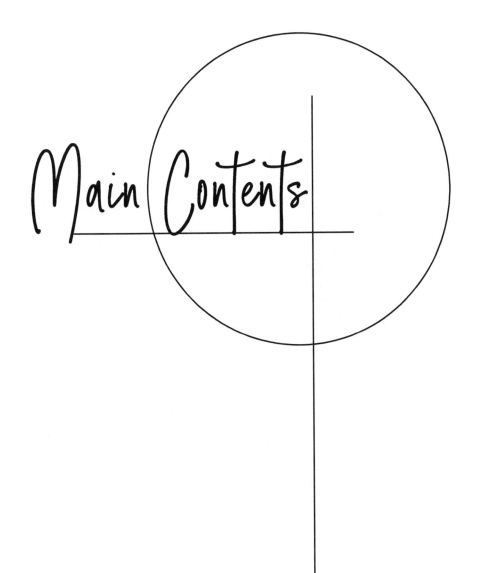

Main Contents

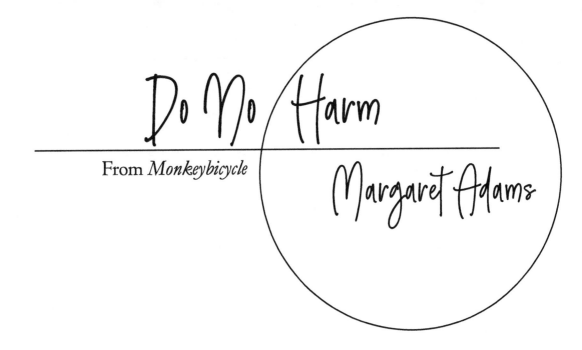

Do No Harm

From *Monkeybicycle*

Margaret Adams

AT 3:17 PM EST Ben McKinnon walked into the Emergency Room at County Hospital and announced that, in eight to twelve hours, he would die.

The staff at County were used to people walking in from the street and hollering tidings of their own impending doom, but not with such unnerving calm, or with a total lack of apparent symptoms. McKinnon spoke simply and patiently to the triage nurse. "I've taken 50 mg of colchicine," he said. "Over ten hours ago. Too late for you to do anything, and I'd rather you didn't try, but I would like some morphine later on." He produced the empty bottles as proof, handing them over in a neatly folded white paper bag.

"Okay," she said. She passed the message to Vasquez, the resident on duty, and paged social work.

Dr. Nick Vasquez wasn't exactly a veteran of the Emergency Room, but after just two years there he'd seen plenty of suicide attempts. There were the people who had eaten bottles of Aspirin and come in once their ears had begun to ring, saying they'd changed their minds, they wanted to live. Then there were those brought in by paramedics, middle-aged men who'd shot the roofs of their own mouths off, faceless patients rushed to often-useless surgeries before ending up vegetating in critical care. These latter cases, he'd felt, were the worst. He wasn't one of those doctors who scoffed at the teenagers who came in scared and sad after taking four over-the-counter Tylenol pills—one of those doctors who said, *don't waste our time, come back when you're serious about killing yourself.* But when putting an artificial airway in a man whose self-inflicted facial wreckage was so complete that the next step was a CT scan to see if he even *had* a full brain stem still, Vasquez struggled. Even after all of his training, part of him occasionally wondered whether people knew what they were doing when they pulled the trigger, and maybe should be allowed to do it. This part would rise unbidden in his consciousness, along with an acute awareness of how much time they spent on someone whose quality of life wouldn't, after this, be anything Nick would wish on his worst enemy. *Do no harm, do no harm, do no harm* he'd repeat in his head while restraining limbs and pumping stomachs. He couldn't tell if the mantra was comforting or ironic. *Give me a car accident or a homicide attempt any day, he thought. But not another old guy with half of his face gone.*

Vasquez had never seen this, though. Never an overdose without symptoms or agitation—not vomiting, not afraid, not pale or restless. Ben McKinnon looked fine. He lay quietly on the bed, his wrists hanging easily in the Velcro restraints. Nick felt almost embarrassed by the mandatory protocol. Around them, Emergency Room chaos raged; urine pooled under the triage bay curtain, but McKinnon remained calm.

Colchicine was a weird choice, something else Nick had never seen before. He called Toxicology. Through the partially-open curtain, he could see McKinnon's bed, a security guard, and the medical assistant who was checking McKinnon's pulses. Nick turned the empty bottles over in his hands while the line rang. Each bottle had been prescribed by a different provider. Colchicine was a common drug for gout—an old medicine for an old disease, not generally considered dangerous, but definitely toxic in large doses. About fifty milligrams in all, he realized, adding the pills up in his head. *Jesus*, he thought. *That's a lot of colchicine.* The toxicologist at the other end of the hospital picked up on the sixth ring.

"Hey," Nick said. "We've got a thirty-eight-year-old white male down here who says he took 50 mg of colchicine about ten hours ago."

The medical assistant tried to catch his eye from across the hallway, an odd look on her face. "Nick." The Emergency Room din muffled her words, but her mouth clearly shaped his name.

"50 mg of colchicine? Ten hours ago?" There was a pause on the line. "Nothing you can do," the toxicologist said.

"Nothing?" Nick peered up at the fluorescent-lit ceiling. He found it helpful to stare at the lights when he was upset. He had two years of memories, now, of those parallel lines of cost-effective, faintly buzzing brilliance, associated with the kinds of situations he couldn't have imagined while studying for the MCAT, and with trying to burn out his own more hopeless thoughts.

"You can't pump his stomach—it metabolized in an hour. You can't give him charcoal. You can't dialyze it out of him. There's nothing you can do."

"Nick," the medical assistant mouthed at him. She was still standing over McKinnon, and she had her hand on something clipped to his belt, a white rectangular card.

"There must be something."

"There isn't. He's got—it's been ten hours since he took it? He's got another twelve hours before his organs shut down. He'll start vomiting in four."

"Jesus," Nick said. "Okay." Then, "That's exactly what he said."

"Yeah," the toxicologist said. "He's either really smart or really unlucky. Can't undo colchicine."

"Nick," the medical assistant said one more time. She had left the bedside and come over to his workstation, and now held up an identification badge: *Ben McKinnon, MD, Toxicology Department*.

"Thank you," Nick said into the phone. "You've been very helpful." And then he hung up.

Nick sat for a few moments, then stood slowly, aware of a high whine in his head. He looked down at his own scrub-clad legs and stained sneakers, told himself to bounce on his toes as he usually did to center himself, but didn't move. He could feel the weight of his own badge clipped to his pocket, a slight ache in the small of his back. Nearby another phone rang. On the other side of the triage bay, someone's lungs vibrated with a deep, hacking cough. Ben McKinnon, toxicologist, had eight to twelve hours to live. And Nick Vasquez, Emergency Department resident, had the short distance between his desk and McKinnon's bed to figure out what he'd say to this patient who was also a provider. To a person who he would think about, but never talk about, in his own dark moments for years to come. To a man who had used his training to commit such harm.

"I'm going to order morphine," he said out loud to no one, his voice clearer than it had been all day.

Margaret Adams' stories and essays have appeared in *Threepenny Review, Joyland Magazine, The Pinch Journal, Monkeybicycle,* and *The Baltimore Review,* among other publications. She is the winner of the *Blue Mesa Review* 2018 Nonfiction Contest and the *Pacifica Literary Review* 2017 Fiction Contest. Originally from Maine, she currently lives on the AZ/NM border in the Navajo Nation where she works as a family nurse practitioner. Her website is www.margaret-adams.com.

buffalo

From New Zealand Poetry Society's *the unnecessary invention of punctuation*

Johanna Aitchison

WHILE YOU & NOOR ARE waiting outside the Cook Street Dairy
for your dhosa you ask her, "What kind of tea do you drink
in Pakistan? Do you use cow's milk or other kinds of milk?"
"Buffalo milk," says Noor. "They have buffalo in Pakistan?
Buffalo. *Buffalo.*" The more you say it, the funnier it sounds.
"My mother-in-law lives in a village with her buffalo," says Noor,
"Everyone is always giving her sons a hard time & saying, 'why
do you not look after your mother? Why do you leave her to live
with a buffalo?' But she loves that buffalo. Whenever someone
invites her to come visit, she says, 'but I have to feed the buffalo.
She loves that buffalo more than her children.'" When your son leaves,
you will get yourself a buffalo. You will watch YouTube videos on how
to care for your buffalo. You will google 'music to soothe your buffalo'
& 'buffalo grooming hints'. You will become president of the Society
For Awareness of Buffalo Welfare. You will invent 57 new words
for the sound of buffalo hooves on bitumen. All of your outfits
will be curated to match her reddish hair. Your buffalo will weep
in the corner of your lawn whenever you leave, but she will do so
quietly. Your nights will ripen into village parties. "These people,"
you cry, as you twirl & twirl, "Where were you all before?"
You can see the gathered backs of the herd tearing up the lawn,
they are sharing out the winds of the savannah. With their milk
you toast the moon: to the sky whose rhythm you thought you'd lost

forever. To the drum, which has taken on new hooves & got to beating.
To the buffaloes: you appoint them Chief Shredders of the torn grass;
you appoint them High Forrest Eaters. Let us stand, let us stomp,
let us split open the skull's house & roam again.

Johanna Aitchison is a writer from Aotearoa-New Zealand, who lives in Ashhurst, Manawatu. She was a member of the 2015 Fall Residency on the International Writing Program at the University of Iowa. Johanna has published three volumes of poetry, the latest of which is Miss Dust (2015). Her poetry has been anthologized in *Best of Best New Zealand Poems* (2011), *Essential New Zealand Poems* (2015), and *Manifesto Aotearoa: 101 Political Poems* (2017). Johanna is currently enrolled as a doctoral candidate at Massey University, examining anagrams and erasures in hybrid poetry. She is a sometime marathoner and ocean swimmer.

Lasting Impression

From *The Collagist*

Ryunosuke Akutagawa

Translated by Ryan C.K. Choi

I RECENTLY ACCEPTED A commission to write about the mountain town of Ikaho, despite having spent only one night there during high school on a hiking trip with two friends up Mt. Myōgi and Mt. Akagi. I recall little about the town itself and even less about its famed views and hot springs. I have but a vague memory of riding a rickety train up the mountainside and being uneasy about the rusted tracks webbed with bush and vine and the lack of straps to hold. After arriving in town, we found a room at a nondescript inn where we happened to make the acquaintance of a sophisticated, middle-aged man who was staying in the room next to ours. He was, by his eager admission, a regular at these hot springs, claiming they possessed special powers of rejuvenation that were the secret to his youthful appearance. We accompanied him to the hot springs no less than six times the following day and after our last bath our bodies were so withered we could barely steady ourselves for the walk back—the halls of the inn seemed to elongate and twist before us, and I remember nearly fainting. Once we had settled in our rooms, we found that we were mysteriously unable to relax. As soon as the sun set, the four of us packed our bags, checked out of the inn and trekked over to Takasaki Station where my friends and I were embarrassed to find we couldn't afford our fares to Ueno. We spent too much money on the hot springs and the inn. We confessed our predicament to the man, who, with no hesitation, gifted us one hundred and twenty sen, then bid us farewell. As I said above, I have little memory of Ikaho and its majestic waterfalls and valleys, and when the topic of its renowned hot springs comes up, I find myself thinking of this man whom we met, and how each time we soaked in the waters together he carried on at nauseating length about his plans to design and manufacture a compact single-seat automobile and become one of the country's wealthiest men. Just today in the papers, I read an article about the invention of a two-seat automobile, and began to wonder about the man, for I have yet to read about a single-seat automobile being made.

Ryūnosuke Akutagawa (1892 - 1927), born in Tokyo, Japan, was the author of more than 350 works of fiction and non-fiction. Japan's premier literary award for emerging writers, the Akutagawa Prize, is named after him.

Ryan C. K. Choi lives in Honolulu, Hawai'i, where he was born and raised.

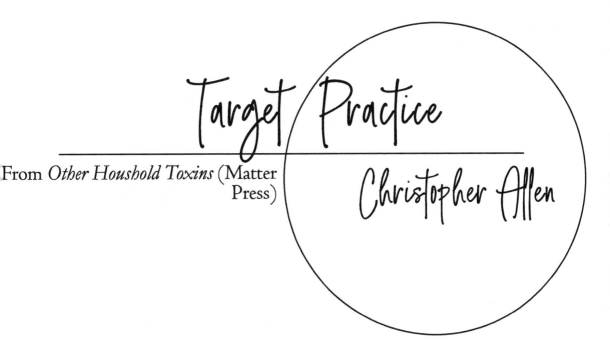

Target Practice

From *Other Houshold Toxins* (Matter Press)

Christopher Allen

TODAY

THE TARGETS ARE locked out, told to snatch some air, move those legs and arms, play your schoolyard games, but stay away from the house in the trees. Don't jump the ditch, don't cavort with that loner Kyle who shoots kids with his fingers.

Two targets hang pteropine from the pull-up bars. One points at a sliver of Kyle lining the broad shadow of a Hackberry. The other target says *Ignore him, and he'll go away* loud so Kyle can hear. He slips into shadow, draws a hand and shoots. Twice. Says *pwewwww pwewwww*. Smoke curls from a gun only Kyle can see. He never misses. His backyard's crap for throwing a football with a dad—too many trees, not enough dads—bit it jams for a jungle war.

Brandon

is Kyle's big half-brother. He's growing facial hair because his mother says men with beards have something to hide. He's fifteen today. His dad left a present leaning on the mailbox. A restraining order says he can't come closer. The gun is long and badass, but it's not the kind you lock up. It's the kind that shoots BBs and pellets that look like roly-polies. It's the kind a fifteen-year-old pumps till his fingers blister and his shoulder goes numb, the kind that shoots a dime-sized hole in the drywall of his room. The kind that comes with a note that says *Don't Tell Your Mama.*

Tomorrow

is Brandon's first day at Hardee's. He'll lock his door and hang a sign—*Don't Come In or I'll keel you*—to guard his Iron Maiden records, a magazine called *Jugs*, a nickel bag of pot in his closet, and now the gun. But Kyle can pick any lock: his mom's condom drawer, the ammo can with her alimony and child support papers from dads, the cabinet with the gin. The lock on Brandon's door is junk, which Kyle will crack with a pair of tweezers tomorrow.

Pumped 10 times, the gun and Kyle will stretch out together, a one-piece plastic soldier. As his cheek warms to the gun's hard stock, the grassless ground will cool Kyle's hairless middle. He'll close one eye and track a target in pink tights from swings to seesaw to pull-up bar. He'll aim at the feet: to wound and take prisoner. He'll shoot and miss and lie flat against his gun. It will press against his groin, and he'll wonder what his own father looks like, if he'll show up one day to linger 50 yards away. He'll cock the gun again, shoot and miss. He'll do this five times with the five roly-polies Brandon will never miss because Brandon is always high.

The targets won't look around to see where the *pwewwww* came from. They won't notice the pellet-sized hole in the wooden post inches from their dangling pink Keds. They'll scream and laugh; they'll do flips from things. They'll ignore Kyle's war in the trees until Kyle's big half-brother gets a shotgun next year.

Christopher Allen is the author of the flash fiction collection *Other Household Toxins* (Matter Press, 2018). His work has appeared in *Indiana Review, Split Lip Magazine, Jellyfish Review* and lots of other good places. He is a nomad.

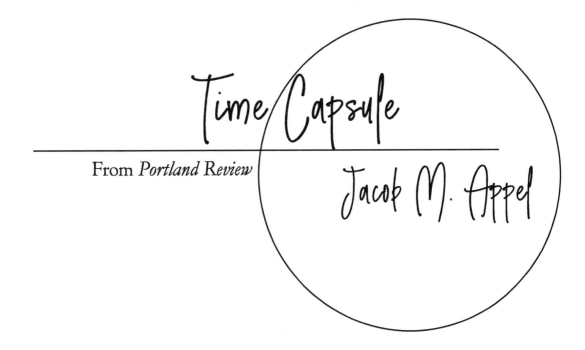

Time Capsule

From *Portland Review*

Jacob M. Appel

WE DIDN'T PAY MUCH attention at first to the time capsule. It was one of those ideas concocted by senior management—like double-decker office cubicles and visit your clients at home day—destined to be ballyhooed and then quickly forgotten. Yet as the firm's hundredth anniversary approached, coverall-clad workmen excavated a shaft in the courtyard and paneled the walls with reinforced concrete. "Send a message to the future," read the sign above the bunker, the words echoed in Spanish and braille. "All employees welcome to participate."

To set an example, the chairman invited us to a mandatory lunch-hour ribbon-cutting, where he volunteered his own contributions: copies of the New York Times and Wall Street Journal, a CD of Birgit Nilsson channeling Aida, a calendar featuring lithographs of poker-playing dogs, and several cases of our own product, fresh off the assembly line. "Nothing says more about our world today," he announced, "than our soaring triumphs in music and art, except possibly your efforts to improve the daily lives of all Americans." After the chairman set his trove inside the time capsule, the firm's president deposited a two-dollar bill, a portrait of the pope, and one of our corporate windbreakers. Several executive vice presidents followed with their own offerings: photographs of film and sports stars, caps and 59 with our company logo, a coffee mug shaped like a penguin. We suppressed our laughter and hurried back to our offices.

We didn't think about the time capsule again for several days. Then we received a message from the leadership team: "Our time capsule provides a once-in-a-lifetime opportunity to communicate with future generations and you are expected to contribute." Starkweather from marketing printed out the message and dropped it into the shaft, saying, "It's a start."

But we were loyal employees, so we did our part. One of the engineers had his children draw greeting cards for our distant progeny with crayons. A clerk from customer relations brought in a crate of large-print books he had intended to donate to the public library. The two security officers on the night shift combed the lost-and-found for suitable donations, finally settling upon a marginally functional umbrella and a lady's wool glove. When management raised no objections to these offerings, Parker from research and development appeared one morning with his ex-wife's abandoned shoes. Wadsworth contributed his late sister's evening gowns. Miss Robustelli, the receptionist from the staffing agency, added her deceased father's underwear and socks.

Later, O'Sullivan, who'd gone out on disability for nearly a year after his kidney transplant, tossed in used pill bottles from his medicine chest. "Better than having them lying around the house," he explained. Rubin donated a jug of malt liquor. Hernandez from distribution slid in several X-rated magazines. Patrossian sprinkled his daughter's ashes into the mix and we all felt very bad for him.

Some of us received a second message from leadership: "You have not yet contributed to the time capsule. Your failure to take advantage of this opportunity continues to be noted." That prompted a second wave of donations. Hutchinson cursed and tossed in his prosthetic leg. Horvath handed over surplus kittens from his Siamese's litter. Eldridge, who'd initially been among the loudest in mocking the project, provided his demented mother-in-law. The third message from leadership thanked those who had not contributed for their service to the firm, and asked them to clear out their desks before the start of business on Monday.

On the way out of the office, several of our downsized colleagues jumped into the time capsule. In solidarity, we followed. First one by one, then entire 60 Portland Review departments. "We're all together in this," declared Starkweather, who was also the union rep. He led chants all morning, picketing across the bunker with placards. Most of us played cards (canasta, pinochle, euchre) and calculated what our pensions would amount to in one hundred years—"if they're still solvent," said Wadsworth. He was always a doomsayer. A communications intern set up a television.

Hutchinson's wife brought him his supper (roast beef) in a brown paper bag, and Parker's ex served him with a subpoena over the deserted shoes. Eldridge's mother-in-law contracted pneumonia (viral) and had to be removed on a stretcher. We were sorry to see her go, sorry that she wouldn't be part of our message to the next century.

As for the rest of us, we're all in—even the chairman, who has commandeered a corner alcove. I only hope that, when the time comes, future generations are able to glean an accurate sense of who we are.

Jacob M. Appel is the author of three literary novels including *Millard Salter's Last Day* (Simon & Schuster/Gallery, 2017), eight short story collections, an essay collection, a cozy mystery, a thriller and a volume of poems. He currently teaches at the Mount Sinai School of Medicine in New York City. More at: www.jacobmappel.com.

He She It They

From National Flash Fiction Day (NZ)

Anita Arlov

HE'S GRAVEN. SHE'S GILT. He was glass-bottle-fed. She was weaned a china doll. He cuts loose. She's unmoored. He picks her Mexican daisies. She reads him Ines de la Cruz. He's on Cloud Nine. She's Man in the Moon. He's finger inlet, bracken, orca, syrup. She's Matariki, moss, cowrie-shell, Hula Hoop. She sleeps in his spoon. He wakes her toes-first. He fries her tomatoes. She peels in the sun. He books Dunedin. She knits him a scarf. He takes on a greyhound. She collects horseshoes. He plants rosemary. She goes to pottery.

He lets slip a white lie. She grows black moons. He slaps his face. She slaps her mouth. He's power cut, sleet, cacophony, sludge. She's burnt toast, high humidity, rent increase, aerosol. He's more-pork cry. She's wild rabbit spoor. He flattens a possum. She wouldn't be caught dead. He's a slot screw. She's a Phillips driver. He's wet towels, velcro, bad breath, block-buster. She's hair-ball, silverfish, traffic fine, art house. He's Saturday. She's Friday. He's long lost tribe. She's street barbeque. He's barbed tomcat. She's treed queen. He pings a nerve. She's a live wire. He's haemochrome. She's bleached bone.

He's breast of water. She's landfall. He's tin can. She's can opener. He's focaccia, nail gun, folk lore, archipelago. She's manuka honey, neon light, kelp forest, quantum theory. He's wind gust. She's window. He's motu. She's hopscotch. He's dinghy. She's jetty. He's indigo. She's India Ink. He's vinyl, rope bridge, home-cooked-meal, equal pay. She's open fire, green belt, skylight, long weekend. He's paper-scissors-rock. She's tic-tac-toe. He's sober driver. She's wine on special. He hangs it out. She brings it in. He catches the backbeat. She pours on the slant. He's Battle of Britain. She's fly.

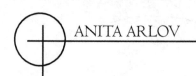

Anita Arlov lives in Auckland, New Zealand. She emcees Inside Out Open Mic For Writers, a monthly gig welcoming fresh work from prose writers and poets, with musician guests. She convened the organizing team of the NZ Poetry Conference & Festival 2017. "He She It They" won first prize and "Ming the Other" won Auckland regional prize in New Zealand's National Flash Fiction Day Competition 2018. *NZ Poetry Yearbook, Broadsheet, Poetical Bridges/Poduri Lirice, Flash Frontier, Takahe* and *Bonsai: best small stories from Aotearoa, New Zealand* are some of the journals where her poems or flashes can be found.

Gator Butchering for Beginners

From *Electric Literature*

Kristen Arnett

IT'S EASY ENOUGH TO slip the skin. Wedge your knife below the bumpy ridge of spine to separate cartilage from fat; loosen tendon from pink, sticky meat. Flay everything open. Pry free the heart. It takes some nerve. What I mean is, it'll hurt, but you can get at what you crave if you want it badly enough.

Start with the head.

The initial incision should be sharp, precise. Don't hesitate. This will be the toughest part. Do you know how hard it is to end a thing? They'll say: *Wait.* They'll say: *I still love you. Remember making out in your car after work? How we named the dog three times before anything stuck? That weekend at the beach we fed birds and one landed on your bare shoulder, then sang for us?* That's a gator mating call; a bellow, rippling vibrations meant to stun prey. Heft the knife and feel for an artery. Nothing's worse than something left half dead, bleeding-howling, so go for the throat. It'll help if you drink enough beforehand to razor-sharpen your words. Slip someone else's name into bed between the two of you. Thrust the dagger called apathy and slice without hesitation. After: hack free the skull. Keep it at your bedside, a gentle reminder not to call at 2am.

Next: the belly.

Bodies aren't meant to be opened from the middle. Gutting's ugly work, airing what's decayed in secret. Gators contort to ingest. They do the Death Roll, a dance of twisted necks, diving to drown their partner before swallowing whole. Cut open a belly and a history spills out: past food lodged in coiled intestines, innards stuffed with a romantic dinner, remnants of a long-ago night you wedged your mouth against something slick and drew out all the pleasure for yourself. Dig into the bowels of the fridge and uncover the last pizza you bought together. Final jar of pickles, solitary spear floating lonely. Deodorant left behind in the medicine cabinet, fuzzy lick of memory on the tip of your tongue from suckling a breast and mistakenly catching the

edge of an armpit. Once clean, the meat here is tender, but it'll always carry the sickly-sweet aftertaste of rot.

Harvest the worthwhile scrape: the tail.

Everyone knows that to outrun a gator you sprint zigzag, but to catch one you have to sneak up from behind. Kneel on its back like a supplicant; brace yourself against its hind end. Ask anyone: all good meat resides in the rump. That beefy, thrashing muscle designed to sweep you off your feet. Below its rubbery hide is the flesh you've been craving. *Do you wanna get a drink*, you ask, cutting carefully to the chase. Forget middle names, Christmas gifts, the flavor of icing on that first birthday cake you shared. Blot out the memory of an unshaved ankle rubbing against your calf under body-warmed sheets. There's only the sweet, tangy bite of what you've been missing. Something savory you haven't had in years. Let your teeth strike bone, jaws tender with need, salivating. Swallow the meat whole and then drive home alone. Dive beneath sheets that smell only of you. Wallow there, a solitary beast.

Digest.

Kristen Arnett is a queer fiction and essay writer. She won the 2017 Coil Book Award for her debut short fiction collection, *Felt in the Jaw*, and was awarded *Ninth Letter*'s 2015 Literary Award in Fiction. She's a columnist for *Literary Hub* and her work has appeared at *North American Review, The Normal School, Gulf Coast, McSweeneys, PBS Newshour, TriQuarterly, Guernica, Electric Literature, Bennington Review, Tin House Flash Fridays, The Guardian, Salon, The Rumpus*, and elsewhere. Her debut novel, *Mostly Dead Things*, was published by Tin House Books in June 2019. You can find her on twitter here: @Kristen_Arnett

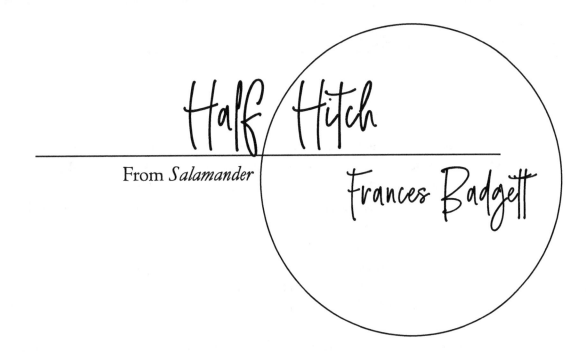

Half Hitch

From *Salamander*

Frances Badgett

Spring

WHAT PASSES FOR WEATHER is cold and slick, the spit and runnel of raindrops. Padilla Bay reflects early sprigs of forsythia, yellow spikes bouncing on stems. A hardness in the clouds, an unwavering blank grayness that enters my skull. Your hands are scarlet from cold, working the knots, timber hitch, half hitch, bowline. I still your fingers and I blow warmth. The rain agitates the water into ripples. Unforgiving wet rope slips in your palm. You make it simple and drop the coil. The boat drifts a little on its line.

Later we find the barn. We nestle in hay like animals curled against each other. I smell rain on your neck. Dampness. My jacket rustles on yours. A first kiss should have a name. Something Greek. We linger here, cold and stinging noses. The wind rattles roof shingles, lifts them like wings. Summer won't be long, though it feels a mile from this cold kiss. And with summer comes an ocean call of fish runs and trawlers. And beyond that an endless nothing of distance. The blue-sky days of cheerful breezes and glaring blooms will bring emptiness. Absence. And the long silence that follows, a stranger's promise of some day, some day, calling like a bird only stopping on its migration.

You whisper in my ear the names of tides—bore, neap, rip—and tell me you have dogs named for them. High and Low? A hacked laugh from the cigarette and salt tangle of your lungs. The coils of my ear are moist from your breath, cooling in the draft. I want to tell you not to go. You are, when you close your eyes, already there. Your legs steadying on the deck, your hand and the rudder welded together in a single sweep.

Summer

The ends will not meet. Tug the sash loose and let it fall, there is more here than just sodden heat and belly. A ribcage flutter that grows into shadows, a girl. Techs are not supposed to tell, but they do. Her hair is a wild, wet halo, her legs above her, curled, small footprint against the wall. She floats in a tiny sea, bubble rising from her lips. I stagger into the sun, half-smile, half-longing. I can't know yet that your boat is taking water, storm surge over the bow.

I settle into a booth and feed us both the most wholesome food I can find in a diner, limp collards dotted with bacon, and I am trying to tell you this, conjuring your face so that you might somehow hear. You once said we had to end it because you like being away. You don't like having to return with tendrils, tethers, knots, nets. You like the clean slice of the bow through chop.

I try to picture where you are at this moment, the ocean heaving your boat in swells, the trail of gulls seeking spoils. You told me the wet deck was more dangerous than hooks and nets, the pitch and slip of your feet. Instinct draws a hand to my belly, her thud against my palm. Strong kicks, they said. You are unreachable in some river, some tumbled rocky salmon run. Your phone is out of service or dead. The line is slack in my ear.

Fall

You come back quiet. She tugs at your hair, stares into your eyes. You blink. This is not what you meant, you say. There is too much ocean in you. Mornings, you walk the shore and stare into the whitecaps as if they might birth your dead crew, one by one. We plank and smoke salmon. We grill cod. We can tuna with carrots. She smiles when you walk toward her. You call her Girl, afraid of the net of a name. You turn to me and smile, a tight-lipped attempt at not leaving us both, a stab at happiness. I wave, my eyes caught in her curls.

Antun was your favorite of the crew. You want to name her Ana for him, you want the churn and stroke of the engine to live in her pulse. You liked the way he sang with the radio, the crazed shock of his hair, perfect vertical. You want me to be him. You want all of us to be him. She slaps her salmon with her palm, and it sends you into gales, reminding you of Antun, of the long hours drifting, churning away from here. She upturns her milk and puts her glass on her head, drops catching on her shoulders. You see her now as yours. We sign the certificate "Ana" as she chews your pen.

You tell me you can't wait to get her out there, to show her that a horizon never arrives. Like us, you whisper. I hear you over the fan. She pulls the collar of your shirt and buries her face. You hand her back to me and walk to the yard, door still open, salt brine air wafting in.

Winter

You place her on the deck in her red boots and untie the bowline. We are in a small space of calm between arguments, your body still tense, hands still thrashing. It is too cold for her out here. The water is deadly cold and we cannot swim. You have no life jacket. You pull me on board and tend to the engine, the rudder. We chug away from the dock, the tension eases off your shoulders, your face. The wind braces, and you howl into it. She howls, too. She teeters on the edge of the boat, hugging the air.

The islands rise and fall on the horizon, a light rain soaking us. You turn us toward home, humming a song you shared with your crew. You once said they were the only people you ever really loved. You said it to me. The salt stings our faces. I tuck her face under my arm and hold her, warming us both. You are gentle at the dock, lifting her carefully and placing her just so. You kiss my cheek before tying the boat, over-under-over of your cold, stiff fingers.

Just before bed, she rolls into the warm reach of the fire's halo. You snatch her up, hold her to the light. She smiles back and kicks, a game. I place a finger on the page and look up, the two of you. Your hands are softening without the daily scrape of saltwater and cold air. She rests on your shoulder, slip of drool. I watch you both longer than you know. She is almost asleep. Then asleep.

Frances Badgett is the fiction editor of *Contrary Magazine*. Her work has appeared in *SmokeLong Quarterly*, *Anomaly* (formerly Drunken Boat), *Word Riot*, *Matchbook*, *Atticus Review*, *JMWW*, *Salamander*, and elsewhere. Two of her stories have made the *Wigleaf* 50 longlist. She grew up in Lexington, Virginia and has a B.A. from Hollins University and an M.F.A. from Vermont College of Fine Arts. She lives in Bellingham, Washington with her husband and daughter, and is currently working on a novel set in the Pacific Northwest. Her website is francesbadgett.com.

A Pinch of Saffron

From *AFREADA*

Ally Abdallah Baharoon

HER SMILE WAS WIDER and brighter on Thursdays. Yasmeen looked on as the children of Gerezani and neighbouring districts came around to knock on her doors. Some were mannered, others less so, but they all arrived with one purpose – receiving their weekly *kashata*, coconut candy, given out by the lady on Lumumba street. They seemed to like it and that made her happy. Maybe because they were free treats; she liked to believe it was the pinch of saffron in them. She started giving out *kashata* when she first heard of Musa's death via the Gerezani grapevine many Thursdays ago. Her previously avowed husband-to-be was no more.

When she first encountered Musa, he was one of the growing number of Arab entrepreneurs in Dar es Salaam. Musa fell in love the moment he saw her walking in the busy streets of Kariakoo and boldly approached her like a hopeful venture capitalist looking for opportunities.

He was the man who was going to marry her except that his mother declared that she would recuse herself from the wedding preparations and subsequently disown him if he followed through. His mother threatened to withhold her blessings, albeit with no explicit reasons. She promised to find him a 'nice Arab girl' but it had been seven years now and there was no sign of this mirage.

Yasmeen had been the love of his life but Musa's naïve business acumen blinded him from seeing that his mother was not a fan of those with too much melanin. His mother hid her prejudice behind practicality, citing that it would be easier for everyone involved if he married a fellow Arab.

When he was finally introduced to the nice Arab girl, Musa abided by his mother's wishes and wedded her within weeks. On his anniversary, he passed away under mysterious circumstances. His mother followed suit a week later. The nice Arab girl was now a wealthy Arab girl after absconding with the family riches.

News goes around fast in Gerezani and the pace at which these incredulous events occurred amazed even the most stoic.

Now, the lady on Lumumba Street laughed every time she remembered Musa's incessant questioning. 'Are you a virgin, Yasmeen? I must know,' he would inquire every so often. That had been his burning question. His explorative spirit followed him in romance as it did in business. He wanted to be the first. She would smile and nod a deceitful yes, thinking it would be best for him to discover an ordinary truth when they consummated their marriage.

Today, as she handed out the *kashata*, half a dozen wrapped in each plastic bag, she realised that it had been twelve years now and time had done its work.

The smiles of the children refrained her from telling them that she would not be doing this anymore. Maybe they would find out for themselves next week by the silence in the house.

Ally Abdallah Baharoon was born and raised in Tanzania. He is an English grad and a performing writer with a passion for stories, humour and live shows. As an intergalactic journalist, Ally seeks opportunities to bring his, according to one review, "invigorating blend of compassion and absurdity" to a diverse list of projects, making the leap from the page to both the stage and screen. The experiences Ally narrates are inexhaustibly inspired by his home district, Gerezani, an imaginative galaxy where he and his *shwanga* family live for cleansing moments of joy.

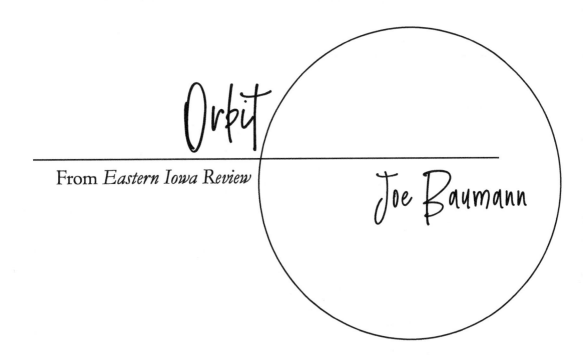

Orbit

From *Eastern Iowa Review*

Joe Baumann

SHEILA IS FAILING ELEVENTH grade math because she cannot stop staring at Fergus McMillan's blowhole. Okay, so she knows that the fibrous bulb of skin that juts out from the back of his neck isn't really a blowhole—nothing ever spumes out or gets sucked in—but the hard flesh is folded over on itself in a grumpy scowl so it looks close enough to the real thing. She spends fourth period eyeballing it, counting the freckles along Fergus's skin that surround the growth like witches crowding around a cauldron. Sometimes she imagines lines connecting those blurpy blemishes, creating new constellations that she names after her sister's stuffed animals: Marcie Mouse, Teddy Blondie, Narbo the Dragon.

Fergus is tiny, stooped, his neck and chin swallowed by a crooked clavicle, and he constantly has food stuck in his braces, remnants of the bologna and cheese sandwiches he eats at lunch speckling his teeth and making his breath smell like the meat department at the grocery store. His hair, unkempt and curlicued under the green trucker hats he wears every day, is the color of a sun-withered apple. He trips over himself as he gathers up his books, shoving them into a faded Teenage Mutant Ninja Turtles backpack that Sheila is pretty sure he owns unironically. She's almost certain he's partially cross-eyed.

And yet she thinks about him. She dreams of Fergus's alabaster skin, exposed as he lies draped next to her on a bed dressed in red satin sheets the color of blood. That skin: always hidden away under soda-stained polo shirts and a long-sleeved white Henley that he tugs down over his wrists with fingernails a quarter inch longer than any other boy's, yellowed like a smoker's. In Sheila's dreams he kisses her and his dry lips taste like sardines, but she wakes up breathless and moved, her stomach queasy like everything in her body has shifted to one side, a fist pressed and throbbing between her legs. She knows she should be pining after Jackson Sanders, the tall, blond football star whose skin is the color of caramel, his muscles the shape of

contracted snakes from surfing all summer. Or perhaps Peter Nelson, who, while not particularly athletic, smokes cigarettes as he hops into his father's ancient Mustang after the final bell rings, black hair pomaded into a swoop like a water slide. Or Ricky Anderson, the lacrosse king who somehow makes windbreakers look sexy.

No, Fergus McMillan, blowhole and all, chases her through her daydreams and haunts her diary entries. In English class she hears his spit-encrusted voice while fat Mrs. Farwig recites Shakespeare's sonnets, and she pictures his tongue sliding with dexterous ease over the iambic pentameter, voice pitching and rushing at just the right moments. Sheila knows she should talk to him, tap him on the shoulder and ask if he wants to study for their upcoming quiz on parabolas and derivatives, but when she thinks about the feel of his bones beneath her fingers, the breakable pliancy of his body that must be like touching crepe paper, she becomes queasy and unsure. She shudders. This, after all, is love, isn't it? Like faith, it is absent reason, a kaleidoscopic, dizzy confusion, like when she was nine and skidded off her bike and clomped her head against the grainy, broken sidewalk. A pleasing nausea, blending sour-sweet vertigo and the coppery taste of pressure placed on a blue-black bruise, followed her for a week. So, she tells herself, she'll admire Fergus from afar, waiting for his blowhole to whisper her name, to create a gust of air that the two of them can ride up into the sky, where they'll be able to taste the stars and marry the moonlight in the wordless black, whirling an elliptic track around the sun in a silent vacuum, a place where sight and smell count for nothing.

Joe Baumann's fiction and essays have appeared in *Electric Literature, Electric Spec, On Spec, Barrelhouse, Zone 3, Hawai'i Review, Eleven Eleven*, and many others. He is the author of *Ivory Children*, published in 2013 by Red Bird Chapbooks. He possesses a PhD in English from the University of Louisiana-Lafayette and teaches composition, creative writing, and literature at St. Charles Community College in Cottleville, Missouri. He has been nominated for three *Pushcart Prizes* and was nominated for inclusion in *Best American Short Stories* 2016.

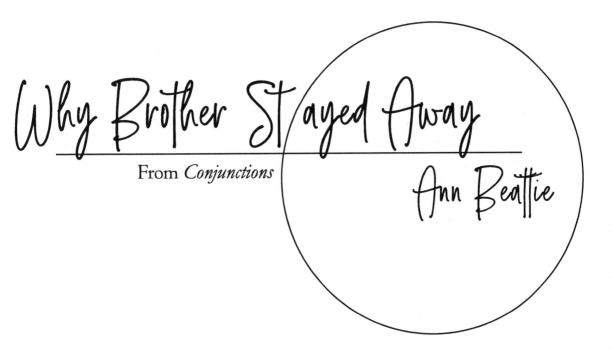

Why Brother Stayed Away

From *Conjunctions*

Ann Beattie

THE MOMENT HAD COME to see if it was true that Grumpa had a collection of ties lined with pictures of what her brother called "naughty ladies." Her brother lived in Buffalo and had not volunteered to have any involvement in cleaning up their grandparents' house. That had fallen to her and her husband. Only three ties hung on a hook inside the wardrobe. She examined the lining of the first. Weren't the women supposed to be naked, even if only from the waist up? Was Grumpa so lame that he was showing his men friends a picture of a woman wearing a scarf wrapped around her tits? Or a girl smiling over her bare shoulder from under a sunhat? The third tie was lined with a drawing of a carved pumpkin, smoking a pipe.

Her husband reached around her, opened the door of the wardrobe, and fingered Grumpa's polka-dot robe, his scuff slippers barely visible on the dark floor beneath it, and a couple of poorly hung, sagging sweaters. There were other clothes mashed together. With one finger, she separated a striped shirt from a wrinkled vest Grumpa had sometimes worn on holidays, his father's watch fob dangling an ornate, gold-filled watch, tucked inside a pocket.

In the secret shed—well; it was hardly a secret that the shed stood at the back of the property under the maple tree that had once been hit by lightning; only its contents were unknown because of the padlock. She watched with little interest as the screws were drilled out of the hinges. They fell on the ground as he walked off to do the next chore.

Call me if you find a dead body, he said. Sure, she replied, she certainly would. She stepped in. The shed was remarkably uncluttered. There was a lawn mower. A bicycle entirely missing its front tire, the back one deflated. A box. Inside the box, various tools, some of them rusty. A barbecue fork. An old issue of *Life* magazine with Richard Nixon on the cover. There was a dead body: the rotted carcass of a squirrel, the tip of its tail still bushy, like a groomed poodle.

Received information was that Grumpa had put the cash from the sale of his business into his wife's sewing basket, but that was not to be found on any shelf, in the attic, in the shed, in the garage, or anywhere else. In the garage, however, a cedar box was found, unlocked. Inside was half a pack of Camels, a cork coaster imprinted with the words Ben Bow, a splayed toothbrush with blackened bristles that had been used for something other than brushing teeth, Murine, a bottle of solidified glue, a white pill with no marking, and a small calendar (1962) from a local gas station. Also a penny, a dime, a tin soldier about the size of her husband's thumbnail, and two buttons.

The screwdriver was required to remove the latches on a wooden box dragged out from under the bed. "Voilà!" he said, walking out. She thought the box looked too rugged to contain, for example, her grandmother's wedding dress. It contained a quilt, log cabin pattern, twin bed size, nice. There was also a second quilt, badly folded. That one was not quite equal in size, but also intended for a twin bed. There was a faint, very faint, scent of lavender that disappeared as her nose pressed into the fabric.

Twenty minutes early, the man showed up who'd bought Grumpa's "antique" Ford truck and was having it hauled away. He stood around, one hand jingling change in his pant pocket. The flatbed arrived. Some twitchy guy loaded with chains jumped out. He and his young helper, or son, or whatever he was underneath all those tattoos, got the black truck onto the flatbed in no time, and just like that, they were gone. The check had cleared the day before. The man drove away in his Saab without even waving.

In the dream she has that night, Nixon requests, by engraved invitation, her presence at the White House. Well, dreams can sometimes be like smoking perilously strong weed. Like she'd be invited to the White House! Like Nixon would send a carriage for her, pulled by prancing white horses! Cinderella, off to a fabulous evening, wearing her finest gown, the night just a bit chilly. Fuckin' Ambien, she thinks, or dreams. The quilt warms her as she bounces in the back.

(She clutches the duvet.)

Through the gates she goes! Mrs. Nixon, wearing a midcalf fur coat, waves a gloved hand. She and President Nixon approach. The driver opens her door. He offers a gloved hand. A horse snorts, raising its head.

(This is her husband, snoring.)

She steps out, her satin slipper as beautiful as Mrs. Nixon's shoes with sparkling buckles. She swirls, to delight the adults. She's a child again. She opens her cape, exposing the deep blue lining. Big mistake! The velvet's imprinted with dancing figures: long-legged showgirls, high-heeled, bare breasted, red lipsticked, one with her butt stuck out, another whose lips coquettishly kiss a rosebud.

The Nixons are flabbergasted. Then they laugh so hard they frighten the horses, who run away, the driver helpless as his carriage disappears. All smiles vanish. Nixon narrows his eyes. What to do? She can't even flee without the carriage. Imploringly, she turns to Mrs. Nixon. But she's vanished, fur coat, splendid shoes, and all. Desperately, she turns toward the president. Men in military uniforms flank him. They're everywhere, a child's soldiers grown life-sized. Go ahead then, Nixon says to one of them: that driver fellow lost his carriage. Now he's gotta be beheaded. Who's our swordsman? Or will we have to have a firing squad and so forth?

She's sputtering spit, she finds, as she awakens and wipes her fingers across her mouth. Her weight is on one hip; she's propped awkwardly on her elbow, her nightgown tangled, the duvet, as always, sliding off the bed. Her husband sleeps.

She forgets the dream until she's about to toss the *Life* magazine down on a pile of someone's recycling in the trash room that stinks of mold mingled with pine, when she looks at Nixon's jowly face. Such an awful, dishonest man. He even extended a war because it better suited his purposes. In that instant, she realizes that her husband found the money. He must have found it, and not said so. Why else be so incurious about everything from the old man's ties to the contents of the shed? "Call me if you find a dead body." All he did was drill latches and walk away.

I'm going back to take another look, he says, picking up the car keys from the hall table as she reenters the apartment. Half senile or not, your grandmother insisted to her dying day that he'd hidden a vast sum of money in her sewing basket. It's a sewing basket I'm looking for, not a needle in a haystack. What's that look supposed to mean? Remember I'm the one who's giving up my weekends doing this, not your brother.

Ann Beattie's stories were first collected in *Distortions*, (1976). She has published 21 books, most recently, *A Wonderful Stroke of Luck* (2019). She tries to go to the gym most days.

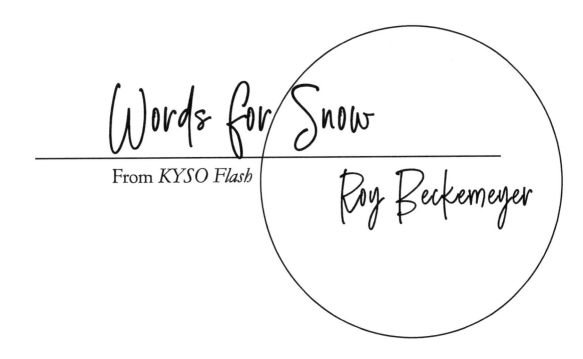

Words for Snow

From *KYSO Flash*

Roy Beckemeyer

The white bears have already forgotten the continent of ice; they think they have dwelt forever on this archipelago of small and scattered islands.

> —The Yupik, indigenous Arctic people traditionally residing in Siberia, Saint Lawrence Island and the Diomede Islands

EACH OF THE MANY Yupik words for snow will be written on a sliver of willow bark, placed in a seal-bladder sac. Year after year words will be pulled out, one by one, gummed by a toothless elder. Blubber-oil lights will flicker on their faces as they tell the words. This is how the people will remember, once the snow has gone: they will recall blizzards when they see the white cataracts cloud in an old woman's eyes; when an old man says the word *qetrar*, the children will repeat it as he describes the feel of the crust of snow crunching and yielding to the cushion beneath. This is how the people will remember when white is known only as the color of clouds, when the land is only mud and stone, when the Arctic Sea remains lapis-blue the entire winter long.

Roy Beckemeyer's latest poetry collection is *Stage Whispers* (Meadowlark Books, 2018). *Amanuensis Angel* (Spartan Press, 2018), is comprised of ekphrastic poems inspired by abstract, surrealist, and other artists' depictions of angels. *Music I Once Could Dance To: Poems* (Coal City Press, 2014) was a 2015 Kansas Notable Book. He recently co-edited (with Caryn Mirriam-

Goldberg) *Kansas Time+Place: An Anthology of Heartland Poetry* (Little Balkans Press, 2017). Beckemeyer lives in Wichita, Kansas and is a retired engineer and scientific journal editor. His work has been nominated for *Pushcart*, *Best of the Net*, and *Best Small Fictions* awards.

The Goat-Headed Girl

From *Spilled Milk*

Matt Bell

BECAUSE SHE HAD BEEN been born with the head of the goat, it fell to the older child to protect her from the leers of the other boys, their gross intentions. (In those days it was not past the men of the bogs to find pleasure in the fields, and the goat-girl stirred such odder wants, suggested combinations previously unknown.) As a child, the older fed the younger handfuls of grass and oats, let her chew the sleeves of his school uniform. Later he tied a loop around her neck and led her to other villages, where he hoped there might be another similarly cursed, or else a righteous man who might love her true despite her shape. Everywhere there were shepherds who promised the older gold for a single night with the younger but the older wanted more for his sad sister than the paid trysts these men offered. The siblings walked and walked. They saw many sights, many strange manners of men, but no other goatheads. In her nervousness, the younger chewed their clothes to rags, and soon no one would receive them, not even in the lands that professed to still hold dear the old rituals of hospitality and charity. Still the younger suckled her brother's hems, until she gnawed loose their last threads. On the road their nakedness increased their danger, for it was only her face that was odd, and the rest of her was without equal in the land. The older thought he had never seen anything more beautiful than when his younger bathed in the cold rivers of the land. He did not desire his sister—he was not that way—but the sight of her did make him wish for another, one much like her, a goat-headed girl he might call his own without the breaking of law or taboo or right-shaped sibling love.

At night the younger laid her odd head upon the older's chest and bleated sadly. He stroked her long ears and he fingered her collar and he made her promises, told her tales until she laughed. Even when she was joyous her voice wasn't a kind noise. If he talked long enough she would fall asleep against him and beneath her warmth he would begin to believe. Such was

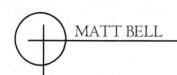

the nature of dreams, in that still early season of life. But what season ever lasts? When the men of the land finally came for his sister, the older fought them with fist and stick and little knife, but in the end he was just a boy, not yet grown into the hardness of truly disappointed men, and so what happened next was hardly his fault, despite how he blamed himself in all the years to come, those wandering years in which he stumbled from village to village, leading no sister at all, still dragging behind him a frayed rope, knotted tight to an empty leather collar.

Matt Bell is the author of the novels *Scrapper* and *In the House upon the Dirt between the Lake and the Woods*, as well as the short story collection *A Tree or a Person or a Wall*, a non-fiction book about the classic video game Baldur's Gate II, and several other titles. His writing has appeared in *The New York Times*, *Tin House*, *Conjunctions*, *Fairy Tale Review*, *American Short Fiction*, and many other publications. A native of Michigan, he teaches in the Creative Writing Program at Arizona State University.

The Ballad of Frankie Baker

From *Little Fiction/Big Truths*

DeMisty D. Bellinger

Frankie Baker, grey as a Missouri storm, stood so tall the room grew close. She yelled, "He wasn't named no Johnny. You listening to those songs on the Victrola and the radio. His name was Allen and he was nothing but a struggling, loser pimp who I thought loved me." She swiftly moved from anger to tears, her sobs came quick and transformed her to a small, lesser thing. She was now a woman who put too much of herself into a prospect worth nothing. "Guess you'd call me his whore. But he was mine. My man! He played piano."

She sat down and turned away from us. Her tired, black hand reached up and caressed the padded walls. Then the other hand joined in. Her fingers played invisible notes, her left hand striding along the lower register. "Ragtime. It was still fairly new. He made up songs, too."

She stopped playing her soft piano, then turned to us, looked at us over her shoulder. "The girl wasn't named Nellie Bly. That's them Victrola and radio y'all hearing. She was another whore. And I didn't shoot him there. I shot him at home because he tried to stab me. I shot him as God would have me do. That's why I'm still alive. I'm a Christian woman."

Miss Baker pulled a folded-up piece of newsprint from her bosom. Unfolded it with care. "They all got it wrong," she said. "I was nice and thick. Beautiful." She passed me the sheet and I see a print of the Thomas Hart Benton painting. "That woman they depicted there is as thin as a whisper. She shoots Allen in his back. I shot that motherfucker in the chest a couple of times. He too evil to die right away. And look at that woman. That's how they make us look. That wasn't me! I was beautiful."

I gave her the engraving back.

"I had curls," she said.

DeMisty D. Bellinger's writing has appeared in many places, including *The Rumpus*, and *Blue Fifth Review*, and *Necessary Fiction*. Her poetry chapbook, *Rubbing Elbows*, is available from Finishing Line Press. Her work has been nominated for Best of the Net and for a *Pushcart*. Besides writing, DeMisty teaches creative writing, women's studies, and African American studies. She lives in Massachusetts with her husband and twin daughters.

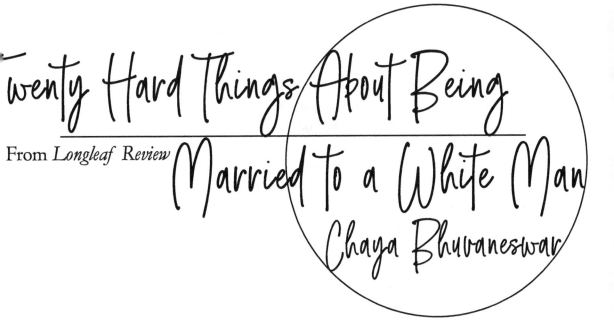

Twenty Hard Things About Being Married to a White Man

From *Longleaf Review*

Chaya Bhuvaneswar

1. YOU NOT ONLY GET mistaken for your children's nanny, but for the mean-looking, barely competent nanny, who can't manage to smile back when the white lady behind you in line smiles and asks the white-appearing children, "Are you children being good for your nanny?"

2. If your white husband is a liberal, your desire to serve him and let him dominate you is a sign of your wrong-headed, oppressive upbringing; and if he's conservative, your only problem is that you think too much.

3. If he's Christian, he wants you to know that he respects your culture completely. Only, come on, it's Christmas. *Everybody* celebrates Christmas. *Everyone.*

4. If he's Jewish, all he wants you to know is 1) you've helped him really break his mother's heart and 2) it's never too late to convert, which would placate his mother and save your children.

5. He sees nothing wrong with kissing his dog, then kissing you not that much later.

6. He cries when his dog has to get shots at the vet, but not every time it's mentioned on the news that a Muslim American girl was recently murdered in Virginia.

7. He and his mother enjoyed Jewel in the Crown, the PBS miniseries of decades ago that showed a white colonial officer whipping an Indian subject.

     You and your mother: not so much.

8. Especially if he's an academic, or a doctor, or some other white-collar graduate-degree'd professional, he'll say he enjoys spending time with your male friends who aren't white; he will feel relieved when those male friends eventually date white women.

9. If he's deeply in love with you, but doesn't know your parents' or grandparents' (or way back ancestors') native language, he will at some point try learning it. This will seem humble, as romantic as a man getting down on bended knee. But it is not. If he learns more than a few simple sentences, at some point, he will start correcting you.

10. If he spent years studying some aspect of what you think of as "your" culture, he won't waste time arguing with you about whether it's really your culture, or whether you know enough about it. Instead he'll make clothing suggestions—sarongs, saris, dashikis, dreads, natural hair instead of extensions—and he'll study you.

11. There might not be a lot of talk; it might be mainly a physical relationship, one that's both pleasurable and fun. But if he's not that much of a talker, he might not do more than laugh uncomfortably when others, both strangers and maybe even some of his friends, say things that are racist to his face.

12. No matter how beautiful, smart, noble, or accomplished you are, there is the possibility that he will always pity you, because the one thing you can't be is a white male.

13. He could feel good about making you "really" American: assimilated, integrated, intermarried, not standing apart.

14. He could judge you much more harshly for being haughty or even bitchy than he'd judge a white woman, because he secretly thinks you should be grateful he picked you.

15. If he's a keeper, he'll stand up to his mother if he has to and make sure she gets it that you aren't the "exotic mistress," or a fancy little "touch of the tarbrush," or any of the other phrases from the TV movie Queenie that you could watch a million times, sitting on the couch with him with your feet in his lap, even while you complain that Mia Sara "white-washed" the role of the Anglo-Indian Merle Oberon character, a role that should've been cast with an actress of color.

16. But if he's not a keeper, you might end up having to think of him as an adventure, and like after any other kind of adventure, you could wake up in a strange bed with a tattoo in an unexpected place, mouth full of apologies and explanations, but in the end no way to excuse

marrying someone you knew, you suspected, was racist deep down, although you didn't know for sure, not till the 2016 elections.

17. He's already made a secret plan of how he'll keep the kids in the US, to be raised by him and his mother, if you end up getting deported or detained and he becomes a single parent.

18. He might not realize that he's white, or he might feel upset with you for constantly mentioning it. Or, worst of all, he'll pity you for "still bringing that up," though it has been so many years, though both of you have made the commitment of marriage. He might even think consciously, "I just wish she didn't have that chip on her shoulder."

19. If he's a liberal, while he's against capital punishment and donated willingly to Black Lives Matter, he doesn't want your little girl to date a man of color who's a rapper, not really. Because of rap's misogynist lyrics, no other reason, he will say.

     If he's a conservative, he has a gun ready to scare away any man who tries to date her who's "not the right sort."

20. But even though he'd feel proud if she chose a white husband, since that would mean that she's choosing a man who might have some other similarity to him—even if her choosing a white man means that he has been a great father—deep down he doesn't want her to choose any husband.

     Because your daughter is still his little, exotic, princessy, lovely and unique little girl, and no man, white or of color, is ever going to be fine enough for her.

     Even if, after college, she gets a job with a biracial family as their children's nanny.

Chaya Bhuvaneswar is a practicing physician, writer and PEN American award finalist whose work has appeared or is forthcoming in *Narrative Magazine, Tin House, Electric Literature, The Millions, Joyland, Large Hearted Boy, Chattahoochee Review, Michigan Quarterly Review, The Awl,* and elsewhere, with poetry in the *Florida Review, sidereal, Natural Bridge, Apt Magazine, Hobart, Ithaca Lit, Quiddity* and elsewhere. *White Dancing Elephants* (Dzanc) her debut story collection was a

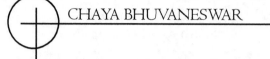

Kirkus Reviews Best Book of 2018. Her poetry and prose juxtapose Hindu epics, other myths and histories, and the survival of sexual harassment and racialized sexual violence by diverse women of color.

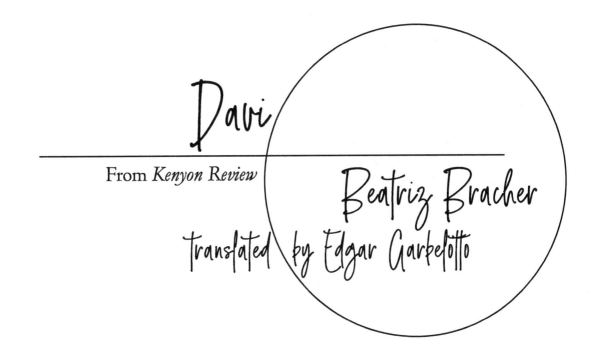

Davi

From *Kenyon Review*

Beatriz Bracher

Translated by Edgar Garbelotto

(having you sleeping by my side was all I ever wanted)

1

DAVI LOOKS AT WHAT is happening in front of him. His mouth is open. He can't breathe. He looks, but he can't see. He is twelve.

A man is on the ground, the black shoe of another man kicking him in the guts, the stomach, the large and small intestines. A stream of blood runs through his sinuses and gushes out of his mouth. It stains his gray-and-white-striped shirt and sky-blue tie a vivid red. A thick liquid forms a puddle on his dark suit, on the asphalt. The man turns on his stomach, protects his face with his hands. He gets kicked in the kidneys and ribs. The flesh around his internal organs can no longer cushion the sound, and the boy hears a noise louder than branches snapping in two.

Of course there are voices and car noises. The kicking man opens his mouth and yells, but the boy can't hear it. He only sees drops of saliva flying. The man on the ground contorts himself and closes his fists. The asphalt is rough. The boy hears "puff, puff." Liver, spleen, and internal hemorrhage come to mind. The man's shirt is stained with blood. Somebody will have to work hard to clean it. If this man wants to kill my father, he should kick him in the neck. The boy imagines the various bones of his father's neck breaking, and it makes his teeth shiver. His stomach contracts. A wave of acid burns in his throat and dies in his mouth. The boy's thoughts swirl.

The body on the ground hasn't stopped moving. The man turns it on its back. Davi looks at his father's face. The face is smeared with blood and rough from the asphalt, but it is a beautiful face. He understands that the face is beautiful; it's a face that pacifies him. His father's open eyes don't say anything. The boy blinks, wants to close his own eyes, but they open again. The man who is killing his father breathes deeply, bends his knees and jumps. His shoe is millimeters from landing on his father's face, and the boy's gaze finally moves from the ground and finds a tinted window where he sees his own reflection. The noises return, sharp now, and break the endless links between him, the words, and all the things related to his father's death. The last instant his memory keeps is the boy's face howling in the tinted glass of the bank window.

2

From the car, Davi sees the palm trees of the Botanic Gardens to his right, the wall of the Jockey Club on his left, the red traffic light in front of him and, far away, Pedra da Gávea. In the rearview mirror, he sees Christ the Redeemer on the Corcovado.

Davi and Flora wait for the green light. Some boys walk on the sidewalk to the left, they appear and disappear in the side mirror. They cross the street, pass in the rearview mirror, and disappear on Rua Pacheco Leão. A young white woman approaches Davi's window with a placard around her neck saying something about the Brazilian cinema and the movie director Glauber Rocha. Two young men hold a banner, letters in black and red: CINEMA IS COOL. The young woman says: Do you want to help Brazilian cinema? We don't have any money to finish the movie. Davi shakes his head. In front of his car, on the back of a small truck full of construction waste, there is a placard that reads: WE TAKE TRASH 2576-3535. Sitting on the trash, a black man swings a rusty fish knife between his legs. In the rearview mirror, Davi sees workers drilling in the street. Tiny shards of black asphalt fly through the air, and signs indicate: MEN AT WORK. CAUTION. DETOUR. A young worker is resting, sitting on the curb. His profile looks like a work of Russian futurist art. A little girl with curly hair and olive skin sells gum to the car in the right lane. She hangs on the car window, and her feet do a dance that reminds him of the hands of seventies' rock 'n' roll singers. A boy sells candy. Other boys offer boxes of strawberries that are too ripe. The light turns green.

3

Davi steps gently on the gas; he doesn't see Flora's face. He looks ahead, drives the car through the slow traffic and says, Sometimes, I don't see him but I know it's him that I'm dreaming of, in the middle of another story, his red eyes, even though they may be calm, even in the face of an old woman, even if they are not red in that moment, they appear and wake me up frightened. Yesterday, it was in a crowded street, he had his back to me, he walked embracing a woman, his hands held and caressed her waist, slowly.

I woke up and you were far away. I needed to hold you tight, bite you. I needed you last night, and you weren't there. It seemed like I was going to fall into my own heart if I couldn't hold you. There was a never-ending black hole in the middle of my chest, and I was going to

fall. I had vertigo, I had to grab onto my bed, dig my nails into the sheets. I woke up and you were sleeping so beautifully. I cried because you slept so beautifully. I knew, I knew that I could, but I didn't want to wake you up. Having you sleeping by my side was all I ever wanted.

Beatriz Bracher is a Brazilian author of four novels, including *Anatomia do paraíso* (*Anatomy of Paradise*, 2015), which won the São Paulo Literature Prize and the Rio de Janeiro Literature Prize. Her book *Meu Amor* (*My Love*) won the Clarice Lispector Award from the National Library Foundation for best short story collection in 2009. She was the editor of the magazine *34 Letra*s, specialized in literature and philosophy, and one of the founders of the publisher Editora 34. Her books have been published in Germany, Uruguay, and the United States (*I Didn't Talk*, New Directions, 2018).

Edgar Garbelotto is a writer and translator born in Brazil and based in the U.S. for the past 20 years. His translation of João Gilberto Noll's novel LORD was published by Two Lines Press in 2019. His work has appeared in the *Kenyon Review Online, Asymptote, Two Lines Press, Ninth Letter, Little Patuxent Review,* and elsewhere. He holds an MFA in Creative Writing from the University of Illinois. *Terra Incognita*, written in both Portuguese and English, is his debut novel.

How to Burn a Bridge Job Aid

From *Neil and Other Stories*
(Whisky Tit) and Heather Press

J. Bradley

HOW TO BURN A Bridge Job Aid

Use	Use this job aid to burn a metaphorical bridge.
Contents	·Define: bridge ·Overview ·Burn a bridge
Define: bridge	For the context of this job aid, a bridge symbolizes connection. Some of the most frequently used idioms involving bridges are as follows: ·Bridging the gap. ·Water under the bridge. ·We'll cross that bridge when we get there. ·Building bridges.
Overview	You burn a bridge to ensure: ·You cannot be followed. ·You cannot go back to what you have abandoned. Your reasons for burning a bridge are valid, even when everyone else disagrees with you.

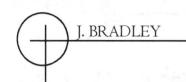

Follow these steps to burn a bridge.

Step	Action
1	Identify what you can do to irreparably harm the relationship.
2	Are you able to live with the consequences of your actions? <table><tr><td>If ...</td><td>Then ...</td></tr><tr><td>Yes</td><td>Go to step 3.</td></tr><tr><td>No</td><td>Reassess this relationship for what is worth saving. **END OF PROCEDURE**</td></tr></table>
3	Do you want to burn the bridge in person? <table><tr><td>If ...</td><td>Then ...</td></tr><tr><td>No</td><td>Go to step 4.</td></tr><tr><td>Yes</td><td>Bring a friend to help you escape as the bridge blackens, the planks fall beneath your feet while you run towards the other side. If you do not have a friend willing to help you escape, consider burning the bridge remotely.</td></tr></table>
4	Perform what will irreparably harm the relationship.
5	Is the bridge burnt? <table><tr><td>If ...</td><td>Then ...</td></tr><tr><td>Yes</td><td>Go to step 6.</td></tr><tr><td>No</td><td>Do you still want to burn this bridge? <table><tr><td>If ...</td><td>Then ...</td></tr><tr><td>Yes</td><td>Repeat steps 1-5.</td></tr><tr><td>No</td><td>Reassess this relationship for what is worth saving. **END OF PROCEDURE**</td></tr></table></td></tr></table>
6	Are you able to live with the consequences of your actions? <table><tr><td>If ...</td><td colspan="2">Then ...</td></tr><tr><td>Yes</td><td>a.</td><td>Take comfort in your reasons when asked why you did it.</td></tr><tr><td></td><td>b.</td><td>Note how you burnt this bridge in the event you need to burn another one that looks just like it.</td></tr><tr><td>No</td><td colspan="2">Live with the regret until it subsides to a manageable level. If the regret is still unmanageable after more than 90 days, refer to the How to Repair a Burnt Bridge Job Aid for further instructions.</td></tr></table> **END OF PROCEDURE**

J. Bradley is the author of *Neil And Other Stories* (Whiskey Tit Books, 2018) and *Greetings From America: Letters from the Trade War* (Whiskey Tit Books, 2019). He lives at jbradleywrites.com.

In Which We Drive The

From *JMWW*

Transpeninsular, Mexico 1

Lori Sambol Brody

WE SAY *WE'RE IN between jobs* since I walked out of serving retirees at Denny's and he slipped some money from Pep Boy's cash register at the end of his shift. Skipping out of Carpintaria is the best thing to do and we've got itchy soles and figure that Juneau does too, although she just started to walk. I can't remember all the towns I've left, army bases and towns of stucco and integrated circuits, each place not where I'm supposed to be. He grew up in this narrow strip between sea and mountains; each year the town grows smaller. So we jump into the Subaru station wagon and the hula girl on the dashboard starts bobbing and Juneau sings to it. We head south along the coast, shooting through the border at midnight. You can tell when San Diego becomes Tijuana, big box stores and 7-11s ceding to downtown casinos and shanties clinging to hills. We drive south, past the beaches with skyscraper condominiums half-built and abandoned, past K-38 where he used to shoot fireworks off and surf as a teenager, through Rosarito and Ensenada. He says, *There's too many gringos there.* We drive through the town with sidewalks paved with clamshells, the town where turkey vultures tear the guts of bloated cattle, the town of shrines to the dead, bristling with roadside crosses. This is our lesson: we must keep moving. The hula girl dances through the town known for its *carnitas*; we fly by women in men's shoes waiting on customers at oil-clothed tables, until something starts knocking in the engine. Down a pitted road, where the mechanic lies in a ditch under our Subaru. *Basuru,* he says. But he fixes it. His daughter drives figure-eights on a Big Wheel she's grown too big for and Juneau circles her. Juneau wants a Big Wheel too. We stay at a beach where whale-watching *pangas* cleave the lagoon that once boiled thick and hot with blood. For only a day, then we drive to the town gringos built; on art gallery walls hang self-portraits of American woman enamored by their mustaches. At a campsite on a beach covered with deflated puffer fish and devil's horns, waves driven by a hurricane hundreds of miles away snap his surfboard in two. I want to drive north, find a home; he wants to take the ferry from La Paz to the mainland. The money he liberated, not much to begin with, is already mostly spent on gas, *cacahuates con chile y limón*, and Tecate. *You're never happy*, he says. We raise our voices until Juneau cries, then she sleeps between us in the back of the Subaru. In the middle of the night, he turns to me and whispers, *Let's go north*. His hand cups Juneau's head. We drive through sunlight and moonlight, taking turns at the wheel. A white hawk surveys from the top of a saguaro. We drive off the highway down a washboard dirt road to an abandoned onyx quarry. A schoolhouse built of creamy onyx stands roofless. We leave Juneau sleeping in her booster seat with the hula girl in her arms. The wind whistles between us. We pick up pieces of stone striated like yellow layered cake. Theda Bara's bathtub was carved from this marble. He calls out but the wind snatches his words away. He pantomimes taking a bite from a stone. Maybe I say, *Don't break your teeth*. It doesn't matter because he can't hear me. The direction of the wind changes and I hear Juneau. She's screaming, face red in the window of the station wagon. *Mama Papa gone*, she says. The hula girl abandoned on the upholstery. The wind blows and we are so still. Her tears wet my shoulder. I say, *We would never leave you, never leave you.*

Lori Sambol Brody's stories have been published in *SmokeLong Quarterly*, *Wigleaf*, *Little Fiction*, and the *New Orleans Review*, among others, and were chosen as the Longform fiction pick-of-the-week and for *Best Small Fictions* 2018. She has driven through Baja in a Basuru and collected onyx from an abandoned quarry. She is working on two flash novellas.

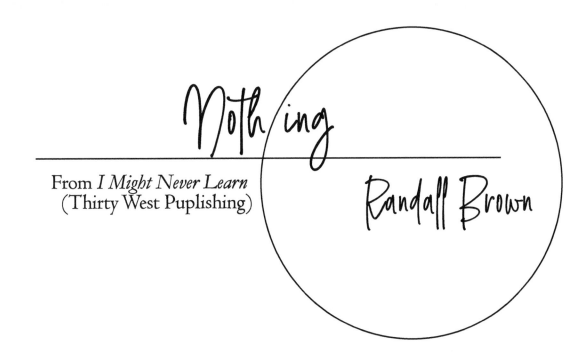

Nothing

From *I Might Never Learn*
(Thirty West Puplishing)

Randall Brown

NO, SHE SAID, IT has to do with money, the way you waste it. I did have lots of money in college. We sold the pot Alex's friend Fed Exed from Arizona. It had red hairs. I ate sushi a lot, bought Ray Ban sunglasses, entire catalogs: The Replacements, The Smiths, Dylan. I bought a Trans-Am. I drove Sara to the Mountain Club in New Hampshire; we hiked and ate mushrooms that tasted like cow shit, or how we imagined cow shit to taste. The leaves burned on the paths. I handed Sara a wadded pocket of crumpled money. That's when she called me a rake. I should've said something instead, something about the things I surrounded myself with, the world going to seed because of it. Sara—her red hair alit like signals across mountains—left me alone a few feet from the peak. I watched her descend, and I thought about what was behind the money and other things, too: the fall of leaves, the sun and stars, all of it.

Randall Brown is the author of the award-winning collection *Mad to Live,* his essay on (very) short fiction appears in *The Rose Metal Press Field Guide to Writing Flash Fiction,* and he appears in the *Best Small Fictions* 2015 & 2017, *The Norton Anthology of Hint Fiction,* and *The Norton Anthology of Microfiction.* He founded and directs *FlashFiction.Net* and has been published and anthologized widely, both online and in print. He is also the founder and managing editor of Matter Press and its *Journal of Compressed Creative Arts.* He received his MFA from Vermont College.

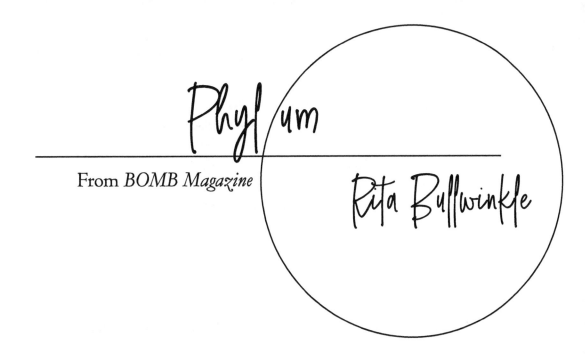

Phylum

From *BOMB Magazine*

Rita Bullwinkle

I WAS THE TYPE of man who got his ears cleaned. I was the type of woman who didn't like dogs. We lived together in a house on a street that was the color of asphalt. I told you what I thought of you. I told you to leave me alone. You didn't own the house. I never liked our street. It smelled like cough syrup. I like living in a place that smells good.

I was the type of man who went to board meetings. I was the type of woman who liked gouda cheese. We lived together in an apartment next to a deli. I stole money from your wallet. I knew you hated how I dressed. I snuck out in the night and went to Harlem. The thing about cities is anyone can go anywhere and never be seen. We both knew it made the game easier. We both liked knowing there was a game.

I was the type of woman who liked swimming in hotel pools. I was the type of man who liked listening to plays. We didn't have children. You listened to Mozart and Bach, and always said you loved classical music, but I knew, and you knew that you don't know any other composers. I like John Lennon. That isn't a composer. Says who?

I was the type of man who walked out into the night and took my hair in my hands and dropped to my knees and wept. I was the type of woman who recycled every scrap of waste I ever produced because the thought that I was slowly killing our planet made me feel like my intestines were climbing up my throat and out my mouth. We clung to each other mostly out of fear.

I was the type of woman who looked out the window and saw a parade of elephants and cats and hogs. I was the type of man who cut his food in half so many times that my bites were the size of raisins. We lived together in a hand-built structure in Vermont. We both knew conversation wasn't for us. You didn't speak for a year. Is that too long of a time not to speak?

I was the type of woman who carved local stones into arrows and cooked snakes into stews and looked at the sky with longing. I was the type of man who sucked juice out of straws and cooked enough grand meals to make anybody love me. We both rotted in the sand of a far-off beach. Our skin fell from our bodies and the sun bleached what was left of us until children found our remains and made them into playthings. The castles of our bones had moats and the moon pulled the tides so close to us that water came and knocked at the door of our dead bodies. You wanted to go with the moon. I was happy to stay in the sand. What you wanted didn't matter in the end because in the end we were both taken by the sea.

Rita Bullwinkel is the author of the story collection *Belly Up*, which won the 2018 Believer Book Award, and has been translated into Italian and Greek. Bullwinkel's writing has been published in *Tin House, Conjunctions, BOMB, Vice, NOON,* and *Guernica.* She is a recipient of grants and fellowships from The MacDowell Colony, Brown University, Vanderbilt University, Hawthornden Castle, and The Helene Wurlitzer Foundation. Both her fiction and translation have been nominated for a Pushcart Prize. She lives in San Francisco.

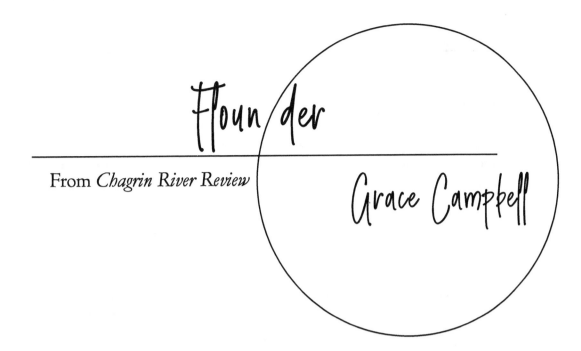

Flounder

From *Chagrin River Review*

Grace Campbell

HE HAS ONE OF those rich dads who wanted to teach him the value of a dollar, so David got a job in the kitchen of the catering place and worked his way up which is how come the dinner he has made me is, at least in my mind, supposed to be really good. Only it is fish, which I haven't expected and I just can't get with fish, can you blame me?

I eat four bites. It tastes like when I used to do little experiments with Elmer's Glue, like stick a whole bottle in the freezer then cut it into tiny slivers. Which, of course, I ate. So I know what I'm talking about here, mostly on a textural level. But it has taken really long for David to make the fish. During which time we have gone through a seven course meal of wine, wine, wine, wine, wine, wine and wine. Which is how come the fish goes into his stomach without making a bight in the buoy line of the gaze so obviously anchored to the hem of my miniskirt. Which is how come we end up on the couch.

You could say I get up from my seat again and again to walk across the room and switch the cd so David can watch me in my skirt. Or you could say I do it to draw some space between me and the fish, because it's not like I can hide it under my plate and mash it down, which worked pretty well back in the Elmer's Glue days. You could say that the whole reason for the fish and the wine and the music and the skirt is the plain fact of the couch. Though you could argue that I might have changed my mind about the dinner had I known it was going to be fish. And I might have changed my mind about the couch had I known David would put his hands on me, saying *I bet you think I won't do this* and me laughing under the broiler coil of his face, starting to say *I bet you won't--*

--but inside the space of a malbec hiccup, David's hand is working its way up me because David knows the value of a bet. The labor causes his face to collect little colonies of strained sweat like the descaled surface of the who-knows-what-kind of sea fowl as he pulls it

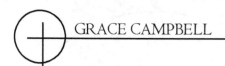

from the heat blast of four hundred degrees Fahrenheit and pronounces it done. Were it any other enterprise, I would move to wipe the mark of his effort from its written place on the wall of his forehead but he guessed wrong about the fish and I guessed wrong about the couch and when you hide your *no* under your dinner plate and try to mash it into oblivion it's not really a *no*, is it.

Grace Campbell is a founding writer and editor at *Black River Press* and the fiction editor at *5x5 Literary Magazine*. She was awarded a 2018 June Dodge Fellowship at The Mineral School. She is the author of the chapbook *Girlie Shorts* (2018). Her chapbook, *FWIW*, was a finalist for the Turnbuckle Chapbook Competition at Split Lip Press. She was also awarded third prize in the *Atticus Review* Creative Nonfiction Flash Competition. Her work has appeared widely, in such journals as *New Flash Fiction Review, Gravel, Jellyfish, Foliate Oak*, and *Spry*. She enjoys tinted lip balm and extremely sharp scissors.

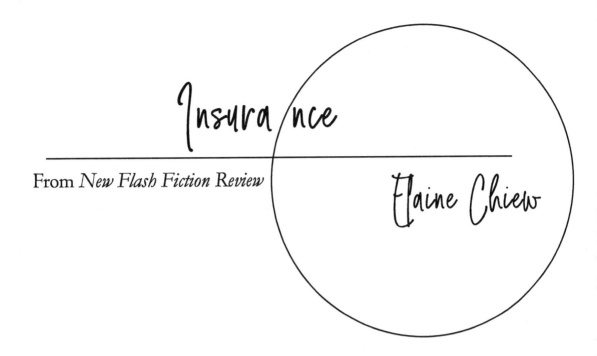

Insurance

From *New Flash Fiction Review*

Elaine Chiew

YOU GO DIVING WITH him in the Bahamas as a leap of faith, even though you're not sure whether it's a leap of faith in yourself or in him or in your togetherness. It's new still in your relationship; you'd met him at a medical conference, out lounging on a cabana. He had drawn up close, in his tan linen jacket and sharply-creased blue trousers, and asked if he could buy you a drink. Not that you are looking for a relationship, or even a carefree fuck, because your mother is in her last stages of Alzheimer's and it's just you and her but between shuttling on the commuters' train from her home of assisted living and your job in insurance sales, you'd begun to find chit-chat with strangers nauseating. But there was something about his blue eyes and shaggy hair that spelled an aura of wanting to please and you thought to yourself, oh why the hell not? Your mother would disapprove of his slight put-on dishevelment and crude jokes. When it's just the two of you, he is altogether more serious, more real, more himself, but he truly comes alive when the audience is ten or more. Then he would sing Nessun Dorma in a faux baritone (which your mother would find kitschy or attempt a ballerina stunt and split his pants). But your mother will never meet him, or if she does, she will never remember.

So you think of him as insurance. A kind of biological safety net, safe enough to risk an underwater world where you go diving with him. You are such a terrible swimmer that once you'd sunk to the bottom of a kid's pool at the swimming club and thought you were drowning and surfaced and screamed for help and when people rushed over and someone finally pulled you out, you claimed a leg cramp because you were so embarrassed.

Down now in these murky watery depths, you panic and start hyperventilating. Water rushes into your mask. Your heart drops to a new plumbing depth. Someone grabs your shoulder and then holds your hand and guides you with finger gestures on how to empty your mask of water. You suck in lungful after lungful of oxygen and begin to feel giddy. All you can see behind his mask are his eyes, but not the expression in them because there is a film of moisture over everything. A school of fish swims past and you think you've never seen anything more beautiful in your life. You think the man holding your hand is a godsend, and you wonder if he isn't the diving instructor, with his rapid gesturing and purposeful movements. There, before you, are schools of marine bioluminescence. Florets of musky coral. Plumes of purple anemones. Membraned jellyfish, lit from within, rising as clouded fumes. Seawhip. Polyps like thousands of eyes. They sense your dark presence. An entire school of fish changes direction. Your lungs swell, you feel the massive ache in your jaw even before you hear the snap upon bone. What is blue becomes red, then black. You are neither fish nor human now. There is no name, no memory, for the undersea monster you've become. You power through subterranean coves, your body sleek, aerodynamic. Swimming. Finning. The water closing over you is icy, instantly numbing. Your sleek tail torque, you rappel down to seabed level.

When you finally surface, you are delirious.

You tell this man it's the most amazing trip of your life. The two of you are sitting eating lunch at a seafood place with all the other divers, and that's when you learn two things: the school of fish is barracuda, and the man who had held your hand is no instructor but the man you are dating for insurance. You burst out laughing and you simply can't stop. Everyone around you first smiles indulgently, including the man you are dating, and then their smiles become more hesitant, and the way their smiles start to fade made your epiglottis seize up and you almost choke on your mouthful of tilapia.

Elaine Chiew is a writer and a visual arts researcher. She is a two-time winner of The Bridport Prize, amidst other prizes and shortlistings. Her short story collection *The Heartsick Diaspora* is forthcoming from Myriad Editions (U.K.) and Penguin Random House (SEA) in October 2019. She is also the compiler and editor of *Cooked Up: Food Fiction From Around the World* (New Internationalist, 2015), and her fiction has appeared in numerous anthologies and journals. In October 2017, she was Writer in Residence at SOTA Singapore. She received an MA in Asian Art History from Goldsmiths, University of London in 2017.

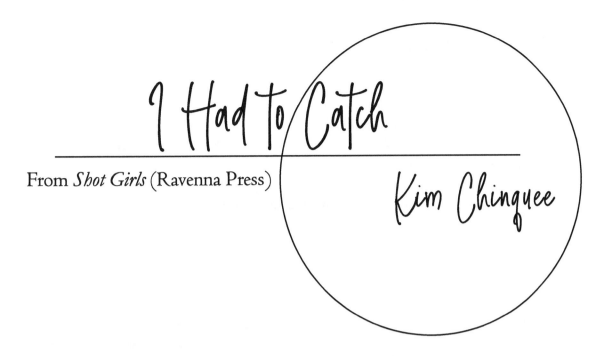

I Had to Catch

From *Shot Girls* (Ravenna Press)

Kim Chinquee

I KNOCKED ON THE door eight times. A cow bellowed on the other side of the door. I pushed the little board up over the latch. It was an old barn, gray and wooden, one my grandparents had built, or maybe the ones before them.

My breath pushed into the cold air. I had on a hat, mittens, and the boots I wore when I fed the calves every morning before I had to catch the school bus. I knew what it meant when a cow was separate from the others that roamed indoors and out—I'd spent a lot of time up in the hayloft, tossing the bales of hay that I helped my dad harvest—every summer, after picking stones from the dirt and throwing them onto a wagon to get tossed onto the stone pile that had existed since whenever—the fields would grow, and once it was time again, we'd go out with whatever the machine was called, and I'd catch the hay straight from the baler that would wrap the bales with twine.

The baler would throw the bales, shooting them like vomit.

I'd do my best to catch them, using my arms, and on the wagon, I'd put them in stacks. My hands were calloused. I was tough—and though I was a girl, I didn't care that my legs were scarred from scratches. A few times, my dad ordered me to drive the tractor, but I got so bored just sitting there, worrying I was driving crooked; then just like I imagined, my dad came at me yelling, taking over, not even trying to correct me.

After the wagon was full, we'd toss the bales onto another machine, and escalator that carried the bales up to the loft, dropping them in random places that we'd have to mound up later.

I loved the loft, where there was an opening looking down into the cow barn, to their indoor feeders. Sometimes I'd just sit there, watching them as they roamed, pooping, laying, chewing up their cuds. Sometimes I dropped them extra hay. I'm not sure why I did that.

I imagined jumping down myself.

We were all about producing.

After unlatching the door, I saw the special cow who always ate my hay. She stood with her legs spread.

I think I heard her moan.

Bits of corn lay on the ground. All around me creatures scattered.

Kim Chinquee's sixth collection *Wetsuit* was published with Ravenna Press in March 2019. She is a two time *Pushcart Prize* recipient, Senior Editor of *New World Writing*, Chief Editor of *ELJ (Elm Leaves Journal)*, and she co-directs the writing major at SUNY-Buffalo State.

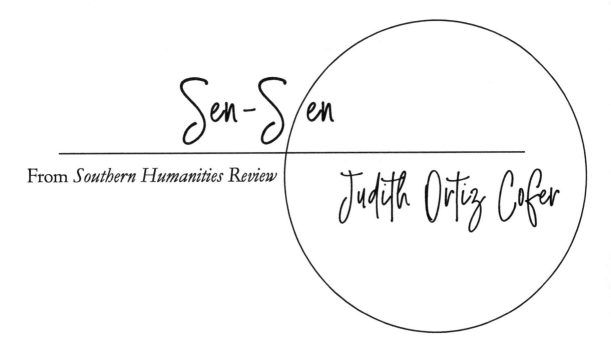

Sen-Sen

From *Southern Humanities Review*

Judith Ortiz Cofer

WHEN MY FATHER CAME back from the dead, he announced himself in the room to my mother as the smell of Sen-Sen the first breath mint. He'd tear open one corner of the little envelope and tap out one of the tiny black squares that smelled of perfume. I recently read that this "breath-fragrance" was registered as a cosmetic in the late nineteenth century by a perfume manufacturer. It tasted like raw licorice once it melted on your tongue. Papi would buy Sen-Sens when he was planning a night out with los amigos. Mother hated those nights, which she suspected included mujeres—why else would he need to perfume his breath? I can still see how she scrunched up her face when he took them out of his pocket, usually when he came to kiss me good-night. I smelled the strong scent and learned to associate it with both his obvious excitement at escaping the demands of home, wife, and children for one night, and my mother's festering anger at the manly prerogative of a night out in freshly ironed guyabera, creased pants, and scented breath. She was angry that she had sweated over the ironing board, that she had outfitted him for a party she could not attend.

Sen-Sen is what wafts into her living room one night when we were decades beyond his early death, when all that was left of him was in a box of photos we'd been looking at that afternoon. Sen-Sen. We'd summoned him by saying his name again and again, and my father is back as his perfumed breath, and the smell of Niagara starch on freshly ironed clothes. He came back as el hombre de la casa, el jefe, who risked my mother's ire and her sarcastic dismissal of the friends he could not disappoint, compadres who must not be allowed to think that she had domesticated him.

"Do you want people to think you have me sentado en el baul?" The question must have hung in the air between them. Did she shrug and say, "No me importa lo que digan la gente"? She often said she didn't care what people might say, but she would also warn me about what others might say about my misbehaviors. I grasped her meaning, but sentado en el baul was a phrase I did not understand as a young child to mean beaten-down. Why would he fear people saying that his wife has him sitting on his suitcase? Ready to kick him out? Sen-Sen—I tasted it once and spit it out; it was like eating a bit of charcoal dipped in the cheap dime-store perfume, Evening in Paris.

And on this night, thirty years beyond his death, my mother hurries to switch the fan on. Her gaze is turned inward when she returns to her chair. By the deep breath she takes, I know that she has taken him in, and in her long exhale, I hear her letting him go, inevitably, into the night again. Sen-Sen.

―――――――――――

Judith Ortiz Cofer was an award-winning novelist, essayist, and poet. She is the author of *Peregrina*, *An Island Like you: Stories of the Barrio*, *The Latin Deli: Prose and Poetry*, *A Love Story Beginning in Spanish*, and numerous other works across poetry, fiction, nonfiction, young adult literature, and children's literature. Her work has been anthologized in *Best American Essays*, *Best American Short Stories*, *The Norton Book of Women's Lives*, and *The Norton Introduction to Poetry*. Cofer passed away at her home in Georgia on December 30, 2016.

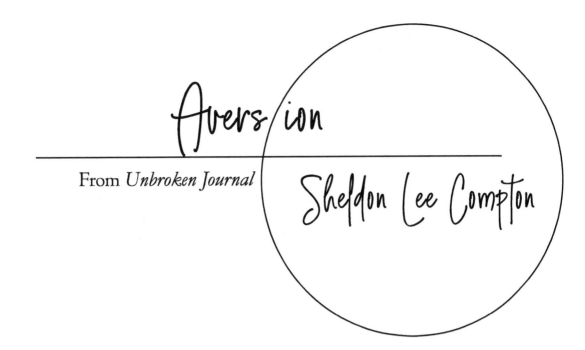

Aversion

From *Unbroken Journal*

Sheldon Lee Compton

EGGS. EGG. ANYTHING WHITE. Anything oval. Come to think of it, anything yellow or white and oval. Or scrambled all over, you know, sort of thrown around and fluffy? And yellow and white, the two of them together. With white specks all through the yellow, smelling of butter. In fact, butter itself. Because butter can send me straight toward the egg cliff and then all the rest of it comes into play, sort of swells up inside me, and to bathroom I go, knees first. Styrofoam, too. Like the cartons. Cartons and cartons of eggs. Too much Styrofoam in one place can eventually do it—opening a box from the mail, for example, with all those little egg-shaped bits of Styrofoam, ohmygod. Chickens can put me there more than you'd think and the shape of a fingernail, if I'm in that certain frame of mind, the moon on nights with fog blurring the edges of everything, and even before life, the womb an imperfect circle, the womb brought to life in part by the terrible egg. But it all leads back to eggs. So many things do now. Amy loved loved my scrambled eggs. I made them for her near the end. I handed her a full plate while she sat on the toilet. She liked that I did that sometimes, the way I seemed impatient to have her taste my eggs. She sat on the toilet, the opening hugging at her white thighs, her legs delicately spread apart a little more than usual, her jogging pants tossed around her ankles, holding the plate balanced in the palm of her hand. She stared at me for a long, long time. How can I explain it? I can't, really. There's only the egg. Anything white. Anything oval or yellow and white or scrambled around or butter or the smell of butter or bathrooms, with those toilets endlessly capped with lids of white, hollow ovals. The perfect smooth white of thighs at complete rest or goddess blue eyes watching me break apart one crack after another and another and another. And it continues. One crack and then another and another and another, all born from the last with the next creating one more until, thankgod, there's nothing left to break and nothing left altogether.

Sheldon Lee Compton is the author of five books of fiction and poetry. His third novel, *Dysphoria: An Appalachian Gothic*, was published by Cowboy Jamboree Press this past spring. West Virginia University Press will soon publish his first nonfiction book, *The Orchard Is Full of Sound: On Breece D'J Pancake and Appalachia*. His stories have appeared in *BULL: Men's Fiction*, *Vending Machine Press*, *X-RAY Literary Magazine*, and *New World Writing*, among others. He lives in Pike County, Kentucky.

The Convent

From *The Rumpus*

Maggie Cooper

THE NUNS WERE KNOWN across Europe for their preserves, which were exquisite, concocted in small batches from freshly plucked alpine fruits. In glass jars, the jams and jellies glistened on breakfast tables from Vladivostok to Copenhagen, and in the orchards around the mountain convent the nuns weighed ripe pears in their palms like full breasts.

What was preserved: the fruit, the summer sweetness of a company of women in the orchard sunshine, the memory of the sisters who had stood over the pots in the months before. In the convent kitchens, the sisters peeled and cored, chopped and macerated, practicing their witchcraft of pectin and hard work. The sour taste of a drop of blood became a finger-pricked counterpoint to the perfume of apricots and plums. The recipes had been passed across the years with only the slightest adjustments—a dash of nutmeg, a touch of anise.

As the moon waxed and waned over the walls of the convent, the sisters polished new jars and poured them full of curds, coulis, and marmalades. They dreamed of orchards that went on for acres, a kitchen with hundreds of pots and pans, a group of women who traveled far and wide to gather the world's bounty: the mango and the quince, the Chinese gooseberry with its fragrant scent and pale green flesh.

It happened gradually at first: a forgotten pot hardening with sugar burned black, a batch of jars bursting into shards as they were carried into the cool of the store room. There were fewer of them than there had been once, for the world outside the convent had grown tired of nuns, and jams came now from enormous factories, where the only song was the electrified hum of silver machines whirring.

Yet the sisters were not to be dissuaded. Instead, they brewed stronger concoctions—dark fig pastes, a cherry jam thick with smoky spices. For so long now, they had cast their love out from the convent in hundreds of glass jars, offering up the fruits of their labors. For so long, they had read from the scriptures and given their thanks for the fruit of the tree bleeding juice against Eve's teeth. It was true, wasn't it, that the less-perfect fruits tasted sweetest after stewing—that there was no jostled peach or half-squashed berry that could not be redeemed?

So they had all believed, for they were themselves the bruised apples of the world, not loved enough by the families who had left them by the convent gates, the husbands that had pushed them out when their wombs had not borne the fruit of a human child. In the convent, every woman had her role to play in the big, bustling kitchens, her voice one of many raised in song along the raspberry vines.

Now the raspberries shriveled amongst the leaves, and the sisters' numbers dwindled so that matins rang thin in the hall, and in the kitchens, pots stood cold and empty. In Vladivostok, an old woman sighed at the memory of a piece of toast she had eaten as a young woman in love, shining with dark berries. When a blight in the orchards turned the cherries to dark rot, the sisters had no choice but to empty their stores and carry the last jars up to the long wooden table that ran down one wall of the kitchen.

Something in the world had gone sour, too sour to be remedied by a spoonful of jelly—too bitter even for the nuns with their strong potions and deep, heavy pots. So they prepared the last recipe, their voices raised in a final song. Perhaps, this could still preserve them, the slow stewing of the fruit, the passing of the pot from one sister to another. They waited patiently for it to cool and set, then dipped their spoons in and lifted the jam to their lips, sweet and heavy like an ending.

Maggie Cooper graduated from the M.F.A. writing program at the University of North Carolina at Greensboro and attended the Clarion Science Fiction and Fantasy Writers' Workshop in 2016. Her work has appeared in *The Rumpus*, *Lilith Magazine*, and *Inch*. You may follow her on Twitter @frecklywench.

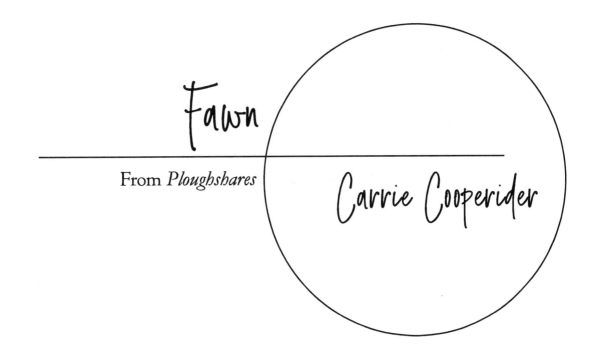

Fawn

From *Ploughshares*

Carrie Cooperider

NO, NO, NO—THAT'S not how it goes. I'm putting too many words in. Start again. I should tell it so that it begins with silence, with snow; show you the frozen speckle-strewn fawn I found at wood's edge behind the cabin's bark-stripped walls. I should tell it so that a six-year-old can understand, because that's what I was and that's all I knew.

I drew my breath in when I saw it, and felt the hairs in my nose stiffen to needles. Snow caked the cable stitch of my mittens and my fingers made fists inside. My toes were icebergs floating somewhere off the coast of my feet, unfelt, and my thighs were stinging hot with cold. I released my breath into fog. The fawn stood on unbending legs, muffled in its last snowfall; no answering steam came from its muzzle. Tiny icicles dangled from its snout and belly and I walked closer to touch my bare fingers to the frozen eyelashes that sparkled around an unblinking eye. Its head was bent to the left distance—looking where? Listening for what? The little deer had just stopped, it seemed, mid-step, mid-thought, the odor of snow still in its nostrils. The sudden spring storm had made the fawn too cold to walk any farther, its blood growing slushy and slow until its will to move left it. How long did the fawn's mother wait for her child to overcome his stubborn foolishness before bounding away into the grove of fir, turning her head one last time to look back, then vanishing into the dim wood?

The fingers of my uncovered hand grew stiff. I could not find my mitten. I must have dropped it when I pulled it off to touch the deer's spiky eyelashes, and it now lay hidden in the same-colored snow. Mother would be cross about the lost mitten, but it was already near-dark.

Leave it then, leave it and go home, to warmth and supper and Mother. Mother, who would be starting to miss me—wouldn't she? Mother, who might be angry enough to send me straight to bed but too tired to take up the switch beside the door. Mother, who, I imagined, would just now be turning her head from some task to peer through the window's false

brightness, seeking out, among the deep blue shadows, her dear heart, her own dear darling—oh, wouldn't she be?

Carrie Cooperider' s short fiction, essays, and interviews have been published in *Ploughshares, The Antioch Review, NY Tyrant, Autre, The Southampton Review, 3:AM, Cabinet Magazine, Speak, The Los Angeles Review of Books,* and *Best Small Fictions* 2017. She lives in New York City and is a graduate of the Bennington Writing Seminars.

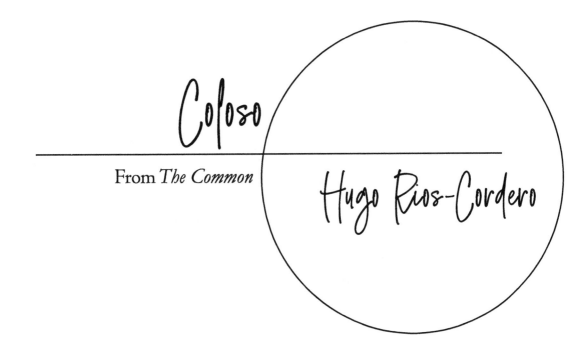

Coloso

From *The Common*

Hugo Rios-Cordero

IN THE SAME WAY that some structures carry time on their shoulders, we too want to observe its traces. Every place, of course, has anchors that halt time as it passes by. In Europe, the huge cathedrals are mute and impotent witnesses of history. Likewise, the old sugar mills of Puerto Rico remain to remind us of an era that, while gone, is still harbored within them. These metal monsters, abandoned to their rusty luck, become sanctuaries of memory. The mill Coloso, one of the last of the dying titans, is now only a grey silhouette lost in the green and twisted landscape of the valley.

But it is not as empty as it seems.

Few know that, out there, the days are longer. The light barely filters through the scaffolding. The elongated girders, black with corrosion, barely remember the workers' strikes and their almost mythical foundations. Now the only inhabitants are the wind and stray dogs. The vacant workers' quarters have lost their original soot, returning to a more human tone provided by nature, but at the same time they are ceasing to exist, sinking into the farthest province of oblivion. Once, these walls silently observed the departure of trucks full to the brim with sugar, the warehouses stocked with canes, the smell of molasses, the whistle blows, and then, finally, the last zafra. But these are very old memories, anachronisms of a time long gone. Recently, Coloso has become the site of a body.

I don't know if it arrived by accident, or was it murder? I couldn't tell if the marks on the skin were signs of a natural or a criminal death. It does not matter. The body had the luck or misfortune to fall through a crack, an unused corner with difficult access, an avatar of architectural waste.

When I found it, it was still fresh. I know I should have reported it. I imagined relatives, friends, looking expectantly through the window or waiting by the phone for news.

However, I decided to hold on to it. And visit it daily. For a moment I thought about hiding it, but then I figured that if it had not been found by now, it would never be. I just looked at it, untouched, undisturbed, envying its quietness. I spent long hours watching the erasure of its features. For a time there was a strong smell, but later it became natural and mixed well with the aromas of iron and history that permeated the environment. It looked so embracing of the corrosion that was integrating it into the ground. A banquet of insects and maggots had gathered and unhurriedly worked to dispatch the remains. Shortly the body became a dark brown silhouette on the verdant ground, in which you could barely distinguish the ghost of a smile. I was with it all along the way. I believe it was Chesterton who said that those who have witnessed disintegration can better understand life. I don't know if that's true, but everything seems different to me now. The sugar mill is still there, with the same obstinate ossification of metal boredly watching the years pass. The birds, like a cinematographic cliché, continue singing; they still nest on the beams, and time keeps dragging its essence through the scaffolding. Sometimes I go back in the afternoons and spend long hours looking at the space once and still occupied (in some organic way) by the body. I think I miss it.

Ríos-Cordero earned his doctorate degree from Rutgers University, N.J. in Comparative Literature and a master's degree in English from the University of Puerto Rico at Mayaguez. He teaches film studies at Miami University, Oxford, Ohio. He has published three books: Two short story collections: *Marcos Sin Retratos (Frames)* and *A lo Lejos el Cielo (Heaven; In the Distance.)* and one poetry collection, *Al Otro Lado de Tus Párpados (The Other Side of Your Eyelids)*. Rios-Cordero is currently working on a novel/screenplay, *Dragones de Papel (Paper Dragons)*.

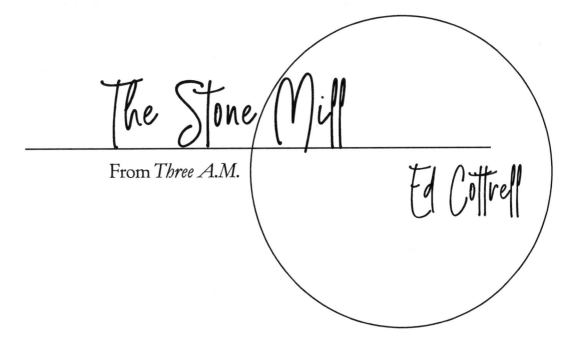

The Stone Mill

From *Three A.M.*

Ed Cottrell

I WANTED TO SEE the machinery that produces grit, the stone specks that go into chicken feed. So I climbed the fence, broke in. Now I'm inside but I'm nowhere really: a kind of industrial barn, built from corrugated steel, a roof that arches like a ribcage. Every corner of this structure is filled with the movement of breath.

It will speak. But I'm waiting for the question. Because it holds a question, I think, but it won't assume into language. There is the echo, the '*!' – '*!' of stones being split apart.

It's not hard to understand the process that takes place here – the mechanics by which stones are chewed into a dark, sand-like matter, pounded by revolving hammers – and the necessity of grit is itself simple. Dusty handfuls of this are added to chickenfeed because the birds have no teeth, they need it to digest. If a chicken has no grit, or is fed the wrong kind, it cannot produce eggshells. The chicken will lay a soft egg with nothing to contain it but a pale membrane.

Does a chicken know what it is doing when it eats a piece of processed stone, holding it with the tip of its beak? That is not the question.

A young woman operates the machinery. She wears a mask and overalls, covered in the dust of the mill. When she saw me first she said, 'Ha! What are you doing here?' but I had no good answer. 'I'm waiting,' I told her. Just waiting. But how long ago was that? How long have I been waiting now? What's the point of marking time? I rationalize it: if the building were simply to talk, it might hurt. It has a sensitive tongue, too much feeling. It traps every storm in its chest. I should listen and make sense of the consonants falling through the radiator.

I remember: from outside I'd watched the stones rolling into the entryway, clattering down the steel chute; the crazed roar. Every time I heard a stone go '*!' inside the mill, I had the sincere feeling that the detonation had taken place in my chest. The space between each blast was just less than a second, there were perhaps eighty of these blasts per minute. Each noise was a stone being reduced to mealed rock.

I remember: outside the mill, I listened while staring down into an abandoned bathtub half-filled with rainwater. Aluminum cans, partly filled, floated on the surface, insulated from the mechanical noise that shook the ground. The water in the cans was clean, still and bright; light striking them collected inside – as if they were cargo boats carrying sunlight.

There is a pause in the noise, then a whirring: the building is catching its breath. I'm certain – it is reaching after speech! The walls turn into cheeks. Air stirs in the throat. There: the mill is inhaling slowly, its cartilage creaks. But it is only a resting breath; and if anything, the slight breath only distils this speechlessness.

A stone goes '*!'

I watch pale dust clouds flickering through the entry-hatch – the rock's ghost floats towards the light, drawn along a pathway of sun.

Still it will not speak. It contains a question too insubstantial to discover. Greater questions are everywhere abundant. They demand to be asked.

This question must be nanoscopic, lost somewhere in this airy space.

A thousand years of speechlessness pass. It says nothing. I am leaving the stone mill, an expert in nothing.

The woman who operates the machinery (perhaps it is her great great great great granddaughter) says goodbye. She takes two handfuls of water, pressing her palms carefully together, then shows this to me. But when I look, hardly long enough to see my reflection, she drops the water and shouts, '*' just as a stone is detonated. 'The sad thing is,' she says, 'that all of them have words living inside. And when they're processed, they go silent.'

Outside the mill I wash my hands, covered in dust, dipping them to the wrist in the rainwater

filling the bathtub, floating the aluminum cans. The water chokes. Thin mud runs from my skin and drifts beneath an aluminum hull. A cloud passes overhead and the light cargo vanishes. A moment later the cloud is gone, and the glistening cargo reappears. Two aluminum cans touch, chattering in the water.

Another stone rolls down the chute, into the mill, with a sweet rhythm it thrashes on the metal, and then – '*!'

Ed Cottrell's fiction has appeared in *3:AM*, *Brittle Star*, *Structo* and other journals. He was the 2018 winner of the Desperate Literature Prize for short fiction, and was shortlisted for the London Short Story Prize in 2017. He was selected for the Escalator Writing Programme in 2014 (National Centre for Writing), and the Platform development programme in 2017 (Spread the Word, London). In 2015 he was a writer in residence at Toji Cultural Foundation, South Korea. He is currently working on a first collection and a novel.

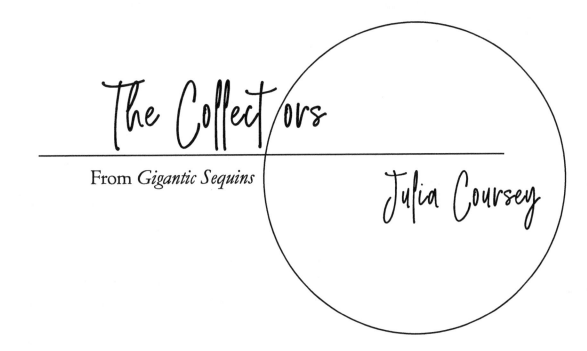

The Collectors

From *Gigantic Sequins*

Julia Coursey

SARAH FELL IN LOVE with almost anything. The object of her affections had often been an object--a wooden hairbrush with boar bristles had been her first great love, a puddle at the end of the driveway her most fleeting. Some of these lovers she kept in a cigar box (which she loved for the smell that hung about it years after its contents had been smoked): an antique hatpin, a perfectly round rubber ball, a crescent of fingernail, a sampler jar of salsa.

When she happened to fall in love with a person, she would usually also fall for one or more of the things they kept around them. Early in the infatuation, she would slip the item into a pocket and keep it on her person for the duration of the crush. But this only worked for rather small things--what was she to do, for example, when she became enamored of Matt Rothfeld's trampoline?

Sarah replayed the impact of his athletic socks on the shiny material, focusing on the moan of the springs, the way it gave under him and then hurled him skyward once more. Having recently acquired her license, she had access to the minivan. It was a simple matter of dismantling the apparatus under the cover of night--she had the whole thing taken care of in under three hours and was back home in time for her morning swim practice.

The trampoline took up residence in the basement rumpus room, awkwardly concealed under a pile of trash bags that held her mother's most recent attempts at decluttering, where it was soon joined by other large scale paramours. There was a traffic cone pilfered from the construction site near her high school, a steamer trunk, the Gillespie's riding lawnmower. Although her parents rarely went into the basement, Sarah knew it was only a matter of time before they discovered her hoard.

It was simple enough to turn to petty crime to finance her spatial needs, being an excellent thief by this point. She would park near the regional train station and leave her suburb a few times a week, exploring new neighborhoods, inventing new ways to steal and then bringing any spoils back to her storage unit. After a few months of this, she splurged on a warehouse, where she was able to finally set up the trampoline and bounce on it in peace. Any interest she had had in Matt had been reinvested in the object after she had heard that he had gotten a blowjob from Maddie Conrad at Jennifer Richardson's graduation party.

Sarah worked hard to improve her skills and was soon in high demand on the black market. Art theft was a particularly lucrative area for her, though quite dangerous. Even though she was adept at avoiding museum security systems, the absence of a piece of art was certain to be noticed almost immediately. She began leaving official looking note cards claiming that the missing object was being loaned to another museum, which usually bought her about a week to get out of whatever country she happened to be stealing in--but this was a sloppy solution.

Lea could fall in love with almost any experience. Her favorites at the time of meeting Sarah were snapping fistfuls of pasta in half, followed closely by applying blush. She loved more involved experiences as well--herding sheep, skin diving, roller derby, spelunking, reviewing products on Amazon--but she found she could accumulate and repeat the small ones so much more easily. Lea's skill as a painter had come about as a result of several years spent trying to experience the lives of particular artists--renting a place in Mallorca and painting like Miro had been her favorite, but the Georgia O'Keeffe period was the one that she thought about the most.

Sarah had reached out to a few forgers on the dark web, offering them a substantial cut of the proceeds for exquisite replicas of the object she was supposed to steal. In the beginning she worked with several different artists, but eventually it became clear that the only one who would do was Lea. Sarah would get a job and then the two of them would scout the museum, Lea sketching the painting and Sarah milling around; noting the various weak points in the security system. Lea would recreate the work, then Sarah would make the switch. The two of them would drop off their haul and spend a few days experiencing the strangest things each place had to offer and combing flea markets for bizarre objects. Sarah's company was pleasant enough, but Lea began to get the sense that she was being collected. Someday, perhaps, she'd end up in that warehouse, bouncing on the trampoline until her socks wore through.

Julia Coursey holds an MFA fromt the University of Alabama and the winner of the *Gigantic Sequins* 7th Annual Flash Fiction Contest. Her work has recently appeared in *Booth*, *The Collagist*, *Joyland*, and *Psychopomp*. She's currently in the final stages of polishing a novel about whales, ghosts, and whales that are ghosts.

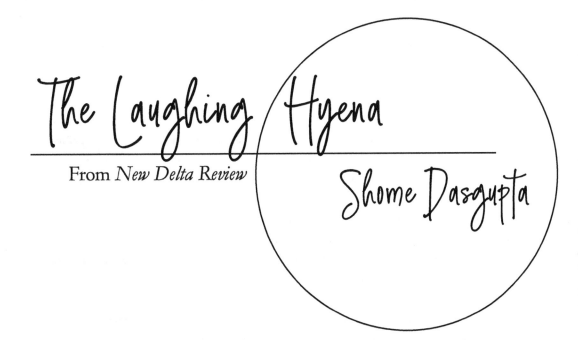

The Laughing Hyena

From *New Delta Review*

Shome Dasgupta

EVERY MORNING, WHEN I would look out the window of the living room just after waking up, I would see a laughing hyena peering through. It had been doing this for the past two months, always on time, always there in the morning.

My daughter thought it was our guardian angel. My wife thought it wanted to eat our daughter. I didn't know what I thought. Every time I tilted my head, it tilted its head, like I was looking at a mirror.

When the thick snow came down, I thought for sure the laughing hyena wouldn't be there, but I saw its head poking out of a bed of snow. My daughter wanted to let it in. My wife wanted to kill it. I didn't know what I wanted to do.

That was a few weeks ago, and it was still coming up to the window. How come it doesn't laugh? my daughter said. Perhaps we're not all that funny, I replied. They don't laugh, my wife said. It just sounds like they're laughing.

The next morning, my daughter was in the living room, facing the window and performing for the laughing hyena. She was holding a rolling pin, pretending it was a mic as she was giving a stand-up routine. The animal looked at her, its head following her back and forth. Donuts, what about donuts? she said and laughed. Her jokes were horribly cute. I chuckled to make her feel better. The laughing hyena remained silent. Fix the table for breakfast, my wife said.

The next morning, just as the sun was breaking, I got out of bed, hearing sounds coming from the living room. My daughter was there, dressed in a makeshift clown outfit, in my overalls and wearing a knotted tie, her face covered in my wife's cosmetics. She was jumping up and down and doing somersaults, rolling across the floor. The laughing hyena tilted its head left and right, remaining silent. Why won't it laugh? my daughter said. My wife had a headache.

You're doing great, I said.

A week later, I could tell my daughter was getting frustrated from not being able to make the laughing hyena laugh. Just leave it alone, my wife said. I think it's laughing on the inside, I said. Keep going. I love it. My daughter said, I'm just going to leave it alone. Good, my wife said. Sometimes, you're just not funny, my daughter said. She walked out of the living room with her head facing the ceiling.

That night in bed, I kept the lamp on late. I was writing on a piece of scrap paper. My wife was aggravated. What are you doing? she said. I said, I'm writing. I've never even seen you hold a pen before, my wife said. Do you have to do that now? I said, I do and she flipped over, covering her head with the blanket, groaning. Just go to sleep, my wife said. I didn't say anything. Go to sleep, she said again. Almost finished, I said.

I woke up early the following morning, just as the dew was warming, and went to the living room. The lights were off. I put them on and saw the laughing hyena peering through, its eyes sad. I went to my daughter's room — she was still sleeping — and rubbed her shoulder. She opened her eyes. Let's go to the living room and try this, I said, holding up the piece of scrap paper. Her eyes were large and wide. Without speaking, without hesitation, she got out of bed. I love you so much, I said.

We went to the living room. I tore the paper in half. It's a skit, I said. My daughter was excited. We acted and performed a dialogue. My daughter was loving it, though the laughing hyena didn't laugh. We were loud, and I was trying my best not to cry, playing with my daughter, seeing her so happy. My wife woke up. I could hear her footsteps in the hallway before entering the living room. My daughter continued to act out the scene. Stop, my wife said. Just stop — this is just stupid. The look my daughter gave, I will never forget. And I should have never have said it, not in front of her, but it just came out. My daughter started to cry. My wife dropped the coffee mug, and it shattered against the wooden floor. The laughing hyena started to laugh, cackling, its eyes glowing as it went up and down on its hind legs.

My daughter rubbed her eyes. Encore, Daddy. Encore.

Shome Dasgupta is the author of *i am here And You Are Gone* (Winner Of The 2010 OW Press Fiction Chapbook Contest), *The Seagull And The Urn* (HarperCollins India, 2013) which has been republished in the UK by Accent Press as *The Sea Singer* (2016), *Anklet And Other Stories* (Golden Antelope Press, 2017), *Pretend I Am Someone You Like* (University of West Alabama's Livingston Press, 2018), and *Mute* (Tolsun Books, 2018). He currently serves as the Series Editor for the *Wigleaf* Top 50. He lives in Lafayette, LA, and can be found at www.shomedome.com.

On the Train to Stavanger

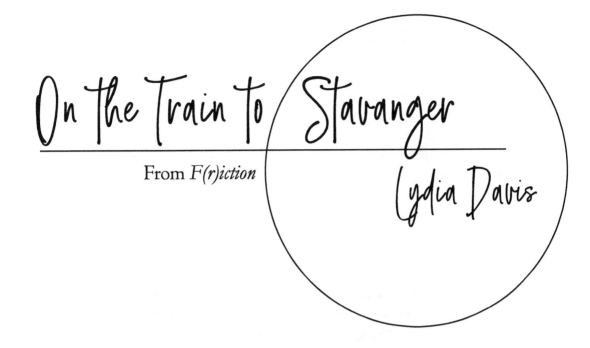

From *F(r)iction*

Lydia Davis

TWO OF THE THINGS I will do on this train ride, I think, as I settle down in my seat, are look out the window at the scenery and listen to conversations around me, hoping to improve my understanding of spoken Norwegian. I lean forward to listen to the couple who are sitting in the seats in front of me, but then they stop talking. I turn to my left to look out the window, but then the train enters a tunnel.

I lean forward again to listen to the conversation in front of me, which has resumed. The couple exchange a few remarks which I don't understand. Then, at the next station, one of them stands up, says goodbye to the other, and gets off. I turn to my left again to look out the window, but the window has fogged over.

Another pair get on, put their things down in the empty seats in front of me, walk away to another car to buy coffee, come back, sit down, laugh together, and start babbling. I lean forward to listen, though they are perhaps talking too fast for me. But abruptly, now, he has his laptop open and she has her iPhone in hand, and they stop talking.

Then three people, across the aisle and two seats ahead, start to chatter to one another, but they are too far away for me to distinguish a single word. After that, all at once, around me, everyone starts chattering and talking over one another so that I can make out nothing. Ten, abruptly, everyone falls silent.

While this is happening, I think with regret how I could also have taken pictures out the window. There is one nice little shallow valley, for instance, with a white house, a red barn, dark woods in the background, a lake in front, and the sun shining on it all. But I have not brought my camera. After that, there are fir trees, a scrubby hillside, and sheep grazing. Ten there are, between Egersund and Bryne, some bare, rocky, scrubby terrain that feels high up, and I think we are on a mountaintop, because I have no idea of the geography here. It turns out that

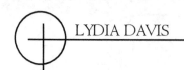

we are not on a mountain top but down by the sea. I could have brought along a detailed map in order to follow our route, but I forgot to prepare one. It is less populated here, not really at all, even by animals—which I know are called dyr in Norwegian. The rocks in the fields are not so different from sheep in the fields. I could have photographed them, but I have not brought even my iPhone.

Lydia Davis's most recent collection of stories is *Can't and Won't* (Farrar, Straus & Giroux, 2014). She is also the author of *The Collected Stories* (FSG, 2009), as well as translations of Proust's *Swann's Way* (Viking Penguin, 2002) and Flaubert's *Madame Bovary* (Viking Penguin, 2010), among other works. Her translation from the Dutch of the very short stories of A.L. Snijders appeared in 2016 in a bi-lingual edition published by AFdH in The Netherlands. Her translation of Proust's *Letters to His Neighbor* appeared in 2017 from New Directions. A collection of her essays is forthcoming in 2019.

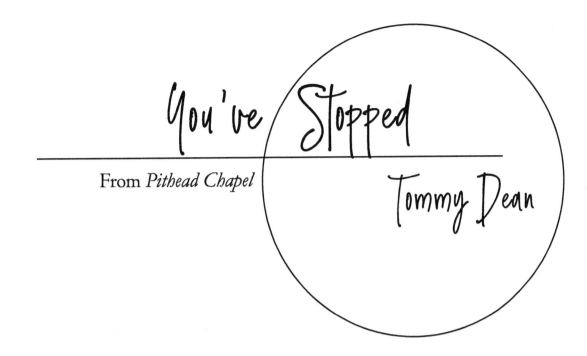

You've Stopped

From *Pithead Chapel*

Tommy Dean

YOU'VE STOPPED AKING ME to marry you. I think, finally, this is a good thing. We're the last people on Earth, you cry into my ribs, your nose stopping on each ridge of bone like a gate unlatching. We don't know that's true, I say, but the air in this bunker is getting heavy with our foul smelling humidity. We're just springs rebounding and recoiling, thrusting our hands out in the dark, mauling the air, waiting to connect.

You've stopped gorging on top ramen and bubble gum. The floor is littered with wrappers, slick with noodles, and those little peas that cling to the bottom of my shoes. I keep them on because I can't give up the idea of running, my calves refusing to give up, the muscles popping and stretching below me, warning of attrition. There's nowhere to run, I whisper, punching them twice a day anyway. You do love me, you say, mistaking my regrets as compliments.

You've stopped checking the latch on the containment door. The fear of being invaded has become the trampled dust, the network of shoe imprints you trace across the floor, pacing to keep the edge of possibility fresh in your mind. This you refuse to stop, coming closer and closer to my hip, my knees. Proximity, when we lived above, often created desire. But now you dart, zig and zag like a goldfish in too small of a bowl. I miss your skin by millimeters.

You've stopped talking, your voice caking over with fallen dust motes because you refused to wear the hospital masks I had provided. Then how will we kiss, you asked at my first suggestion. Survival, at first, felt flirty, like finding ourselves alone in a hotel while everyone else was at the beach. Now, I'm pretty sure the beach doesn't exist. You still assume the world is out there, waiting for us, that we've merely stepped off the page of this fairy tale you've been writing in your head.

You've stopped waking up unless prodded by my fingers checking your neck for a pulse.

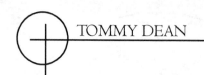

A bear in hibernation, eyelids caked in allergy and lethargy. Even your heart has slowed. I whisper I love you, a hundred times a day, seizing on the lightning bug blip of your heart as it pushes back against my palm, its own failing cadence letting me know that I'm too late.

Tommy Dean lives in Indiana with his wife and two children. He is the author of a flash fiction chapbook entitled *Special Like the People on TV* from Redbird Chapbooks. He is the Flash Fiction Section Editor at *Craft Literary*. He has been previously published in the *BULL Magazine*, *The MacGuffin*, *JMWW*, *Spartan*, *Pithead Chapel*, and *New Flash Fiction Review*. His story "You've Stopped" was selected by Dan Chaon to be included in *Best Microfiction* 2019. Find him @TommyDeanWriter on Twitter.

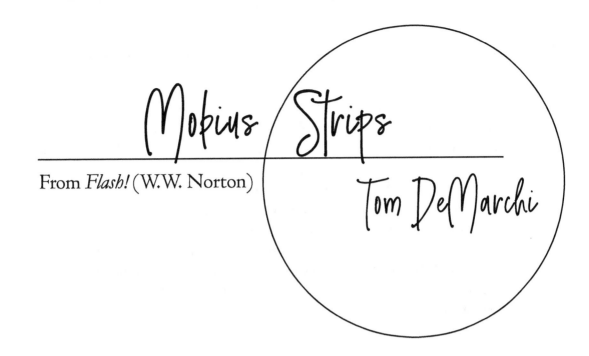

Möbius Strips

From *Flash!* (W.W. Norton)

Tom DeMarchi

THE DORRS ARE BOLTED, the windows sealed—of this I'm sure, just as I'm sure that Rosemary's lying beside me, beneath an itchy afghan in a bed I've slept in since I was eleven years old, a bed I had shipped via train from Peabody to Fresno to Miami, back to Peabody, back to my parents' aluminum-insulated ranch that's currently getting pelted with snow. Rosemary's jugular pulses in the red glow of my digital clock, and I wonder if the whistle I hear is wind blowing through a crack in the window, air through Rosemary's nostrils, or the B&M railroad chugging past the reservoir three blocks away, or if I'm dreaming of the past, of July 1979, when Mark X—what was that boy's name?—and I hiked home after swimming in the reservoir and lined the tracks with pennies, watched the 2:19 whizz past, blow dry our hair, spit copper tears at our feet.

My father shuffles down the hallway to the front door. I picture him twisting the knob, unlocking and locking the deadbolt, traipsing from window to window, unlatching and latching.

He stops in the dining room, presses palms and forehead to glass, stares at the plowed snow barricading his driveway. He sighs at the thought of shoveling in a few hours, when his stomach will churn coffee and Cheerios. A shiver sends him back down the hall to my bedroom door where he pauses.

My mother, a nurse, says the human brain is a series of Möbius strips lined with locked filing cabinets, that neural atrophy causes us to begin losing keys at age twenty-three. My mother says crossword puzzles, a steady diet of blueberries, long walks, needlepoint, and thick history books keep those keys jingling on our hips, keep the hallways lit. My mother posits this theory weekly, as if it just occurred to her.

I wonder if my father's standing in the hallway because he's wondering if he locked the front door. Names of old golfing buddies, where he put his glasses, his age: just some of the

things my father chases down dark hallways. I wonder if he wonders if he's showing signs of Alzheimer's, like Mr. Otto, a neighbor once arrested for pissing against the wall of the 7-Eleven, and who, like my father just last week, reported his car stolen after he'd forgotten where he parked.

I wonder whether I'll remember this moment: Rosemary's pulsing jugular, B&M's fading whistle, my father frozen in the hallway, cold fingertips pressing his forehead, and me—now—disentangling myself from the afghan's itchy embrace, easing into my slippers, opening my bedroom door, startling my father into saying "Jesus!," planting my index finger on his lips, taking his hand, leading him from window to window, door to door, jiggling doorknobs and testing locks, securing the house so both of us can sleep without any regard for the snow piling up outside.

Tom DeMarchi teaches in the Department of Language & Literature at Florida Gulf Coast University in Fort Myers, Florida. His work has appeared in *The Writer's Chronicle*, *The Miami Herald*, *Quick Fiction*, *The Pinch*, *Gulfshore Life*, *The Southeast Review*, and other publications. In 2019, he published *Möbius Strips and Other Stories* (Rain Chain Press). When not writing, teaching, sleeping, or cataloguing his music collection, you'll find Tom reading biographies of jazz musicians and dead presidents, watching his son play soccer, or meeting with colleagues to discuss the Sanibel Island Writers Conference, which he directs. Because of his haircut and monochromatic fashion sense, he is often mistaken for a police officer.

My Father's Girlfriend

From *matchbook*

Leonora Desar

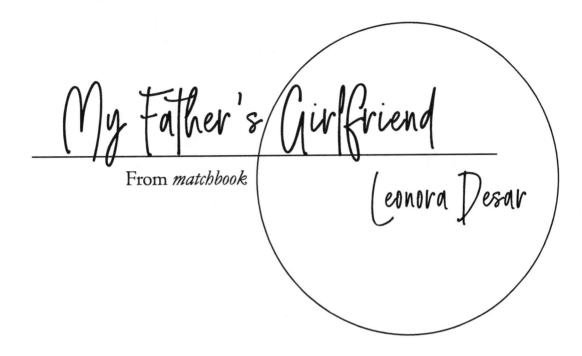

MY FATHER'S GIRLFRIEND HAD a secret ring. She had many. It was a dial tone when they first met. They didn't need words, he could just pick up the phone, and they would know each other. He stood there and twisted the cord, and the perfume came, it wrapped around his neck. It smelled like cognac and blueberries. It smelled like cashmere.

It was two and a half when she wanted him to fuck her. Two long rings and a fast one. The first two were a slow deep kiss, the half was a peck, it meant, get over here. When they were fighting it was just a peck, there were three of them. Sometimes I could see a bird flying across the room. She pecked at my father, and he rolled his eyes. My mother said, what's that, my father said, it's just a bird. She had a carrot top of hair like a mohawk. It was spiky like her eyes. She smelled like cigarettes, and she left a ring of lipstick around my father.

When she was done being fucked the ring was slow. You couldn't really hear it, but it was there, the slowness. It sounded like a woman drinking alone, the way she got up and pretended to walk straight. The slowness was the getting up, it was walking across the room. It was that moment she took looking at the phone, wondering if she should call him or my mother.

After she killed herself the phone still rang. It was slower, fainter. It smelled like lipstick, and then it was just a dial tone. My father stood there twisting the cord. The lipstick twisted all around us.

Leonora Desar's work has appeared or is forthcoming in *matchbook, River Styx, Passages North, Mid-American Review, Black Warrior Review Online, Wigleaf, SmokeLong Quarterly, Harpur Palate, Hobart, Best Microfiction* 2019, and elsewhere. She won third place in *River Styx's* microfiction competition and was a runner/up finalist in *Quarter After Eight's* Robert J. DeMott Short Prose contest, judged by Stuart Dybek. She was recently nominated for the *Pushcart Prize* and has been recognized as a finalist by *Glimmer Train, Crazyhorse, Mid-American Review, Black Warrior Review,* and elsewhere. She lives in Brooklyn and holds an MS from the Columbia Journalism School.

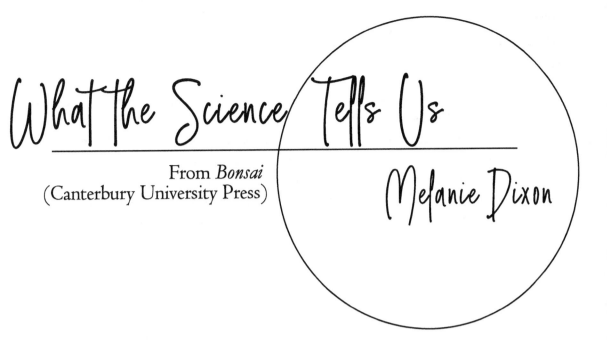

What the Science Tells Us

From *Bonsai*
(Canterbury University Press)

Melanie Dixon

THE SCIENCE TELL US that 8 out of 10 cats prefer Whiskas, that there is a 50:50 chance of having a boy or a girl, that ovulating women wear red. Science tells us that a big earthquake is overdue in Wellington, that suicide is one of the most common causes of death for teenagers, that you're safer if you wear a seatbelt.

Science tells us that love is real, people fall in and out as easily as getting on or off a bus. If you're single, it's only bad luck. Does that make you feel any better? Science tells us that boy meets girl, Romeo will fall in love with Juliet, and an infinite number of monkeys will tell us the same thing.

Plants grow towards the sun, darkness is the absence of light, black is not white. Science puts two highly reactive gases together to make a molecule we can't live without. It tells us a cat in a box can be simultaneously dead and alive.

Science gives us quarks, mesons, gravitons, anti-matter, black dwarves. It tells us we're all made of particles from the last supernova. Every human being. Star dust.

But science can't make my morning coffee, or scratch my back in the shower. It can't ask me about my day. It can't tell me why you left.

Science tells us we are made of string in a multidimensional space-time continuum. It gives us infinite worlds with infinite outcomes.

In a parallel universe, we are still together.

Melanie Dixon is an award-winning short story writer, novelist, poet, and creative writing tutor, based in New Zealand. Melanie writes literary fiction for adults as well as contemporary fiction and fantasy for younger readers, and has had work published and anthologized internationally. Melanie holds degrees from the University of York and Oxford University, and is a graduate of Hagley Writers' Institute. She is currently associate director at the School for Young Writers and editor of Write On. When she's not writing or curled up with a book, you can find Melanie planning her next outdoor adventure with her family. www.melaniedixon.com.

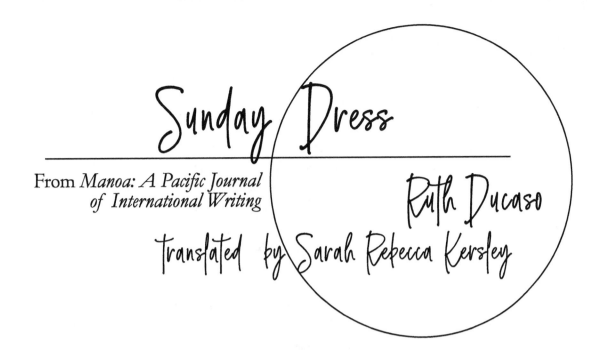

Sunday Dress

From *Manoa: A Pacific Journal of International Writing*

Ruth Ducaso

Translated by Sarah Rebecca Kersley

NISSINHA HAD BEEN PREGNANT thirteen times. She hadn't wanted any of them. But she'd had all thirteen. Thirteen offspring were born in that house. Among the farm workers it was the loveliest house. The biggest. Nissinha's husband was the best looking. The biggest. He went about the farm in a white suit and white shoes. If this had been the favela, he'd have been a samba man. But on the farm, he was a laborer. None of this meant anything to Nissinha. Nissinha didn't want to give birth. Nissinha gave birth every year. All Nissinha was, was pregnant. Nissinha couldn't be alone. Nissinha complained about the worm she'd had for ten years: "It's the worms!" said Nissinha, in response to any problem that arose.

Nissinha's rage only got bigger. The offspring brought themselves up. Nissinha wanted to be alone. She yearned for human solitude. Nissinha didn't know how to live, whatever that might be. Nissinha wanted one of those worms to bring her a gift: the undoing of life. As they didn't stop coming, they could at least give her this joy. She began to wish for this gift with the fourth offspring. Five, six, seven. Every year was the same for Nissinha. And nothing was hers. They didn't bring her anything. Nissinha hid her belly.

That Sunday, in the little sixth month of the thirteenth time, Nissinha paid a visit to the neighbors with her offspring in tow. A neighbor noted: "Nissinha, look at that belly! This one's a li'l boy!" This was hurtful to Nissinha, who didn't say anything. Followed by her misunderstood little ones, Nissinha walked home. The biggest house. It was Sunday. The day of pain in the street. The biggest husband was licking his pain in the store. And Nissinha?! She got home. She walked firmly, kicking aside everything in her way and scouring the rooms. She found the shiny scissors, and the ace! The children looked at their mother. All they could see was the pack of cards falling, colorful. A colorless floor. A colorful floor. A child's toy. The children squabbled over the pieces. The scissors were in Nissinha's hands, and the dress that

had given away her pregnancy was torn: she didn't have the courage to do anything else, not even to push out the thirteenth.

Having finally received her gift, Nissinha left this injured Sunday dress for those who would remember. The biggest husband made every day into a Sunday and licked himself relentlessly. The offspring spread themselves out randomly over the other days of the week.

Luciany Aparecida (Ruth Ducaso) is a Brazilian writer, born in 1982 in Vale do Jiquiriçá, Bahia. She holds a PhD in literature, and is a university lecturer in Brazilian literature and literary theory and criticism. She is co- founder and curator of the PANTIM Small press and Collective. She writes using three different aesthetic signatures: Ruth Ducaso, Margô Paraíso, and Antônio Peixôtro. She was awarded a creative writing grant from the Brazilian National Library Foundation/ FUNARTE in 2012. In 2013, she was selected by the Bahian State Cultural Foundation (FUNCEB) for a creative writing grant, resulting in her book *Contos Ordinários de Melancholia* (Ordinary tales of melancholy) (paraLeLo13S, 2017). In 2015, she was one of the writers-in-residence at the Sacatar Institute. She is also the author of the zine *Auto-retrato* (PANTIM Edições, 2018), and the book *Ezequiel* (PANTIM Edições, 2018). Website: https://lucianyaparecida.art.br

Sarah Rebecca Kersley is a poet, translator, editor, and bookseller. She was born in the UK in 1976 and holds an MA degree from the University of Glasgow. She has lived and worked in Bahia, Brazil, for over a decade. Her translations of work by Brazilian contemporary writers have appeared in journals such as *Two Lines: World Writing in Translation* (Center for the Art of Translation); *The Critical Flame; Flaneur Magazine; Asymptote* and *Mãnoa Journal.* Her own poems—written in Portuguese—have appeared widely, inclding in *O Globo* (página Risco); *Revista Pessoa; Revista Modo de Usar & co.; Jornal RelevO; Revista Oblique,* and *Mãnoa Journal.* She is the author of the poetry book *Tipografia Oceânica* (paraLeLo13S, 2017) and the memoir-biography *Sábado* (paraLeLo13S, 2018), both forthcoming in English. She co-founded Livraria Boto-cor-de-rosa, an independent bookshop, cultural space and small press dedicated to contemporary literature, in the city of Salvador, where she is based.

Three Witch Haibun

From *Raleigh Review*

Logan February

VENGEANCE. AN ARROW FLIES out from the gap between my teeth. Which means it came from my belly. I'm trying to say I did it to myself. Sometimes, the shame wraps itself around my throat, and I try to lie. I say my mother killed witches' birds and fed them to us for dinner. Let me tell the truth, from the beginning. In Yorùbá, àjé pupa, the red witch, holds a knife in each hand, the only one with the power to kill. I picture her submerged in dark water, like my brain. A circling of acid, shifting poles. A kill switch in my own hand. Almost as malevolent as her is the black witch, àjé dúdú. She curses and haunts and follows. Like the eyes in my country, when I am touching the boys I love. These people terrify me. They would kill me if they could. They can't — that is for me to do. Nothing is safe, except to say this: the black lights a match, seething against everything queer. Later, I found the white witch. Àjé funfun. Protector, bearer of peace. Not God, no. Here, God is a spectator. One among many strange, luckless beings. The white witch weaves haven magic. But this is the truth of how it happened: When I was a child, I spoke as a child, gathered pebbles as a child, strung up my catapult as a child. When I was a child, I shot down the birds, I confess. After that, I put away childish things: my catapult, my songs, my protection spell. And now, they come for me.

first, the poison, red
is calling for my warm blood
it wants to end me

gathering bad wind
the heavy evil lingers
and raises a fist

until everything
in this strom the ruins my head
then stands still as dawn

Logan February is a Nigerian poet. His work has appeared or is forthcoming in *Washington Square Review, The Southeast Review, The Adroit Journal, Paperbag, Raleigh Review,* and more. He is a *Pushcart* and *Best of the Net* nominee, and his debut collection, *Mannequin in the Nude* (PANK Books, 2019) was a finalist for the Sillerman First Book Prize for African Poets. He is the author of two chapbooks, and the Associate Director of Winter Tangerine's Dovesong Labs. You can find him at loganfebruary.com.

There Will Only Be One Funeral

From *wildness*

Benjamin McPherson Ficklin

IF YOU HEAD SOUTH along a foothill of the Siskiyou Mountain Range, you might see a maple leaf detach and spiral downward, leaving the tree it once was to become singular, rigid, delicate, lying on a rock amidst tall brown grass, eventually succumbing to time and becoming dust, detritus, much more. You might notice it, though just as easily you might see a hunk of madrone bark peel back to reveal amber skin smoother than human epidermis. You might hear a scream. You might hear the high idle of a pickup truck as you trot between the manzanitas and Oregon grape, turning from this outcropping into a valley furry with moss. Perhaps the creek runs off the mountains' snowfall on a rainy day. But if you heard the scream, it's a sunny Autumn afternoon, and the creek is not yet a creek; it's a series of pools blooming clouds of mosquitoes. In the gulley rises a path, muddy and wide enough for an automobile, steep enough that the humans trundling up the slope with plastic tubs in their hands have to lean forward and plant each step carefully. Depending on your ears, you might hear the pudgy blonde guy in black overalls and cowboy boots wheeze the phrase "Oh fuck" around his lit cigarette—he notices, after leaping out his vehicle, where his emergency brake is not. You might know his name is Teddy Kilpatrick but that everyone calls him boss or Little Ted. Little Ted because farther up the hill from him and his slipping truck is Big Ted. Theodore Kalani sitting in his XXL camping chair between the cousins Marta and Margherita who might be speaking Italian while Big Ted shucks nugs off three-foot-long stems into one of the bins. The cousins might be shucking too, or maybe they're rolling cigarettes while Reggina Urbanska or Gabriel Luna-Colombo heft the just-harvested weed from the plants to the shuckers. Or maybe it's early Summer when you're sniffing along a trail; you might smell the burnt odor of the ponderosas or the smoke from a nearby forest fire; you might see the seven rows of plants thick with kolas growing longer in the sun. But the scream occurs in the Fall. And your olfaction might be overwhelmed by the marijuana and the madrone berries steaming half-digested in piles of bear shit. You might look down from whatever tree you're perched on to see half the plants stripped of flowers, green skeletons. If you're one of the thirty-eight dweedlers, you might gasp as you look toward the shrieking LSD Lian. She stands above the slipping truck with a view of the muddy hill. Or maybe you're a juvenile turkey on a paved road, one turkey from a flock of nineteen, and you might be pecking the freshly crunched carcass of your mother when the scream turns all your heads in fear. Just as easily you might be a gray fox eating a Jerusalem cricket, or you might be the cricket feeling your abdomen ripped from your thorax. You might be an old rabbit with a broken leg trying to run from a coyote. You might be, at the moment Ed Conner turns to see who's screaming, a three-day-old roadkilled skunk. Or an ant. Yes. Maybe you're an ant amidst thousands hopelessly defending your home from a black bear. Or you might be a fern crushed by a tire. Or, eleven seconds after the scream, you might be a human with a muddy face shattered, a spine snapped. Or you might be the tick buried in Ed Conner's hairy back as he inhales his chew upon seeing his brother sitting in the mud at the base of the hill. Or you might be Karyssa-Jlyn sitting on the couch in your trailer, pulling a hit from a bong, and next to you might be Little Teddy and he doesn't know you're pregnant, and you won't tell him because you're ashamed of him for not joining the other dweedlers in mourning the ramifications of his fuck up. If the maple leaves are dropping from the life they once were, then you might be James Conner struggling to pull your prosthetic leg out of the hill's grime, your empty plastic bin beside you. Your ascent paused. You might have a nice view of the foothills full of mist. You might think you've never seen leaves so large. That might be your last thought before you hear LSD Lian scream, turning back just in time to see the truck. You might be alive for now. Or you might fly over the frantic gulley full of trapped fog to land on a madrone growing cockeyed on an outcropping farther South. You might be the snow-capped Siskiyous. You might be the mud or the pink sun at twilight.

Benjamin McPherson Ficklin will never surrender—Benjamin McPherson Ficklin will always love you.

Lawrie Shrapnel

From National Flash Fiction Day (NZ)

Jan FitzGerald

HIS NAME WAS LAWRIE Chapel but people called him Lawrie Shrapnel, because of the plate in his head. It was a garlic bulb head, not an egg like other old men's.

He lived on the school boundary and we were forbidden to talk to him because he liked to watch us playing. Sometimes when the duty teacher was called inside, the boys would kick the ball into his property and as he stumbled through blackberry to retrieve it, we'd flock over to the fence to check out that weird head.

Malcom Rowe reckoned the plate inside would look like something from his Meccano set. Sometimes Lawrie Shrapnel would catch up with my friend, Rosemary, and me biking to school. Riding "no hands," arms extended in classic vaudeville style, he'd belt out the musical hit song "Rose Marie," to faces red with laughter.

"Most days," he told the butcher, "I feel like a horse has kicked me in the head. Other times, it's as if my skull has lifted and I hear this tinkling, like a Tibetan bell, a long way away and the clouds talking to me."

When the minister asked him if he believed in God he said he believed in Dylan Thomas and the Mekong Delta.

One autumn my friends and I biked into town to watch our fathers in the Anzac Parade. Eventually my dad marched past and winked, and behind him in the next row, we spotted Lawrie Shrapnel, doing little half-skips to keep in step. A swathe of medals like stars and rainbows hung across his chest.

And the funny thing is, none of us actually noticed what he wore on his head.

JAN FITZGERALD

Jan FitzGerald (b. 1950) is a long established New Zealand poet with publication in most New Zealand literary journals including *Poetry NZ, NZ Books, Catalyst, Takahē,* and *Landfall,* and overseas in *Poetry Australia, The London Magazine, Orbis* (UK), *Acumen* (UK) and *Brilliant Flash Fiction* (USA). Jan works as a full-time artist in Napier, and has three poetry books published: *Flying Against the Arrow* (Wolfdale Publishing 2005), *On a Day like This* (Steele Roberts 2010) and *Wayfinder* (Steele Roberts 2017).

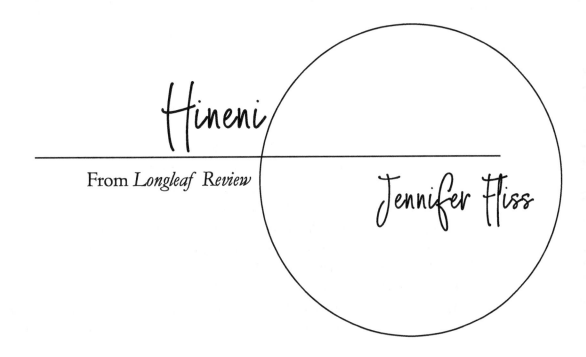

Hineni

From *Longleaf Review*

Jennifer Fliss

I AM HERE. MY grandmother is dead.

I like it when my gums bleed. When I spit peppermint and a string of fire red trails in the sink. When I bruise, a yellow gray blossom flowers beneath my skin. The blood is so close and yet, hidden. I pluck and I pop and I squeeze to try to get everything out.

"What are you doing?" my husband asks. I stare into the mirror, tweezer in hand. I am plucking errant hairs. But are they errant? Placed there by G-d. Or by Mother Nature. I shouldn't even be looking in the mirror; we are sitting *shiva*.

My grandmother was eleven when liberated from Auschwitz. When I was eight, my parents were killed in a car accident. I went to live with my *savta*. When she plucked lice from my head at ten, she said the parasites had been the only thing in the camp that let her know she was alive.

Arbeit Macht Frei, she would say to me, when she insisted I do homework. Later I learned she co-opted the iron saying over the gates of her death camp. Work makes you free.

Nothing makes you free.

She had gone first to Israel and then to Brooklyn. Human relations were nothing like the give and take of a parasitic relationship, she said. She and my grandfather divorced before it was common; left him behind in Ra'anana.

"Just tweezing," I tell my husband.

"There's nothing left to tweeze." He takes the utensil from my hand. Brushes his thumb over the bare and tender space above my eyes.

We get into bed and I feel a hair above my right eye. It's sturdy, upright and thick. I want to get out of bed and pull it out. It feels so alien there. Alone. Tomorrow is the funeral.

It's only been twenty-four hours. In Jewish tradition, it all happens so quickly. My husband turns to me. Says *stay*.

It is not long before his snores fill the air, his arm slung over my chest. I stir; he grumbles and holds me tighter. I cannot think of anything else. The hair. The foreign object. My hair. Her hair. The curls. The shaving. The lice. The sores. The moment a man tells you you are free but can you believe them is this a trick and who will watch me I am only a child and I have no one but the parasites on my body. What will happen when I clean them away?

I fall asleep. The next morning, we say the mourner's kaddish, a prayer I know by heart. I see my grandmother in a picture frame. Scowling, as she did, but with light in her eyes and I think if she can, so can I.

The night of my parents' funeral, she told me that the most important thing you can tell people, dead or alive, is that you are here. On this earth. To live what they could not or what they will not. *Hineni*, she said and made me say it out loud.

Hineni, I tell the me in the mirror, and I leave the single hair above my eyes where it grows.

Jennifer Fliss is a Seattle-based writer with over 150 stories and essays that have appeared in *PANK*, *The Minnesota Review*, *The Rumpus*, *The Washington Post*, and elsewhere. She is the 2018/2019 Pen Parentis Fellow and a 2019 recipient of a Grant for Artist Project award from Artist's Trust. She has been nominated three times for *The Pushcart Prize* and is an alumna *Tin House* Summer and Winter workshops. She can be found on Twitter at @writesforlife or via her website, www.jenniferflisscreative.com.

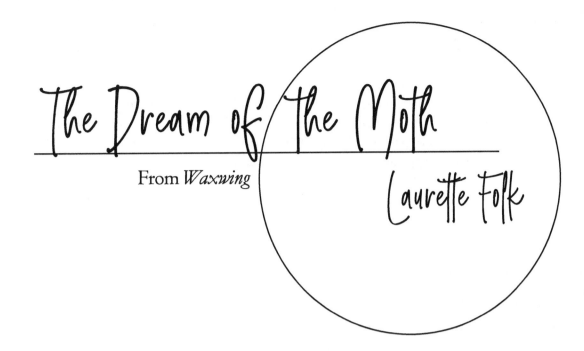

The Dream of the Moth

From *Waxwing*

Laurette Folk

HE CHOPPED ME INTO exactly twenty pieces. He was a man I had known most of my life, my mother's lover, a rich man, a man with a deep, furrowing brow and strong arms and chaffed hands. I can tell you that the world bloomed into stars as red as blood. He laid the pieces of me out on the basement floor in the dirt, where the spiders crouch and wait. When he went away, the pieces of me shifted, and he came back and chopped some more. This happened for three days, the shifting and the chopping, until I was one thousand pieces glistening like sunlight on shattered glass. He gathered me together and piled me into a chest with dancing women carved into the grain. When he came back to bury the chest, I burrowed into his mind like a worm in wood eating away at each thought and desire.

Eventually, the medicine men came with special teas and locked him in a room in the country where only the hills could hear his screams.

In the cool dark chest, I had the dream of the little moth. I slipped my paper wings through a crack in the wood and wiggled through the crevices of the Earth. Up I fluttered, dancing, flying, up to his rooms where the concubines glided and perfumed their bodies with the finest herbs. Up I fluttered to the roof, measuring my wings against gravity, above congregations of learned men and dray beasts, up to the delicate vapors of the clouds where below me a lake mirrored all the sky's best intentions.

Laurette Folk's fiction, essays, and poems have been published in *Upstreet, Waxwing, Gravel, Flash Fiction Magazine, Mom Egg Review, Pacific Review, Boston Globe Magazine,* among others.

Her novel, *A Portal to Vibrancy*, was published by Big Table in June 2014 and won the Independent Press Award for New Adult Fiction. *Totem Beasts*, her collection of poetry and flash fiction, was published by Big Table in May 2017. She is a graduate of the Vermont College MFA in Writing program. www.laurettefolk.com.

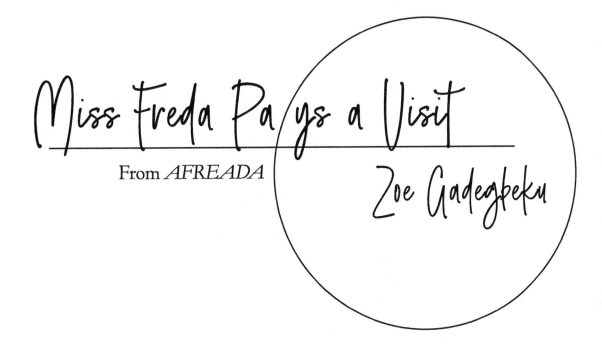

Miss Freda Pays a Visit

From *AFREADA*

Zoe Gadegbeku

ON THE THIRD DAY she came to visit, all the sharp edges in my house fell to pieces. I discovered them hour by painful hour, as I moved from dusty corridor, to bath, to wood-floored bedroom dotted with several months' worth of shed hair and fluff. Sewing scissors– their gold handle rusted over with neglect– sat scattered on my work table; screw, blades, and finger rests spread far from each other as though they had never been whole. The old-time straight razor I used to shave my head was also apart from itself, its cutting edge bent in half like it was made of paper and not steel. Even the keys jammed into my room's locks were dull around their teeth.

"The keys too? Is that not a bit much?"

My voice scratched its way out of my mouth, hoarse from lack of use, but she behaved as though she hadn't heard me.

"Miss Freda?"

She was still, just as she had been on her first two visits, careful not to make any forceful movements that would topple the unsteady kitchen stool she sat on. She usually stayed no more than three hours, sighing whisper-soft every few minutes, and rearranging her lean arms across her chest when she grew stiff.

"Girl. You are still mourning? Still trying to end yourself?"

Her voice lilted and chimed like a dinner bell, but there was some sort of distortion to the sound. It was almost as if my head was submerged in water, and I was listening to her through the muffle. I stood silent in front of her, watching the 4 o'clock sunlight spilling lazy orange warmth over the window sill and onto my feet, narrow and much-veined just like hers.

"Miss Freda, didn't you die?"

She ignored me. We might as well have been taking part in two different conversations, running parallel and eventually away from one another.

"Anyway, I deadened the keys too, just in case. It would be torturous to go that way, but I thought you might still try."

She laughed to herself like high heels kicking on concrete and added, "You this child of ours."

"Of ours? I'm no one's but my very own."

Miss Freda kissed her teeth and rolled her eyes so far up and back I thought they would stick.

"Girl. You think you made yourself the way you stitch those clothes? You think you hold yourself together all on your own?

As she spoke, she adjusted the yellow film of fabric she wore for a dress. The way she called me *Girl* made me forget my real name. I knew she was the aunt that followed her sister, my distant and unloving mother into sickness and then death years ago, but I felt more lifeless before her brazen self. What did she want with me?

"Give the sharp edges a rest, girl. You are all of us. You are a wide sky inside too stifling a house. Let me show you—"

Zoë Gadegbeku is a Ghanaian writer living in Boston. She was a fellow in the 2017 Callaloo Creative Writing Workshop at UWI-Cave Hill, Barbados. She received her MFA in Creative Writing from Emerson College. Currently, she is the Senior Editor of *Transition Magazine* at the Hutchins Center, and the Communications Assistant at the Center on the Developing Child, both at Harvard University. Her work has appeared in *Saraba Magazine*, *AFREADA*, *Blackbird*, and *The Washington Post* among other publications. Her essay "My Secondhand Lonely" (*Slice Magazine*, *Longreads*) was included on the notable list in the 2018 edition of the *Best American Essays*.

Curse of Ham

From *Driftwood Press*

Nicholas Nakai Garcia

THEY HAD THE REGALIA you'd expect: gold chains, big crosses, and studs in they teeth, jewels dangling, gold rings on ever finger, gold all over like Mansa Musa, little black tears on they cheeks, black tattoos, which I simply don't understand cuz ink dudn't show on black skin. Some kept they sunglasses on—big ones that covered they faces—and, course, they had they britches pulled down, nether garments wrinkled out for God to see, and they was just as loud as all get out, no mind to other folks set beside them. But they could eat, or so claims Walter. They'un ordered everthin on the menu twice, and he iddn't know where they hid it since every one of them was skin and bones, but, here again, the blacks are that way. It's how they're bred—long and lanky—cuz that's the way Ham must've been when Noah sent him off, and that's a compliment to em. For the rest of how we associate with blacks, well, you heard me tell it already, but here I come to tell it again: the blacks got affinities, and crime aint just a one of em. You've seen the rudeness in mothers who aint a lick of sense till you figure they all screwloose, and kids get so far as fifth grade till they're upsettin the police, and we all heard this kind of story how many times since the mess up in Ferguson. These boys wasn't no different, cuz they were talking about a rap video they aimed to make off in Colfax, Louisiana, and I thought: what in Colfax is there to put on film for? Well, turns out they wanted to film there cuz of the massacre that happened to the blacks in 18-somethin'r other, and they said they goin down there to raise the dead and set em loose on the Earth. For revenge I take it. I asked Walter if he told them boys—since they aint ever cracked a school book—that slavery's been over with a good long while. But Walter said he couldn't get a word in edgewise cuz they was rappers. He said Thelma, who was takin they orders, heard em ramblin curses, and understand this: she like to fell backwards if she iddn't see with her own two eyes one of them boys throwin chicken bones across the table through a ring of salt, mumblin things under his breath like he was overtook.

When I heard that I aimed to go down and tell Ms Thelma that they aint done nuthin but truck with the devil on they own souls to get a scare out of her, so she ought not to worry nothin. But Walter said the second them boys left, he called pastor Lynch down to have a word. I said, Walter, why you'un called Lynch and not sheriff McDermish, and he said it's cuz the law aint a thing to what presence they brung in the diner that night. So Lynch'un went and divined the diner with his hand and a bible, and he come out and said Walter should shut down for a day or two to get the devil out, and Walter was scared enough to do it. He'un closed shop, and I thought, well, this here is serious now, so I went on the internet to look up more about Colfax and what them boys was meant to do out there, and whether I needed to prepare for doom or something like it. I read up on how all them freedmen got killed defending the courthouse, and how the White Legionnaires used a cannon on em all, and how the blacks surrendered, and the whites maimed em, and how they'un dumped all their bodies in the Red River till it dammed. They didn't prod the clog, they just let the mud set atop them till it made a bridge. Readin all that was a mistake. I'un turned the computer off and lay down for bed and had a wicked dream I won't surely forget, cuz there I seen a great big grave dug up, the dirt of it piled like a mountain, the grave so big it was like a stone quarry in the middle of the woods, and there them black boys was standin at the edge of it, rappin into it, enchantin the crypt, and I couldn't see too good as it was nighttime in the dream, but something big rose up from that hole in the world like we do from a bath, and it'un took to walkin across the forest as high as a building stands, and it looked around to get its bearings, and I saw it was a great big black thing, mouth hangin open, its eyes glowin yellow, and it went on walkin into the cities of the south and commenced to steppin all over em, fires eruptin under each step of those barefeet—this colossus negro—and you could see the little traces of the army guns way down below lightin up the dark like morsecode, but they iddnt have no effect cuz he just kept steppin all over us and settin fires, like red hot craters when he lifted his feet, and I knew them rappers was grandbabies of slaves, and they wasn't waitin for no reparations.

Nicholas Nakai Garcia has been published in *Driftwood Press*, *Cagibi*, and *1888 Magazine*. He was guest editor of fiction for *Driftwood Press 6.1*. He lives in Los Angeles, California, writing screenplays and his first novel, making films, producing music, and mountaineering when there's snow.

The Last of the Sama-sellang

From *Cha: An Asian Literary Journal*

Sigrid Gayangos

FOR MORE THAN A week I had waited for the weather to clear so I could make the two-hour banca ride across the Basilan Strait, past the two Santa Cruz islands, and through the narrow passage surrounded by enormous mangroves with thick, gnarled roots. Our tiny banca carved a course between shrubs with wraith-like silhouettes, their seemingly impregnable tangle of interlocking branches discouraged even the most daring wanderer.

A turn onto the path revealed Mr. Tsai's house on bamboo stilts, with the descending blood-red sun as the imposing backdrop across miles of undisturbed waters. Previously, day after stormy day had passed, accompanied by a turbulent sea that spewed violent waves. But today, everything was still.

The guide switched off the engine of the motorboat, and for some time the puttering sound lingered as if endless upon the air. As the last crackle ricocheted into the distance, I suddenly noticed the mingled scent of decay and salt that overwhelmed the islet before us. I cursed under my breath, dreading that perhaps we had arrived a day too late.

I was standing at the foot of Mr. Tsai's house, where a number of oysters of varying sizes had already encroached on the present site. Without a moment's hesitation, I headed up the flimsy makeshift stairs and went in. The smell of rot was stronger there. I was welcomed by a spartan but meticulously arranged living space, in the middle of which was an outdoor inflatable pool for kids filled with what seemed like briny water. Cluster flies, huge ones with blue and yellow sheen on the thorax, hovered around the room.

Inside the pool was a creature that looked like a human-whale chimera gone wrong: its eyes sunken into dark holes; a tear on its face, which could only be the mouth, revealed many sharp, fang-like teeth; its skin (or was it scale?) was blue-gray all over, all six feet of it, with patches of pink and green on certain areas. Next to the pool, Mr. Tsai knelt and caressed the head of the wheezing creature.

"This…this is the sama-sellang?" I asked.

Mr. Tsai gestured for me to approach, "Sorry to disappoint. What were you expecting?"

"No, not disappointed. I'm just surprised, is all."

Mr. Tsai continued to fuss over the creature, as if momentarily forgetting that I was standing there.

So I cleared my throat and added, "I've read so many things about them, especially on the underground trade of their gem-like scales. I was expecting something more colorful, I suppose."

"If you had come a week earlier, then you would've seen some of its famed scales. This one fetched its owner a hundred-thousand deal from a Malaysian trader--and that's already from the dull, sickly mound they managed to collect from its last shed."

"But the scales should grow back like fingernails, right?"

"Normally, yes. But this one has been repeatedly scaled, I'm afraid it's beyond recovery. You see these?" Mr. Tsai asked, pointing at the areas that were a ripe shade of pink with green ooze dripping out, "These are burns from the blade. It takes at least five weeks for them to grow back their scales. Ah, but human greed knows no waiting time. They scraped and scraped and scraped."

As I crouched before the ailing creature, I realized how incredibly enormous it was, with my two hands barely enough to cover a side of its face. It was still the stuff of folktales-- the ancient sea dwellers who tamed waves and sunk ships, who whispered to and ordered winds according to their whims, who were as old as the southern islands and seas themselves. Yet now, here was one of them, stretched out in a rainbow-colored plastic pool with mouth half open. Its body limp; its breathing weak and labored.

"Will it live? My motorboat is still outside. We can take it to the City Vet," I offered.

"It won't last long." The old, scrawny man held the sama-sellang's limb-like pectoral fins. He gestured again for me to come closer. Mr. Tsai, I then noticed, was dressed formally for a sunny day on a deserted islet. His hair was oiled and neatly combed, parted in the middle. He wore a neat cotton shirt, dark pants with an elegant sash of red and gold around the waist.

I knelt beside him and found myself unable to resist the urge to lay my hand on the sama-sellang's heaving chest. It did not recoil at my touch. I was struck by the warmth of its body. This was neither plastic caricature nor just the object of many songs and legends. This was a living creature, the last of its kind. Its hot mass continued to pulse under my palm, struggling to persist despite the cruelty that it had endured.

"I am so sorry," I whispered.

"There was nothing you could do," Mr. Tsai said as he continued to caress the creature. Its sallow skin seemed to glimmer where the old man's hand had traced a path, and for a moment I thought I caught a glimpse of a fraction of its previous radiance. It was magnificent, still. Even lying prostrate, it seemed ready to levitate any time, leave the rickety hut, and descend back to the deep where it truly belonged.

"Will you report this to the city council?"

The old man shook his head, "It belongs to the ocean. We are not worthy of their purity."

A shudder ran through the sama-sellang's belly and it whimpered.

"Ssshhh...rest now," Mr. Tsai murmured.

I found my hand suddenly reaching out for the vial of amber liquid that we seemed to have forgotten in my belt bag. It was supposed to help the creature sleep easy.

As if sensing my unease, the sama-sellang's eyes popped in a wide accusing stare and its tongue rolled from its mouth. Flies that gathered around us had doubled in number, as if sensing an unusual feast was before them. With its last remaining strength, the sama-sellang pushed closer to the old man.

"Take it easy, rest now," Mr. Tsai repeated, getting into the briny pool himself, as he leaned closer and clasped the dying creature's hands.

Outside, the cicadas sang and the wind whistled. The waves joined in a mournful ebbing and flowing. The sama-sellang's breath grew fitful. Its mouth rattled; its leg-like lower fins clattered in one electric spasm. I continued to rub its back and give it whatever little comfort I could provide. There was not much I could do except wait.

Mr. Tsai leaned his forehead against the sama-sellang's. The creature's eyes peeled open for the last time and sought his face. Their bodies had merged into one: one forehead to another, hands and fins, sallow skin and intricate patterns on the old man's sash.

The sama-sellang let out a final sound, a cry that was at once pitiful and terrifying. It reverberated around the tiny house, and as the echo died away, so did the beating under my hand. And then, darkness descended unannounced.

Mr. Tsai continued to hold the creature in his embrace. I rose as quietly as I could, and headed to the makeshift stairs that faced the quiet sea.

Sigrid Marianne Gayangos was born and raised in Zamboanga City, Philippines. Her works have been anthologized in *Mindanao Odysseys: A Collection of Travel Essays, Fantasy: Fiction for Young Adults, Maximum Volume: Best New Philippine Fiction 3* and *Philippine Speculative Fiction 12*, among other places. She is currently working on her first collection of short stories.

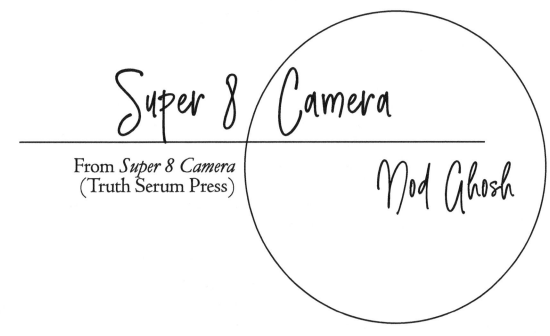

Super 8 Camera

From *Super 8 Camera*
(Truth Serum Press)

Nod Ghosh

HE CAME HOME ONE day with a Super 8 movie camera. When he placed the silver gadget on the table, we crowded around to get a better look. My sister pressed a button and nothing happened.

"How much will the film cost?" my mother asked. "And the developing. It's not just the price of the camera." Her face elongated with anxiety. It hadn't been that long since we'd fallen on hard times.

My father had been to an auction.

Auctions were where he acquired much of the paraphernalia that filled the windowless rooms in our wide and rambling house.

Despite her initial reticence, my mother was interested. She stroked the chrome-plated logo, peeped through the viewfinder.

"It looks good." She pointed out features here and there. "How do you make it work?"

"It needs the right batteries."

"Hai Raam! You haven't seen it working? How do you know it's not broken?" My mother flicked her husband an accusatory stare.

"I got it for a very good price," he said, as if that was the only explanation required.

Although it was the first time my father had brought home a movie camera, it wasn't the first time he'd come home with unexpected purchases. Often he returned from the auction house with multiple unnecessary items. Cupboards overflowed. Objects sang out their uselessness like adverts.

Here I am. The ninth bicycle, rotting and chainless.

Thought you had enough reading lamps? You can never have too many! Here we are, with spent bulbs and burnt out plugs.

I am the inside of a piano. I look like a harp. I am as tuneless and irretrievably useless.

A broken television set? Don't throw me away! Somebody, somewhere might be able to repair me.

Table leg? Useless as a bone without a dog? But my wood is beautiful. I could be made into something wonderful.

Handle-less pans. Handle-less pans. Porridge burnt onto the bottom, blackened soot bases. Someone once loved us, handle-less pans. We will be loved again.

My brother asked if Dad would film him practicing football.

My sister asked whether she could use it to make a movie. She started planning roles for each of her many friends.

My mother said we already had so many things in our lives that didn't work.

That night I dreamed of making my first feature. All the friends I didn't have would have starring roles. The film would be about a lost girl who was found, then lost again.

It didn't matter that the camera wasn't working. Buttons had been pushed, and a chain of events unleashed.

It didn't matter, because the story was already beginning to unfold, because somewhere, somehow, it had already happened in real life.

"Super 8 Camera" is taken from Nod Ghosh's novella-in-flash *The Crazed Wind*, published by Truth Serum Press in 2018. Other work appears in anthologies *Sleep is A Beautiful Colour* (U.K. 2017 NFFD), *Leaving the Red Zone* (Clerestory Press, 2016), *Love on the Road 2015* (Liberties Press) and *Landmarks* (U.K. 2015 NFFD). Originally from the U.K., Nod lives in New Zealand and is a graduate of the Hagley Writers' Institute in Christchurch. Further details: http://www.nodghosh.com/about/

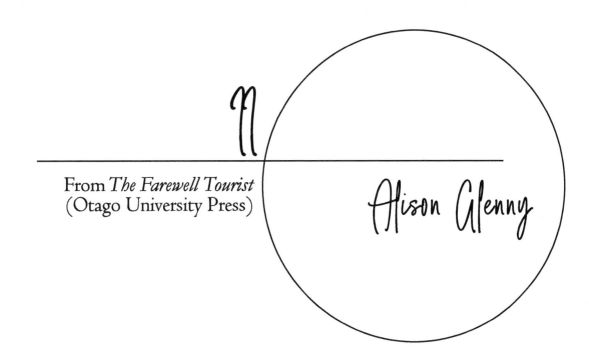

From *The Farewell Tourist*
(Otago University Press)

Alison Glenny

HE CONSIDERED HER BODY to be a little machine, remarkable
for its feats of transmission. Encouraged to speak into the
trumpet, she was startled to hear her voice emerge as clicks,
groans, and a strange whistling sound. She pretended to be
the wind, and he enacted a magnetic storm around her. In
the final act, she helped him demonstrate the tent.
Emerging over and over from the triangle of canvas, each
time to fresh applause.

Alison Glenny lives in Paekākāriki, just north of Wellington, the capital city of Aotearoa/New
Zealand. She holds an MA in Creative Writing from Victoria University of Wellington, and a
post-graduate Certificate in Antarctic Studies from the University of Canterbury. The piece
included here comes from her Antarctic-themed collection of hybrid prose poems, *The Farewell
Tourist*, which was published by Otago University Press in 2018.

The Cup

From *Mascara*

Xiaoshuai Gou

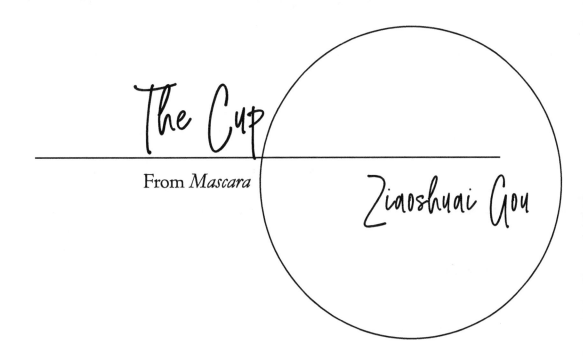

THE CUP ITSELF WOULDN'T amount to much significance to any stranger: crude ceramic, plain design, with a kid happily pursuing dragonflies under the summer sun. It was randomly picked up at a reject shop by the pregnant mother. The joy flowing on the kid's face perhaps had something to do with it.

A skinny boy was born at the end of March. It was the first time the pregnant mother became a real mother, and many things had to be learned from the start and properly handled. The difficulty caused by the absence of a father was aggravated by the fact that the new mother soon turned out to be milkless. All manner of baby formulas were then brought to her, from various countries, and via the hands of all kinds of people. The cup was useful for the first time, and the mother diligently washed it after each time the formula was fed to her baby.

Two months later, the content of the cup began to change. At first, formulas were still the staple of it, with occasional pills crushed into them to add extra nutrients for the proper growth of the newborn. Then things changed to almost the complete opposite. Pill powders of all brands and colors started to take hold of the cup, while non-stop coughs of the baby boy rendered the formula feeding increasingly pointless. With the same diligence, and with growing amounts of quiet tears, the mother continued to wash the cup. But a stubborn dark stain was still irreversibly engraved into its interior wall of once milky smoothness.

Then came the summer. The coughing finally subjected the infant boy to the 24/7 protection of the hospital ICU and the vigilance of its nurses. Pills stopped being crushed. Full tins of formula were stashed away without the prospect of ever being opened again in the future. Suddenly all things ceased to be of any meaning. The mother's distress grew more and more visible every time she watched her baby son through the ICU windows, until eventually she was declared as suffering from severe postnatal depression, and was subsequently

hospitalised in the same hospital as that of her infant son. The cup washing was abandoned.

The next summer differed from those preceding it with its excessive rainfall. This posed a serious problem for the old grandma who had a flower garden at her back yard. For the bulk of the summer, she had to juggle constantly between visiting the hospital where her depressed daughter was showing clear signs of recovery, and salvaging the small garden frequently in danger of being washed away by the heavy rain. Luckily her efforts paid off in the end. Both her daughter and the garden survived the rainfall spell at the end of summer. And as did her late grandson's tiny grave at the north corner of the garden, with a solitary ceramic cup placed in front and mounted with dirt and rain water.

Xiaoshuai Gou was born and raised in China. Currently pursuing a Bachelor of Arts degree at the University of South Australia, he works primarily as a translator between English and Chinese, and as a teacher of English as a second language. His work appeared in *Mascara Literary Review* and several other publications based in China.

Juliet Changes Her Mind

From *Electric Literature*

Amelia Gray

IT WAS RIGHT AROUND the moment all seemed lost and her man lay dead on her lap, the moment the friar had left her to do whatever, when the candles addressed their warmth to her alone, their crackling sound like angel wings, like insects pinched above the flame, the moment her lover's lips lost their warmth, and the slab felt extremely slablike, cold as the crypt around her, which she had chosen as the best location for this performance but was lately feeling a bit dramatic and—she could admit—a little silly, the candles smoking up the place and dripping wax all over, walls lined with wrapped figures of the proud familial dead, this place being so gross and forbidden even from her most wicked cousins' most wicked dares that she had never so much as touched its heavy iron door and now here she was camping out, long after dark with a man's body pinning her, it seemed, to the slab; pushing him off required setting down his dagger, but at last he slumped aside, and his head when it tipped from the low-set stone bumped on the floor like a fresh summer melon and she saw him then for what he was, a dead boy in his own grave, glory fading with the night, candle wax stuck to the long lashes she had loved until that moment. When she pulled herself up and felt the pins and needles of feeling come back to her legs, she cried out with a keen and sudden sense of everything, of the whole glorious world filled to bursting, wild and ready for her and, stumbling over herself, made a break for the iron door and the east, where life itself would rise to meet her with the sun.

Amelia Gray is the author of five books, most recently *Isadora* (FSG). Her fiction and essays have appeared in *The New Yorker*, *The New York Times*, *The Wall Street Journal*, *Tin House*, and *VICE*. She is a winner of the NYPL Young Lion and of FC2's Ronald Sukenick Innovative Fiction Prize, and a finalist for the PEN/Faulkner Award for Fiction. She lives in Los Angeles.

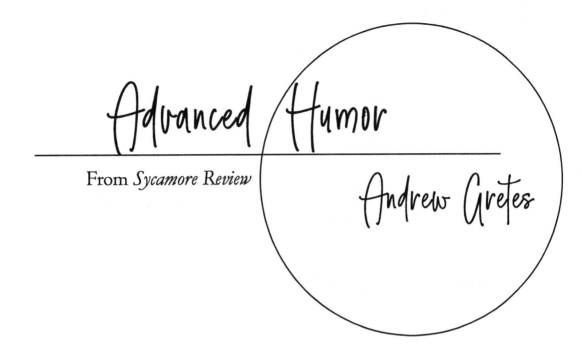

Advanced Humor

From *Sycamore Review*

Andrew Gretes

IT SOUNDED LIKE A   joke. The university didn't even offer Introduction to Humor or Intermediate Humor. Just Philosophy 421: Advanced Humor. No prerequisites.

Intrigued, Jason signed up. Lovesick, I followed. It was our last semester before graduating. My plan: to slide witty, ostensibly-improvised notes to Jason for four months and then seal the deal in May with a note reading, "Let's copulate?!" wagering a two-year friendship on an orgasm.

The class was humorless. The professor was a self-described insomniac, a physicist-turned-philosopher who drew cobwebs of space-time on the chalkboard, equating punchlines with wormholes.

On the first day of class, I sat beside Jason and practiced my power pose: chin titled, doe-eyed, smiling, no teeth, shoulders turned, ankles crossed, arms akimbo. Irresistible, so long as I avoided moving, talking, breathing.

Jason held up the syllabus and asked the professor, "Where are we going?" He was referring to the field trip underlined on the last page of the syllabus. In lieu of a final exam, the field trip was worth half our grade.

The professor said, "Ideally?"

"Sure."

"Another dimension." The bags under the professor's eyes were pronounced, bulging, like a second pair of eyes that had yet to open.

Two weeks into the semester, Jason stopped taking notes. He sat in his chair, hunched, navel-gazing, literally.

The professor spent forty minutes analyzing why slipping on a banana peel was funny, how the transformation from subject to object was incongruous.

I wrote in my notebook: *We laugh because we are not what we should be.* Clueless as to what this meant, I raised my hand, an antennae seeking reception. "I, uh, I don't follow."

The professor said, "When you slip on a banana peel, you become a thing. Rachel, you're *not* a thing."

I blushed. Even questioned my identity. *Rachel ≠ thing?* The sentiment was beautiful, if not uncomfortable. I was so used to being a thing. Thing to be shaved, perfumed, painted, ogled, filled. Thing seeking thing-collector.

I laughed.

The professor frowned.

I said, "What world do you live in?"

Jason told me his advisor had miscalculated. Apparently, he was three credits over the minimum requirement to graduate. "Honestly," he said, "I'm thinking about dropping Advanced Humor."

I begged Jason to reconsider, offering a favor, any favor.

He said, "Anything?"

I contorted into my power pose.

Jason touched my shoulders gently, almost quivering. He said, "Jesus, Rachel, are you having a stroke?"

When Jason dropped the class, I was left with no bullseye to distract me. Fear—that opportunist—knocked. Rachel—that sucker—unlocked the deadbolt to her amygdala. Hello loans! Welcome spinsterhood!

Desperate, I latched on to Advanced Humor, daydreaming about the mysterious field trip at the end of the semester. A new red dot appeared in the horizon, and I shot forward. I consoled myself: *Every target comes equipped with complimentary blinders.*

Months later, the day arrived. As a class, we took a bus, two subway trains, walked four blocks, and entered a comedy club. The professor told us to sit, listen, and wait. There were pictures of World War II tanks on the wall. Apparently, a pun on "tanked"—what the comedians were trying to avoid. There were scented candles on the tables, ranging from "crotch rot" to "napalm in the morning." Luckily, no candles smelled as advertised. Lastly, there was a velvet curtain behind the stage. No one emerged from it. It just hung there—red, pleated, shut—veiling a question mark.

To earn an A on the final exam, we couldn't leave the comedy club until we saw "it." We had no idea what "it" was. So we waited, ordered drinks, and listened to jokes about irritable bowel syndrome, toll booth operators, and animal-cuddling dictators. Eventually, the last comic stepped offstage, the patrons trickled out, and the staff locked the doors with us—Advanced Humor—inside.

That's when the owner of the club—a man with a mustache, a paunch, and a grin—approached. He chitchatted with the professor like they were old friends. The two used ambiguous pronouns. "Ready for *it*?" "I live for *it*." "*It* nourishes." "*It* awaits."

Sheepish, we followed the owner and the professor onstage and watched them pull back the red curtain to reveal a bay window. The vista beyond the window was bountiful, serene, luminous. Imagine a keyhole into Saturn.

The professor said, "Call it what you will. An alternate dimension. A counter-world. Oz." We waited for the professor to say something more illuminating. He didn't. Not that I blamed him. I sympathized. There's a reason Dorothy says to Toto, "We're *not* in Kansas anymore." It's easier to describe what's missing.

Beyond the glass of the bay window, there was no flatulence. No workers bottled inside toll booths for ten hour shifts, dispensing change like human vending machines. No dictators tickling kittens while watching their own people being hacked into human cutlets. No power poses. No things. Just the "should" to our "is." The shadow of our jokes.

The owner of the comedy club stroked the bay window, smearing the glass with his fat fingers. He said, "You know, it wasn't always this size. It actually began as a shard of glass, no bigger than a penny. Then it grew into a porthole. And now it's a bay window. With every joke, the portal gapes a little wider, like a mouth."

I stepped closer. On the other side—in "Oz"—I could see a girl gracefully leaping over a banana peel. We made eye contact. The girl approached, lifted her finger, and touched a tiny crack in the glass. I wanted to welcome her, become her, fan her in our general direction, so I sucked in the fumes of our world and laughed.

Andrew Gretes is the author of *How to Dispose of Dead Elephants* (Sandstone Press 2014). His fiction has appeared or is forthcoming in *New England Review, Willow Springs, Pleiades, Sycamore Review,* and other journals. He teaches and lives in Washington D.C.

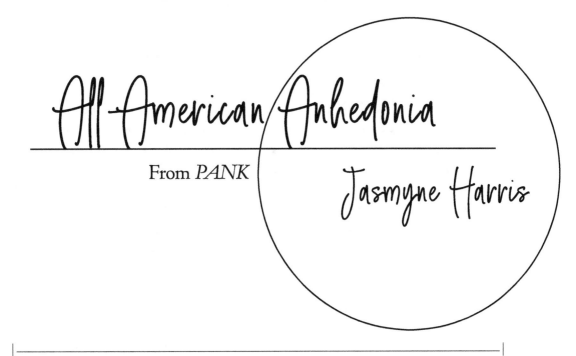

All-American Anhedonia

From *PANK*

Jasmyne Harris

THIS IS THE DISTANCE between Theodore and a table of desserts. What he wants most is the baklava. If he were to close the distance between him and it, this baklava would be his 211th. Theodore keeps precise count of his many cravings and conquests. You cannot see him, I know, but do not mistake him. Theodore is All-American. His broad shoulders and strong jaw make for an appealing stock photograph advertisement. Can you see him now? Yes, yes. Americana. All-American, they say, and we all know what they mean.

This is the distance between Theodore and his two sisters who stand on either side of the dessert table. One is more beautiful than the other. The eldest, Bianca, is slim, plain, and delicate. The other has not yet developed breasts or hips and because of this, Theodore rarely regards her presence at all. Theodore often wonders where he fits between these two. They do not touch any of the items that fill the table. For this, he is grateful. Theodore watches the hands of his sisters and imagines them creeping their dainty fingers onto dessert trays. He imagines strangling the smaller one. It is true that the desserts are not his alone. In theory, he can taste a profiterole cocooned between the roof of his mouth and tongue and feel its weight in his stomach. Its sweetness is an authority, and much stronger than truth. He is too far away.

This is the distance between Theodore and the clock that ticks above the dessert table. In one hour, Theodore is meant to be at practice with his lacrosse teammates Christopher, Franklin,

Tomás, and Gregory. All the boys resemble one another and he sometimes forgets their names. You may have missed it, but Theodore has devoured both a strudel and streusel in his short steps. They sit in his stomach dissatisfied and whole. They make him heavy. They make him drowsy, you see. Of course you do. No person could resist. If the other boys were here, they would already be at the table with their hardened grubby fingers stabbing and molesting the key lime pie, fudge, and banana pudding dishes. He is not like them. Theodore takes his time. While others indulge in alcohol and prostitutes and animal slaughter, Theodore only submits to the whims of his sweet tooth. He is weighed down by their commandments, but he must make room. He wants to vomit so that he may have more.

|———————————————————————|

This is the distance between Theodore and the chocolate-sprinkled brigadeiro that speaks to him and only him and says, *eat me*. Soothing tones of a lone velvet cacao tongue. Can you hear it? It lifts itself up into the air, its body dusting the floor, and into Theodore's right eye. It pushes the others down. Down it goes, full-bodied and defiant. It desires to be the last and final object of desire. Theodore is too full now. The table whispers to him with sugar and flour and butter on its breath, you cannot be full. You have not eaten a thing, Theodore. What is this lust?

|————————————————|

This is the distance between Theodore and American apple pie. If he has it, which he will, this will be his 33rd slice of apple pie. This is peculiar, no? The All-American had never indulged in the patriotic idol until his 16th year when his housekeeper left a slice at his bedside where he lay in recovery. Theodore's parents, who live one floor above him, had always held their children at a beggar's distance. Theodore cannot remember their names. He is sure it is something like Bob and Nancy or Clark and Susan. His mother, let's call her Nancy because Theodore likes that name, happened to show at one of Theodore's games. She held a pair of binoculars to her face and wiggled a few fingers at him. It startled him so that he made a false move. Another player hit him and he flew and spun and jerked in the air. The others swarmed like ants across the green field to his aid. She was still seated when he looked up, the binoculars having become her new eyes. Her lips were slightly parted, not in anxiety or dread, but in delight.

|—————————|

This is the distance between Theodore and a stack of sticky baklava. A susurrus arises from the flaky phyllo wings. Miniscule, light flutters lift its honey-drenched body up and away from the table to deliver itself unto the tip of Theodore's tongue. It is the ultimate honor. It is speaking, saying his name. A microscopic voice it is, and Theodore looks around to see who else can hear. His sister to the right stands despondently, fingering her phone and looking so deeply into its luminescent screen that her shoulders hunch forward, willing herself into the screen, to be the screen. Be the screen, be the screen, the baklava says. Where there is gravity, there is madness.

|——————|

This is the distance between Theodore and his sister Bianca. He is closer now and can hear her hums. He used to enjoy the sound of them vibrating within her narrow throat. She is bored, but not bored enough to look at him. Theodore suspects she hadn't in a few months. Babka, cham cham, peach cobbler, and rum balls lay coolly on decorated silver trays. Theodore watches Bianca ignore the desserts he cannot. He imagines stuffing her mouth with crème brûlée. The caramel layer shattering and breaking her poised face, sending tawny shards into the folds of her collared blouse, perhaps even puncturing her lung. She would have to notice him then.

X

Theodore is X. There is no more distance between him and anything. Theodore is suspended in a space where everything is simultaneously close and far. Perhaps Theodore has been swallowed and consumed in excessive amounts. Both his hands are sticky and wet. Remnants of caramel, vanilla, pecans, raisins, sugar, and chocolate line his palms. Bianca is yelling his name and he can taste the baklava on his lips. It taste like nothing. Are you happy now? Theodore asks. Behind him are the claps of one hundred men and women. They could be celebrating him. They could be celebrating anyone. They could be celebrating nothing.

—

Jasmyne J. Harris is a writer in St. Louis, MO. Her work has been featured in *Bayou Magazine*, *Sharp & Sugar Tooth: Women Up To No Good*, and *PANK Magazine*.

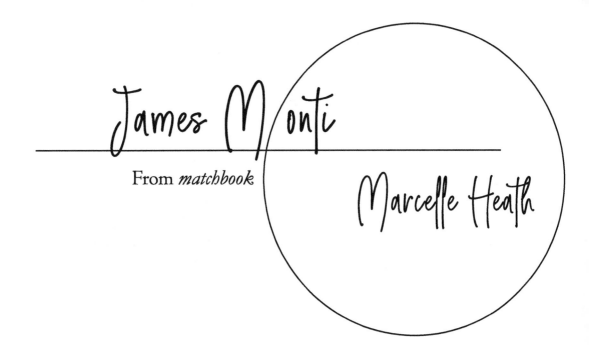

James Monti

From *matchbook*

Marcelle Heath

IF YOU'RE LUCKY, YOU'RE made beautiful by the future. No one will find out that for a period you loved your neighbor's dog more than your own. Or that you once struck your sister so hard she passed out. No one will know about the affair you had right after you were married. Or that the final words to your demented father were *Please die*. No one will discover that, every day for fifteen months, your search terms were "James Monti," "James Monti married," "James Monti wife." In the future, your name will pop up in conversations about Jackie Kennedy, the subject of a fictional memoir you wrote and sent to all your friends. They will remember the time you asked one of their children if he remembered you in his dreams, the time you flew to Oslo by mistake. Three hours in, you thought, this could be your one chance. You could disappear like your aunt did after Mount St. Helens erupted in 1980. She was covering the story for The Columbian, and everyone assumed she perished in the disaster. Her girlfriend found her living as a pig farmer in Little Rock some twenty years later. When you disembark in Oslo, you eat fish soup and drink three beers. You have twenty thousand dollars, the bulk of which you inherited from your father, and an eleven-year-old daughter. You take a car to the Viking Ship Museum. At the Oseberg ship, you read about the burial chamber for two women, which included two tents, four sleighs, fifteen horses, six dogs, and two cows. You check in at a hotel on Tjuvholmen, or "Thief Island," so named for its seedy past. The next day, you book a flight back. You go not because you miss home but because you suspect that you will not. The story will change, the missed hours attributed to illness and jet lag. You will remember the gripping beast engravings, their cartoon eyes and open mouths. You won't travel abroad again, but you will die on a plane, soon after your divorce, on your way to see James Monti. Your remains will be packed up by your daughter, who will put off doing anything with them, and moved from Los Angeles to Kansas City to Detroit and back. Here, a wildfire in the San Fernando Valley will claim you, your daughter, and thirty horses, a funeral pyre worthy of Valhalla.

Marcelle Heath is a fiction writer and editor. Her work has appeared in *Joyland, Kenyon Review Online, matchbook, Nat. Brut, NOÖ, Split Lip Magazine, Wigleaf,* and other journals. Her short story collection, *Nine Times Gretchen King is Mistaken,* was a semifinalist for YesYes Books 2017 Pamet River Prize. She is former Series Editor of *Wigleaf* Top 50 (very) Short Fictions and Managing Editor of *VIDA Review,* and curates Apparel for Authors, an Instagram interview series on writers, fashion, and the public sphere. Marcelle lives with her family in Portland, Oregon.

Whatever They Told You Not to Be

From *805 Lit and Art*

Natalie Hernandez

LA LLORONA, LA MALINCHE, La Whatever they told you not to be. Anna says she saw you crying at Lucky's on Friday, and man they believe her. He told your mother he just wanted his family back, and you closed your lips as she told you on the phone what women like you get. Nothing. But nothing would always be better than so many somethings. This is where you were raised. This is where you never wanted to stay.

The day you left, you clutched that red satchel of yours full of things you thought were somethings. A shot glass from Mexico. You'd never been and you didn't drink. You said thanks anyway, thanks Dad. He calls you gringa when you straighten your hair or when you use the word like or that one time you asked for sour cream. Dinner is sniffles. It's watery eyes and burned tongues. It's the risk of choking on misplaced, overlooked, not unintentional chicken bones. And your uncle pretends his nose isn't running, but that's how you know it's good, and you gringa pretend too. Mija is for loved daughters. Blanca. Blanca is for you.

So you drink ginger ale at Lucky's, the bar downtown that's open late, the only one. Shoes belong to the liquor waxed floor, and twenty-two year olds belong to numb lips. The bouncer bends your ID back and forth, and he asks you to say your name. It's the same when you go to the airport and TSA pulls you aside, has you move each limb here and there, pats you down, rolls your hands for residue. They don't make a sound and you the pro don't either. You want a blanca name to match your blanca skin.

Anna says what they want to hear. What you wished was true. But you sat down at the bar. You smiled, laughed, and made easy look damn fucking easy.

You know it was him. That it wasn't some stranger ransacking your second story apartment you barely can afford, so you don't even bother with the cops. He didn't take a goddamn thing. It was just a reminder that he could.

If you had a man, if you never left him, this never would've happened, because married women don't get robbed, your mother tells you that night. She doesn't hang up until you say I love you, and you almost don't.

There's kids, Anna says. Kids need a home with a mother and a father. She's worried, real worried, cause she saw you fall off a bar stool at Lucky's from all the whiskey you were drinking. And Marco told her you never feed the kids. Nada, but some potato chips every once in a while. Your mother drives four hours to tell you this and check your cupboards and fridge.

That night at Lucky's, you decide to walk home, and that's when you hear her. She's down there off the trail just near the canal. It's the wind, but you swear you hear all three. It's morning when a bicyclist breaks your stare and interrupts the story you've told yourself all night. When you were eight you stayed out too late at the park playing baseball with the boys who lived down the street. It was dark when you got home, so your father said he wanted to tell you a bedtime story. The first and only one he ever did. At night when it was late, there was a woman to be afraid of, the one who took children, and blamed it all on a man.

Marco never said sorry after his fingers left your neck. You listen to her cry the way your mother used to when your father drank too much. The way you never could. La Llorona, La Malinche, La Whatever they told you not to be.

Natalie Hernandez graduated from the University of California, Irvine with a degree in English. While there she participated in creative writing workshops. She currently lives in the San Francisco Bay area overusing the word "hella."

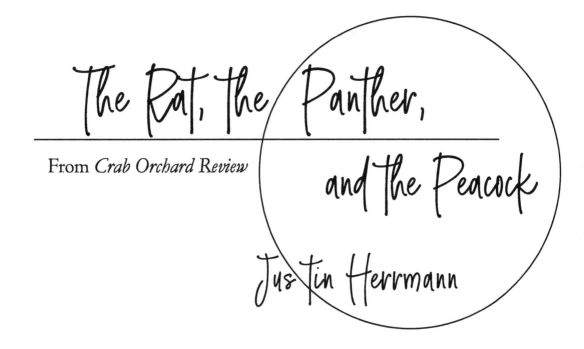

The Rat, the Panther, and the Peacock

From *Crab Orchard Review*

Justin Herrmann

WE AREN'T ALLOWED TO touch skuas or any other wildlife. Skuas look like dirt-colored seagulls, but are the size of chickens or infants and eat fish, trash, and smaller birds on the coast of Antarctica. As a janitor at McMurdo, the largest Antarctic research station, I can eat four times a day. Prime rib on Sundays. Lobster on holidays. My coworker Samantha McCallister introduced me to, among other things, Frosty Boy, the twentyfour hour soft serve machine. I gained twenty pounds my first season.

Early that season I sauntered toward my dorm holding a sprinkled sugar cookie. As I brought the cookie to my mouth, it was torn from my thick-gloved hand. The skua's beak or claw nicked my cheek. Samantha watched from the deck of her dorm.

"Hard way to learn that lesson," she said. Then, "You're bleeding." She insisted skuas carry disease and took me to her room, which smelled like wet socks and was shared with three galley workers, all on duty. She cleaned the cut on my face with Heaven Hill vodka. Then she poured vodka in blue plastic galley cups and handed me a stick of gum.

"Chewing gum while you drink this cheap stuff," she said, "makes it taste like you're drinking the fancy flavored kind."

The bar, Southern Exposure, opens three mornings a week for night shifters. There's three guys to every girl at McMurdo. Other men would buy Samantha drinks, Samantha who described her own face as a cloud with glasses. Because I'd leave with her when the bar closed most mornings, men called me fortunate. I was still married back then to a good woman in the Midwest, though with each weekly phone call, there was less to say.

Skuas congregate at food-waste bins behind the galley. My third season a skua stuck its head inside a no. 10 can that'd been knocked from a food-waste bin. It was going after dregs of tomato paste. A loader hauling a pallet of Amstel Light may or may not have known about the

skua before he ran the can over. The equipment operator was terminated.

Samantha didn't return to McMurdo after her first season. I wrote a few letters early on to keep her informed about things down here. After a while Crab Orchard Review u 45 Justin Herrmann I stopped writing. Sea ice grows thinner each year, but human life changes little in the Antarctic.

My fourth season a Skua showed up at South Pole Station, some 800 miles from McMurdo. Nothing other than bacteria naturally lives at the very bottom of the world. The unfortunate bird likely followed the annual traverse that hauls over 100,000 gallons of fuel to South Pole. Too far to make it back to the sea, the bird was discovered in a heap near the summer dorms. Maybe a lost gamble, something in the bird's blood telling it creatures headed this direction become easy meals.

Waste at McMurdo is separated into more than a dozen categories including mixed paper, non-ferrous light metal, food waste, and so on. Most waste is shipped off the continent annually. There's a category known as skua. It's for useful reusable items like clothing, books, toiletries. Many nights after we'd clean Crary Lab bathrooms, me and Samantha would check the skua bins in all thirteen dorms. Once I found a Member's Only jacket. I gave it to Samantha for Christmas. She wore it the rest of the season. She gave me a beaded necklace with a thin, curved bone hanging from it that she found in skua.

"Surely," she said, "nothing promises a blessed life like a lucky raccoon dong."

Samantha once told me the skua is the rat, the panther, and the peacock of the Antarctic. Today I received an email that read, Mike, everyone loved Samantha. She was special. It turns out she didn't love herself as much as we all did. I'm sorry. I scavenged through skua. I was meticulous. I found that same Member's Only jacket. I dug through the pockets, hoping for a sign. Deep within the lining, through a small hole in the silky pocket, there was a piece of hard gum, wadded back in its Juicy Fruit foil. Of course I took the gum from that foil. I rubbed it between my thumb and forefinger. I left the dorm, walked through the galley pad and faced the congregation of skuas perched on the food waste bin. I offered, the gum on my open palm, waiting.

Justin Herrmann is the author of the story collection *Highway One, Antarctica* (MadHat Press 2014). He's a *River Styx* Micro-Fiction Contest winner and his stories have appeared in journals including *Crab Orchard Review, Washington Square Review, SmokeLong Quarterly,* and *New Flash Fiction Review.* He has an MFA from University of Alaska Anchorage, and spent 24 months living and working with good people at McMurdo Station, Antarctica. Come drink a beer with him next time you're in Kotzebue, Alaska.

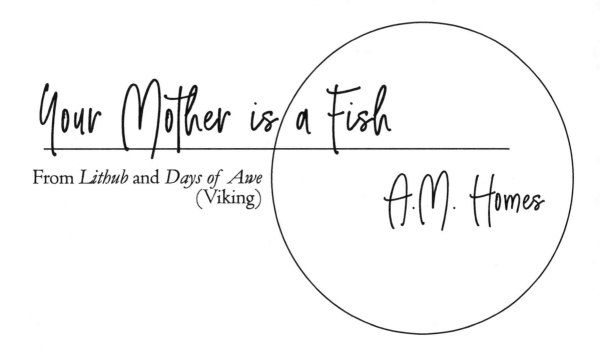

Your Mother is a Fish

From *Lithub* and *Days of Awe*
(Viking)

A. M. Homes

À L'OEUVRE ON RECONNAIT l'artisan. You can tell an artist by his handiwork.

She is sewing a story, stitching a tale, line by line. This one is about her great grandmother who sewed herself a mermaid costume and swam to America. The journey was long, arduous and by the time she arrived at the state of Maine, her costume had fused to her flesh. She had a dressmaker split the center seam, separating her legs so she could walk, and she went through life with her legs covered in thick green scales, a brocade, fossilized by the sea into leathery chaps like a cowboy would wear. Men found her scales incredibly attractive; it was considered good luck to rub her thighs. They all wanted only one thing, to get into the space between the scales, the alligator purse that had been perfectly protected. The sweat of their palms stung her skin; she found them repulsive.

She moved to Massachusetts and took a part time job doing women's work sewing tassles on loafers in a shoe factory.

Suck cock, suck cock, the sound of the sewing machine.

At a country circus, she met Ray, a boy with powdery hands, like buttery talc, who worked the spinning cups in a traveling show. His mother was a bearded lady, his father the world's tallest

man. His beloved uncle Meurice, a merman, who died long ago, was laid out, taxidermied in a glass vitrine that traveled wherever the family went—a quarter a peek.

Ray asked her about her homeland and she told him about the veiled life, she told him there were places she couldn't go, she told him she was invisible there—people only saw what they wanted to see, they didn't look very far. She told Ray that when she left she knew she would never go back. Her family wept as she sewed herself into her disguise, their tears filled the river that floated her down to the sea—her home was lost to history. As she told Ray the story of her past, her eyes filled and heavy tears dripped plink, plunk onto Uncle Meurice's vitrine. Ray wiped the vitrine dry and never asked her about it again.

When their daughter was born with an extraordinarily long needle sharp index finger—that featured a boney eye for thread to pass through, they thought it a plus. They named her Penelope. She could thread herself through fabric, through wood, and drill though metal. Penelope was incredibly good at math, winning a scholarship to a prestigious engineering school. She graduated with honors and took jobs building ships, airplanes, skyscrapers. Their son, Morris, named after Ray's famed mer-uncle, was born with wings transparent fire-resistant flesh webbing from his arms to his ribs. His shirts had to be custom made. A more successful Icarus, Morris made the first successful ship-less solo flight into space and returned with an incredible tan. At a very young age he married an ornithologist and they nested on the top floor of a high rise.

"Yours is a family of unusual traces," a soothsaying neighbor said.

"We are bred to survive," Ray answered, accidentally clipping the woman with his weed wacker, lacerating her ankles. "It is evolution—we keep what we need, we lose the rest."

Morris had an irrational fear of infants of all kinds and so he and his wife lived with their two ancient Labradors, their deaf screaming cockatoo, and various geriatric gray parrots and macaws all adopted at an advanced age. They opened their doors to all elderly animals, "Don't put your pet out to pasture, give it a new life at Ye Olde Animal Haus," was the slogan on their matchbooks.

Penelope, so smart and successful, was lonely. Strolling the seaport, she met a sailor from far away; they married that night and immediately returned to the water. Packing to go, her mother gave her the family heirloom the scrap saved from the grandmother's center seam. Penelope recognizing its significance, affixed it to her skin–a scaly merkin mounted with crazy glue.

Given the family's history it came as no surprise when Penelope's parents received word via carrier pigeon that identical twins had born on an island off Key West with gills and organs of both sexes—identical hermaphrodites Tasiña and Tasi.

"Great grandchildren!" the newly minted great-grandmother announced to the ladies of her sewing circle, leaving out the spawny details. The sewing circle clucked approvingly. Long ago when she joined the sewing circle, she told anyone crass and curious enough to ask about her scales that she was a burn victim. It was easier for people to understand and she wasn't looking for trouble.

A stitch in time saves nine, a fish in time, saves mine.

Thimbles and Threads, the ladies called themselves—a ministry that stitched for salvation; "Charity Never Faileth—Sew What's New? They knitted hats for cancer patients, socks for orphans, afghans for Afghans, lap blankets for cold old women and men, the grandmother donning a thimble to darn watch caps for the Christmas at Sea, "Leave No Keppe Cold," a Jewish military relief organization.

But soon Penelope's sailor mate met a bad end. Not used to living on land, he had gone ashore and failed to look both ways when crossing train tracks and even though the conductor slammed on the brakes nothing was spared, and his bodily mash was returned to the sea in a potato sack covered with salt tear

A youthful widow, single mother, a woman with needs of her own. Penelope began an affair with a dolphin. In a dispatch to her mother she described him as a great conversationalist, incredibly loving, and gifted in special ways. "He can curl his member like a finger beckoning . . . I won't say more lest you think me crude. Swimming with him reminds me of when I used to dance standing on daddy's feet, waltzing in time. For the moment, I am content to live as a fish."

Her sailor's children Tasina and Tasi matured quickly and were ready to replicate—each able to complete the process entirely on their own. To her dismay, Tasi, her he/she daughter, declined she felt the need to hang on to herself to be in essence, copyrighted, but Tasina her she/male son turned out little ones by the dozen. Some stayed on land, some on the sea, some sold sea shells, another had fleas, four go to Harvard, two go to Yale, a dozen go to Trinity and one goes to jail. Another spends his days surfing big waves in Hawaii and the oldest is a federal judge swearing in people who promise not to tell tall tales. Tasi, having spent so many years raising children found it difficult to get a job and worked as a temporary secretary—She/He's pretty but can she/he type? Penelope, now twice widowed, having had enough of it all, returns to the city. A septagenarian who looks forty, well preserved from a life in salt water, she comes back to New York. Having learned a thing or two from her kids, she tells everyone that she wants to be called Tom. She packs plastic bought on the Lower East Side at Babes in Toyland and tends bar down by the water at a place called, Henrietta Hudson's, spinning her yarns to any available ear. One of the girls at the bar tells her the story of a straight businesswoman who packs just because she feels it gives her a competitive edge. "No one knows what you've got tucked in your pants until you get hit by a train," she says and Penelope Tom nods knowingly.

One night spindly Sarah Spider, a sex therapist, sits down next to Penelope Tom near closing time and starts spinning a handsome web. Penelope Tom admires the handiwork and the mating dance begins. "It's been so long I wouldn't know where to begin," Penelope Tom confesses, as Sarah's expert hand travels up her thigh. She remembers the sensation her mermaid mother spoke about and having inherited her hypersensitivity and not forgetting that she's still got the old scaly merkin crazy glued over the spot, she feels her/his packy getting moist and squishy. Sarah spins a wicked web, leading Penelope Tom back to her apartment after closing up shop. Sarah ties her/him up and down and is just about to cuff her to the bed when Penelope Tom realizes that there's more to it than that. Lost between her legs, a latex hot head, Sarah is a cannibal and a carnivore and she's the midnight snack. As Sarah is using her pincers to pry the merkin loose, Penelope Tom comes to her senses and with her elongated index finger—the needle nail grown tough over time is now like an ivory tooth—pierces Sarah's shell. The stabbed spider spurts bug juice everywhere.

Penelope Tom takes a taxi to her granddaughter Tess's house in Harlem, leaving her cock and balls behind, hoping she can hide out for a while. Tess, a fashion designer, has a boyfriend who, nostalgic for the ontogenetic past of life in the womb, internalizes the water—he drinks his morning urine. It harkens back to the water of his early life, the amniotic, the oceanic. His habit has prompted many women to leave him. Tess just nods, she brings him a tall glass to pee in, "Bottoms up," she says, liking the way his penis fills the glass, like a soda syphon "Aqua vitae."

While recovering at Tess's, Penelope Tom catches up on her reading and finds that while on it's journey, the space rover Opportunity discovered evidence of water on the surface of Mars and is intrigued at the idea that at some unknown time in the distant past there was life on the red planet. She gets it in her head to do one thing before she dies—with her engineering skills she will build the Bimodal Nuclear Thermal Rocket.

Because of her age, because she is a woman (before she is a man), because of all of history and everything that has come before, she is once again invisible. No one notices the little old lady man in Harlem building sewing herself a space ship. Nautilus Neptune. She confides in Tess, who supplies heat resistant fabric and helps her grandmother saw off her index finger needle, which they affix to the space ship as an evolved antenna of Darwinian evolution. As she's preparing to go, she affixes what has become the family seal, the historic remnant of scaly merkin to the nose of the Nocturnal. On the appointed day, Tess stands on the roof of the building and lights the long fuse. Wearing welder's goggles she watches as her grandmother takes off, a bright blast, an eruption, carrying the past into the future with a sonic boom that echoes around the world.

A. M. Homes is the author of the memoir *The Mistress's Daughter* and the novels *This Book Will Save Your Life*, *Music for Torching*, *The End of Alice*, *In a Country of Mothers*, and *Jack*, as well as the story collections *The Safety of Objects* and *Things You Should Know*. She lives in New York City.

Diction (a glossary of terms)

From *Room*

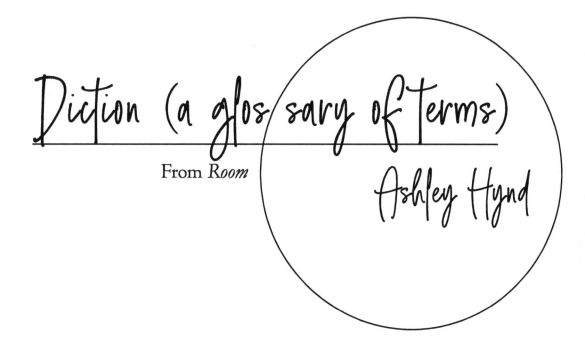

AUNT: *F.* FROM THE Latin *amita*

1. small creatures that can carry more than their share **1.2** stand-in mothers (who can't hold seventeen hours of labour over you) **2.** photo filler used for major childhood moments: christenings, communions, etc. **3.** *antonym* ex-aunts: members of the family easily erased by divorce

Brother: *m.* from the Latin *frater*

1. a mythological creature said to beat up boys when they break your heart **2.** *synonym* brotherhood: the reason why your cousins always gang up on you in a fight

Babcia: *f.* not to be confused with *babka*

1. a Polish grandmother who makes hand-made Care Bears for her unborn grandchildren then dies two months before you are born (you think I would have loved her)

Cousins: *uni.* from the Latin *consobrinus*

1. competition for the mashed potatoes at thanksgiving **2.** temporary siblings **3.** the reason for the block option on Facebook **4.** an episode of *Jerry Springer* on crack cocaine

Daughter: *f.* from the Greek *thugatēr*

1. a princess who can do no wrong and always gets her way **2.** the black sheep always to blame for family fights **2.2** a constant strain on resources such as food, finances, and freedom **3.** a continuous cycle of oppression forced upon women since birth (sometimes referred to as fresh-starts)

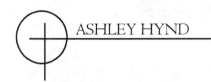

Father: *m.* from the Latin *pater*
1. an angry- absent- narcissistic- yet-charismatic- male- role- model of your formative years **1.2** the reason you drop out of high school at sixteen to get a job **3.** PTSD waiting to happen

Grandfather: *m.* from the Latin *grandis + pater*
1. a man who died from cancer the year your sister was born **1.2** the owner of the cologne bottles on the back of your grandmother's toilet (which haven't moved in fifteen years) **1.3** an otherwise story-less member of the family (but mommy learned to love abuse somewhere)

Grandmother: *f.* from the Latin *grandis + mater*
1. a mythological creature rumoured to bake cookies **1.2** the only reason for family gatherings **1.3** a fragile little woman who gave you twenty dollars and a funeral for your thirteenth birthday

Mother: *f.* from the Latin *mater*
1. an emotionally absent woman who incubated you **1.2** a body on a one-way train to the States **2.** a cackle-tongued woman of wisdom with a dash of drama **3.** the strongest woman you have ever known (aside from possibly yourself)

Pépé: *m.* not to be confused with *papa*
1. a French Canadian grandfather on your father's side **1.2** your best friend until the age of four **1.3** your first experience with trauma (turns out he wasn't sleeping)

Sister: *f.* from the Latin *soror*
1. rumoured to have loved you once when she was two **1.2** smacked an old lady in the nursery of the hospital saying "my baby!" **1.3** the child used to make the second child feel like a mistake ("why can't you be more like your sister")

Uncle: *m.* from the Latin *avunculus*
1. the point where you cave under pressure **2.** stand-in fathers who actually hung your school pictures **3.** the reason you thought *Beauty and the Beast* was romantic **4.** *antonym* ex-uncle: taboo or family secret

---

Ashley Hynd is a poet with mixed ancestry who lives on the Haldimand Tract and respects the Attawandron, Anishnawbe, and Haudenosaunee relationships with the land. Like many people

with mixed heritage the knowledge of her history is unclear. According to the stories in her family they are of Anishnawbe, Cherokee and metis decent. Her writing currently grapples with the erasure of her history and is as much an act of reclamation as it is a call of accountability for what has been lost. She was longlisted for *The CBC Poetry Prize* (2018), shortlisted for *ARC Poem of the Year* (2018), and won the *Pacific Spirit Poetry Prize* (2017). Her poetry has appeared in *ARC, Canthius, Room, Prism International, SubTerrain, Grain* and is forthcoming in *Cv2* and *Vallum*. Ashley sits on the editorial board for *Canthius Literary Journal* and runs a monthly brunch for writers called Poets & Pancakes.

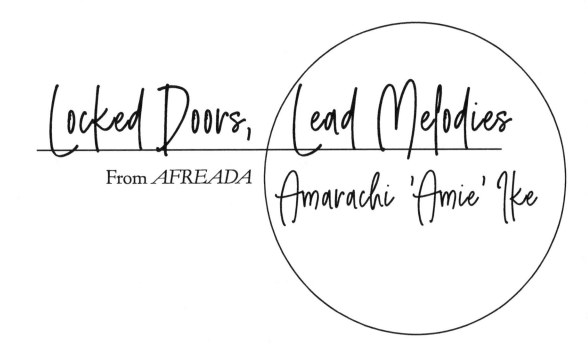

Locked Doors, Lead Melodies

From *AFREADA*

Amarachi 'Amie' Ike

THERE IS AN OLD market woman growing inside of me.

My mother weeps for me the night I birth blood. I feel the turbulence of an ocean in my womb being emptied. She says I have become a woman and I want to celebrate my womanhood but my brother looks morose and my father has fear in his eyes. She grabs hold of me and whispers, "if a boy touches you…", then she stops to analyze the canvas on my uniform. I am nine years old.

Now, I am fifteen. I grow the seeds of my womanhood and harvest a new body. It is my transfiguration. I harvest along with my body, an insecurity and an uncertainty of self. It is habit to recite affirmations. And with affirmations, I learn silence and submissiveness.

There is a place of tranquility. I was sixteen when I stopped following the backside of my mother through crevasses of the market. The day I have my feet for guidance, a man eats of this harvest of my body. He grabs hold of its fruits in the ruckus of this selling place. And the women throw their bodies backward, but for one who is staring. She is seated on a wooden stool with a barrow before her. She looks at me, whispers some instructions. I hear her say bow. I hear her say scream the kind of scream that puts prematurely born men into the gutters. So, I let out a piercing sound and watch my goliath whimper.

There is a place of trouble. It is on the lap of a man. The market woman will wait at the door of my matrimony while my parents revel in what's left of my dowry. She has taught me well. I'm twenty-four, she says, my aspirations should not die on his bed. My husband did not promise me love. He promised me his honesty, his sons. I told him I wanted daughters. He laughed.

My uncertainty in marriage leads me to the market. I contort my way through waves of people and unlock the doors that led me here, listening. I hear her say she is tired. Her spirit leaves me when I place her hand on my back, and she lets out her last breath. It spells out a name Nneoma, "good mother". I say I will name the market woman growing inside of me *Nneoma*. A woman has made me a woman.

Now, a crowd circles the figure in the distance. He has tattered clothing and hair like cocoa plantation dusted in earth. He folds with his hands to his ears. My heart forgets to beat. Beat, I whisper. And he lets out a piercing sound. It's a melody in fact. I hear it. I see it. It's beautiful because it is not silence.

Amarachi "Amie" Ike is a fiction writer and undergraduate of the University of Nigeria, Enugu Campus. She has been published on several online platforms, including *Ile Alo* and *The Short Story Project*. She writes to inspire, entertain and incite conversations.

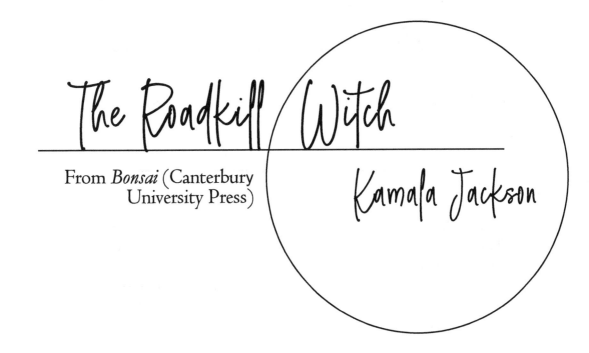

The Roadkill Witch

From *Bonsai* (Canterbury University Press)

Kamala Jackson

WENDY WAS OUT WEARING her high-vis vest before the morning traffic started. In winter she wore the cap with LED lights, much more practical than carrying a torch. But it was almost November and all she needed was a spade.

The first casualty she came across had a thick pelt, a crushed skull, and little white fingers splayed and stiff. Dried blood stuck the head to the tarmac. Using the spade, she gently loosened that contact and slid the blade under the body. She carried it to the side of the road.

"We'll find a nice spot for you."

The soil was easy. She lined the trench with the thick, glossy leaves and the blue flowers of vinca growing in the ditch. She lowered the body with care and covered it, smoothing the surface.

"Rest in peace."

The dead were a rabbit with a damaged hind leg, two more possums and a cat with a broken back. The poor mite was skin and bone, with the rusty brown fur of the local ferals.

Wendy stood up and eased her back. A car swerved fast round the corner, music blaring, lads yahooing.

"It's that roadkill witch."

She didn't hear the jeers, see the finger. A cataclysmic event was happening in her chest.

The ambulance driver, without local knowledge, followed his satnav. He took the metal road with its steep inclines, sudden dips, potholes, shoals of gravel on the bends. Wendy's bones were shaken and shaken.

The hospital was noisy, the lights glaring. A nurse tried to put a line in a "wandering vein". When Wendy was left with the beeping monitors, the drips dripping, the tubes in her

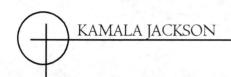

nose, she closed her eyes and conjured up soft, dark earth, mosses and the drifting scent of jasmine.

Kamala Jackson has Kiwi and U.K. heritage. She was born in India and given an Indian name. She has an M.A.(Hons) in English from the University of Auckland, and a degree in Creative Writing from AUT University, also in Auckland. She has travelled in Europe, the Middle East and South Asia. Her working life has been all about words: editing manuscripts, selling books and writing. Her stories have been broadcast on national radio. *We Are One*, a novel in manuscript, was showcased by The Literary Consultancy in 2018.

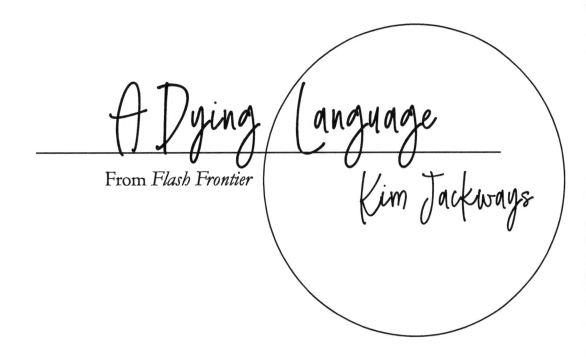

A Dying Language

From *Flash Frontier*

Kim Jackways

MY GRANDMOTHER'S FEET SPIKED up like monuments. Still cold, despite the starchy blankets and the heat. The hum and beep of the machines just made her swear under her breath when she woke. Her heart may be failing but her tongue still whipped.

Before she shrank, I sat on the dusty mats, a frieze of springbok dancing around the grotty walls. Mother murmured that the floor was dirty. I popped out my headphones, *hip hop beats can wait*, and asked Grandmother to teach me.

She pressed her lips together and expelled air with an explosive click, like a dream punctured on waking. I tried to echo her but my lip piercing was all bulky and metallic. My parents watched. Crazy, they seemed to say. Think of the future.

Nobody uses the glottis these days. Slippery as aloe, the concepts slid past: *The ostrich egg method of getting water, the perfect amount of Hoodia cactus to suppress thirst, how a young girl left her village to marry a boy.*

Then she asked for water. Any more than a sip and she choked. I fed her my tears but it was never enough. The clock ticked faster, like all the sounds I couldn't save. Click. Tock.

Late. Too late. I knelt at her feet as her tongue lolled, and her agile lips went slack. And the feet of a tribal elder were no longer respected, but tagged and bagged in crisp white.

Kim Jackways is a New Zealand writer, who loves the challenge of the short form. A series of massive earthquakes in her hometown spurred her to follow her passions – language and travel.

She left the office job behind, for a year in France with her family. While there, she began writing a novel set in 18th century Provence. She draws on her background in Linguistics and Psychology, in order to understand human nature.

Weather Proverbs

From *Streetlight Mag* — Ingrid Jendrzejewski

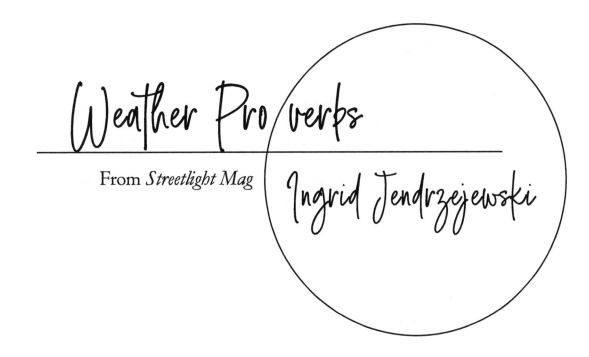

Mare's tails and mackerel scales Make tall ships take in their sails.

SHE'S STUDIED THE WEATHER and knows about clouds which is why her lips are thin and tight. She does not want to tell him about the promotion. Tonight, she will prepare a nice dinner, but chop the onions too quickly. Blood from her little finger will mingle with Bolognese.

When the sky fills with altocumulus and cirrus clouds, a warm front is approaching. Although the day might be pleasant, it's time to batten down the hatches: soon, conditions will be favourable for storms.

When the ass begins to bray, Surely rain will come that day.

He is happy for her but he is also not happy for her. He will not say that he is not happy for her but instead will complain about these things in this order: the weather, the season, the neighbour's barking dog, the tightness of his interview suit around his waist, the quantity of onions in her pasta sauce. She will try to make a joke, but it will backfire.

When a storm is approaching, air pressure plummets. Some organisms are sensitive to minute changes in the environment, changes that humans can't detect. Beware the daisy who closes her eye. Beware the swallow who flies low. Beware a ring around the moon.

The sharper the blast The sooner 'tis past.

Neither of them expect him to hit her but he does. She will emit a sharp, startled cry and he will look at his hand as if it belongs to something else. "I didn't mean," he will say. "I don't know what," he will continue. When they go to bed, she will feel him look at her back with weak, wet eyes. He will pull her so close she cannot escape the smells of dinner and toothpaste on his breath.

Strong winds build fast, rage hard, then pass. Storms that catch one by surprise are likely to blow over before there is time to find an umbrella.

Clear moon, frost soon.

She is still awake when the pale sunlight creeps into the bedroom through the sides of the curtains. She is stiff from lying still through the night. Soon, it will be time for her to get out of bed, to ready herself for work. She will not wake him when she slips out of his arms, out of their bed. She will not turn on the lights when she gets dressed. She will not kiss his forehead before she leaves the house.

On clear nights, the Earth's surface cools rapidly. With no clouds to get in the way, heat from the ground radiates up and disappears into space. If the temperature is cold enough, the ground will freeze. It is important to know the sky: some things, no matter how many storms they weather, are undone by a single frost.

Ingrid Jendrzejewski studied creative writing and English literature at the University of Evansville, then physics at the University of Cambridge. Her work has been published in places like *Passages North*, *The Los Angeles Review*, *The Conium Review*, *Jellyfish Review*, and *Flash Frontier*, and her novella-in-flash *Things I Dream About When I'm Not Sleeping* was published by Ad Hoc Fiction. She currently serves as co-director of National Flash Fiction Day (UK), editor-in-chief of *FlashBack Fiction* and a flash editor at *JMWW*. Links to Ingrid's work can be found at www.ingridj.com and she tweets @LunchOnTuesday.

Santo Spirito, 1577

From *Flashback Fiction*

Michele Finn Johnson

MY PARENTS CONSIGN MY eldest sister, Paola, to Venice's Santo Spirito convent. There is no dowry for Paola and so her duty is our salvation. When they took her away, Paola's nails dragged across the front door's casement, leaving ten tiny scratch marks.

To visit Paola, I have to walk through neighbourhoods where the prostitutes live. I wear my moretta; I clench its button between my teeth, but no one seems to notice me anyway. I am never mistaken for an unscrupulous woman.

Paola tells me to stop judging people, that it is not Christian-like. I don't tell Paola that she looks like a stray dog with her nun hair chopped in uneven wedges.
The prostitutes wear yellow ribbons, but I can tell them apart from honest women by the cut of their gamurra, their scent of anise and smoke.

I ask Paola if she misses home. She will not answer me. I ask if the nuns have already removed her tongue, thinking Paola might laugh like she used to at jugglers and slow cows, but she stays silent for a long while. "I miss cigarettes," she says, finally. "Will you bring me some?"

One day I forget my moretta, and a yellow-ribboned woman tells me I look just like my sister. I think she is just a crazy woman, but then she calls me tiny Paola.
There are only two more months before Paola takes her final vows. She says I can continue to visit, but we will have to be completely silent.

My last visit before Paola is to take her vows, I hand her the bundle of cigarettes that I've smuggled inside of my gamurra. Paola grabs the cigarettes and slides them under her habit; she looks around for others before she speaks in a flood of words. She tells me about a tunnel under the walls of Santo Spirito, how the nuns crawl through it in the evenings, spilling straight into the yellow-ribboned parish; how she smokes and drinks vino novella until she stumbles; how she is keeping the company of several men. When we say goodbye, Paola's eyes close and

her hands fold around themselves until they dissolve into her sleeves.

I walk home from the convent at dusk. I suck my moretta close to my face; I cannot be seen. The yellow-ribboned women look less like prostitutes and more like nuns with their hard eyes and raggedy hair.

I reach the edge of the yellow-ribbon parish, and I let the moretta drop into my hands. A strong breeze bangs against my naked face. It is dark when I get home—too dark to make out Paola's scratch marks on the casement. I reach out with my open palm, try to find some trace of something that I know for certain, but all I feel is the curved warp of oak.

Michele Finn Johnson's writing has appeared or is forthcoming in *Colorado Review, Mid-American Review, Booth, The Adroit Journal, DIAGRAM, Barrelhouse, SmokeLong Quarterly,* and elsewhere. Her work has been nominated several times for a *Pushcart Prize, Best of the Net, Best Small Fictions,* and *Best Microfiction* and won an AWP Intro Journals Award in nonfiction. Michele lives in Tucson and serves as assistant fiction editor at *Split Lip Magazine.* Find her online at michelefinnjohnson.com and @m_finn_johnson.

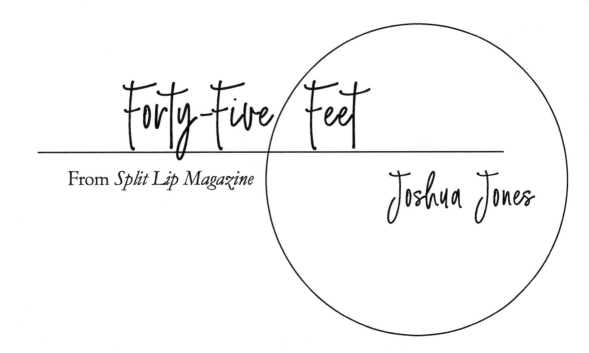

Forty-Five Feet

From *Split Lip Magazine*

Joshua Jones

OVER HALF THE STRING is swallowed, its remaining twenty feet coiled in the man's lap. He's skinny, this would-be yogi, his flesh taut about his ribs, sunburnt and flaking. It's been years since he fashioned the string from a long strip of cloth—twisted it into a braid and knotted it every five inches. Each cleanse, he soaks the string in a solution of proteins and amino acids, flavors it with beet extract and cardamom oil until it is stained brown and red. Now the string dangles from his lips like a bloody stream of drool. Three more days to swallow—days of meditation, of lucid dreams, of penance.

Tomorrow the mustached landlady will shout at him through the thin door: his rent's overdue, the neighbors are complaining about the smell again. He no longer notices the mélange of fermenting cabbage, sweat, and urine distilling in the seven glass jars lining the sill of his only window, of his only room. His landlady refuses to believe anybody buys the distillate, but once he hands her half the rent money, a transaction that always leaves him feeling weak and sinful, she will shift to her post-payment shouting, the heat from her aura cooling, souring. He will try to press a tisane of lemongrass and licorice root into her palm along with the soiled bills, but she'll throw it back at his bare chest and tell him to put some clothes on, a robe or anything. She won't look at the string spooling from his mouth. Will not know where to cast her eyes. His eyes, too, will fall to her feet and her legs that threaten to burst from her nylons like trussed sausages. They disappear into the folds of her long sleeve dresses, always so dark against her pale skin. Sometimes a gold cross will peek from below her second chin, and he will remember that she, too, is a woman of God.

When ten feet of string remain, he will wake from another vision, this one of him making love to the landlady, her girth crushing his frail frame, breaking his ribs, pressing the air from his lungs until he is empty, emptier than he's ever been before. He will stripe his back with

a sheaf of bulrushes, his arm swinging mechanically until a white cloud envelops him and he can hear the roar of the ocean.

When less than six inches hangs from his mouth, he will walk to the beach and commit his visions to murals in the sand. With the heel of his foot, he'll dig concentric circles and sweeping curves. He won't look up as joggers scatter the patterns, as they avert their eyes from his nakedness. When the cloud behind his eyes dissolves from white to red and the harsh cries of gulls give way to the shouts of the park police, he will wrap a sheet about his waist and check the plastic cup for offerings. Dollar bills and cigarette butts and shells and perhaps a necklace of black beads that he could offer his landlady the following week, if only she would allow it to rest between her breasts.

By the time she shouts at him again, the string will have begun to pass. He will count backwards as he exhales, will keep his pulse from matching the steady pounding at his door. He cannot bear to answer and will continue to pull the cleansing string inch by inch. It will emerge perfectly white, the color of sand, of gulls, of doughy flesh.

Joshua Jones' writing has appeared in *Barrelhouse, The Cincinnati Review, CRAFT, Necessary Fiction, SmokeLong Quarterly, Split Lip Magazine, The Tishman Review,* and elsewhere. He lives in Maryland.

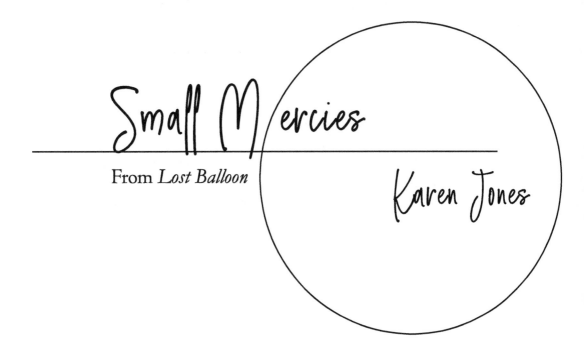

Small Mercies

From *Lost Balloon*

Karen Jones

WHEN YOU PLAY MONOPOLY with your brothers, let them win, she says. Boys don't like to lose, especially not to girls. She's patting her face with a powder pad, as though her features will fall off if they're not pressed in place. When she's out at a dance, I sneak into her room and play at being her, being beautiful, being good with make-up. When a boy asks you out, always say yes. It doesn't matter if he's not the best looking, the cleverest, the funniest – it takes a lot of courage for a boy to ask a girl out, so be grateful and always, always say yes to boys. I take her lipstick and pout as I smear the scarlet grease over my too-thin lips on my too-fat face with its barely-there eyes. I can never look like her, but I can do as I'm told. And so, I did. I said yes to boys. All the boys. The ugly boys, the short boys, the boys who smell like sewers and the boys with urgency mapped out in spots on their red faces. When your brothers get up in the morning, draw their curtains, make their beds – be useful. The liquid eyeliner almost makes me have eyes. Not eyes like hers – not violet, not startling, but at least existing. My mother made me easy – a thing she never was to me. I'm sure it wasn't her intention, but I was nothing if not obedient, so I said yes over and over again. Until I finally got it, finally realized what I'd become. I used her cold cream to erase the face I'd painted. Then I said no. I said no over and over again. But the boys told me they'd heard about me and no really meant yes, and did what they wanted anyway. That hurt more, so I went back to being the girl my mother made me – the yes-girl, the old-before-her-years girl, the never-as-pretty-as-her-mother-so-beggars-can't-be-choosers girl. Now she complains that I never gave her grandchildren. Oh, but I did, Mother Dear. So many half-formed girls that neither of us got to hold or mould. Small mercies, Mother. Be grateful.

Karen Jones is a prose writer from Glasgow, Scotland, with a preference for flash and short fiction. She has been successful in writing competitions including *Mslexia, Flash 500, Words WithJam, New Writer, Writers' Forum* and *Ad Hoc Fiction*. Her work has featured in *Nottingham Review, Lost Balloon, New Flash Fiction Review* and several other ezines. Her stories appear in numerous anthologies including *Bath Short Story Award, To Hull and Back* and *Bath Flash Fiction* Volumes 2 and 3. Her work has been nominated for *Best of the Net, Best Microfictions, Best Small Fictions* and a *Pushcart Prize*.

Blue-Eyed, Brown Aunt

From *Two Sisters Writing*

Babitha Marina Justin

MY AUNT, MEENAKSHI *CHERIYAMMA*, had an unusual pair of blue-green eyes. Growing up with those eyes must have been traumatic for her. A girl from Kerala, she had blue eyes which contrasted with her deep chocolate brown skin. This was almost unheard of. Everyone thought she was a witch. When she died, they buried her ashes under the Astoria tree and worshipped her like a goddess; a less important one that too, as she was worshipped on a single day in a year.

Cheriyamma shared her room with me. I inherited her looks, but I missed out on her blue-green eyes. I craved for them even in my sleep, as I knew that her eyes made her look as ravishing as the sea. Incidentally, I was the only one who found her beautiful, as I was the first one to find her dead in our room. One day, I came back from my school and started telling her about my day. There was nothing unusual in her posture lying on her bed with her bluish-green eyes open; but when she didn't answer a series of questions, I shook her cold body and cried out for my mother. *Cheriyamma* was thirty-two.

No one knew how she died, there was no struggle on her face, but a calm peace written all over. Looking at her, we could not believe that she had stopped breathing. My father, who doubled-up as a village doctor, checked her pulse, and her heart beat with a German stethoscope, shook his head and pursed his lips. Then, he tried to close her eyelids, but they refused to close. They cremated her with a pair of eyeshades which originally belonged to my grandfather. The entire family used those unusually dark eyeshades whenever one of the family members contracted conjunctivitis. My father wanted the shades to be cremated along with *Cheriyamma*, and my weeping grandmother wondered aloud what we will do during the next conjunctivitis season.

Unlike my family, I was quite pained at *Cheriyamma's* passing. Everyone was kind of relieved because the entire village thought there was something evil in her. No man ever dared to approach her with a marriage proposal. *Ammumma*, my grandmother, believed that her stars were all in the wrong place. Incidentally, there were nights when even I thought there was something mysterious and evil in her behavior. On raven dark nights, I often heard her open the creaky door and walk into woods behind the house. I trembled with fear and waited for her to return.

Once, when she came back, I mustered the courage and asked her where she went with her hair fragrant and open at night. Her eyes gleamed like fireflies and she said, she went to the nearby tree where a Gandharva appeared on new moon days. I was terrified. After that night, I was particularly vigilant whenever she got dressed on new moon nights and I lie waiting for her to come back safe after meeting the Gandharva. At times I even heard the Gandharva's voice whispering to her, and I imagined him gliding down from the tree to drop her back safe.

My grandmother who was a repository of stories sensed nothing wrong when I asked her about Gandharvas.

"*Ammumme*, how do Gandharvas look?"

"Incredibly handsome! They have sculpted bodies and beautiful voices. Human beings don't look half as good as them."

"Have you seen them *Ammumme*?"

"God forbid! If I had met one of them, I would have been seduced and taken along with him. The women they leave behind become insane, fantasizing them and missing them all the time."

I was gripped by fear.

"Meenakshi *Cheriyamma* meets a Gandharva very often."

Ammumma frowned. When I told her that Meenakshi *Cheriyamma* meets him every new moon day, she shut me up.

"He doesn't go behind blue-eyed witches. Don't keep imagining things, you go and study!" She shooed me away.

Cheriyamma's Gandharva started visiting her on other nights as well. I heard him talk to *Cheriyamma* for a long time before they disappeared into the snake shrine. Cheriyamma was deliriously happy after meeting him and I thought that the Gandharva should be unimaginably beautiful.

"*Cheriyamme*, will you ask the Gandharva to sing a song for me?"

"How do you know he sings?"

"*Ammumma* told me that he can sing in a heavenly voice."

My aunt looked preoccupied for a while.

Then she asked me with emerald shafts dancing in her blue eyes, "Would you like to meet him?"

"Yes, of course!" I clapped my hands with joy.

"Don't tell anyone you met him, ok?"

I nodded feverishly, and my locks too danced along, like springs set on music.

That moonless night, *Cheriyamma* took me out to meet the Gandharva. I saw his silhouette from a distance and my heart started beating fast.

I was quite disappointed meeting him because I could not see his superhuman beauty in the dark.

His form looked too human and vulnerable.

"Gandharva, can you sing a song for me?" I asked.

"If I sing, the entire neighborhood will wake up, and then they will search for me. I appear only in front of special people."

I thought the Gandharva sounded too human as well, his voice resembled Kannettan's. Kannettan came to our house every morning to milk cows, and all of a sudden, I felt even the Gandharva resembled Kannettan.

Kannettan was not bad looking, he was tall, strong and well-built. *Ammumma* told me he is from a lower caste and I am not supposed to be friends with him. But whenever Kannettan was free, he let me touch the calves and once he even taught me to milk a cow.

Cheriyamma shut me up when I told her about the Gandharva's uncanny resemblance to Kannettan. She once again strictly forbade me to tell about this meeting to anyone. The Gandharva will be furious, she said.

After meeting the Gandharva, I started sleeping peacefully knowing that *Cheriyamma* is in safe hands. One night, I woke up to a ruckus. My parents surprised *Cheriamma* and her Gandharva, and they tied them up and beat them. *Cheriyamma* was locked her up in the loft afterwards.

I took her food up to the loft. Her blue eyes were glued to a distant vacuum and once she asked me if Kannettan still came to milk the cows.

"Kannettan disappeared all of a sudden," I told her. "There's a new man to milk the cows." What I didn't tell her was the rumour that Kannettan had gone missing from the village.

"I want you to bring me something kept under my bed."

I ferreted out a packet from under her bed. *Cheriyamma* opened it and took out a golden filigreed saree.

"This is my bridal wear, I want to wear this when my Gandharva comes to take me away. Will you please unbolt the loft door?" she asked.

The saree had the colour of her eyes.

I unbolted the door with a thumping heart. When I returned home, I was quite relieved to see her lying on the bed with open eyes.

She looked dark and beautiful in her bridal dress, and the calm on her face nestled on her unblinking blue-green eyes.

Babitha Marina Justin is from Kerala, South India. Her poems and short stories have appeared in *Eclectica, Fulcrum, The Scriblerus, Inlandia, The Punch Magazine, Constellations* and many other journals. Her first collection of poetry, *Of Fireflies, Guns and the Hills,* was published in 2015. Her first novel, *Maria's Swamp: The Bigness of Small Lies,* was published in April, 2019.

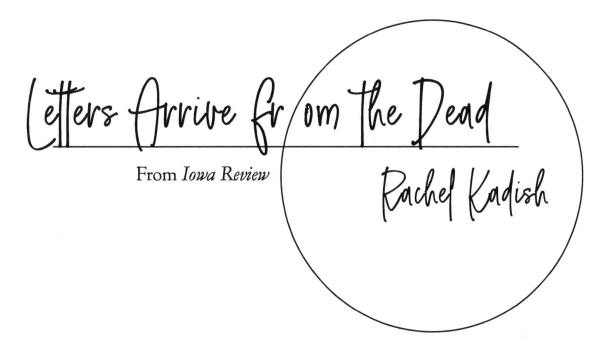

Letters Arrive from the Dead

From *Iowa Review*

Rachel Kadish

WHEN LETTERS ARRIVE FROM the dead, the postmarks are often in error. Envelopes are backdated or bear stamps from improbable places. This stands to reason; the dead are notorious fibbers. They have reputations to protect, or to invent, and certain inconvenient legacies to dismantle.

In the temporary village in which they're housed before moving on, the dead close out old business, study their new obligations, and acquire necessary paperwork. Each has been allotted a certain amount of time to set affairs in order, and most work diligently, if grimly, toward this departure date, though inevitably some linger longer. (So what if they outstay their visas? Who will hold them to it?) For the most part, they remain decorous—yet even those who are, frankly, hooligans do not steal from the living, vandalize heirlooms, or poison food, nor do they murder, make appliances malfunction, shatter glass. The fantasy that the dead do such things is libel. It's not that the dead never wish harm on the living, but that their gestures are ineffective. True, they're capable of visiting the living in altered form, but most choose not to on account of the draining fatigue that results, the inner ear problems that last days, the aching joints that are hardly worth what's achieved: a brief whisper that goes unheard in a noisy setting, or a brick, thrown with unfathomable effort, that nonetheless misses (the dead have execrable aim). Ultimately, even the fiercest recognize the futility of such modes of communication.

In their desire to settle their last affairs with the living, they retreat, in the end, to this post office, which promises to dispatch their messages without need for ghostly visitations. Here, at last, they press their points much as the living do: wearily, obediently, coloring within the lines of bureaucracy—because who can be troubled to do otherwise?

In the dim, dusty post office, the drowsy clerk flexes his wrist, stamps his heavy stamp. The creaking desk chair, the unoiled wheel that sticks, the sigh of the small, lumbar pillow as it takes his weight. The dead, shuffling in a queue that ends at his desk, mail admonishments, rebukes, samples of tea. Their messages to the living are opaque—they know the censor in the adjoining office must be appeased. Besides, who wants to report the literal truth of their dull status in this transit village, when more newsworthy and impressive experiences await in the next phase? Still, communications must be sent—there are arguments to be settled, exhortations and endearments to convey. Nor are the dead above the occasional passive-aggressive missive: the postcard reading *Wish you were here.*

(The postcard arrives in a dream. Waking, the living scramble to interpret: what lies beneath these four words? What deeper meaning may be intuited? Psychiatrists are visited, old diaries are dredged, sage is burned.)

Dreams, while the most common delivery system, are not the only one. Airplane contrails, owls, drifting smoke—anything seen out of the corner of an eye will do. Communications breach the world of the living in the form of a familiar perfume or a whorl of dust or dry leaves blowing into an alley on a windless day. A passing bus splashes mud across the new shirt purchased for a date with her—was it a warning from the other side? The living readily attribute such phenomena to certain departed kin, friends, or enemies—attributions that are often inaccurate. Studying the receipts noting the interpretation of their messages, the dead cannot be faulted for feeling at times maligned, even plagiarized.

At his desk with its dockets, dreaming of vacation, the clerk assesses each item with practiced skepticism. Certain things are not permitted: hazardous materials, messages that violate confidentiality laws. Surely by now the dead—the never-ending line of them traversing the long hall toward his desk—must know the routine. Yet the clientele is ungrateful. Why was she served before me? I wasn't told my letter would be censored. My package is but a small one; it contains no harmful objects; it contains nothing that would harm a soul.

The stamp, the creak of bureaucracy, the ticking clock. He himself works long hours, his salary is paltry—yet he makes no complaint, for who would listen? We all know a better system would be possible, if we were starting from scratch.

Please it won't harm them. To know what I finally know, now.

Five minutes to closing you'll have to come back tomorrow.

Now and then a message is returned to sender, unopened. Only then, as the sender makes his way toward the door, clutching his receipt, do the dead pause in their bickering and part in silence, to make way for the bereaved.

Rachel Kadish's most recent novel, *The Weight of Ink*, was awarded a National Jewish Book Award, the Julia Ward Howe Fiction Prize, and the Association of Jewish Libraries' Fiction

Award. Her work has been read on National Public Radio and has appeared in *The New York Times*, *Salon*, *Paris Review*, *Iowa Review*, and the *Pushcart Prize Anthology*. She has been the Koret Writer-in-Residence at Stanford University and a fiction fellow of the National Endowment for the Arts and the Massachusetts Cultural Council. She lives outside Boston and teaches in the Lesley University MFA Program in Creative Writing.

Film: Nox Transfer

From *Conjunctions*

Karla Kelsey

—for Paul Chan and *Pillowspohia (after Ghostface)*

THE FILM BEGINS SILVER, white, and black as two nude bodies make their way down the beach to a sea scattered with geranium heads a layer of petals overtaking us, one male and one female, as the wave does. Wave and wave until petals pull under and sky darkens moon over water and then a strobe of light and waves and waves differentiating you from me, you are the male body walking out of the sea. Walking out and holding

a gun to your temple caught in strobe light. This I did not expect the gun the gun and where did the female body go who would rush you, push you to the ground the gun the gun wrested and flung firing out nothing over sand. Where did she/I go I am air I am salt in air I don't see her and the heavy perfume of flowers okay-okay semi-ordinary, as was the dark-moon-light-strobe, but the gun

the man his head and the shot returning her still nude and cradling cradling and stuffing flower petals in her mouth keening with beach glass in her mouth this I cannot and I did not, I did not agree to film these figures I did not agree to watch to say we to say I to say you—

NOX

To refilm this with what if instead or what if the second time around the male body naked and silver holds a bouquet of geraniums, gray scale, alternative to gun and pungent flower-flower he rises out of the sea with his geraniums with his sex

or perhaps this vision holds a possible future, the story of how in the future the geraniums will come to be scattered at sea, how in the future blood into sand, how in the future salt and the woman and so they are not-yet and I can stop them the dark-moon-strobe and the emerging I can. If I swallow the emerging I can prevent the gun the gun and so I will not ingest these red these pink these white petals torn from centers and scattered. I will not the beach glass I will not the boat the wedding the bouquet thrown over the side. I will not in a white dress. I will not a child

in white shorts on the patio tasting geranium petals, a geranium because great-grandfather brought them from the homeland. Instead insist no heritage but sex by touch by tongue and no memory. No sea. Blindfold instead of wedding boat let us camp out in the corner of this

lantern flickering over concrete erosion and no past and only body body and body body and body body. Bodied—

NOX

Nevertheless one body male and one body female spat out to sea. Spat out to the promenade off-season and she/I in white dress. The wooden carousel horses protected by a glass pavilion. Off season restaurant and salt and a young woman approaching out of the dark with the high wide forehead of divination. A young woman approaching I love because she

is part-you and she is not me. She is nothing of me, she is you but not as a man but as a young woman. She approaches and she approaches. You who had been the male body are a young woman approaching and the moment I say violence effaced by calliope she/you are holding a gun to your temple she/you say geranium and median I am the medium of this vision, the young woman you in the black hoodie

zipped and cold along the waterfront and too cold we left her lonely so alone and cold and a gun. A gun a gun my mouth striking the throat's o of no of come home she holds a gun let us pause this moment let us ask let us implore without going any further let us plead this gun be a water gun, let it be a pink plastic gun let it be a trick gun a trick gun firing out cheap silk flowers let it be stated for the record I have heard the lesson the lesson has been recorded no need for the gun no need and no need—

NOX

Let us begin the film again and again the male body naked, singular, but not outside this time this time in a room, contours shadowed. The body shadowed. And I enter in a geranium-patterned robe, desert to room all the moisture collecting along my skin a dewy flower the male body erect and

the room still. A crystalline arc of water against curtainless window reflecting back sheets salt-dank, down pillows mourning their geese, the male body emerged out of storm wave that overtook the promenade again and again pounding until by salt and rhythm

concrete disintegrates, granule from granule, neurons adrift and what was red was infused with white and so became pink. Body and body. Body and body we fuck and we sex but after continues your death mask pink quartz a pink desert after the war had dried out the sea in your future death I am a desert sea a desert sea a desert sea. But the daughter: the daughter released—

NOX

Let us begin the film again punctuating cloud barrier to witness a constellation disintegrate simultaneous with a constellation in the brain. The hoodie zipped against empty space empty arms empty hood in wind. Synapses unleashing. And from the gun a crystalline arc of water. And syllables, not a sentence, syllables overtake, culminate in cosmic raving cosmic silence—

NOX

Let us begin the film again: I wait a body of water a body that had been female absorbing male and naked sprawled across the desert I was encouraging the geraniums to overtake the room, this is in the future, the future room of glass louvers, bunches of geraniums gathered in water glasses, I male/female in geranium robe your/my neurons drifting—

Karla Kelsey is a poet, essayist, and editor whose work weaves together the lyric with philosophy and history. She has published three books of poetry: *A Conjoined Book* (Omnidawn, 2014), *Iteration Nets* (Ahsahta, 2010), and *Knowledge, Forms, the Aviary* (Ahsahta, 2006) selected by Carolyn Forché for the Sawtooth Poetry Prize. *Blood Feather*, her fourth book of poetry is forthcoming from Tupelo Press and in 2020 Ahsahta Press will publish *On Certainty*. Her book of experimental essays, *Of Sphere*, was selected by Carla Harryman for the 2016 Essay Press Prize and was published in 2017. From 2010-2017 she edited *The Constant Critic*, Fence Books' online journal of poetry reviews. A recipient of a Fulbright Scholars grant, she has taught in Budapest, Hungary, and is Professor of Creative Writing at Susquehanna University's Writers Institute.

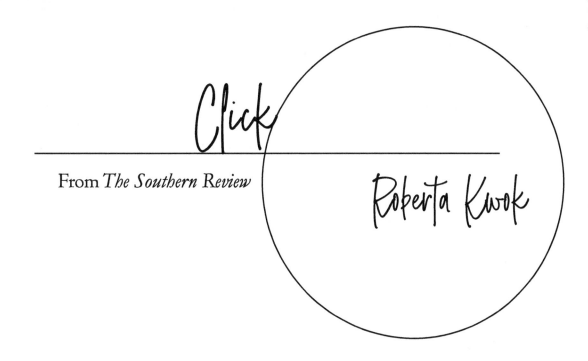

Click

From *The Southern Review*

Roberta Kwok

IN 1975, BILL CURTSINGER took the first underwater photographs of the narwhal, a whale species called the unicorn of the sea because the males have a long, slender tusk. These rarely seen animals live in the deep waters of the High Arctic. About a decade after Curtsinger's expedition, a girl named Kristin Laidre saw one of the photographs in a library book.

He is twenty years old when the letter arrives. A college student in Arizona. He has come west from the edge of the Pine Barrens in New Jersey, a sprawling forest of cranberries and tiger beetles and lady's slipper orchids, where he swam in a lake that seemed as wide as an ocean.

He knows how to use a gun, has shot deer and ducks. But Vietnam is no place for him. He joins the Navy, then talks his way into a photography unit. They send him to an underwater testing site off the Bahamas—the Tongue of the Ocean— where he dangles submerged above an abyss of water, the bottom thousands of feet away and invisible, snapping pictures of submarines as they glide by and poking whitetip sharks with a stick. He flies in a jet that takes off from an aircraft carrier near Puerto Rico. He volunteers to serve in Antarctica, where the sun does not set for the next four months, and watches for seals in a steel observation chamber below the ice.

Years later, he travels to the other end of the world and camps on a rocky beach in the Arctic. The hills are bare. He swims into the bay with his camera, and the green gloom is nothing but emptiness until the narwhal appears before him, as if someone has clicked Next on a slide projector. The tusk is not white as he expected, but black. There are more—chattering and cooing at him, pale flesh speckled like stones overgrown with dark moss. He is not afraid. He has thirty-six shots and he uses them all.

The word narwhal may have originated from the Old Norse words nár and hvalr, meaning "corpse whale." Sailors saw the flesh of a drowned man. But the horns became the stuff of scepters, the cups of kings. Its full name is Monodon monoceros: one tooth, one horn.

She knows the names of all the whales. She is perhaps ten years old, and her bedroom is covered with posters of them. It is the mid-1980s in upstate New York. When she goes to the library, past the card catalog to the very bottom shelf in the back, there it is—a giant sea-green book. She slides into an underwater world and sees the outstretched fins of a humpback, the dark, dripping curtain of a fluke. On one page is a mother narwhal with her calf, a mottled mermaid tail caught as they are turning away from the camera.

She lives in a town of dancers and opera singers. Things change. She becomes a ballerina, moves across the country after high school to join a company. Every day her body repeats the same movements in the same order. She plays a flower, a snowflake, a monster with the head of a fish.

Then her ankle is injured and nothing feels right, not even walking to the grocery store. Three surgeries and she accepts that it is over. She returns to the whales and flies one summer with other scientists to Ottawa and then to Resolute Bay and from there in a tiny bush plane to an island in the Canadian Arctic. They set their nets in the bay and wait. When a narwhal is caught, they jump into their boats and pin an electronic device to a ridge on the animal's back, the skin firm and cold.

She keeps going back. Hunters save the stomachs of dead narwhals for her and she cuts them open: slimy, reeking pink balloons. Beaks, bones, rocks. Out on the ice, her team drills a hole and lowers instruments into the water. Now she can hear their squeaks and grunts and buzzing and whistles. They are miles from anything, and she knows it is them.

The narwhal leaves the island and swims through a strait into Lancaster Sound and then into Baffin Bay, ahead of the creeping sea ice. It dives for halibut and squid. Every time it surfaces, the device on its back transmits signals to a satellite in outer space, an aluminum vessel sailing far above Earth.

He keeps taking photographs. An ancient shipwreck in the Aegean Sea, a worn sword, a ceramic cup fashioned after a ram's head. The folded billows of a jellyfish, elegant as an evening gown.

She flies high over the frozen ocean for what feels like forever and sees nothing but ice and cracks of black water. Then a shiny bead appears far below—it is coming up to breathe. "One narwhal," she says into the recorder, and waits for the next one.

Roberta Kwok is a freelance science writer who has contributed to *The New York Times*, *NewYorker.com*, *The Southern Review*, *Nature*, *Audubon*, and *U.S. News & World Report*. She earned an M.F.A. in creative writing from Indiana University Bloomington and a graduate certificate in science communication from the University of California, Santa Cruz. She lives near Seattle.

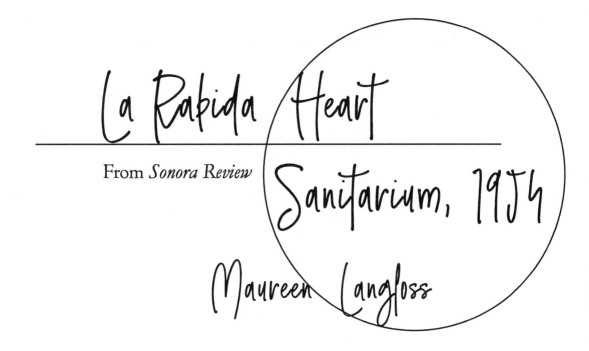

La Rabida Heart Sanitarium, 1954

From *Sonora Review*

Maureen Langloss

THE NURSES FORBID US from touching our feet to the floor. We were to stay in bed. So we made the tiles below a river and rode our mattresses across them like boats into dark tunnels. Sometimes we'd emerge to the other side, surrounded by mountains that flinched as we approached. Even the landmasses feared us, what we could do to them.

We were six. Six when you learn to tie a shoe, read a primer, twist a tooth until it breaks from its root. *Teeth are like bones exposed to air*, Elizabeth told me. She would say things like that, smart true things that I carry with me still.

Still was the air. Quiet, ground down. The food would come on trays, the nurses in masks. *Eat, eat*, they'd say. But food tasted of phlegm, of stone. It was too hot or too cold. Swallowing made our throats ache. We crossed lines on the wall to mark the time. 210 for me, 176 for Elizabeth. I couldn't see her bones when she first arrived, but there they were now, poking out at sharp angles.

Sometimes I'd stand up in my bed, reach as far as I could. If I stretch, stretch, stretched I could open the door a crack without leaving the boat. I could check if the infirmary spies were on duty. When the watchman took a break, I could clasp my bread in my hand. I could leap, fly, land. The boat rocked less with two girls aboard. The extra weight tethered us to the earth, steadied the current of our hearts.

I pressed my roll into Elizabeth's palm. *At least try the bread*, I said. *I know you like the bread.* She chewed slowly, her jaws determined but weary. Worn down by fever. *When I get home*, she said. *It will be spring, and I'll walk to the gulley to pick two daffodils. The kind you put to your chin to turn it yellow. One for each of us.*

I fell asleep beside her and dreamt of baskets filled with sunlight. Sister Claire arrived at half past three, smelling of sacrament, to give us our reading lesson. She wasn't stern like the nurses, and always brought a fairy tale to read after we'd practiced our vowel sounds. The A and the I and the E of things.

Tsk, tsk, my girls, she whispered. *Look at you, tangled up together like a ball of yarn. God doesn't want you to tax those sweet hearts by climbing in and out of bed.*

I opened my eyes just as the color dropped out of Sister Claire's cheeks. She made the sign of the cross, bashful and quick. She kissed her fingers, squeezed my hand. Then she lifted Elizabeth gently from my arms and carried her, wilted, to the door.

The next day, Sister Claire brought me a book of poems with a lamb on the front. Anna Jane moved into the bed next to mine. She didn't want to ride in boats. She was eight, her mouth full of permanent teeth. She thought the two extra years meant she knew more than I. But she didn't know the half.

With the spring, a shipment of penicillin arrived for the children who had rheumatic fever. A nurse delivered the medicine to me via syringe. I set my feet down on the river and walked out the La Rabida door.

Maureen Langloss is a lawyer-turned-writer and mother-of-three living in New York City. She serves as the Flash Fiction Editor at *Split Lip Magazine*. Her writing has appeared in *CHEAP POP*, *Gulf Coast*, *Little Fiction*, *The Journal*, *Wigleaf*, and elsewhere. Her work has been nominated for a *Pushcart Prize* and *Best of the Net*. Find her online at maureenlangloss.com or on Twitter @maureenlangloss.

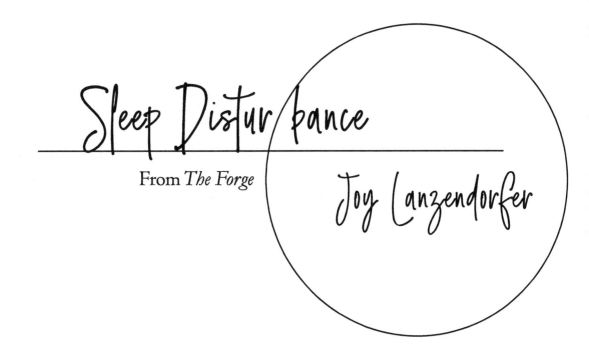

Sleep Disturbance

From *The Forge*

Joy Lanzendorfer

THEY SAY WE'RE PRIMATES, but you looked like a bear as you padded through the blue light of my neighbourhood, naked. Through a slat in the blinds, I saw your hairy chest, the jiggling fat over your hulking bones, and the hard strata of muscles on your limbs. The sprinklers were frothing over the grass and onto the sidewalk, but you lumbered through the water and past my house. Your eyes were open, I thought. Then again, maybe not.

Above the box elder, the crows mobbed. Their noise had pulled me out of bed, where I'd been trying to sleep since 2 a.m. Don't calculate the hours, I would think. Don't think about how, if you went to sleep right now, you'd have three hours rest before you had to get up again. Don't think about your dad dying. Don't think about how old you are or how little you've done with your life or how tired you'll be tomorrow. Don't think, don't think. But I did. Finally, the crows erupted like a thunderstorm outside and I gave up. Now here you were, drifting like fog through my suburb, the only clothes on your body a knit cap that in the weird light could have been gray or could have been brown.

The crows didn't bother you and you didn't bother the crows as they heaved through the air like tossed balls. At the end of the street, you opened the unlocked door of a 1970s Chevy and climbed in the back seat. I saw the hunching of your body as you shut the door and lay down. As I stared through the slat, waiting for you to show yourself again, I became aware of the light growing around me, and the rustle of my family nearing the end of sleep, like a dripping faucet.

Later, when I came out to go to work, there was no sign of you. The car was empty, the locks pressed down. Where did you go, and when? I know I saw you, a shadow man moving past my vision. The crows were my witness. But now, as the neighbor pulls his garbage can across the street so that the wheels grind against the gravel, the crows are quiet. They have abandoned me, along with the night. There is nothing to do but get on with the day.

Joy Lanzendorfer's work has appeared in *The New York Times*, *The Washington Post*, *Tin House*, *Ploughshares*, NPR, *Smithsonian*, *The Atlantic*, *Poetry Foundation*, and *The Guardian*. She's received awards and grants from Speculative Literature Foundation, Cuttyhunk Writers Residency, WildAcres, and others.

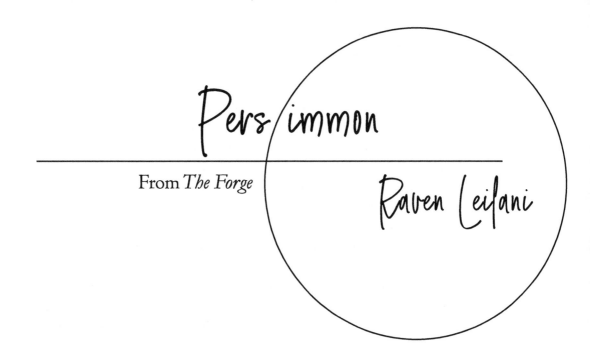

Persimmon

From *The Forge*

Raven Leilani

THE FIRST TIME SHE speaks to you, you are on the toilet. You are both at a party, and she is waiting for a polite time to go home. Underneath the stall, you see her reach into her sock and pull out a wrinkled joint. *How much longer*, she says, a curl of smoke hanging above her stall like a question mark. *Twenty-three minutes*, you say, like you're tired of parties. Like you get invited to enough parties to be tired of them, and are not in fact, holed up in the stall to cry.

You will leave the party together and quickly engage in the sort of casual, mucoid intimacy particular to women. You will talk about all of the things that come out of your bodies. The phlegm and the toe jam and the dark knots of blood. And it will be nothing. It will be like nice to meet you, like how do you do. You've done this before. Met a woman like you never, ever meet a man, that is, with your mouth all the way open, begging her to take your teeth.

She is black and moony, and her boyfriend looks a lot like yours. There are white women on tv who love each other. They come in twos and fours and they all have boyfriends too. The boyfriends are all incidental, a procession of haircuts that pale against the metropolitan fog. They last for approximately twenty-one minutes, and then the women link hands over champagne and orange juice. Woman #4 says, *don't tell anyone where we buried the body.* Woman #2 says, *okay but what about my shoes.* Woman #1 keeps her silence. She knows the entire world is built around her. She stares dreamily into the distance with the irregular posture of a self-conscious focal point, does not hear Woman #3, who says, *we should just get rid of them all.*

When you do the online tests, you are always Woman #3. The one who is most stable and least fun, whose dialogue is arch and spare and merely functions as the underlying rhythm for the rest of the cast. So when she takes off her clothes in front of you, you are primed to play your role. Primed to be loose and unimpressed, even when she sits next to you and thumbs the buttons on your coat.

What's happening is you are circling a question. You are playing Call of Duty from different parts of town, slipping off your bras, and crouching to reload your guns. She used to be a medic, but now she is a bombardier, swearing at children through her headset as bunker busters ripple through an enemy camp. You take a bullet, respawn, and pick her up in your jeep. She cradles C4 against her chest and asks you the question, her avatar's eyes pink with dust and smoke. She says, *what is the terrible and irreversible thing?* The terrible and irreversible thing being the red meat of female friendship, where you reveal a central act of violence and the ensuing mutiny of your mind. But you are selfish. You are black, and everyone already thinks suffering is the best thing you can do. Instead of answering the question, you drive the jeep over a landmine, and on the way out, a twelve year old from Brussels calls you both a couple of cunts.

You go grocery shopping together and fill the cart with ice-cream and cake. You eat the cake with your hands, pull up your shirts and let your bellies distend. You call her a whore just to see how it feels. And when she smiles, you do it again.

But there is no mechanism inside you that tells you when to stop. And she doesn't want you to. She goads you along, offers her throat. She draws you into the bathroom after a concert and rephrases the question, excited by your ugliness and certain of its source. She grins in the nicotine light and sets down her beer. She says, *how much longer,* and backs you into the stall. And before you get home, you buy a single tomato. You stand over the sink and eat it in the dark. You turn on the lights in a panic, your hand laced with the juice of an imposter fruit.

Raven Leilani's work has appeared in *Granta, Narrative Magazine, New England Review, McSweeney's, Florida Review,* and *Conjunctions.* Work is forthcoming in *Cosmonauts Avenue.* She was selected for the 30 under 30 list for *Narrative Magazine,* and she is currently an MFA candidate at NYU.

Anton's Saga

From *3 Elements Literary Review*

Mare Leonard

RAIN OR SHINE, ANTON sent out billows of sentimental songs into the dandelion-dotted fields of Suzdal, a village 60 miles east of Moscow, where 40 years after the siege of Stalingrad, everyone remembered the starvation, the slaughter, and the less-than-score- settling imprisonment of General Von Paulus in their monastery. Some men spit on the steps, but never spoke of more sadistic retaliations, needing to work from dawn until dusk to scrape by, to haul in truckloads of potatoes to feed their families.

Children in babushkas, old women in polyester dresses, men in stained overalls cried when Anton played "Katusha" on his accordion every hour, reminding the villagers of the *never-to-be-forgotten* war. Everyone bowed to Anton with respect but knew of his defect, knew that at birth his brain did not *fuse*, understood the word fuse because of the electrical systems in their tractors, understood the intricacies of machinery, accepted their need to plow and plant onions and beets to meet their quota for the five-year plan. They understood the beauty of onion-domed spires and came to believe Anton possessed a hidden power because they could read the hour by the moment Anton scraped his clogs along the cobblestones in the morning and the night.

Every day, he greeted them all with the only words he knew, *Do svidaniya*, goodbye, and they replied, *Do svidanya*, Anton.

Mare Leonard lives and works in the Hudson Valley where she is an Associate of the Institute for Writing and Thinking and the MAT programs at Bard College. She has published chapbooks

of poetry at *2River, Pudding House, Antrim House Press* and *Red Ochre Lit* and *The Dark Inside My Hooded Coat* is available from Finishing Line Press and from her website Mare Leonard.com. Finally, she was nominated for a *Pushcart* in 2018 for a poem published in *The Pickled Body.*

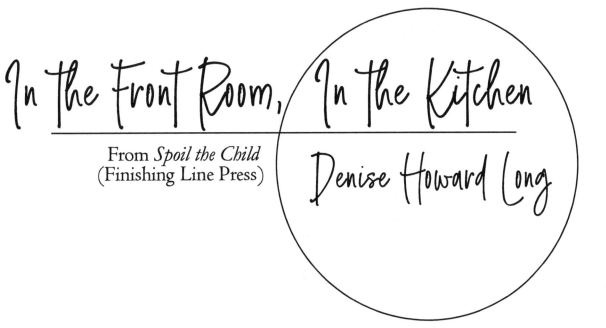

In the Front Room, In the Kitchen

From *Spoil the Child*
(Finishing Line Press)

Denise Howard Long

IN THE FRONT ROOM of the house, the sheet they have placed over the mirror on the mantel has pulled loose. It hangs down just enough so that a strip of afternoon sun disturbs the shadows lurking in the corner of the room. Near another dusty corner, half-empty pill bottles still clutter a basket.

Along one wall, straight-backed chairs remain at attention. The cushions are pale blue leather, smooth like an unblemished egg. In those chairs, the family sat for seven days while friends and family filed through.

A year ago, this floor was covered with a tapestry rug, a swirling pattern of purples, blues, and gray. The children, when they had been small, found shapes and animals and faces in the colors of that rug—the way most kids did with clouds in the sky. To one side, a baby grand piano had once sat, but after the accident, they had to make room for the bed with the metal railing and back that lifted up and down with the press of a button.

Because the rug has not found its way back into the room, ruts show in the wooden floor. Ruts from the wheelchair, from the rolling bed, from the machines, machines, machines. Deeply gashed wheel tracks travel toward the doorsill, leading out to where the sun shines more freely. Where it's not held back by heavy curtains.

Near the front door, the staircase sits silent. Family photographs line the wall along the stairs, many hanging crooked from rubbed shoulders and stomping feet. Near the bottom, is a wedding portrait: white lace, gray tux, roses the pink of a newborn's cheeks. Up the stairs, the family grows—three people, then four, then five. Then, the pictures stop several steps away from the second floor.

Down the hall from the stairs is the kitchen. There, yellow gingham curtains hang limp over the sink. The air in the room is stale. The floor is etched with layers of footprints. Stacks of mail are piled on the table. Dishes and cups and mugs and silverware clutter the counter; some are dirty, most are clean, but none of them has found its way back into place in the cabinets and drawers.

In the kitchen are more family pictures. Not like the formal portraits by the stairs, with their combed hair and pressed clothes. These are snapshots of life pinned haphazardly to a corkboard over the breakfast nook. The parents holding hands at the top of the Empire State Building on their twentieth anniversary. Neither is looking at the camera, only at each other. The older son in marching band, his tuba hugging his tall, slender body. The feather in his uniform cap jaunts to the side, mirroring his crooked smile. The daughter in a silvery leotard with smoothed back hair. She scowls at whoever is taking the picture, but poses just the same. Her pale limbs stretch out beyond the picture's edge.

But the photo of the younger son is torn at the corners where it's been taken down and pinned back up. In it, he's riding his motorbike, sailing through the air over a dirt track. The family has all looked at it, knowing that he is flying there against the sharp blue sky, as if he gives no thoughts to ever coming back down.

Denise Howard Long is the author of the flash fiction chapbook *Spoil the Child* (2018, Finishing Line Press) and her fiction has appeared in *PANK, SmokeLong Quarterly, Pithead Chapel, Evansville Review, Blue Monday Review,* and elsewhere. Her story "What We See" was selected by Aimee Bender for inclusion in *Best Small Fictions* 2018. Her work was named runner-up for the Larry Brown Short Story Award and she's been granted residencies from Hedgebrook and Dorland Mountain Arts Colony. Originally from Illinois, Denise currently lives in Nebraska, with her husband and two sons. You can visit her at www.denisehlong.com.

Siren

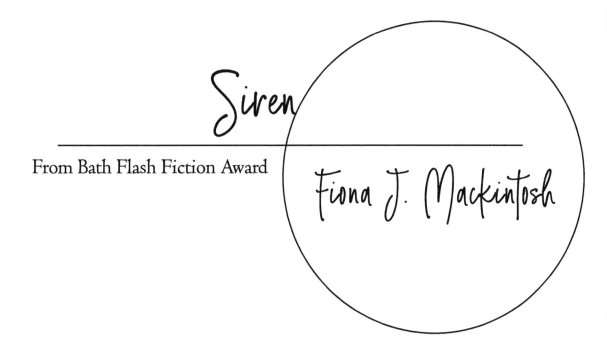

From Bath Flash Fiction Award

IN THE WET SLAP of the haar, the lassies slit the herring mouth to tail and pack them into briny barrels. I see her head move among the rest, brown curls escaping from her shawl. She has the juice of silver fishes in her veins - it's in the raised blue of her wrists, her raw fingers, in the taste of oysters when I lick her down below, her skirt canted up and knees apart.

They say despair can be a man's making, but that's not how it feels to me. I give her everything I have - primrose plants, stockings, greenhouse fruits — and everything I am, a stiff-collared man behind a counter at the bank. She says my palms smell of money and loves their smoothness on her skin, but then she sees the brown sails coming, the lads home from the draves, swaggering in their thigh-high boots. She rests her elbows on the bar, pink mouth open, as this one tells of breaching humpbacks and that one tells of waves the height of mountains. I loathe their muckled arms and sunburnt faces and wish them at the bottom of the sea.

She knows the only times I venture out are on the calmest days, sometimes to cast a line and once a year to watch the puffins hatch. It's not an epic life, not one likely to inspire the poets. But when the *Reaper* goes down with all hands lost, it's my door she comes to and cleaves herself to me from head to heel. She says, "I ned a man who willnae leave me wantin'." Afterwards, cross-legged on the bed, she hangs a pair of cherries over her ear and, giddy with my unexpected luck, I take them in my mouth, stones and all.

Fiona J. Mackintosh is a Scottish-American writer living near Washington D.C. whose fiction has been published on both sides of the Atlantic. In 2018, she won the Fish Flash Fiction Prize,

the October Bath Flash Fiction Award, and the Autumn Reflex Fiction Prize. Two of her pieces were selected for *Best Microfiction* 2019. Her short stories have been listed for the Bristol, Galley Beggar, and Exeter Short Story Prizes, and she was honored to receive an Individual Artist's Award from the Maryland State Arts Council in 2016. She is writing a five-novel series about 20th century Britain entitled *Albion's Millennium*.

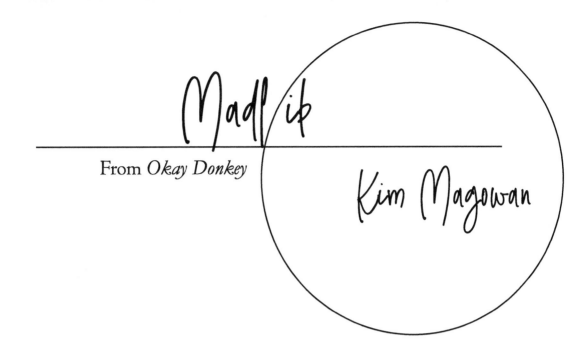

Mad Lib

From *Okay Donkey*

Kim Magowan

MOM, WHEN YOU WERE at the <u>FERRIS WHEEL</u> Saturday, Ron <u>BENT</u> the <u>CLOCK</u>, so I couldn't <u>HICCUP</u>. He put his <u>KNEECAP</u> over my <u>EYEBROW</u>, so I couldn't even <u>GIGGLE</u>. Then he stuck his <u>ELBOWS</u> inside my <u>EAR</u>. I <u>JUGGLED</u> and <u>JUGGLED</u>. Remember, you asked why my <u>TEETH</u> were so <u>TURQUOISE</u>? I know you <u>MIX</u> Ron is <u>FIZZY</u>, but really, he's a <u>KANGAROO</u>. Mom, I don't <u>SNORT</u> you, I know how <u>SUGARY</u> you've been, but I fucking <u>CARTWHEEL</u> him. Ron said if I <u>KNITTED</u> you, he would <u>FLY</u> me, and besides, you would never <u>WHISPER</u> me. So, do you <u>SNIFF</u> me?

Kim Magowan is the author of the short story collection *Undoing* (2018), which won the 2017 Moon City Press Fiction Award, and the novel *The Light Source* (2019) from 7.13 Books. Her fiction has been published in *Atticus Review, Cleaver, The Gettysburg Review, New World Writing, SmokeLong Quarterly,* and many other journals. She lives in San Francisco and teaches in the Department of Literatures and Languages at Mills College. You can find her on Twitter (@kimmagowan) or read more of her work at www.kimmagowan.com.

No Future in Oysters

From *New World Writing*

John Mancini

MY FATHER WAS AN oysterman just like his father before him—and just like I would have become had things not turned out the way they did. By the end of the sixties, the Bay was in poor shape, and the men who worked the water and drank at the bars at the marina could see the writing was on the wall. Action groups were starting to form around the idea of "saving" the Bay—whatever that meant—and the careers it sustained, but by the time "environmentalism" entered the popular imagination, after decades of industrial pollution and runoff from local steel factories, the Chesapeake had seen such a decline in oysters, crabs and rock fish that most of the old dredgers were already out of business—and those of us who weren't would soon be driven to retirement by mechanical dredging.

I spent most of my childhood riding in my father's skipjack with my brother Glen, watching the tongers gather the catch from the floor of the Bay and haul it up and dump it on the culling board to be sorted. When I was old enough, I kept my tan by working on the boat alongside the men. By then, my father was reluctantly using the dredge to work the deeper waters—"Life has a way of sucking you in," he liked to say, meaning if you weren't willing to improvise, you'd have to compromise. "You've got to learn to adapt," he said. "Just look at the Indian. He didn't vanish. He just changed colors." My father claimed to be one-eighth Indian, which would have made me one-sixteenth Indian had it been true, but I don't think it was. He used to tell me our ancestors were outlaws, that they'd belonged to a war loving sub-tribe of the Algonquin on the Eastern Shore, a tribe that shared with their northern neighbors a love of fishing and of fighting—only one of which I had done well. I was not much of a fighter. When U.S. troops invaded Cambodia, I joined the reserves before the draft could take me—no one was getting 4-H those days, and blue-collar boys from the Bay were among the first to ship out.

The year Hurricane Camille devastated the oyster population, my brother died in a boating accident—one that had nothing to do with oyster dredging and everything to do with diving into Stoney Creek at low tide. After Glen's death, my father stopped asking me to join him on the boat, didn't want me thinking about becoming a dredger—didn't want me on the Bay, period. He started drinking more, working the water less. He spent his time at the Pearl down at the marina, bitching about mechanical dredgers and Nixon, buying rounds for his friends when he could, and selling a little pot to make ends meet—but he was slowly falling into a blackness that would last throughout the winter.

The following spring he asked me to join him on a road trip to Texas. It was a rare invitation—I had long known him to vanish for weeks at a time without explanation—and it was an invitation that I accepted if for no other reason than to change the scenery. The sameness of Silver Sands had begun to make my brain go flat, in eighteen years I'd never been farther south than D.C., and despite our differences I was still willing to follow my father anywhere he wanted to go—whether out on the Bay or over the Allegheny Mountains. So we drove together, father and son, down through West Virginia, and we stopped over in Tennessee where he had some friends who ran a small motel and diner called the Royal Arms. He was "checking on his orders," he said. He planned to make another stop here on our way back north, but for now our destination was Laredo, on the Rio Grande, where we were going to see an old friend of his, someone he wanted me to meet.

Twenty hours later, the road had taken its toll and the vastness of the desert was making me dizzy just to look at. The emptiness on all sides was like something out of an old western, the scrub brush and clumps of ponderosa pine, the sage brush-dotted gullies and zigzagging gorge dissolving into the Technicolor distance. I knew I was out of my element, but I put my trust in my father, for whom this was no strange territory. I knew he had been here before.

The first bales we brought back from the ranch in Laredo had been humped across the border by young boys barely in their teens—the so-called "Acapulco Gold" they carried, with its bright orange hairs, resembling gold nuggets that had been compressed into solid bricks the size of shoeboxes and wrapped in burlap and tied with twine. The bales filled the flatbed of my father's Chevy and stayed lashed down with a length of tarp that snapped in the wind all the way back to Tennessee—where we unloaded half the product as planned—and then on again to Maryland.

Though I did not realize it at the time, a new family business was being forged, one that didn't require long days on the water and one that would eventually prove quite profitable for me—though it was not without its hazards. Eventually, I would serve ten years of a twenty year sentence for possession and distribution. But going to prison was just another matter of learning to adapt. I'd learned that from my father, a man who made one thing clear to me on that trip all those years ago, something he advised me to chew on a while before I made up my mind. After all, becoming an outlaw was not for everyone, and it was a hard truth—one you could really break your teeth on if you weren't careful—one that he had come himself to believe as the only logical solution to a problem that he had not caused. All the way to Baltimore, he repeated it like a theme: There was no future in oysters. Marijuana, however, was a different story.

John Mancini has published short fiction and poetry in *New England Review, Atlanta Review, Natural Bridge,* and other journals. His small fictions have appeared online in *SmokeLong Quarterly, New Flash Fiction Review, HOOT, Literary Orphans,* and elsewhere. He earned an MFA from San Francisco State University and an MA from the University of Southern Mississippi. A songwriter and musician, his songs have received film and television placement worldwide. Read more of his work at www.johnmanciniwrites.com.

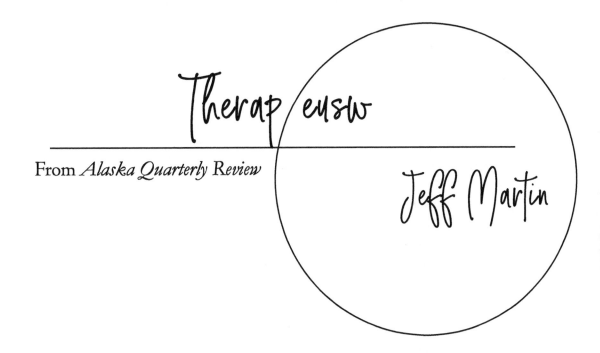

Therapeusw

From *Alaska Quarterly Review*

Jeff Martin

IN THE FALL A bunch of fathers die and we're all taking ancient Greek. Mrs. V explains there is no "yes", there is no "no". Are you going to the marketplace? she asks us. We are going to the marketplace, we say. Do you worship the goddess? she asks. We do not worship the goddess, we say. But there is also a dance that weekend, so we are mostly lying.

The fathers die like fuses, one after another. There are four in the end, and Mrs. V talks about proportions. This is disproportionate, she says. In a class of seventeen, what are the odds? Rahul says they must be pretty good and he looks terrible because his dad is one of them.

There's no way to kill someone in ancient Greek. It's very precise, we learn. I bring about your death, we say. You have brought about my death. I write a note to Ginny Hayes. Is she going to the dance, I ask. She is going to the dance, she says. Will she go to the dance with me? I ask. She does not answer. I write again. You are bringing about my death, I say.

Rahul doesn't ask anyone to the dance. No, he says, I'm θάνατος inside. It would be good to try, I say. What's the worst that could happen? And he looks at me because the odds are four in seventeen that the worst could happen.

There's an entire page of verbs just for fear. We look at them on the bus ride home. This is very precise, I say. Rahul is chewing gum because it keeps him from puking. He has been chewing gum for weeks. I fear, I say. Me, too, he says. Outside it is October and the light is way too short.

I write another note to Ginny Hayes. This one is in Greek. I tell her she is a goddess who can heal me. Θεραπεύσω, I say. Therapeusw. I am being healed. She does the worst thing possible, which is write back in English.

Rahul's dad was in the garden when his death was brought about. Rahul says it was his heart or his lungs, it was hard to tell. He was planting basil. I don't even like basil, Rahul says.

It makes everything taste awful. I can't admit I don't know what basil is, so I agree.

On the last day of October I write another note to Ginny Hayes. Last chance, I say. If you decline, I will whip the seas with my anger. You will whip the seas with your anger, she writes back. This is my τιμή, I say, this is my honor. You will whip the seas with your anger, she says.

That night Rahul and I walk through a field near the school. We're too old to trick or treat. The corn cobs crackle underfoot.

Θεραπεύσω? I say.

Rahul is chewing gum. No, he says, I fear. I am in the act of fearing.

Jeff Martin's stories have appeared in *New England Review*, *Alaska Quarterly Review*, *storySouth*, and *No Tokens Journal*, among others. He co-directs the University of Virginia's Young Writers Workshop and can be found online at readjeffmartin.com.

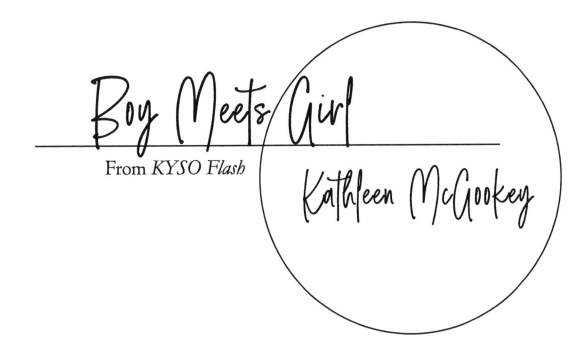

Boy Meets Girl

From *KYSO Flash*

Kathleen McGookey

IN A TWINKLING, THE the girl turned into a sparrow, the boy into a wren. No, girl into ocean waves churning, boy into froth, wind, sunlight glinting on shore. Or boy into rooster, girl into fox. Possibly a hunting party gathered. Possibly another suitor and maiden hid in the wood and watched the chase while the girl slowly combed her luxurious red hair. The boy and girl moved like flames glimpsed from the corner of an eye. It might have been mercy, that escape from such monstrous desire. But not as comets ablaze across the velvet night. No, not as moonlight resting lightly on any body of water. Maybe boy into lightning, girl into struck rock. Maybe girl into oak, boy into ivy, into moss, climbing up, trailing down. Does it matter?

Kathleen McGookey's fourth book of prose poems, *Instructions for My Imposter*, is forthcoming from Press 53. Her chapbook *Nineteen Letters* is available from BatCat Press. Her work has appeared in journals including *Crazyhorse, Denver Quarterly, Epoch, Field, Indiana Review, Ploughshares, The Prose Poem: An International Journal, Prairie Schooner, Quarterly West, Rhino, Seneca Review,* and *West Branch*. She has published three other books of poems, two chapbooks, and We'll See, translations of French poet Georges Godeau's prose poems. She lives in Middleville, Michigan, with her family.

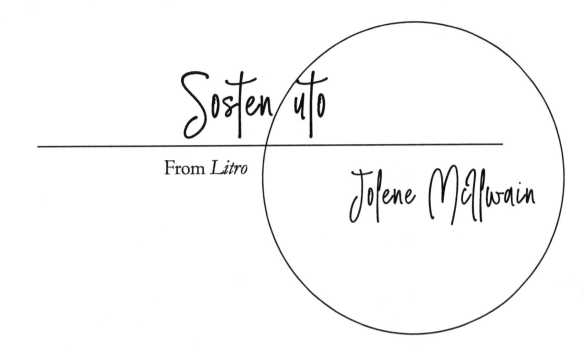

Sostenuto

From *Litro*

Jolene McIlwain

THERE WAS THIS SECTION of Dvorak's Symphony No. 9 he could play—a little piano riff from the largo movement he'd kick out when he thought about that woman he knew he shouldn't think about at his real job. He feared there he might hurt. Hurt someone. Hurt something. Might lose his job for being distracted, messing up. But here, long after all happy hour suits left, when the regulars were keeping their heads down, when Cubbie was counting money and glasses and filling coaster holders, and right before last call, he played it. It felt right then. It felt like a Crown Royal rim, licked wet.

They had met in the hallway of this place when he was much younger and she was broken, a waft of warm whiskey. She fell onto him, like sound itself, continued to strike him, for three months like a felt hammer, soft and hard. She was both strings and percussion. He knew he didn't love her. He loved his wife, the woman having daughter after daughter, the woman filled with milk and kindness, open eyes and smile, his soft pedal, his una corda.

But lately, and for some time now, he's considered it may have been the only time he'd really felt love. What he lived before and after her—with his wife and daughters—was commitment. A completely different pedal. Different effect. Different sound altogether. Love with this woman he met in the hallway offered more octaves, hidden extra keys below hinged lids.

Since those nights when this woman taught him about another place where sorrow was sharp, and laughter was insanely regular, and movement between emotions so quick and surprising it left him spent, he had to learn to shift back to his life, his place, his contract with level responsibility. And with this move he'd grown closed and heavy, burdened with life, a home full of girls who became women, wives, mothers and then, slowly and quickly left him.

His wife fretted over the dotted harlequin bugs on their cauliflower plants, the hairline faults of their plastered ceiling. So, he scraped off the black and white eggs, lined up like little keys on the undersides of leaves. He spackled.

But he allowed a small spot for this woman he'd met in the hallway.

It was just that lately the memory of her broke through that placed where it was tucked safely in his head. She poured out of him somewhere above his ear. Left a gaping hole there his wife was sure to notice, again. He was becoming reckless with despair restoring jacks and hammers, capstan screws. These broken pianos reminded him, too often, of her, this unsteady steady woman who made him liquid and tender.

His wife's name drew him in first. Her father, his instructor, mentioned her one day as he practiced Chopin's Preludes, No. 7, A minor. Octava was nineteen; he was twenty-one. After their first date—tickets her father could not use to the symphony—they played chopsticks, her fingers stumbling over the keys, the side of her arm barely brushing the side of his. "She'll be your metronome," her father had said, toasting them at their wedding.

Just a few weeks into it with this woman in the hallway, his wife found out. She said she understood, said she'd allow him to leave her if that's what he needed. But he stayed. Left playing piano at that bar every night and took on two jobs, one tuning and repairing uprights and Grands, and one cleaning long hallways of the music hall with a mop and rolling bucket of grey water. He made enough money to take good care of his wife, his girls, and still played just one night a month, only for tips. She allowed him this, reluctantly.

And so once a month he remembers when he fell in love, when he just played piano. And, the woman? She sweats his drink, slides beside wispy sheets of music, waves around his head, a sound riding on perpetual sustain. And when he's done, when he's had enough, he walks home, unlocks the door, and finds his way back to his bed, his wife, and lays this open spot of his head on the pillow.

Jolene McIlwain's work appears online at *Cincinnati Review, New Orleans Review, Prime Number Magazine, Prairie Schooner, River Teeth, Fourth River,* and elsewhere. Her fiction has been nominated for Pushcarts and Best of the Net and selected as finalist for both *Glimmer Train's* New Writers and Very Short Fiction contests and semi-finalist in *American Short Fiction's* Short and Short(er) fiction contests as well as *Nimrod's* Katherine Anne Porter Prize. She's an associate flash fiction editor at *JMWW* and is currently working on a collection of short stories and a novel set in the hills of the Appalachian plateau of western Pennsylvania.

A post-traumatic god

From *Meniscus*

Heather Mcquillan

TĀWHIRIMATEĀ TRIED TO STAND his ground but was outnumbered. The ground he stood on was his mother's unstable belly, doughy and stretched from so many sons. She let him down in the end, as all mothers do. Let go of his hand.

This he remembers: darkness humid with sweat and the sourness of spilt milk, the hau, the beat, the pulse, pressed tight between his parent's renditions of love, their keening drone, beneath the shouting of his brothers and the TV turned up too loud.

This he remembers: the rupture, the coming into the blue lights and sirens and the whero of eyelid blood when he closes them against the glare. His mother convulsing, his father gone, brothers scattered.

This he remembers: a stranger's hand on his shoulder. The weightlessness of feet that have nowhere to stand. The weight of swallowed words deep in his belly while they click Bic pens.

In resting he is jolted. Thought spirals into cyclone cones — always back to the eye of the storm. He's tried the recommended doses but they don't work for him so he pulls sharply from the bed he shares with a thin-boned woman, takes his clenched fists away from her frail flesh and he runs. His feet tread heavy along his mother's backbone, along the length of the coastline out to the headland, where he howls at a cloud-blacked father-sky and slaps his chest until the skin burns. This he knows: cold air and the taste of blood in his throat and the taste of endorphins that will bring him, finally, to rest.

Tāwhiri sits on the paint-peeled seat outside the takeaway shop. He is waiting for the skinny woman to fetch him back in her beat-up car. Sweat stains the curves of his white singlet. His father is hazy today. His mother has not rumbled for some time. His brothers are pencilled scars on the horizon.

Heather McQuillan, from New Zealand, is a writing teacher and an award-winning novelist for young readers. She writes regularly for *Flash Frontier* and has won awards in New Zealand (National Flash Fiction Day, 2016) and Australia (Meniscus CAL Best Prose Prize, 2018). Her stories have been selected for anthologies including *Best Microfiction* 2019; *Bath Flash Fiction* Volumes Two and Three; *Bonsai: best small stories from Aotearoa, New Zealand,* and *Best Small Fictions* 2017. Heather has a Masters of Creative Writing from Massey University. Her first collection, *Where Oceans Meet,* is published by Reflex Press, 2019.

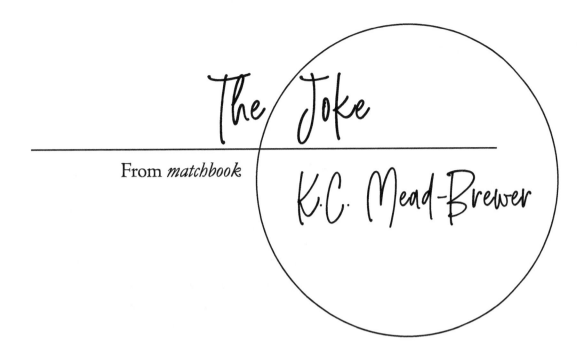

The Joke

From *matchbook*

K.C. Mead-Brewer

I'M ALONE IN MY apartment but I have the TV on so it sounds like a bunch of people are in here talking. This way people in the hall won't walk by and think that I'm alone. I can hear the neighbors laughing through the wall. Is it me? Are they laughing at me? I knew that welcome mat with the parrots wearing sunglasses was too much. Sometimes I look at things to buy and I don't know who I am. Now they're laughing even louder. I press my ear against the white paint—not eggshell or anything; I left it like I found it; Empty Apartment White—and now I can hear the clinking of glasses as well. They're probably not laughing at me if they're drinking and clinking glasses. Probably someone told a joke. Maybe a guest. Guests tell jokes even if they don't come prepared with anything specific. I know because that's how guests work on TV. It's a relief to know they aren't laughing at me and I peel my ear off the wall. My hands jerk at my sides—they don't always know what to do with themselves—so I go to the bookshelf and let them flip through a book. I'm not much of a reader but I spend lots of money on books. The authors don't mind this arrangement. It isn't for the authors that I buy them, anyway. It's not because I'm some fancy supporter of the arts. It's because this way, if anyone comes by, maybe one of the guests from the party next door—maybe they go out for a cigarette and wander back in the wrong door (my door), maybe they come over just to see what I'm watching, maybe my neighbor's cable is on the fritz—they'll look at my stocked bookshelves and they'll think to themselves, Now here is a person who reads. My hands flip quickly through the pages and soon a tall stack of freshly opened and closed books is sticking out of the floor. It occurs to me that books might make for interesting bricks and that maybe I could build an interesting-looking book-thing to show off to any guests who wander by. Maybe if I had an interesting book-thing, like an archway or a fort, then wandering guests wouldn't just wander out again. Maybe they would only leave to go bring other guests in to see what I'd made. You don't need to look at my apartment for very long to know I've got plenty of space for guests and building things. I don't own a lot of extra stuff. This's and that's. I don't collect anything. I don't have any hobbies or special skills. I don't have any topics that I know more about than anyone else. So I start building with the books—not really sure where I'm going with them, just kind of waiting to see what shapes they make on their own—and I realize that maybe watching me build this book-thing might be even more interesting than simply seeing it finished. I turn up the TV as loud as it will go, a nonchalant way to pique the neighbors' curiosity. The little green bars count to 180. I've never done this before and I worry a little that it might hurt the TV somehow. But why would they make a TV that could hurt itself? It's so loud I can't hear my neighbors anymore or even my own voice when I say, Well, that's loud. I start back with building the book-thing. The book covers are trembling like water—that's how loud the TV is—and I'm stacking and I'm stacking and I'm surprised no one's come over yet and the walls are kind of shaking—the TV, it's really loud—and the door and the floor and the windows are all shaking and the book-thing is getting bigger and bigger—I hadn't realized I owned quite THIS many books—and it's only when I get to the very last book, the shelves completely empty, the walls and ceiling and apartment all crumbling the TV is so danged loud, that I see I've built myself a boat. Well, the guests have missed out seeing me build the thing but maybe they'll still be interested if they see me using it. The TV's screaming. Plaster and wood and pipes are all bursting. It's really loud. Is it possible they don't hear it? Aren't they curious yet to come see me, what I'm up to, what I'm watching? I consider trying to paddle the boat around but there aren't any books left to make paddles with and anyway where would I paddle to? I sigh extra loudly but still can't hear myself so I just ignore myself, my bad attitude—my teachers always said I had a bad attitude—and lie down in the boat on my back. The TV's so loud I don't even hear it anymore. The TV's so loud that all I can think or smell or feel are its deep vibrations and it's almost relaxing. I close my eyes and feel the world thrum and it really is almost relaxing. Almost like someone's sitting here with me, and together, we're drifting out to sea.

K.C. Mead-Brewer lives in Baltimore, Maryland. Her fiction appears in *Electric Literature's Recommended Reading*, *Carve Magazine*, *Strange Horizons*, and elsewhere. She is a graduate of the 2018 Clarion Science Fiction & Fantasy Writers' Workshop and of Tin House's 2018 Winter Workshop for Short Fiction. For more information, visit kcmeadbrewer.com.

Beenie Man Asks Who Am I

From Brunel International African Poetry Prize (2018)

& The Jury's Still Out

Momtaza Mehri

THE ZEITGEIST CALLED AND it wants its coins back. Somebody's gonna pay for what the world did to me. Promise or a warning, interpret as intended. You can't mic drop your way out of genocide. Tonight I am looking for an audience, another way of saying I am looking for a weapon. Whichever recoils in my general direction. Whichever I mistake for applause. I would keep my friends close but they turn into my enemies. Such is cruelty made tender. Pop culture is the minutiae of my loneliness. Neon behind the eyes. I glow from the inside out. Jangle to the hips. Each nightly simmer. Zim Zimma. Keys to the Bimma. I came. I saw. I left. Black Caesar. Born into anomaly. The Romans become Ar Rum become the dirt that suckles my preened roses. Verse two by three. To the ends of the earth and they will be beaten again. Overcome. Consider, if you can, today's lone prophecy. Profit I see. Prophet a-sea. Men in and out of water look the same. Suck salt's marrow with every breath. Water & dark bodies haven't been on speaking terms for a while now. This, I was born knowing. Now the land, the land knows how to hold a body. Is well practiced. Welcomes our detritus. Our wet & weathered undoing. Particulates all our secrets. Secret defined as: blank cheques, blood promises, birth rights, bruised calves & everything else that leaves its time-stamp on the wrist. Take these keys as gifts.

I cannot give you a home. Take me as gift.

Momtaza Mehri is a poet and essayist. She is the co-winner of the 2018 Brunel International African Poetry Prize. Her work has been widely anthologized, appearing in *Granta, Artforum,*

Poetry International, Vogue and *Real Life Mag.* She is the former Young People's Laureate for London and columnist-in-residence at the San Francisco Museum of Modern Art's *Open Space.* Her chapbook *Sugah Lump Prayer* was published in 2017.

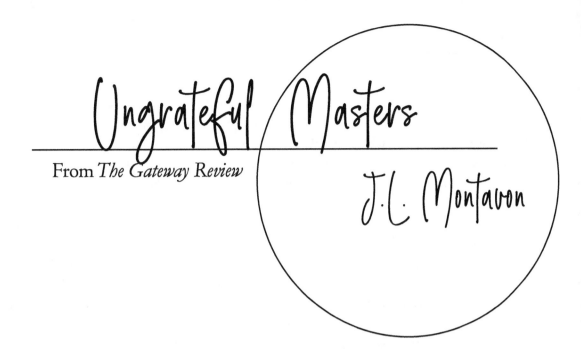

Ungrateful Masters

From *The Gateway Review*

J.L. Montavon

THE UNGRATEFUL MONSTERS ARRIVE in trees, like fruit. But it's our fruit, not the tree's. Mary, my sister, tossed an unhatched one into the trash and got a scolding. Unwelcome as these things were in our house, and in all but the most saintly households, our parents said we had to take care of them and raise them as our own.

We thought different. We came from Mom, not trees.

The people who enter our flickering pea-green television screen, via the ever-attentive rabbit ears on top, said they've studied and studied how the monsters, instead of gestating in the womb, manage to bud and hang and drop and fruit—to no avail. Supposedly they're just like us, but look at how preternaturally pink they are, look at their fat stubby limbs and stupidly wide eyes, like they sprang out of a magazine in the barbershop or grocery store. The magazine with candy-colored covers to make you salivate: "What a plump morsel, how I'd like to hold one in my arms." The magazine doesn't show the squalling and screaming and demanding these things do in your home.

It's no accident they showed up around Christmas, the time when everyone gets goo-goo eyed about babies and gifts. It's our fault, certain people preach, for gussying up Christmas. Sacrilege, the bright lights of many colors, the shiny ornaments, the figurines of fat jolly joy and heavenly flying children. Sacrilege, the feasting and quaffing, the good cheer and gay carols, the sucking of striped canes hung on branches. Hubris, cutting living trees and bringing them, like babes ripped from Creation, inside to gratify our gaudy notion of what we wish them to be—shining lights in dark times, glimmers of hope in the dead of December—instead of respecting the perfect somber silent green standing nobly in the white base that God intended.

The ungrateful monsters almost make you think the preaching might be right. They sprout like ugly ornaments on the trees outside our house. Our pseudo-siblings drop only from live evergreens and do not dance in our eyes with bright colors. No, they're crusty russet pods, a misshapen mix of potato and pine cone, oozing goo as they grow, smelling to high heaven, engorging to a strange fullness until they fall and split open. We hear them in the morning, their unearthly wails, as if the devil has just sphinctered a new demon up through the ground.

Notice how they grow only on private land. Our tender-hearted parents view them as helpless, blissfully ignorant creatures in need of care. But they scheme, oh how they scheme. By dropping on a specific family's property, everyone knows exactly who these beings belong to. They want to nest and infest with someone in particular, not everyone in general.

Mom and Dad are conscientious people and we can never not be grateful for that. But . . . they brought the yowling things inside as part of us, never noticing, as the foundlings grew, how ice cream disappeared from the freezer the moment it was stowed there. Or toilet paper, which Mary thinks they eat. And potato chips. We've seen it, we've peeked from the kitchen door as they put their faces into a bag and vacuum it out, leaving behind an empty, shriveled sack.

We're obliged to play games with our supposed siblings, tetherball and foursquare, Monopoly and the Game of Life, until we let them win.

They have special tastes. Mom caters to them with liver and brains and kidneys for dinner. All we get is extra ketchup to cover the organs.

Every cater enlarges the ingratitude. She knows it and we know it, yet our parents persist in believing in the goodness of anything bearing resemblance to human tissue.

It's the same with families everywhere. The Government's motto AFFIRM LIFE (posted on banners, the words never not in capitals) means that everyone's obliged to care for pods that grow on their property.

The Department of Interior came up with the solution of making public lands the place of birth. Pods were planted anywhere the Government had a right to plant. Someone said the animals who lived there would be hurt and the Government said never mind, this is an emergency, species not human don't matter.

The pods disdained public lands and did not grow. They were crafty, like I said. "The Department of Interior knows nothing about growing interior things," Mary said.

A faction has split from the Government, demanding that all land be made private. That way someone, everywhere, would be obliged to care for the growths. This faction has an extra special reverence for life, they say, but the rest of us don't want to be assigned plots of earth whose issue is our responsibility.

Our parents rebel, in their quiet way. Dad goes out at night to patrol the property. Mary and I see him giving Jenny, the dog, a sniff of the socks of the ungrateful things. We don't know what happens, but we hear from other kids that pods might accidentally be tossed into a pond or run over by a lawnmower or appear under the nose of a hungry dog or cat. Coyotes are no longer shot. Wolves are welcome.

There's talk the Government will be voted out. Their ministers say that if that happens, the Apocalypse will follow. A lot of people think it's already here.

I don't know, maybe these things that fall to the ground from the trees will somehow contribute to our well-being. Maybe they have some secret knowledge that will rescue us. They demand feeding, and praise, and if we offer both to the utmost, maybe they'll save us all.

Mary isn't so sure. We share a birthday. We're looking forward to the next one, our sixteenth, the age at which we'll be allowed to purchase firearms.

J. L. Montavon was born and raised in Denver and lives in San Francisco. The story "Recursions" was chosen by Joan Wickersham as the winner of the 2016 *Salamander* Fiction Prize, and other stories have appeared in *Hobart* and *Prime Number Magazine*.

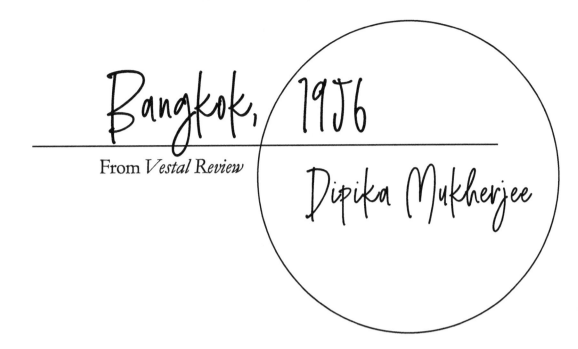

Bangkok, 1956

From *Vestal Review*

Dipika Mukherjee

I WILL NOT BE born for another nine years.

It is my father's first foreign posting; my mother is his bride. She leaves a sprawling home in Calcutta and fifteen playmates to take his hand, crossing black seas to go where he will go. In a house as vast as her natal home there are the two of them, a maid, a gardener's family... only silence speaks her language through cavernous days.

He has not learnt to woo her; they both married when told.

But one day he brings home a sari from the Parsi merchant. *Look*, he says, unfurling a shimmer of cloth on their bed. *The rose color reminded me of you.*

He is color blind.

She sees a snot-green of silk; it reminds her of mold on damp monsoon drains.

She picks up the sari and drapes the pallu coyly over a shoulder. She looks at the ground and says, *This is the most beautiful thing I have ever owned.*

Dipika Mukherjee is an internationally touring writer, sociolinguist, and global nomad. She holds a PhD in English (Sociolinguistics) from Texas A&M University and is the author of the novels *Shambala Junction*, which won the UK Virginia Prize for Fiction, and *Ode to Broken Things*, which was longlisted for the Man Asia Literary Prize. She lives in Chicago and is affiliated to the Buffett Institute for Global Studies at Northwestern University and is Core Faculty at Story Studio Chicago.

How to Not Get Ovarian Cancer: A Guide for Jewish Women

From *The Gateway Review*

Carla Myers

GO BACK IN TIME. Not just to when your parents met, but way before that to the shtetl, where the matchmaker ran out of ideas and suggested a match where a new couple already saw each other every Shabbat dinner. Kill the matchmaker. If you are averse to killing under these circumstances, you are a schlemiel, and I have very little compassion for you, but if you insist, pull the woman aside and show her *Fiddler on the Roof* on your iPhone. Convince her she is not the oldest daughter who marries the tailor but instead is the wild daughter who marries the sexy Russian. Provide a sexy Russian, and officiate the wedding. Important: do not forget to get an on-line wedding officiant license before you go.

If, when you return to the present, you still have that pesky cancer gene, you have failed and must try again. Find each of your great-grandparents as children. Surreptitiously watch them and evaluate their behavior. Make a spreadsheet in Excel and rank them based on their various attributes. Kill number eight on the list. If you can't, don't worry. I find Excel cumbersome too. Instead, pick the one who looks the most 'Jewish'. I would go with scarlet fever to do the deed. It was common and wouldn't look suspicious. It also sounds much more romantic than, say, 'dysentery', so I think it will sound nicer in your autobiography, should you ever choose to write one.

If you still have it, you are running out of options. First, retake the genetic test just to be sure. You wouldn't want to do something rash if you didn't absolutely need to. Now you are left with just your grandparents and parents. Since they are your close family, you may have a problem with the killing, because no matter who you kill at this point, when you return to the present, one quarter to one half of you will be gone, you will probably not really be yourself and that would be unfortunate after all this work. Also, you would have fewer people to drive you to your doctor's appointments that you are clearly now going to have.

So, find a doctor. The doctor will want to attach a helium tank to your bellybutton and blow up your abdomen so much that assistants will have to tie ribbons to your limbs and float you around the hospital corridors like it's the Macy's day parade. In the operating room, the doctor will reach onto your balloon and take out every organ until you are empty in the middle, like a dank cave with drippy stalactites or a bagel. Then the doctor will untie the ribbons, pull a cork out of your vagina and you will zing all over the room, bouncing off walls and ceiling as you deflate. You will end up in a high corner, spluttering, until you finally drop to the floor. It will be hard to tell if you are a patient or a giant pile of stretched-out translucent chicken skin. Before you leave, the doctor will tell you that they might have caught it in time, but it's hard to say. Kill the doctor.

Go home and excise everything else from your life. Drop your friends, ignore your family, and stop coloring your hair. Eat only hard boiled eggs, because they're easy to cook and you don't even have to swallow them. They just line up like greasy kids at a waterslide and slip down your gullet one after another. Throw out every piece of clothing except for a giant pair of workman's coveralls that are so big they don't make contact with the foreign body inside. Make your writing tighter. Now the clock is ticking, so slash at every other word with the scalpel you stole from the dead doctor's hand.

With an undergraduate degree in sculpture and a J.D., Carla Myers followed the most logical path to becoming a writer. This year she retained a significant number of body parts, but not as many as she had hoped. She is the winner of the *Columbia Journal* Evolve Special Issue and a finalist for the 2018 Nancy D. Hargrove Editor's Prize for Fiction and Poetry. Her work has been published in *The Gateway Review, The Jabberwock Review, Patheos, Muse/A Journal, Streetlight, Convivium, Ethel, Sonic Boom, Panoplyzine* and *The Finger.*

Bliss Place

From *Black Warrior Review*

I.

DRIFTWOOD LIES BONE-WHITE in the sand. The sky droops low. Beach houses line the bay like so many glass jars. A stairway winds up the bluff far away, rising like a bad dream in the night. I say to you we should head back. You say there are too many things to know. You are going to the hills to talk with angels.

2.

Many creatures move in the night, scratching their backs against the shingles of our house. The cicadas sound like sprinklers. The child inside of you is not yet viable. You are hoping for twins, but I am certain it is only our dead mother. Your dead mother, you say, mine is alive and well. But a mother, like the eve of something, is both mine and everyone's. In our furry bed, you nuzzle your soft head into my armpit. You clean my ear with your fingertip. Your skin is blue lotuses and white water lilies. I tell you so. We go on listening to the night.

3.

Nobody had lived on the island before. The natives from the mainland would row out in spring to harvest clams and oysters and bury their dead. Mother, too, came here to die. Father died first. These stories are all the same. I was not afraid of the island until you came along, with that child growing inside of you. This was no place for a birth. The creatures wouldn't sleep then. They smelled it on your skin. The tide pulled back, and the beaches laid bare, with all manner of dead things stranded ashore. It was some kind of omen, I knew, so I tried to save a starfish. The thing was glumpy and skin-pink, along its arms were tiny tentacles like thirsty mouths. The sea smelled like it would drown me. I made a mess. The starfish lost a leg.

4.

You found a piece of driftwood in the shape of a whale and showed it to me like some kind of secret. For good luck, you said. You said the island was full of magic. This was your first visit. On the ferry, you had stood on the deck the whole way, from horn blast to horn blast. When you came back to our bench, your eyes were red and your hair wet. Why didn't you come out? you said. I don't know, I said. The way ships cleaved the water always made me sick. From the port, we came directly to the beach. You said the city looked so small from here. You gave me the whale wood to keep in my pocket. You were barefoot and happy.

5.

Because summer has ended, everyone has returned to the city and left us alone on the island. On the other end of the bluff, there's a small town with a post office and a church and your standard coffee shops and diners, but the people there don't count. They're part of the season too, and when the tourists and the tycoons leave, they disappear like ghosts. You say you don't mind the solitude. We walk through the woods to the paved street where glass houses hang precariously from the bluff. There are signs asking us to leave. Private Property, they say, No Trespassing. We count seventeen kittens on the block. You say we should rescue them, or they'll die come winter. I say they'll live. Every year they multiply. All it took was one lost pet, and now a whole pack of wild island cats.

6.

Mother was a singer and father was an alcoholic. They met at a hermitage in New York. When I was born they bought some land upstate and tried to live off it. Mother named the property "Bliss Place." Father salvaged scrap metal from junkyards and never sold any. We grew vegetables, dug a well, pit-fired pottery, knitted sweaters, and my parents failed at everything. Then father got sick. We drove him to a hospital in town and he stayed there a while. I chopped all the firewood that winter. When he came back it was like mother believed Bliss Place would finally work. She was reading all these books on ecology, darning our clothes, over-weeding the garden. Like she could save the Place, and father too. He died anyway. He wanted to. We sold Bliss Place. Mother used the money to build a small house on the island. When she finished building the house, she died too.

7.

Lately, the island has been giving you dreams. Bad ones, without shape or meaning. You curl around your belly and cry and cry. I check the windows for creatures and they run back into the night. I am so tired. I don't know what else to do, so I sit on the bed and touch your hair. It is damp with your sweat. My father's hair was wet, too, the night he died. From snow, I had first

thought, when I pulled him in from the cold. But as he lay there thawing on our wood floor, I knew. I could smell the blood on my hands.

8.

Mother said she found him in the steelyard like that, how long ago she couldn't say. I had to go look for the shotgun. A blizzard was coming in, and I knew if I waited until morning it would be buried too deep. The footpath was harder to follow in the snow. I lost it several times and had to trace back. The woods were so quiet. I missed the coyotes. I missed the black bear. I missed the sweet bobcats. I wanted to meet a wolf. I found the shotgun in a small clearing not far away. I don't know how I didn't hear it. I don't know how she dragged him so far. The snow was falling harder then, and somehow I made my way back.

9.

Come winter our child dies, and we walk the perimeter of the island, breaking frozen sand cakes under our feet. I am not in the mood to talk. The sun is small and red and falling farther south. You say you are afraid. After some time, you go home. After some time, I find that stairway again. It rises tenuously, like scaffolding, like they are trying to repair the bluff, like I am trying to repair my heart. I am sorry about a lot of things, but it doesn't seem to matter. The state ferry comes and goes around the bluff, the last one for the day. What did the angels say to you? I wonder. Was our mother among them? I imagine they spoke only in haiku. I imagine they were so beautiful.

Thirii Myo Kyaw Myint is the author of the novel *The End of Peril, the End of Enmity, the End of Strife, a Haven* (Noemi Press, 2018), which won a Asian/Pacific American Award for Literature, and the family history project *Zat Lun*, which won the 2018 Graywolf Press Nonfiction Prize and is forthcoming from Graywolf Press in 2021. She holds an MFA in prose from the University of Notre Dame, a PhD in creative writing from the University of Denver, and is currently a Visiting Writer at Amherst College.

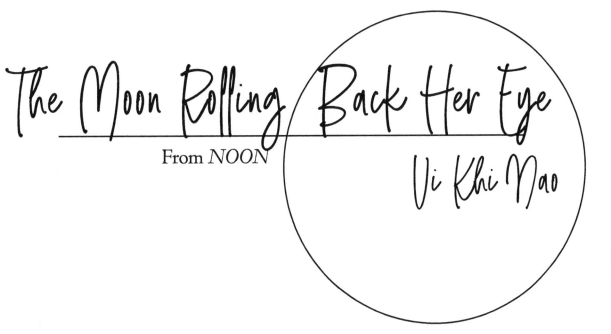

The Moon Rolling Back Her Eye

From *NOON*

Vi Khi Nao

IN MY YOUTH, WE would line up in rows for the boys to fuck us. The orgy den was in a hut. A Laotian hut or was it Cambodian? Our pants dropped to our knees and we gave up our bodies to the young boys. The beds were made out of the spines of bamboo trees and details of the orgy were organized ahead, a playful schema, sometimes with a simple knock on the wood door. I could see the earth through the cracks of the bamboo strips—deep pits and shadows crawling back and forth together as if to weave black cloud baskets to hold our prepubescent sweat and creaks. My mother spent her nights sitting in a gondola in a Cambodian riverbed plotting our seafaring exit route on the Pacific. Sometimes I sat in the gondola with my mother amongst the men. The gondola would rock under the terrified eyelid of the moon, the moon rolling back her eye so that I could see the white part exposed like a witch being fucked into having a nightmare. The men traded with Laotian communists in uniforms with handshakes and briberies. Sometimes I walked three hundred meters to a latrine. Flies flew around the yellowed urine splitting on top of smash-potato shaped shit. I half-welcomed the orgies, but walking to the latrine with flies buzzing and the need to squat in perfect alignment with the wood crates bothered me. I would put this off as long as my eight-year-old body could bear it. The grasses I walked on to get to the latrine were tall and never mowed like the grasses are mowed in the States and they were yellow like a blond girl's hair. Whenever I walked, I walked on the blond girl's hair, feeling her scalp beneath my feet. Sometimes the boys came knocking, wanting to fuck, and I didn't know if I refused or felt bored with the sex event, but something happened. My desire departed from me or perhaps I became troubled with having sex in the middle of the afternoon, when the heat groaned and escalated. I remember bearing false witness about a young boy. We were on our knees, being disciplined, perhaps for having sex too frequently or perhaps a gang of us had started the orgies, or I was leading the membership, or our discipliner, one of

our mothers, asked who spoiled the meal, and I bore false witness. I told our disciplinarian that the young, skinny boy with short black hair, dark like tar, did it. He was whipped nearly to death, bleeding before me by the bamboo stick. He did not speak a single word and did not defend his little body and took the whipping like a courageous gentleman. It took place in the middle of the afternoon, the execution of his punishment. The heat was high and his skin was raw, red thick lines crossed and uncrossed on his tiny thighs.

Vi Khi Nao is the author of *Sheep Machine* (Black Sun Lit, 2018) and *Umbilical Hospital* (Press 1913, 2017), and of the short stories collection, *A Brief Alphabet of Torture*, which won FC2's Ronald Sukenick Innovative Fiction Prize in 2016, the novel, *Fish in Exile* (Coffee House Press, 2016), and the poetry collection, *The Old Philosopher*, which won the Nightboat Books Prize for Poetry in 2014. Her work includes poetry, fiction, film and cross-genre collaboration. Her stories, poems, and drawings have appeared in *NOON*, *Ploughshares*, *Black Warrior Review* and *BOMB*, among others. She holds an MFA in fiction from Brown University.

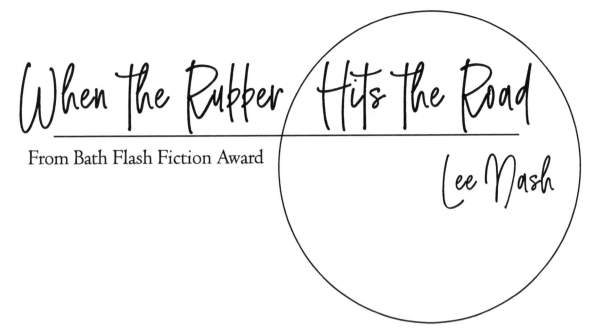

When the Rubber Hits the Road

From Bath Flash Fiction Award

Lee Nash

EVERYTHING CONSPIRED AGAINST HIM: the wind, first stealing the flames he'd kindled and torching his thatched cottage, then tearing away the corrugated iron roof of the home he'd built in its place; the Amazonian climate that finished his mother and sister; the mosquitoes and sandflies, maddening and everywhere. Everything and everyone: his business partner who walked; his long-suffering wife who at last set sail for Blighty, never to see him again, leaving Henry to his new conflict, a chain of coral islands off the coast of New Guinea; Queen Victoria and her version of justice. Still, he managed to pack those 70,000 seeds into the *Amazonas*, safely tucked between banana leaves, and now the wind was with him. Fast forward to the flames that clear the land in Malaysia and Myanmar, China and Cambodia, making room for neat rows of *Hevea brasiliensis*, to the demands of industry, the elastic bands and erasers, the half of all our tyres, engine belts, gloves, electrical wiring, emulsion paints and condoms – rubber smoothing and cooling us all the way. Fast forward once more to the infamous bio-warrior, carrying spores of South American leaf blight; with a nod to Mr Wickham he's brought an ample supply and under a dubious guise. As the aircraft touches down, he bites on a rubber bullet, thinks of the Indian slaves castrated by the barons, the cash-rich labourers' lust for cars, and welcomes the chaos that will ensue. With a measured pace, he walks his infested Wellington boots over the ripe plantations, clipboard in hand, while latex drips from the spiral scores into the waiting cups. The scarred trees recede in every direction; he flexes his leg muscles, still stiff from the flight, and starts to relax. The wind will do the rest.

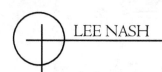

Lee Nash lives in France and freelances as an educator. Her poems have appeared in print and online journals including *Acorn*, *Ambit*, *Angle*, *Magma*, *Mezzo Cammin*, *Orbis*, *Poetry Salzburg Review*, *Slice*, *The Heron's Nest*, and *The Lake*. Her first poetry chapbook, *Ash Keys*, was published by Flutter Press. She is a 2018 Bath Flash Fiction Award prizewinner. You can find out more at leenashpoetry.com.

The Dog Lovers

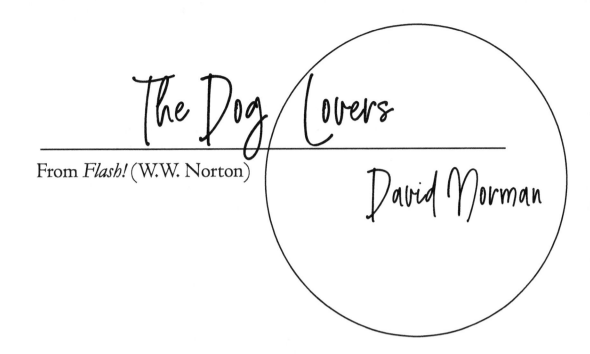

From *Flash!* (W.W. Norton)

David Norman

ON THE ISLAND, I dream I'm a conquistador straight out of one of my father's books. Not Cabeza de Vaca, but his cowardly old friend, Lope de Oviedo. I'm Lope de Oviedo, I tell myself, and in my dream I wake to see Cabeza de Vaca paddling across the bay.

He comes ashore and asks if I'm ready to escape with him back to Pánuco, civilization. His lips tremble as he speaks. Sand and white sea foam hang in his beard. I roll over on my side and shake my head and say, "It's not yet time for me, friend."

My muscles ache from the sickness that has invaded the Island. De Vaca doesn't stay long. He asks me how my captors are treating me and if my health has gotten any better. "No better, no worse," I say. When he leaves, I scavenge for crabs, oysters, fish. For their women I will carry bundled roots on my back and tread barefoot across oyster shells.

At night, I'm always limping just beyond the edge of their campfire. They never welcome me into their circle. I'm nothing more than a shadow of these people the Spaniards call the Dog Lovers. Spying, loping, starved, beaten with sticks, I am my father's least loved character.

The sea is a fire at my back. At dawn the sun bleeds out of the gulf, and the surf leaps and snaps and howls so loud I turn around, thinking it's them, the Dog Lovers. They'll blame me for this sickness, and if I can't cure them, they'll slaughter me. I'll become another victim, buried, unburied, they'll eat my flesh. All night I hear the horrible sound of their ritual weeping.

Often I'm performing some task for their women. Weaving baskets. Sharpening spears. Making a fire. Last night, one of their elders struck me across the head and laughed. She told me to dig a hole and spread her hands to show me how deep. Another woman said what goes in won't come out until we're finished with the others.

I understand their language, but I can't speak it. So I show them how I can't dig unless they let me eat the food I've gathered. I lift my arms, my withered arms, all sinew and bone.

They leave me, and I grow angry. I try to dig, but the sand collapses around my fists. The bottom of the hole rises like the bottom of an hour glass. My fingers throb. Slowly the sand turns to a wet mud that smells like rotting fish. I raise my head, I glance at the moon, the shimmering sea. I should have left with my friend. He won't come back for me.

With the moon and stars burning above, I scratch my message in the sand: Here lies Lope de Oviedo, old coward, gentleman, friend. With the sea and the Dog Lovers wailing, I lower my body into my pit of sand.

David Norman's debut novel, *South of Hannah*, received the commendation award from Impress Books and was published in 2018. His fiction has appeared in *Euphony, Real South, Image, Descant, Gulf Stream, American Literary Review, Southern Humanities Review, Rio Grande Review,* and other publications. He lives in the Texas Hill Country and plays in several local bands as a jazz pianist. Learn more about him at www.davidrnorman.com.

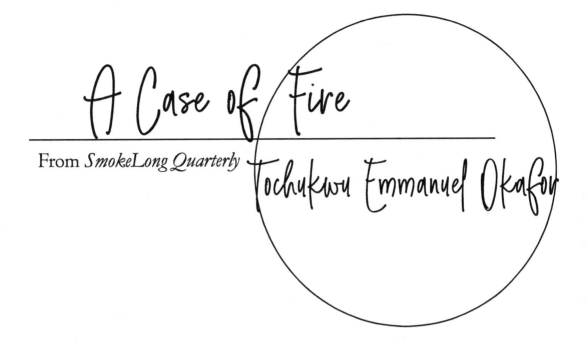

A Case of Fire

From *SmokeLong Quarterly*

Tochukwu Emmanuel Okafor

CONSIDER A CASE OF a man who sets his five-year-old niece ablaze.

The five-year-old niece, her name is Ukamaka. She has plump cheeks with skin the colour of a kola nut, her hair cropped low with a slant parting across the front hairline. She likes to run along the street, past the woman who sells fresh tomatoes and peppers and calls *Ukamaka omo mi*, past the mill that reeks of sweat, sawdust, and dung, past the unpainted bungalow where her female friends once invited her to a play but Ukamaka realizes that a little girl like her should never partake in such sort of child-adult play.

It is Sunday afternoon. The street is empty. Excepting the three Jehovah Witnesses who trudge from door to door, knocking on tar-painted gates, their lips full with the word of God. And a naked child who rolls a tyre down the street beside the open gutter. Ukamaka is running towards the pharmacy store to buy some antibiotics for her ailing mother. By the time she returns—after the Jehovah Witnesses dust their feet in places where they had been rejected, after the naked child bruises his left knee and runs home, crying—Ukamaka's mother is lifeless, stiff, on the worn earth-brown cushion. Ukamaka calls her mother by her name. She shouts, tugs at her mother's breasts, places her right ear on her mother's chest. No sound, no heartbeat, nothing. Ukamaka screams. Her mother has left her alone in this world, the same way her father did a year ago, but, in his case, a train had squashed him into scatterings of fat, flesh, and blood.

She sits by her mother's head, sobbing, whispering stories, when her uncle walks in. This man, we shall call him Uncle Arinze. After Uncle Arinze enters the room, more faces emerge. They cry, shout, pound their chests, complain to God for being so cruel and selfish, He never for once asked Himself how on earth little Ukamaka will survive this world.

She lets them shove her around. From mortuary to funeral mass to a new home with Uncle Arinze, an unmarried man who lives six streets away from Ukamaka's home. Uncle

Arinze allows Ukamaka to play with the children on the street. Some weeks later, Ukamaka begins to shit anywhere she can find. Bushes, dark street corners, school backyard, abandoned vehicles. Anywhere but Uncle Arinze's home. The first time she gets caught is at her friend's mother's barn. When the woman reports the girl to her uncle, he says he will talk some sense into her. On the night of the same day, Ukamaka receives a good beating from Uncle Arinze. Uncle Arinze buys a twenty-page notebook, tells Ukamaka to fill each line with: "I will not poo-poo in people's houses."

Ukamaka knows fully well how to use a flush toilet without supervision. Yet, ever since she lost her parents, she finds a certain kind of joy in shitting in public places—the gentle breeze caressing her buttocks, her spirits unfettered by the walls of a room. No one sees the scars inflicted upon her by Uncle Arinze. No one cares to ask after her.

The second time, Ukamaka shits in a gutter, and when she is apprehended by the local touts, they drag her by her ears to meet Uncle Arinze. The touts demand five thousand naira as fine from Uncle Arinze for Ukamaka's behavior. Uncle Arinze falls on his knees, saying, "I am only a school teacher. I teach in a public primary school. The government does not pay us well enough." The boys leave Ukamaka in the hands of Uncle Arinze. That night, Uncle Arinze heats up an iron bar on a kerosene stove and presses it into Ukamaka's back. The girl screams and screams.

A week later, she shits in an empty class at school. A teacher catches her, says she will report her to her guardian. Ukamaka begs for forgiveness, crying, both knees scraping the ground as she follows the teacher.

The news reaches Uncle Arinze's ears. He thanks the teacher.

He ambles into his room, emerges with a thin cane, and whips Ukamaka.

Ukamaka is crying, pleading. She says she will be of good behavior. She clutches to Uncle Arinze's leg as the man drags her from bedroom to sitting room to the empty front yard. Uncle Arinze has had enough. He ties her with a hessian rope around an avocado tree, drenches her with fuel. The little girl is choking, eyes bloodshot, her body pressing forward. Uncle Arinze lights a matchstick, sends the girl burning. Police arrive an hour later.

Now, Uncle Arinze is weepy. He says to the police, "I did not mean to do it. It was the work of the devil," as he is bounded off to a van, black smoke rising behind him.

Tochukwu Emmanuel Okafor is a Nigerian writer whose work has appeared in *The Guardian*, *Litro*, Harvard University's *Transition*, *Warscapes*, and elsewhere. A 2018 Rhodes Scholar finalist and a 2018 Kathy Fish fellow at *SmokeLong Quarterly*, he won the 2017 Short Story Day Africa prize for Short Fiction. His writing has been shortlisted for the 2017 Awele Creative Trust award, the 2016 Problem House Press Story Prize, and the 2016 *Southern Pacific Review* Fiction Prize. A two-time recipient of the Festus Iyayi Award for Excellence for Prose/Playwriting, he currently lives in the US and is at work on his first novel.

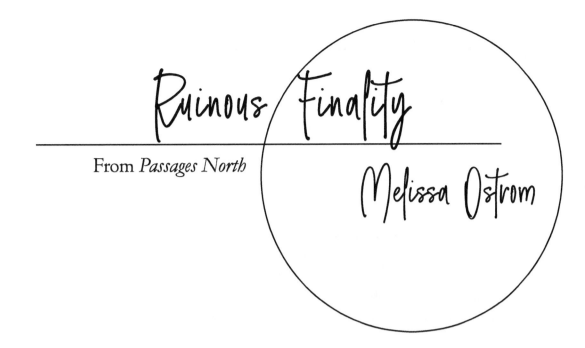

Ruinous Finality

From *Passages North*

Melissa Ostrom

BEGINNINGS PLEASE; ENDINGS SUCK. Since stopping's required, make it suggestive of further starts. Wrap up the tale with an onset: a wedding, child's birth, successful escape from oppression. Dress up declines with some relief, a light breeze. Or fail to mention them at all. The painter in love with his flushed subject forgets the young consumptive's failing lungs and celebrates the music of her breathlessness or argues for the possibility of beauty in death or pronounces poignancy in a life shuttered at its pretty stage. All neatly captured in a painting. Certainly, in the meantime, someone does not inhale without hurting. We know this. Spare us an account of the hurt. If you must hack it out, give us an embassy, a friendly shelter in the treacherous landscape. Maybe plant, at the foot of the deathbed, a hearty secondary character for whom the reader may harbor a little hope. Hope is key. Never mind the tornado. Have you ever seen a green sky? It's gorgeous. (Come on. The winds are wrenching the clapboards off the farmhouse. There goes the cow. Please, provide a cellar for our star. Reveal a cache of gold coins under the bin of potatoes. It's your story. You can do it!) Give a description of a springtime-orchard-turned-winter-fairyland, the branches sheathed in ice. But do you have to go on about the ruined crop? Must the entire village starve? Avoid epidemics. They kill the audience. Without a few survivors to weigh it, joy's more than immeasurable; it's nonexistent. Try this: *The doctor sighed and covered the still body. How sadly and slightly the wasted shape disturbed the blanket's contour. Silence hummed after the last rattling breath. With a cry—a startled sound that belied the knowing, the long, lingering knowing of death's nearness—the sister fell to the floor and buried her head in her arms, wishing she could not think, not remember, not breathe too.* Now, bring the doctor closer to this girl, let him rest his hand on her head, let her raise her wet eyes and welcome his comfort. That's enough. You need not explain the mourning process, burgeon their mutual esteem, share the guest list, spell out the vows, or enliven the marriage bed. Definitely don't hint at the possibility

of the girl following the way of her sickly sister. Of course she will follow. Everyone follows. There is nothing interesting in that.

Melissa Ostrom is the author of the YA novels *The Beloved Wild* (Feiwel & Friends, March 2018) and *Unleaving* (Feiwel & Friends, March 2019). Her short fiction has appeared in *The Florida Review, Fourteen Hills, Juked, The Baltimore Review,* and elsewhere. She teaches part-time at Genesee Community College and lives with her husband and children in Holley, New York. You can find her at melissaostrom.com and on Twitter @melostrom.

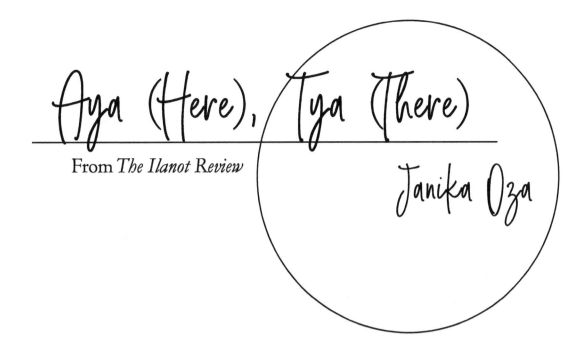

Aya (Here), Tya (There)

From *The Ilanot Review*

Janika Oza

AYA, IT IS GETTING chilly, Ma says on the phone, raining all night. The streets are flooding, and in the morning all the mangoes have fallen from the trees. The air smells like rotten fruit and the mosquitoes are coming out. It's 6:00 AM. Tya?

Aya, I say, 8:00 PM, icy cold, snow on the ground. My boots have lost their waterproof and the subway keeps breaking down. It's been okay, busy. The landlord is threatening again, too many of us to one room. They say we live as animals, but you should see how they keep their pets. Like baby princes. Remind me how you spice your okra?

Tya, where will you find okra? Ma asks. When will you find the time to make it? Come home to learn from me, then get married and make it for your husband. Aya, you can buy it from the corner, make it every day. Tya, who will sell it fresh? They eat pizza and chicken, Amrikans, don't they? They flavour it with butter and salt. Tya, they don't like spicy.

Aya, it's okay, I say. I'm doing fine. The restaurant doesn't ask for papers and the landlord turns a blind eye, so long as I do as I'm told. I know there is the possibility of permanence—an American husband, an admission to graduate school. But these are as imaginary, as distant, as home. Tya, Ma and Baba told everyone when I got into an American college, framed a copy of my student visa on the wall. But they thought I would come back. That aya, I would miss tya, in time returning so they could bring me around to the neighbours and show off my polished English and foreign experience. Sometimes I do miss it. I miss Baba's custom of playing the golden oldies on repeat in the mornings, Ma's way of spicing the okra. I want to ask again, if I need to stir cumin and mustard seed into the hot oil, but I can't remember the word for mustard seed. I feel ashamed, upended. Aya, the restaurant packs me leftovers and the Korean market sells cheap vegetables, I say instead. Aya, I'm eating well.

Baba has taken the phone, wants to know if I'm still writing papers, if I'll be published

soon. Keep trying, he says, you're doing well. You're in America now, he says, tya you have opportunities. Tya, you are making us proud. Remember to call us, he says, before giving Ma back the phone. Tya, Ma says, what else is happening?

Nothing else, I say, aya, everything is okay.

The moon is slipping behind the clouds and the 180 bus rumbles down the street. Pretty soon, I'll be on my way to work the late shift, staying past midnight to scrape chicken bones into the garbage, to sweep away stray chickpeas and wipe greasy fingerprints from menus. Tya, Ma will be brewing morning chai on the stove, grating ginger into the milk to stave off the cooling winds. Baba will sweep mangoes from the front yard like fallen leaves. Aya, in a few weeks, the snow will turn to rain. Tya, the rain will keep coming.

The next time I call home, I will remember, the way the crickets return every dusk. My people's word for mustard seed is rai.

Janika Oza is a writer and educator based in Toronto. She was the winner of the 2019 *Malahat Review* Open Season Award in Fiction for her short story, "Exile", and was longlisted for the 2019 CBC Short Story Prize. She has received fellowships from VONA, Winter Tangerine/Kundiman, and GrubStreet. Her writing is published in a number of journals including *The Columbia Review, Into The Void, Hobart, SmokeLong Quarterly,* and *Looseleaf Magazine,* among others. Find her at www.janikaoza.com.

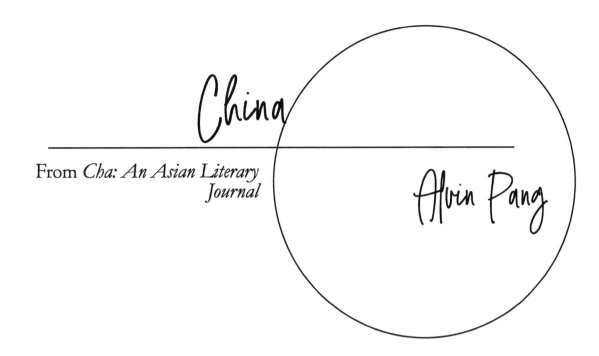

China

From *Cha: An Asian Literary Journal*

Alvin Pang

CHINA WHEN I WAS a kid was grabby relatives who wanted cigarettes in exchange for acknowledgement. Their endorsement seemed to matter to my grands who were born in China. Less so to my Singapore-born parents. Does being raised in another place make such a difference, against the vibranium weave of genetics? My mother-in-law needed glasses; her siblings in Putian did not, ever. China was cheap toys children could afford to be bullied out of in school or have broken to ensure their diligence. It was hairline cracks on vintage porcelain cups, tossed after the grands passed. It was languages we could not afford but hoarded anyway in our mouths: the soft blanket of teochew muay; the cackle of hokkien hay mee. My paternal ah ma swearing "tor jiek heong lou tor jiek guai" whenever we caspered around the apartment, stirring dust and trouble, with visiting cousins. "Zhong nei ga fan shue!" she'd yell if seriously pissed at politics or neighbours or an insolent daughter. China was being smacked with a ruler in school for uttering anything but Mandarin in Chinese class: we learnt early that speech is act, has red welt consequences. China is ah ma with my head on her lap and a chinese-styled ear-scoop deep in one canal, cleaning out wax in the last of the evening light. It is her calling me a good grandson for dropping by her bedside at the hospice, in 1998. China is my ah kong's bald head and tattoos, which I can no longer remember except that he had them. His white singlet and black kungfu pants; his gouged and homemade toolbox, smelling of singer oil and the musk of his able fingers. China was the superhero pugilists who came from China but were told to life by Hong Kong, who leapt from roof to roof in pursuit of truth, justice and the Jiang Hu way; from whose palms dragons burst forward like empowered fireballs, or flaming buddhas, or webs of inner mana. And everything had a philosophy of change and equanimity and loss. The world being put right by those a little beyond the pale. The Emperor for all his majesty could not act to save his best friend or secret sibling: the wandering master, replete with insouciant detachment. China was corrupt officials and lone, legendary lawful magistrates defying pressure from upstairs to let be, who stayed felonious princes with gilded guillotines. Was wronged patriots choosing death over political expedience. Was festivals dedicated to the few good men (usually men: women were often longsuffering, fearless, ruthlessly driven tutor-mothers, or else peerless beauties who brought down kingdoms). And always a feasting: remembrance through shape and lip. Dishes cooked up by poets, and Li Bai drunk under the moon. China in the red; in the tannic scrape of tea Wah Kong gulped down boiling with his bak kut teh. China is the schools he built in his home village: the monuments erected in his name; his ancestral muslim graves; his two wives and eight children, one of them my mother. China is his mahjong games and, on a good night thousand-dollar tips tossed at delighted grandchildren like White Rabbit candy. His six-months-to-live liver cancer, extended by TCM in China to years more of benign confusion and his children falling out over the will. China is Asian values and Taiwanese soaps about family feuds and the handwringing hard-done-by pioneerings and soft, acquisitive, ungrateful progeny. China is first generation makes, second generation keeps, third generation squanders. China is Japanese atrocities in Nanking and Singapore. Is refusing to use Sony products until the 80s. China is being tarred with the same yellow brushstroke. Is go home chink on British sidestreets. Is crosstalk dyed one tongue. Is wayang with no watchers save the dead, stopping by for the month, to keep them out of trouble. Is my sister's name, now unused, a rabbit on a boat. Is the name I share with the national orangutan. Is Confucius Institute. Is PEN's I Am Liu Xiaobo event in Cape Town, with no one else able or willing to read aloud his dustsong. Is knots I loved to pick apart as soon as I received them, the itch of their perfection too much to abide. Is basha, hardbought at the marketplace of history, not shichang. China is top grade longjing sent from Scotland by the expatriates I met at a reading, and the afternoon in which we concurred there are many different ways to be Chinese, and no compulsion. China is my daughter weeping defiant rage at being made to study one. China is boiled herbal soup and pig's brains with rice and red mushroom stew and sea cucumbers and shark's fin and starvation in the '70s. China is mess made do on every continent. China is US dollars on trans-Siberian trains. Is discount pharmacies in downtown Osaka. China is Mao's arms ticking off a watchface. China is the welling and walling up of the past. Is the Beijing Olympics. Is Shanghai jazz clubs. Is concubine villages in Shenzhen. Is maglev trains. Is the new golden horde. Is Marina Bay Sands. Is where Singapore is, states the envelope from Liverpool. I can see China from anywhere I sit. I can see it with my eyes closed. China is the us I cannot scrub off. China is not friend nor foe: it is weather, or will be. China made small enough to put in your pocket. To tweet. Will taste of temple ashes. Will stain me to the bone when I am fire.

Alvin Pang is an award-winning poet and editor based in Singapore. Featured in the *Oxford Companion to Modern Poetry* in English, and the *Penguin Book of the Prose Poem*, his writing has been published in more than twenty languages, including Swedish, Macedonian, Croatian and Slovene. An internationally engaged literary practitioner and speaker, he is a Fellow of the Iowa International Writing Program, and a board member of the International Poetry Studies Institute. His latest book is *What Happened: Poems 1997-2017.*

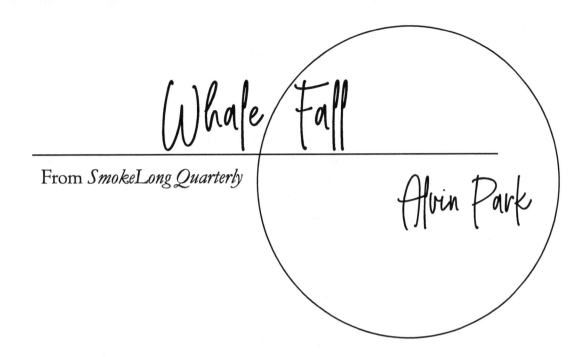

Whale Fall

From *SmokeLong Quarterly*

Alvin Park

SHE AND I WERE one year married when we made the decision and waited for the papers to remove the priest's words and our vows. I told myself we could fix this, that it was because of the village's new hunger.

We'll be better with full stomachs, I said.

With the decision came a body washed ashore. Flippers, baleen, and eyes too small. The creature dug ruts into the sand trying to roll back into the sea, to return to its family. Gasping breaths and a body like a hill. Small geysers from the stale air spit from its head.

I watched the creature starve and choke on the metal-thick air until its eyes unfocused and grayed. Before the other villagers could wake and stumble bleary-eyed and dry-lipped to this new harvest, I slung the axe, hoe, and shovel over my shoulder, tools that once dredged potatoes, cut buckwheat, and softened the rich dirt that had stopped saying *I give*. Now tools for cutting barnacled skin and heavy flesh packed tight into burlap.

Home: I called her from the door and held the sack open as it dripped red, grease, and sweat. She asked, Where did you get this? but took the bag from me without waiting for an answer. Her shirt hung loose and heavy on her shoulders. Her mouth already watered, chewing on imagined meat.

She rinsed the meat until the sea separated from sinew. In the pan, the fat blistered and melted, filling the kitchen with the smell of cold sand and iron. She tossed cubes of poached muscle in shallow bowls with pickled beets. With the blubber, she thickened pots of rice, more grit than grain.

She and I ate together, quiet except for the clank of chopsticks, spoons, the breaths between swallows.

After the meal, I lay on the floor and she sat at the bed, our lips slick with fat. How I wished for her to climb atop me like on our first night, to take me within her and bend so that I could taste that bitter salt of her skin. That she could look on my body bared that night and still desire.

Scientists came to study what was left of the animal on the beach. They split the bone-stretched skin, cut open the stomach, and found tools, dolls, and tables. They found pieces of metal from the city's refinery, jagged shards made for staying, for sticking in dirt and proclaiming dominion.

It was underweight even with the metal, the scientists said, Its meat is toxic.

It was too late for much of the village. Already the fevers, the aches, the unremembering. The priest who had eaten the meat raw as sacrament sat in his bed one morning, questioning the man next to him. He failed to recognize the sloping shoulders or gold ring or rough beard bordering soft lips that repeated *husband husband husband please*.

She spoke of forgetting as a blessing, as breathing. She said, This will make the separating easier.

I hid lists around our bedroom, an exercise in clutching or reminding. In the margins of newspapers, I wrote the color of her eyes, her favorite flower, the shape of the birthmark on her hip. In the Bible, over passages of begetting, I wrote the taste of her lips, her name, over and over, two syllables light as glass, and how often I called her by the first syllable, a sigh across her skin. On the calendar, I marked her birthday, her mother's birthday, and the day that we had first moved here, when she said, I want to live here long enough to hear the boards creak, to mistake the sounds for ghosts.

But the amnesia never came for us. In the week after the creature's arrival, the villagers unlearned their jobs, homes, and names, and I still slept on the floor each night, still dreamed of her lips those first nights when she said, I don't want to become my father, and I said, You won't, you won't, not knowing what she even meant.

I thought her desperate when she took me to the shore with the tools and burlap. The creature had long decomposed. The bones, smoothed by salt and seagull and the tongues of children, stood as archways half-buried in the sand.

Still, she swung the axe at a vertebrae, breaking it like a dish.

Still, she boiled the bone shards in seawater to turn the marrow to soup. How thin and clear the broth. How the bones had little left to give.

Still, she said, Drink this. A taste like cut grass and the memory of milk. How quickly the potion weighted my eyes. How I dreamed of my fingers curled together as one. My skin shone blue in the ocean. I swam with my lips parted and felt her pass through my bristled teeth and down my throat as krill, algae, dandelion petals.

Lips to my left ear, she said, My mother told me that whales grow gold in their chests.

She said, It's nice to imagine the gold in their bodies, all the things formed and left behind.

I said, Would it have been easier to pretend to forget? Would we have been happier?

I said, I should have been better.

I felt her shake her head, the tickle of her hair against my lungs or the hollow of my neck. She said, It's not about being better. It's about what we started with.

Sunset: I awoke from my daze, limbs sticky with sea and sand, reaching for her shape, alone. I would stumble home to where her shoes and tools should have been. I would smooth her empty bedspace searching for what I already knew. The calendar would be missing from its nail.

But there on the shore, where the waves kissed the sand, I called out her name and felt the parts of her still stuck in my neck and knees and baleen teeth, a feeling like waiting or forgetting.

Alvin Park lives and writes in Portland. He's associate fiction editor at *Little Fiction*. His work has been featured in *The Rumpus*, *The Mojave River Review*, *Wyvern Lit*, *Synaesthesia Magazine*, *Wildness*, and more. His parents are Korean. He has a long way to go.

As Petals Fall on Asphalt Roads

From *Adroit*

Aimee Parkison

SOMETIMES THERE'S FOOD ON the plate, but no one wants to eat it. No one wants to eat it, but when everyone is hungry, it's gone. It's gone, and there's music playing, piano music in the parlor where everyone's stomach is rumbling, as if talking wordlessly, complaining about the food that is gone. Complaining about the food that is gone, we stare out the windows at the rain battering the rose of Sharon as petals fall on asphalt roads. As petals fall on asphalt roads, the rain pours harder, the piano music stops, and I remember when I was a child, wondering why my mother never ate at the table, why she only ate alone when everyone else was finished and only if there was food left on the plates, though there often wasn't. Though there often wasn't, I didn't realize why she wasn't eating since because of her artful misdirection I never understood food was in scarce supply in my childhood. Food was in scarce supply in my childhood, but dreams were not on mornings when I woke, remembering the vivid pastel bakery and all the wonderful cakes I had eaten, bright cakes displayed under glass like valuable jeweled sculptures, unlike any cake I had ever seen. Unlike any cake I had ever seen, these dream cakes nourished me when I slept not realizing I was hungry because of how delicious they were. How delicious they were, even though they weren't real and would make real food seem undesirable in comparison, as the dream baker in the child's mind could prepare the unconscious food to feed unrecognized hunger. Unrecognized hunger waited like a friend with the dream baker and the dream cakes as my mother entered the bakery as if nothing was wrong with the fact that I was nude and eating all the cakes. Nude and eating all the cakes, I was never so happy until she asked why I had saved none for her.

Aimee Parkison holds an MFA from Cornell University and is the author of five books of fiction. Her most recent book, *Girl Zoo* (FC2/University of Alabama 2019), is a collaborative experimental story collection co-authored with Carol Guess. Parkison's fourth book, *Refrigerated Music for a Gleaming Woman* (FC2/University of Alabama Press 2017), won the FC2 Catherine Doctorow Innovative Fiction Prize and was named one of *Brooklyn Rails'* Best Books of 2017. Parkison is widely published and known for revisionist approaches to narrative.

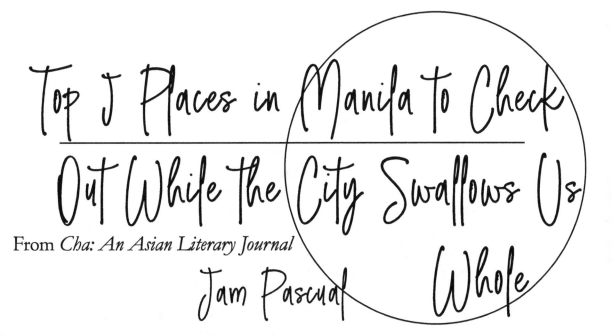

Top 5 Places in Manila to Check Out While the City Swallows Us Whole

From *Cha: An Asian Literary Journal*

Jam Pascual

after spot.ph

FOR WHEN YOU FORGET that history is the wage of ruin. Or for when the next white tourist comes over. Either way, how to be presentable in the face of what conquers? Perhaps we can begin with time, which is unkind to flesh and steel, vomits out the topical, but smoothens out the wrinkles of memory, reminds us that what used to be

5) an ocean aeons ago will eventually kiss the skin of the sun. The way we spend our summers here, we flock our feet to sand soft as the body of the next pitying lover willing to house your sorrow in its heat for the night. The alternative is the bay, and the saltwater breeze filtered through the daily revolutions of the Ferris wheel. Indigo giving way to neon. Call it development, that luminous promise of the modern. But in case you forget that within spitting distance of the dock is

4) the biggest mall in the country, sitting heavy on this place like a glass crown on the liver-spotted scalp of a withering king, they put an actual globe in the middle of the roundabout, because nothing says united nations like an enclosure of neighbouring casinos, the few remaining smoking areas since that damned Executive Order 26. Yes we have sky lights. Yes our smog is bespoke. Yes it is possible to be lost even when you know exactly where you are, if where you are is the last corner unmolested by the shadow promises of a tiger utopia. And if we're talking about the dark, you can drive to

3) that new speakeasy everybody's raving about, and by everybody I mean, whoever dethroned

the yuppies of Gen X from the high council of Gutenberg and gloss. And by the way, it isn't a fucking speakeasy just because it's hard to find. If that were true, I ought to build my own speakeasy, call it After the End of History, or A Day on the Calendar In Which All Your Friends Are Free to Hang, or Decent Fucking Wifi. One time I had this drink called ABC: absinthe, Bacardi, something costly. The language this place speaks is carved from an alphabet of sedatives. Some people say this city was also named after our capacity to thirst—may dila—so open wide, big boy, because isn't everything here just

2) a desert mouth calling out to Abraham for a drop of the last typhoon that promised a clean canvas to begin again with. Still, check out this sky deck. Babylon with a penthouse. A view that also gazes into thee. All these stories beneath us and I still can't find a solid metanarrative to ride the dick of. Better luck in the red light district. Better luck in Congress. I'll let you in on a secret: we turn the wheels of the content machine, we deal beauty, we cast pearls into the nooks where so many snouts before have burrowed into for a scrap of what flourishes in decay. May we never forget what sustains us. Let me speak of the Great

1) Jollibee Drought of 2014, and how for weeks there was no golden skin to tear from the savory morsel of all our tiny dreaming, and how back then we didn't know, I'm sorry, we didn't know the whirring in the back of the kitchen were death rattles, and we were still young enough to believe that turning back time meant we could catch the swing of its nastiest haymakers and throw it down on the mat to twist its limbs and make it consider mercy. No move in the book to get you out of this headlock. Ditch your cyanide molar tactics. It's all teeth.

Jam Pascual was a fellow for poetry for the 56th Silliman University National Writers Workshop and the 15th Iyas National Writers' Workshop. Some of his poems have been published in *Rambutan Literary*, an online journal for Southeast Asian literature. He currently works as a columnist and copy editor for *Young STAR*, the youth section of *The Philippine Star*.

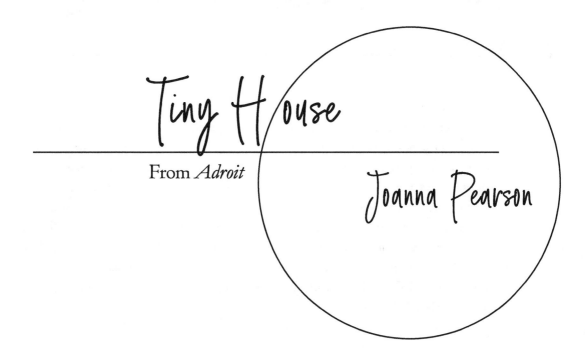

Tiny House

From *Adroit*

Joanna Pearson

WHEN PETRA BRINGS THE flyer home to Joshua, they have been living their new life for almost three months. One would think that in this amount of time, a different energy might have seized them. Their life has been distilled to its purest essence. They drink well water from a well they drilled themselves. Petra has planted a fig tree out front. They have two plates and two bowls that they wash by hand each evening, having sold most of their other belongings. At Petra's insistence, they are vegan. Everything is streamlined, concise, and in this sense, pure. It should be fulfilling. Instead, they are a little bored. Sometimes, Joshua hits his head on the ceiling.

The flyer is the first and only hint that Petra might be considering an actual job. They have cashed in a small savings account from Joshua's grandfather as well as a work injury settlement Petra got when she managed the restaurant. Since then, she has told Joshua that she is not suited to work anyway. She is a nonconformist.

"So that's what you call it," Joshua says. He has recently lost his adjunct gig teaching intro to anthropology to rich kids. He figures this means he is most likely stupid and definitely a failure. He tells Petra this, about having previously mistaken nonconformity for mere failure.

"Only in the world's eyes," Petra says, but with such disinterest that Joshua envies her. As if there are other eyes that matter. He often envies this in her: an ability to accept her own certainties. A perky obliviousness.

"I could do this," Petra says, pointing to the fine print on the flyer. "I'd be good at it."

Joshua pauses momentarily to consider the fact of the flyer itself. Who, after all, still used flyers? Everything was posted online. Joshua and Petra no longer have access to the Internet, except for a few stolen moments Joshua takes for himself at the library. Checking his email now feels like looking up hard-core porn. Petra says the Internet is rotting people's minds, and Joshua cannot help but agree, even from a place of unrequited longing.

"A cuddle partner?" Joshua says. "Really?"

And he is genuinely shocked. For all Petra's notable qualities, she is not cuddly. Not a cuddler, amateur or otherwise. There is no hint of cuddly-ness about her. She has a shock of dark hair and sharp cheekbones and two feral front teeth that abut one another in a way that is wrong and specific and yet somehow sexy. For all he has been and is attracted to her, she is not one to linger in a caress. She is not one to embrace you when, say, you have just learned of your father's suicide. Joshua still does not like to think about the day his sister called to tell him. In retrospect, of course, it made the sense of something fated: his father's long smoldering depression, his reticence, his love of 22-caliber rifles. When Joshua had told Petra what happened, she had frowned momentarily before saying to him with forced buoyancy, "There must be a bright side?"

"Talk about easy money," Petra says.

"It's weird."

"It's a service."

This is the way they tend to talk to one another: two parallel lines. Petra ruffles Joshua's hair.

He startles. Since moving in together, she has touched him even less. Quite amazing, really, the way the distance between them has only seemed to increase in such a tiny space. Joshua is aware each evening of how the pop of floss going into the crevices of his teeth seems to ring out, bell-like, and how every burble of his digestive tract is amplified. It's embarrassing. Is it possible to remain in love in such confines? He has wondered this, a purely theoretical question since Petra has disavowed the very notion of love from the moment he met her.

"Human beings are inherently lonely creatures," Petra opines. "And yet have a shocking inability to do anything about it." It is obvious to Joshua that she sees herself as the exception to this rule. Most of Petra's critical observations exclude herself. She's retracted her hand now, that brief moment of her touch lingering with a kind of electricity on his scalp. "Everyone is touch deprived."

He nods at her, his scalp still thrumming. *Ever since Dad died, you do whatever she says,* his sister had observed before they'd moved out here. For the record, Joshua has always wanted to try this. It is an experiment in living. He is considering a book proposal. He's explained this to his sister, but his sister is a practical woman, an ER nurse. Every day, she touches people with efficiency, although this is a different thing, different entirely.

"You should do it, then," Joshua says, surprising himself. He thinks of Petra curled against some other lonely man, their breath syncing, minutes slipping by while they lie there in shared human warmth, forming their own brief abode.

Petra sighs and shrugs. The air inside is warm and stagnant, redolent of the maple syrup Petra poured into her soy yogurt this morning. Her eyes have gone big and dark and distant, reminding Joshua of a deer, of the last time he'd gone hunting with his father as a boy.

Joshua had been sniffling, afraid, and there was the fallen animal, big and staring up at them with one dark eye. Joshua's father had clapped him on the back and gestured for Joshua to kneel against the deer's white belly, between his fore and hind hooves.

"Get on down there and feel," his father, usually so silent, had said. "I want you to feel it go."

And as Joshua had pressed against the still-warm deer, he was trembling, but he'd made himself small, curling tight on the cold ground and closing his eyes.

Joanna Pearson is the author of the story collection, *Every Human Love* (Acre Books, 2019). Her short stories have appeared in *Alaska Quarterly Review, Colorado Review, Copper Nickel, Ecotone, Kenyon Review online, Mississippi Review, Shenandoah*, as well as other journals, and have been noted as distinguished stories in *Best American Short Stories* and included in *Best of the Net*. She lives in North Carolina with her husband and daughters.

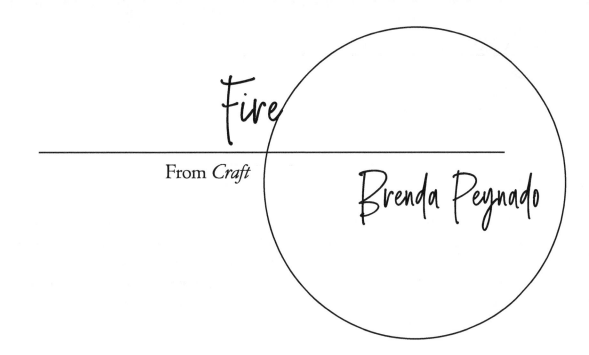

Fire

From *Craft*

Brenda Peynado

WHEN I WAS EIGHT, I watched a fire leap over the forest in glowing arcs and the men in my family battle it away. The fire had taken out farms on the panhandle for a hundred miles each way, from Tallahassee to Pensacola. I had just been put down for bedtime after the family's Sunday dinner when my uncle shook me out of bed and told me, *Go fetch the buckets, girl.*

I ran up to where I could see a glow like orange dawn over the hilltop. The heat almost burned my face off. The fire whizzed from tree to tree in arcs like deadly rainbows. The men passed buckets up the tree line. They were soaking the trees on the border of the farm in violent crashes of foaming water against bark. Trees exploded from boiling sap with deep popping sounds like drums pulling themselves open. I saw one come apart right in front of me, the sap glimmering as it burst, like amber that couldn't take its own history. I, useless with my fistfuls of empty buckets, froze at the top of the hill. I felt like something inside of me was ready to explode. I wanted to stand there until those arcs burned me with the trees. I stared, with the heat on my face, until my father finally screamed at me from the bucket line to *move*. But we were dwarfed against those loud, raging arches, and eventually the water planes got there with their rain.

While we cleared all the underbrush away, my cousin whispered, *I saw you, up there not doing anything.* I wacked him with my bucket and then he grabbed my hair and held me down in the hot mud. *You're just a girl*, he said.

I'm not a girl, I yelled, full of rage and flailing. I pushed him off and ran.

He caught up with me and grabbed my shirt by the fistful and the buttons tore, and he said, *Look, you are a girl*, as if that settled everything and we could never again be friends.

When I walked back home through the crackling woods, I left my shirt open to show what he'd done, to show the sap burning inside, to show how ready I was to burst, to turn others

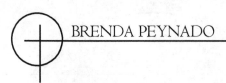

to ash, the word girl meaning *fire*.

———————————————

Brenda Peynado's stories have won an O. Henry Prize, a *Pushcart Prize*, the *Chicago Tribune*'s Nelson Algren Award, a Dana Award, a Fulbright Grant to the Dominican Republic, and other prizes. Her work appears in places such as *The Georgia Review, The Sun, The Southern Review, The Kenyon Review Online,* and *The Threepenny Review.* She received her MFA at Florida State University and her PhD at the University of Cincinnati. Currently, she teaches in the MFA program at the University of Central Florida.

Sleepover/s

From *Hobart*

Ashleigh Bryant Phillips

NICKI CHEWED ON PEN caps and twisted them with her teeth. She tore off pieces and kept them in her mouth. You could see them sitting on her tongue when she talked. I could never figure how she did that without choking.

She came into our class in the fourth grade. She'd just had her appendix taken out and the boys picked on her. Will Fletcher said she smelled like pigs. Her daddy was a hog farmer. His hog houses were back off the road on the way to school. Sometimes on the playground, when the wind blew right on the top of the swings, you could smell them.

Nicki and her family had moved down from Virginia. She had three sisters and they all had lots of freckles and long blonde hair. I'd never seen hair so thick and frizzy before. They all wore worn-out clothes that looked like mine just faded. And they all lived with their mama and daddy in front of their hog houses way back off road on the way to school. You could see their trailer sitting back there every morning. It was yellow down a long dirt path.

And Nicki had a lisp— I'd never heard anybody talk like that. She was the littlest girl in our class. She sat in front of me and her shoulder bones stuck outta her sleeveless tops. She was the second oldest sister.

When they had sleepovers it was like all the girls at school got invited. We played hide-and-go-seek and three girls would squish together in the same spot. One time I got a spot to myself in the kitchen cabinet and I saw a mouse caught in a trap. I screamed then we all screamed and then Nicki's sister Samantha came in there and told us to shut up or we'd wake up their mama and daddy. Samantha was the oldest and we all huddled together hanging outside the storm door to watch her fling that mouse off the porch. It was flying in the air when Nicki said "Look-- it's still wiggling." It's little body shined in the porch light or maybe it was moonlight before it disappeared in the yard. "Poor thing," Samantha said, "It's half dead, half alive."

Samantha always did our makeovers. I loved her to French-braid my hair. She never pulled it too tight. And to make things work good with so many girls, Samantha made a rule that when she was braiding somebody's hair, that girl would be brushing somebody else's hair and getting her ready.

At the first sleepover, Nicki asked me to brush her hair. I remember thinking that I didn't want to hurt her. There was probably lots of tangles in her thick thick frizzy hair, maybe in the little baby hairs up around her neck. But I got all her hair in my hands and smoothed it down her back. Then I started brushing from the bottom, working out the knots. And then once all the knots were gone, I took the brush and ran it down from the top of her head all the way to the bottom. I remember she shook like she had goosebumps then, turned around and giggled, "You're giving me the tinglys."

Samantha told us to hold our breath when she put her mama's nice Mary Kay mascara on us that way we wouldn't blink. And she told us how the lipstick and eyeshadow she gave us went with our season and what that all meant. And she had a special hand mirror with sparkles in it that she used to show us our new look. And then she'd make all the girls who were too scared to get makeovers get up off the living room floor where they were giggling and carrying on, they'd move their sleeping bags out the way, clear us a circle, and we'd walk around it so everyone could see our new look.

And then we'd lay down, so many of us all together. You had to tiptoe not to step on anybody. And we'd watch Titanic and look at Rose's naked body on that fancy couch, her pretty breast heaving under that big necklace. As soon as it was over the Barrett Twins would holler for somebody to rewind it. And we'd watch it again and again-- "the naked part."

In the fall Nicki's daddy got his leg tore off in one of the hog houses. He got caught in a piece of equipment. Every time anybody talked about it all I could think of was how he'd wallowed in pig shit and slosh after his leg had been ripped off, dragging himself through all that mess to get some help, with all the pigs grunting and running around, slick and mud wet.

The school threw a spaghetti supper for him. To raise money so he could get a fake leg. But when he got it, it won't quite right. Like it was too little or something and he hobbled around the best he could at basketball games. And then everyone would go to him on the bottom bleacher and shake his hand and tell him how pretty all his girls were.

Everyone put Nicki's daddy on the prayer list. And Mama gave me black trash bags and told me to put clothes in them I didn't want nomore. She said she was gonna take them to Nicki and her sisters. I filled the bags but didn't go with her. Mama came back and talked all night at supper how Nicki and her sisters smiled when they saw all the clothes, how they started trying them on right there in the middle of the living room floor.

At the lunch table the girls talked about Nicki's new dress, how they thought she looked nicer. It was black and white plaid with yellow sunflower buttons. I didn't tell them that it used to be mine. In class I thought about her shoulder bones, were they sticking out more? And I wanted to brush her hair. She turned around and asked me if she could please borrow a pen. Will Fletcher looked at me and said, "She's gonna eat it." I reached into my pencil box and grabbed a pen that I had chewed on and gave it to her. She took it and started to trace a picture of one of them wild horses running on the beach. She really liked that section in our North Carolina notebook, how those horses swam to shore after shipwrecks and stayed there in their own horse families, taking care of each other for hundreds of years in their own horse way. I watched Nicki work on the wild horses. She'd scratch out the tail and start again to get it right.

The next thing we knew all the sisters stopped coming to school one day. The teacher told us they'd gone back to Virginia. We emptied Nicki's desk out. The boys tipped it over and all her waded up homework and half used notebooks spilled out. Us girls dumped out her pencil box. She didn't really have any crayon colors we needed. She didn't really have many crayons at all. All she had was the regular colors that everybody has, nothing special. But we split them between us anyways. And I stayed and dug for a pen cap to keep.

Ashleigh Bryant Phillips is from Woodland, North Carolina and she wants to thank you for reading her work. Read more at *BULL*, *drDoctor*, *The Nervous Breakdown*, *Parhelion*, *X-R-A-Y*, *Scalawag*, and *Show Your Skin*. Follow her on instagram/twitter at @woodlandraised.

Abstinence Only

From *Passages North*

Meghan Phillips

AFTER THE GIRLS LEFT, the school started to stink. The fug of boy bodies. Old onions and sprouted garlic, a weeks-old Arby's beef and cheese, dirty socks and cum-crusted gym shorts. The girls were all sweet mint gum and cherry blossom hand lotion. Sun-warmed laundry fresh. Shampoo like the ice cream case at the farm show—creamsicle, black raspberry, cake batter, cherry vanilla. After the girls left, the health teacher's warnings took on new meaning. Abstinence was the only way to protect yourself, the only way to really be safe. We thought the girls were playing with us. Some new coy shit to to get us hard enough to rent limos for prom. To surrender letter jackets and chess tournament pins. To make it Facebook official. No fooling around in the percussion closet in the band room before school or soft hands down our waistbands or tongue-sucking, lip-mashing in the parking lot after school. No signs on game day, "Go #14" with a big heart. No texts--I <3 u, bb. After the girls stopped touching licking holding loving us, we were so lost in our sweaty-fisted longing we hardly noticed the girl-shaped gaps in our days. The empty chairs at quiz bowl, at debate, in choir, at lunch. The field hockey field, all unmarked turf. The softball diamond, chalk lines pristine. The stacks of papers passed to the front of the room were half as thick as they once were. Stuck in an endless wet dream, we didn't know on that last day when the teachers had finally had it with no homework, no essays, blank test papers and closed mouths, when they told Allie and Fatima and Bethanne and Liz and Rebecca and Shantae to take their chairs to the hall and sit until they were ready to participate, that the last thing we'd hear from the girls was the scrape of metal legs on asbestos tile. That the last thing we'd see of them was their chairs piled high on the school's front lawn, like branches waiting for a bonfire.

Meghan Phillips is the author of the chapbook, *Abstinence Only* (Barrelhouse, 2019). Her stories and poems have appeared in *Wigleaf*, *Barrelhouse*, and *Strange Horizons*, among others, and have been nominated for the *Best of the Net* anthology, *Best Microfiction*, and *The Pushcart Prize*. She lives in Lancaster, PA with her husband and son.

The Bug Man

From *Alligators at Night* (Ad Hoc Fiction) and Tin House

Meg Pokrass

MA OFTEN SAID THAT despite everything, we were lucky people, because the Bug Man came over to our house for free, sprayed in places nobody had ever seen. Places that we never knew were there.

Happy times were when the Bug Man pulled up, in his strange truck with a giant plastic model spider glued to the top of it.

"Your mother means business," he said to Josh and me, blinking into the sunlight.

"You're one lucky dog," he said to Muttsy.

Once, when he came to spray, he hugged Ma in the side yard. They seemed to want privacy. I watched them from the upstairs bathroom window. Ma looked pretty in his long skinny arms, like a different mother.

I thought that maybe our lives could change. He could marry us, become our father and take us to live in a large, bugless house.

But three days before Christmas, Ma, reading the newspaper, slammed down her coffee cup. It splattered the table, dripped onto the floor.

"Ma, are you okay?"

She sat mesmerized, glaring at the newspaper. I grabbed a roll of paper towels to clean up the brown puddle at her feet.

"Cancer, just like his father who started the goddamn pest company!" Tears rolled quickly down her nose. "He's already gone," she said, sobbing.

I hated the word. "Cancer." She looked bitter and ugly saying it, as though it was stuck between her front teeth. Josh ran outside, good at acting like nothing was wrong.

Watching her cry, my ankles itched. They were already covered with flea bites. Soon,

families of spiders would bubble up through the floorboards.

I cut out the Bug Man's obituary, as if he had belonged to us.

Meg Pokrass is the author of a novella-in-flash from the Rose Metal Press and five flash fiction collections, most recently *Alligators At Night* (Ad Hoc Fiction, 2018). Her work has been anthologized in two *Norton Anthology Readers*, *Best Small Fictions*, 2018, *Wigleaf* Top 50, and has appeared in 350 literary magazines including *Electric Literature* and *Tin House*. She serves as Flash Challenge Editor for *Mslexia Magazine*, Festival Curator for Flash Fiction Festival, U.K., Co-Editor, *Best Microfiction* 2019, and Founding Editor of *New Flash Fiction Review*. Meg teaches flash workshops in various parts of the world. Find out more here: megpokrass.com.

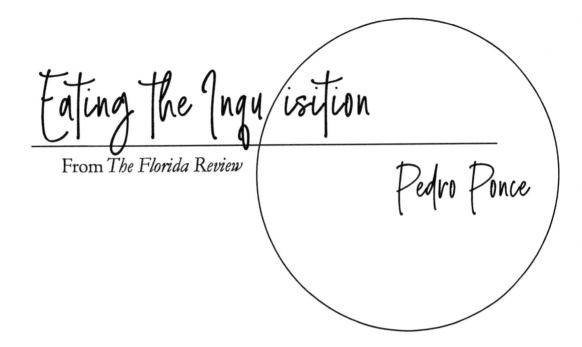

Eating the Inquisition

From *The Florida Review*

Pedro Ponce

I'M EATING THE INQUISITION. My friends look askance, dissembling disgust as I fork a bishop's mitre into my mouth. I sop sauce with ribbons of parchment declaring an auto-da-fé, twirl them on the tines of my fork, burn my tongue on confessions al dente. Dinner conversation limps along over the sound of my mastication. Are you really going to finish all that? someone asks. I could ask for a box, but leftovers inevitably disappoint. The Inquisition must be eaten all at once, piping hot, just as the crowd has assembled in the town square. Fistfuls of kindling distend my stomach with pleasant pain. I will not sleep tonight as my stomach pulps quills and ink pots, knouts and choke pears. I will slump against propped pillows as the crowd inside me screams for justice and, much later, mercy.

Pedro Ponce's short fiction has appeared in numerous journals, including *Split Lip Magazine, Copper Nickel, Gargoyle, Queen Mob's Tea House, Witness, Ecotone,* and *New Flash Fiction Review.* His work has also been anthologized in *Funny Bone: Flashing for Comic Relief, New Micro: Exceptionally Short Fiction, Boundaries Without: The Calumet Editions 2017 Anthology of Speculative Fiction* and *Sudden Fiction Latino: Short-Short Stories from the United States and Latin America.* In 2012, he was awarded a creative writing fellowship from the National Endowment for the Arts. He teaches writing and literary theory at St. Lawrence University.

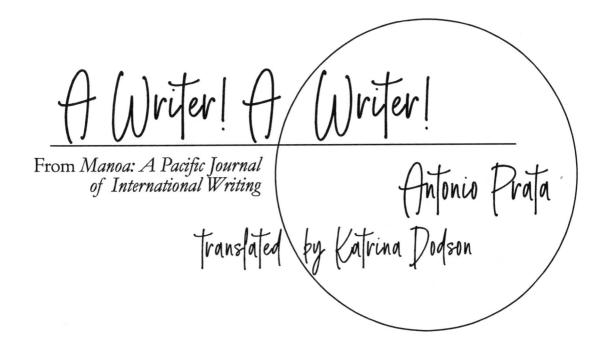

A Writer! A Writer!

From *Manoa: A Pacific Journal of International Writing*

Antonio Prata

Translated by Katrina Dodson

WITH THE NEWSPAPER IN one hand and a Diet Guaraná in the other, I was roaming the streets of Kiev, dodging roadblocks and Molotov cocktails, when the voice on the PA system brought me back to seat 11c: "Attention, passengers, if there's a doctor on board, please alert a flight attendant."

There was that discreet commotion: everyone whispering, peering around, looking for whoever was sick and hoping for a doctor, until, from the back of the aircraft, our hero emerged. He came walking up with a surefooted stride— salt-and-pepper hair, as you'd expect—his vanity cloaked in slight reluctance, like some Clark Kent who, at that moment, was less interested in showing off his superpowers than eating his peanuts.

A flight attendant met him in the middle of the aisle and hurried him over to a plump older woman who was clutching her head and hyperventilating in the first row. The doctor crouched, took her pulse, listened to her chest and back, talked with her in hushed tones, then spoke to the stewardess. They brought over a metal box; he gave the woman a pill and less than ten minutes later went back to his peanuts, under the admiring gaze of everyone on board. Well, almost: my admiration, I must admit, was quickly gnawed away by envy.

Look, by the time the practice of medicine was born with Hippocrates, the tale of Gilgamesh had already been circulating the world for over two millennia. Since time immemorial, while the body was left to its own devices, the soul has been examined by myths, verses, fables—and nevertheless . . . Nevertheless, dear readers, who's ever heard a stewardess ask anxiously, "Attention, passengers, if there's a writer on board, please alert a flight attendant"?

I wouldn't be fazed. I'd shut my newspaper calmly, slip a pen and napkin into my pocket, go over to the plump woman, and crouch by her side. We'd talk in hushed tones. She'd confess to me—who knows? that she was about to reunite with her son after not speaking for ten years; she wanted to tell him something that sounded nice, but wasn't good with words. I'd establish a quick medical history, asking what had led to the fight, her son's name, whether he was more of the MFA or MMA type. Ten I'd throw in a few pleasant memories of their relationship, life a line or two of poetry from Drummond de Andrade—or the Ramones, depending on her taste—and, prior to landing, I'd hand the woman three paragraphs that could make even a rock burst into tears.

On the way back to my seat, passengers would say hello or share similar stories. A young mother would tell me about her cousin the poet who, upon hearing the cries of a waiter while at a restaurant—"A writer, for God's sake, a writer!"—was brought over to a lovesick young man and managed to write his marriage proposal on a card in a bouquet of flowers before his future fiancée came back from the ladies' room. A gentleman would remark upon the wellknown case of the novelist who was on a cruise and, at the pleading of three thousand tourists, had managed to convince two hundred crew members to stop calling them "you guys." I'd smile, ever so slightly, and say, "It's true: if you choose this profession, you've got to be prepared for emergencies." Then I'd politely decline the pack of peanuts offered by my seatmate and return to the bombs of Crimea, with my cup of Guaraná.

Born in São Paulo in 1977, Antonio Prata is one of *Granta's* 2012 Best of Young Brazilian Novelists and widely regarded as a master of the short literary sketch known as the *crónica*. Prata has been a columnist for Brazil's leading daily, *Folha de São Paulo*, for nearly a decade and is the author of a dozen books, including the *crónica* and memoir collections *Meio Intelectual, Meio de Esquerda (Kind of Intellectual, Kind of on the Left*, 2010), winner of the Brasília Literature Prize; *Trinta e Poucos (Thirtysomething*, 2016); and *Nu, de Botas (Nude, in Boots*, 2013). His children's books include *Felizes Quase Sempre (Almost Always Happy*, 2013) and *Jacaré, Não! (Alligator, No!*, 2016).

Katrina Dodson is the translator of *The Complete Stories* by Clarice Lispector, winner of the 2016 PEN Translation Prize and other awards. She is currently adapting her Lispector translation journal into a book and translating the 1928 Brazilian modernist classic, *Macunaíma, the Hero Without Character*, by Mário de Andrade (New Directions). Her writing has appeared in *The Believer, McSweeney's*, and *Guernica*. Dodson holds a PhD in Comparative Literature from the University of California, Berkeley and has been a fellow of the Fulbright Program, National Endowment for the Arts, MacDowell Colony, and Banff Centre. She currently teaches translation at Columbia University.

Born of Driftwood

FromThe Southern Review

Gretchen Steele Pratt

On the Outer Banks in the early 1900s, a migratory sand dune, several stories high, engulfed the small fishing village of Seagull. Two churches, the post office, thirty-five homes, and the one-room schoolhouse were consumed by the dune.

TEACHER IS BUILDING A shack of driftwood, building it on the far shore. We watch from the schoolhouse windows, taking turns with her old silver binoculars. She gathers all manner of driftwood into her apron and sometimes passes by the beach in front of the school but does not turn her face to us.

Born of driftwood endowed with breath we are—began that old story Teacher had to close her eyes to tell. She spreads the wood to dry and eats nothing and takes not a drink but smokes her pipe. Eyes dry as opals and the sand and wind drying her from the inside out—*petrified*, as Teacher would say. Sister says her bones are *anyway filling with sand*.

Where is the lighthouse keeper? The light is out. There had been no beating it to the boats, no crowded bridge. Sister says at the tip of this spit of an island a wave of sand has begun its slow roll down through the land, a tidal wave of sand swallowing the trees right up to the grapevines that hang from the top branches, swallowing the barns and the cows sleeping in them, their nostrils choked with sand—*sand-killed*, as Sister would say. A tidal wave of sand never crashing toward us and no stopping it as long as the hot wind does blow.

And so each night the ghost crabs swarm down the whole shore, we hear the claws and shells scuttling over each other, and do they bother Teacher? And moths beat like birds against the schoolhouse windows. Morning comes and Sister pulls the rope, the bell clangs above us but not to wake Teacher who is already neck high in her cocoon of driftwood and weaving more on.

Mosquitoes the only weather thick most mornings with the sun and we keep the windows closed. Clouds of mosquitoes like ghosts work our little patch of garden. They never bothered with Teacher on our old walks by the marsh passage—her being made of smoke but smokeless—she is, then winking, walking backward to face the line of us through the water grasses though our legs be already welted with bites.

We were waiting for Teacher to harvest the school-yard garden. We all sunk the seeds in the spring and now so long without rain the melons rot on the vines, sunken, sucked looking. good folks is scarce take care of me—the sign we painted in the middle of the garden hanging by one nail.

The buoys gong in the rainless sun-blown squalls. Our books are brittle and everything is so dry. The map of this island curls on the wall. And turning to tinder the pictures of the flora—bald cypress, sweet pepperbush, yaupon, cordgrass, switchgrass, blue-eyed grass.

Teacher will lay us all down one by one limp like just-hatched birds in her nest of driftwood but I don't tell Sister.

Sister spends her days drawing the growing sand wave on the chalkboard. She says it is now entering the island's graveyard the laurel all withered. And the graves being but sand-filled will be gathered up, the coffin tops will dry and crack and pop their nails. Where once was only the shade of oaks and cedars.

At night the slowest breaking of glass, ever closer, pane by pane the wave swallows the homesteads. Our ears are licked by the heat. The ocean grows smaller and farther from us. Teacher must walk farther each day down to the wrack line.

The windows of the schoolhouse grow cloudy with moth ash. We wait. We have shed all manner of clothing. We grow light, waterless in the slow trough of the sand wave. *Bleached as bone*, Sister says. *Bones light as kites.*

It towers at the edge of the school yard, the tall pines crack. No stopping it as long as the hot wind does blow. Burning, but smokeless, smokeless. We can hardly hear the surf, so far has the ocean left us. Teacher will row to us from across the sand in her boat of driftwood. She will gather us in her apron and lay us down curled inside the hull. The sea far away now, emptying itself wave by wave of this white wood.

Gretchen Steele Pratt is the author of *One Island* (Anhinga Press). Her work has recently appeared or is forthcoming in *Southern Review, Beloit Poetry Journal, Fairy Tale Review,* and *Ecotone.* She lives in Matthews, North Carolina, with her husband and three children and she teaches at the University of North Carolina at Charlotte.

Upon Discovering That Cows Can Swim

From *Jellyfish Review*

Santino Prinzi

YOU'RE ON A BOAT on Lake Nicaragua. A tour. Your reflection in the water is murky, like a shadowy chartreuse twin staring up from beneath the surface. You want to touch her, your twin, but you don't. You're always refraining. That's when you hear their breathing, and you're not the only one. Others on the boat have spotted the cows grazing on floating foliage. You look up to see another cow swimming down the creek. She looks majestic, graceful, her horns sharp and glistening. You want to fashion a wreath from wildflowers and crown her. The captain conducting the tour says cows are his favourite animal and he rubs his stomach. You spy the stomach hanging from beneath his t-shirt, that reddish-pink of flesh peeping from polyester. There's nothing friendly about this. The others laugh at his jokes while you contemplate veganism. The swimming cow rests with the others and grazes. You watch, knowing this is the most unusual thing you'll see on this trip. When you have signal on your phone, you'll google to check if cows can swim because you need to know if something this marvellous is real. Because you need to know that something so marvellous can be real.

Santino Prinzi is a Co-Director of National Flash Fiction Day in the UK, a Consulting Editor for *New Flash Fiction Review*, and is one of the founding organizers of the annual Flash Fiction Festival. His flash fiction pamphlet, *There's Something Macrocosmic About All of This* (2018), is available from V-Press, and his flash mini-collection, *Dots and other flashes of perception* (2016), is available from The Nottingham Review Press. To find out more follow him on Twitter (@tinoprinzi) or visit his website: santinoprinzi.com.

No One's Watching

From *Atticus Review*

Melissa Ragsly

GERALDINE HEARD HER MOTHER and father come up with another reason to sell the house. They watched Geraldine dabble at the edge of the surf, her mother straightening a kerchief and her dad in his pullover despite the sun pinching at them with rays like claws. It was time to go eat and Geraldine was still in her swimsuit. Their beach was small, the water level had risen in the past few years. Now there was only a strip of sand before the sod of their yard began. She didn't care if the water came up to the back door, Geraldine told her parents she wouldn't let them sell the house, not to bother calling that broker from the ads on the local news.

Geraldine had put up with changes and she didn't like them. She didn't like when she moved up to the new school and had to memorize a locker combination. She didn't like her new polka-dot bra whose straps would never stay up. She hated how her mother's body was getting smaller as hers grew, as if she was greedy, stealing the flesh that fell away from her mother. She hadn't lived a long life and yet each year that passed forced a universe of change on her. Geraldine was tired of this seemingly unending process of metamorphosis.

When Geraldine was small, her mother would hold her over the surface, dunking her chicklet toes in the foam. The cold jolt of water would send her giggling into her mother's arms, so smooth and glassine, like a waxed cherry. Now her mother was a grid of skin tags from arm to neck, her face pitted and sandpapery, like her father's on Sunday mornings. Only when her mother submerged herself all the way under the salt water and stayed down, did her disease flake off. She seemed momentarily healed, as if the key to survival was almost drowning.

Her parents waited for her to get up but the liquid felt cool like her insides got when she let the tide splash between her legs. She didn't want to leave the spot she made for herself, a hollowed-out divot just big enough for her to sit in. She wiped off the sand glomming onto thin hairs below her knees.

She watched her parents give up and get smaller as they headed towards the horizon of the house. They gave her a five-minute warning but Geraldine couldn't see the temperature of their glares in the sun. If they were kidding or if they were lying about time like parents did.

Geraldine had to pee. Her mother used to tell her to go ahead and pee in the ocean.

No one cares, Geraldine. Just go in your suit.

But everyone's gonna see it all turn yellow.

Honey, no one's watching. I'm the only one here.

Geraldine insisted on being covered. In a satiny pink bathing suit, her mother looked like the smooth inside of a conch. Geraldine squatted and made herself into an easel. She told her mother to look away. And when she was in the middle of letting it all out, the stream unstoppable, her mother would look back at her and they'd lock eyes.

She saw her father waiting for her through the wide mouth of the kitchen window, cooling off under a ceiling fan. She picked up a shell and put it to her ear knowing that he would pick up the wall phone. He was mouthing something, popping off like bacon frying. She barked into the ear-like folds of the shell, *I can't hear you.* He hung up the phone when her mother called out to her from the open door, that it was too late for the Club, she'd draw Geraldine an oatmeal bath and they'd make due with sandwiches.

You're red as a lobster, her mom called out to her.

Lobsters are black before you boil them!

Geraldine sat holding in her pee. The sun flared and fell closer. Geraldine felt hungover from it, like the day after drinking the dregs of rum and pineapple on Christmas. She fell in and out of sleep on the sand, a second or two of grogginess alleviated by discomfort. Her body ached with burn and she considered letting the undertow take her out to cure her of her ills, but her mother's voice would never escape her. She heard her saying that thing people said about what daughters become. She heard it in her head and removed the shell from her ear. Her mother's voice used to be softer. She could harmonize it with the gulls once, until it deepened after a treatment. Her mother was better for a while, but her voice never returned.

Geraldine tried to make it back to the house but only got as far as the grass. It was an okay house on the beach and it would make everything easier to get rid of it. The money. It would change things. *I'm never going to have this again,* she heard herself say and she tried to say it how her mom would. Before.

She'd felt drops from her suit. She couldn't tell if it was still wet from the ocean or if she let out the pee she'd been holding in. She turned and saw her father there big and still as a boulder wrapped in his sweater. Sirens sharpened the air, closing off her ears like how the sun flares so bright it goes from illuminating the world to bleaching it out to nothing.

Melissa Ragsly's work has appeared or forthcoming in *Best American Nonrequired Reading, Iowa Review, Epiphany, Hobart, Joyland, Cosmonauts Avenue* and other journals. She is an Associate Editor for *A Public Space* and a Program Coordinator at the Authors Guild and is currently working on a novel. More can be found at melissaragsly.com.

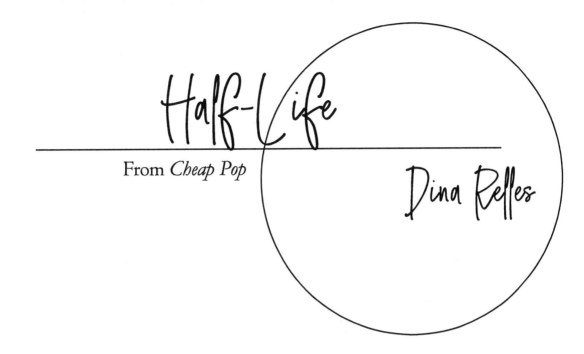

Half-Life

From *Cheap Pop*

Dina Relles

AFTER THE KIDS CRUSH the moth on our driveway, I can see its rich red underwings more clearly. My oldest flits off to destroy an ant hole along the street's edge. My younger son and I stay and stare at the crunched wings and legs, what's now just a shell of a thing.

The sky's cadaver blue and you can hear the first cracks of thunder over the hills that taunt beyond our yard. We run inside ahead of the rain.

"I'm scared," says the littlest, who sleeps on the floor, when the storm wakes him in the middle of the night.

I think, *me too*, but don't say. I sit cross-legged beside him on the carpet, my fingernails, jagged stubs, stroking his soft, hairless back. I'm scared of rain we run from. Of storms that stay at our backs. Of empty nights that fall one into the next. Scared, not of the dying, but of living half a life.

A half-life, in nuclear physics, is the time it takes for something to reduce to half its original value.

That night, I dreamt in metaphor—a man I hardly knew placed his hands on my C-section scars. I woke and wrote in the morning: *We used to chase fireflies in your front yard and now you call me 'old friend.'*

What I want to write is how it feels to be in the night air with someone who's not mine. The suggestive way dew smells before sunrise. The thrill I get from driving too close to the median strip on Brookside Road.

Sometimes I'll undress in front of the black window, lights on, and wonder if anyone's watching.

It's when isotopes become unstable that they begin to decay, emitting radiation in levels that could be harmful.

I took the express train all those years ago, after the boy in Brooklyn let me loose, watched the Raritan River pass through the Plexiglas. I married the man under the mistletoe at the other end of the line. We moved out to the country. Bought a van. Sometimes we take a drive just to be anywhere other than where we've been.

Isotopes can lose enough of their atomic particles to turn from one element into another.

When I'm alone, I play radio music too loud and cry at the sight of cornfields and spend long afternoons on the blacktop with the children circling round.

The term half-life can also refer to any type of decay.

And now I see the kids have crushed—sneaker to asphalt—not a moth, but a spotted lanternfly. A parasite invading where we live, threatening the fruit trees and farms. One thing always gives way to another. Not everything goes on.

What I want to say is: I'm still alive.

Dina L. Relles' work has appeared in *The Atlantic, matchbook, Monkeybicycle, Hobart, CHEAP POP, Passages North, DIAGRAM, River Teeth,* and *Wigleaf,* among others. She is the Nonfiction Editor at *Pidgeonholes* and an Assistant Prose Poetry Editor at *Pithead Chapel.* More at dinarelles.com or @DinaLRelles.

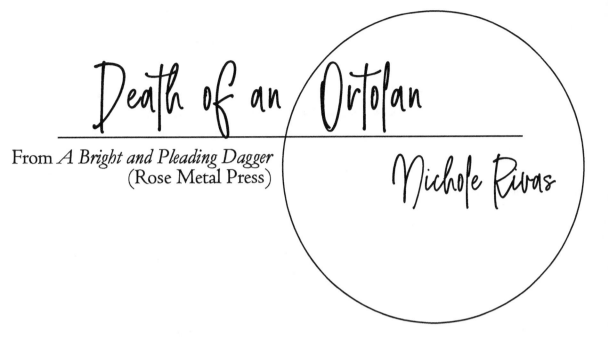

Death of an Ortolan

From *A Bright and Pleading Dagger*
(Rose Metal Press)

Nichole Rivas

ON MY FIRST DATE with Penny I was very nervous because I was only nineteen and Penny was fifty-two. Over coffee, she told me that she was divorced and had two kids, both older than me. Actually, Penny was already a grandmother. She said her grandson's name was Carapace, which I know for certain because I had to ask twice. Penny and I talked a lot about the war, and I said some pretty stupid things that I quickly regretted. But Penny didn't see things that way. *You have a beautiful mind, like a curly Q*, she told me. I had never been on a date with a woman before, and so I hid my hands beneath the table and tore my paper napkin into tiny pieces. I couldn't believe it when Penny said she wanted to see me again. I went home that day and wrote all about it in my diary.

On our second date, Penny and I went to an aquarium. She paid for both of our tickets because I was only working part-time at a pizza shop and making minimum wage. Penny, on the other hand, was a gynecologist. More specifically, she was my gynecologist. When we were watching the piranhas rip apart a human cadaver I said, *Penny, I've been thinking and I'll feel terrible if this turns into something real. I don't have anything to offer you. I'm not even in college.* And I couldn't believe it, but as soon as I said that, Penny grabbed me by the shoulders and kissed me on the lips. Her tongue was like the inside of a tomato. When she pulled away she said, *It's too late, because this is already something real. I love you more than I love my own children.*

On our third date, Penny and I had a picnic and she showed me how to eat an Ortolan. I thought we were just going to have some cheese and maybe some grapes, but she pulled these little balls of foil out of her picnic basket, and when she unwrapped them I saw that they were tiny birds. She explained that they were caught in nets, stabbed in the eyes, fed excessive amounts of grain, drowned in jars of brandy and roasted. I was horrified, which led to a deep, philosophical conversation about good and evil, but before I could get reoriented Penny said,

Hurry up, your Ortolan is getting cold. And I suddenly realized that I didn't want my Ortolan to get cold, even though that morning I'd never even heard of an Ortolan. Penny handed me a cloth napkin to put over my head while I ate the bird bones and all—a tradition. I was so nervous, because this was only the third date with a woman I'd ever been on, let alone a gynecologist, my gynecologist, and it was a good thing those napkins were cloth, or else I would've ripped them to shreds all over again.

Nicole Rivas teaches writing in Savannah, GA and holds an MFA in Creative Writing from The University of Alabama. Her chapbook of flash fiction, *A Bright and Pleading Dagger*, was the winner of the Rose Metal Press 12th Annual Short Short Chapbook Contest. For more, visit www.nicolemrivas.com.

Dientes for Dentures

From *Kenyon Review*

Laura Roque

ABUELA WOULD NEVER SCREAM my name. Not even when I was being an eleven-year-old descarada, strutting my stuff in a uniform skort, a half block in front of her so the seventh and eighth graders would think I had parents that let me walk home alone. (This being after la pobre vieja walked across Hialeah so I wouldn't have to, so Mami wouldn't have to imagine my kidnapping and suffer eighteen anxiety attacks whilst speeding toward Job Two). Whenever Abuela had it up to here with me, when I swiped her sewing scissors and dulled them with canvas paper, when she caught me holding them by the blades like a Victorian barber, or when I lost said scissors indefinitely (usually around crunch time for a seamstress, like Halloween or Noche Buena), Abuela would bark my name, a bark that echoed like she was chasing me in a cave, a bark like a Rottweiler's, like the Rottweiler she fought off with her bare hands in '99 on the corner of La Ocho y La Cincuenta y Nueve. She was seventy-six and gouging the eyes of the freaking Chupacabra in the middle of the street; I was nine and catapulted onto the sidewalk, sent sailing out of harm's way by esa vieja loca. By the time Chupa's owner bolted out of his house, said Rottweiler was without his right eye.

"Señora, señora," Chupa's owner begged, holding the bloody dog by the fat of his neck, "Let's take you to a hospital." I remember him in work boots and faded jeans stained with every shade of paint, shaking so ferociously I thought the stains might liquefy and drip off. Abuela waved him away, threatening him with her owl eyes when he attempted to come to her aid. She inspected her massacred calf with pursed lips, patting the little ivory hairs that had escaped her impeccable sock bun. I was freakishly unscathed, like she'd cast a protection spell before she flung me, sent me floating with magic like some bruja, although she was a devout Jehovah's Witness and would've set the Rottweiler on me for even making a demonic joke like that.

"Abuela, y si tienes rabies?" I'd asked. She didn't respond, just sucked her false teeth.

I know, per Cuban and/or American myth, that if one dreams of teeth loosening from gums and dropping, it means someone close to the dreamer will die. Abuela's been toothless in her sleep since before I was born. Back in Cuba, in her mid-50s, she willingly substituted her dientes for dentures. Mami told me so, over two decades after Abuela maimed the Rottweiler. By then Abuela was speechless and unable to explain herself.

Although Abuela was mi Papá's mother, Mami frequented Seasons Hospice, warmed the turquoise pleather chairs in Abuela's room, more than I did. I made time at least once a week, and the two of us would find ourselves watching la vieja on a bed so white I figured they were trying to give it the appearance of angel wings, make it as close to a chariot to the other side as possible. A broken femur, a surgery to fix it, and the dementia that inspired Abuela to claw at her stitches like they were proof of alien experiments, had her strapped to super-white beds.

"I hate seeing her without her teeth," I said, watching Mami moisten Abuela's tongue with a little sponge. Abuela's eyes were half-closed, but she was asleep. Her mouth was open and wrinkled inward in an uninterrupted black hole, like the well that was her only water source en el campo en Cuba, before Castro's men seized her mother's farm.

"She looks even less like herself," I said. Abuela had suffered a stroke the night before, and half a functioning face wasn't enough to keep dentures in place.

"She's had those false teeth," Mami said, returning the sponge to a glass of water and wiping her hands on her jeans, "since before she was my age, lo sabías?"

"What happened to her real teeth?" I asked.

"She got an infection en Cuba, in one tooth, y le dijo al doctor to take them all out then, pa'l carajo."

"What did Papi say?" I asked.

She sighed, easing herself onto the seat beside me, "Tu Papá already knew that his mother was media loca."

"Because she was a communist?" I asked, as a nurse entered.

"Buenas," the nurse said monotonously, and Mami and I buenas'd back in unison.

"Eso también," Mami said, holding her phone at arm's length to squint at Facebook notifications, her glasses hanging at her chest.

I used to picture Abuela's communism in black and white, imagine old movies of her in a tight, pencil skirt that slithered to a classy just-below-the-knee, a tucked-in blouse with tasteful ruffles, her hair jet-black and cut under large ears, marching with an equally emotional crowd of more slithering pencil skirts and men with bottle-cap glasses, all shouting a todo pulmón, "Fidel, amigo, el pueblo está contigo." I could see Abuela attending meetings of the party, proudly and dutifully giving intel on potential Yankee imperialist traitors to the neighborhood watch.

I could also see Abuela powdering apart like talc when she herself visited the US of A and decided to stay, knowing her only son's future plans fell anywhere between fake passports to building a raft of stolen materials, anything to get to where he openly called "Libertad." Abuela became a US citizen because I was born one, all the while loving Fidel Castro with the same ardent fervor, the same desperate blaze she used to love her only son, the only person who hated communism more than José McCarthy himself.

Mami always said Abuela's Fidel fetish was proof of a mental illness, one she had long before dementia. After the revolution, the guys in green showed up like they owned the place (because they were about to), gave Abuela and her entire family twenty-four hours to evacuate the only home they'd known, and the morning of, her oldest brothers were found in the stables, swinging lifelessly from ropes.

"*Love* Fidel Castro?" Mami said, scoffing at either Fidel or the Cozumel 2016 album on her phone's screen. "Someone who manipulated his people? Made them afraid of things that weren't true to control them? Alguien who turned us against each other so we couldn't abrir los ojos, realize who the real problem was?"

"Cubans love repeating their mistakes," I said. "Look at who they follow here."

Mami set her phone on her lap. She held her glasses between her eyes and me to get a good look at the girl she and her communist mother-in-law raised alone, but together.

I slid my chair from Mami's purview, parked it next to Abuela. I alternated between staring at the fluorescent bulbs and the purple dots my eyes made on the walls before spotting the plastic box on the bedside table. I snatched it, replaced it with my feet, crossed them at the ankles. I shook the box, held it to my ear like a seashell, only instead of the ocean I could hear Abuela's teeth rattling.

Laura Roque is the daughter of Cuban political exiles and was raised in Hialeah, FL. She was honorably mentioned by *Glimmer Train* in 2016 and was first runner-up for FSU's Creative Writing Spotlight award in 2017. In 2018, she was the winner of the *Kenyon Review*'s Short Fiction Contest and *Glimmer Train*'s Fiction Open Contest.

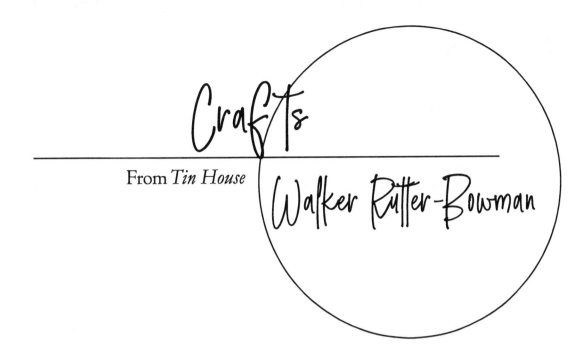

Crafts

From *Tin House*

Walker Rutter-Bowman

GLITTER

I TELL THEM TO glue first. They drag the orange nose of the glue bottle across the paper. I come around with the glitter, see what they've done—words, hearts, animals, suns. I sprinkle the glitter on the glue lines.

"But why can't we do it?" they ask, their little hands reaching for the shaker of glitter.

"I have to be the one do it," I say. "I know how to sprinkle the glitter. If you did it, the glitter would all flump out in a pile. It would be chaos."

"What's chaos?"

"It's when glitter spills everywhere. And then sticks to everything. Sticks to you. To your skin. For weeks, months."

Their eyes go wide. They touch their cheeks, imagine themselves covered in it. Then they look down at their papers, their arcing ridges of sparkle. Their eyes and thoughts move down and in; they pack themselves into the silvery gleam.

CONSTRUCTION PAPER

For Thanksgiving we make turkeys out of construction paper. For the feathers, there are orange, red, and yellow pieces of paper cut into teardrops. For the bodies, there are brown oblongs. For the eyes, there are wiggle eyes. The construction paper rasps when handled. While the kids work, I sit behind my desk, rub my knuckles on a grainy sheet of yellow.

At the Thanksgiving assembly, the kids sing songs about wheat and harvest and

America's institutionalization of neighborly love. *Sowing in the morning, sowing seeds of kindness, sowing in the noontide and the dewy eve.* Their little voices rise. But do they know what a dewy eve even is? Do I? When was the last time I enjoyed a dewy eve? When was the last time, as the dew fell and the night-mist rose, I felt the eve take hold? Their little voices rise again: *We shall come rejoicing.* I dream of wet grass, of sliding beads of water, of jeweled droplets glowing in the long beam of moonlight.

COLORED PENCILS

I could assign the job to one of my students, but I find it so satisfying. I put the pencil in, and the spiral blade tears away at the dull nub. According to the vendor catalog, the sharpener has a "flyaway steel helical cutter system." It rattles as it churns. I plant the pencil's flat end in my palm—feel its spin, its canted wobble. I watch the shavings curl and gather in the clear receptacle. The minutes pass. The sharpener grows warm to the touch, produces a cooked wood-chip smell. I don't notice the students come back from P.E. until Claudia puts a hand on my shoulder. "Mr. Fisher," she says softly. "I think it's sharp now."

WIGGLE EYES

I always thought they were called "Googly Eyes," but when I go to order them, they're listed in the vendor catalog as "Wiggle Eyes." And though one would think they'd be the least realistic part of the children's turkey collages, or their cotton-ball snowmen, or their felt dolls, or their clothespin reindeer, they are, in fact, the most realistic, the truest—wide, lidless, poached in terror, the pupils swiveling in deranged and pointless vigilance.

MARKERS

Every day at snack-time, Jeremy tests the markers. He says, with a workmanlike resolve, "Time to test the markers." He tests a marker, eats a Cheez-It. To test, he makes a mark on a piece of paper. If it is sufficiently wet and inky, he puts the marker back in the marker basket. If it is dried up, scratching out a faint line, Jeremy says "Nope" and throws the marker in the trash.

Some days I think he really cares about the markers. Other days I think he just enjoys the sound of the marker smacking against the inside of the trashcan, thumping the hard plastic and ruffling the loose liner. I like that sound, too. One would think Jeremy's parents work as

quality control technicians at a factory, but no—his father is an actuary, his mother is a local reporter. And one would think Jeremy uses only markers when he colors, but no—only crayons.

POM-POMS

"These are not pom-poms," says Daniel. "These are cotton balls."

"A pom-pom is a type of cotton ball," I say.

"I know the difference," says Daniel, squeezing the cotton ball as though testing a melon.

The students say they do not like this project. They say they do it every year around the holidays, and they just don't like making cotton-ball snowmen. They say they're sick of it. They say they're sick of the the way the glue bunches the fibrous tufts of gauze into stiff clumps. They say they're sick of how easily the balls detach from the paper. They say they're sick of the way the balls bounce soundlessly on the classroom floor. They'd prefer it if they detonated, like snow globes, in a hail of bright and gleaming shards.

"Class, I respect your wishes," I say. "But this year the cotton-ball snowmen fit in perfectly with our Weather unit. For instance, does anyone remember another name for snow?"

"Snowball," says Michael.

"Close," I say, "but no."

"Snow*man*," says Grace.

"No..."

"Precipitation," says Isabel.

"Yes!" I say, writing it on the board. "*Precipitation.*"

"I thought precipitation was rain."

"It is," I say. "It's both rain and snow."

Outside, snow begins to fall—the first snow of the season. The kids rush to the window. I tell them to come back to their desks, finish working on their snowmen.

"But Mr. Fisher," someone says. "This is the real thing!"

"Mr. Fisher, Mr. Fisher! This is precipitation!"

"Children," I say. "Come away from the window. The snow's not going anywhere."

Claudia tugs on my sleeve. "Oh, yes, it is, Mr. Fisher! It's falling!"

Walker Rutter-Bowman received his MFA from Syracuse University. He has received fellowships from the Edward Albee Foundation and the Ucross Foundation. His work has been published or

is forthcoming in *Kenyon Review*, *Tin House Online*, *Nashville Review*, *Harvard Review*, and *Full Stop*. He currently lives in Washington, DC.

Where the Wild Things Are

From *Flash Frontier: An Adventure in Short Fiction*

Andrew Salomon

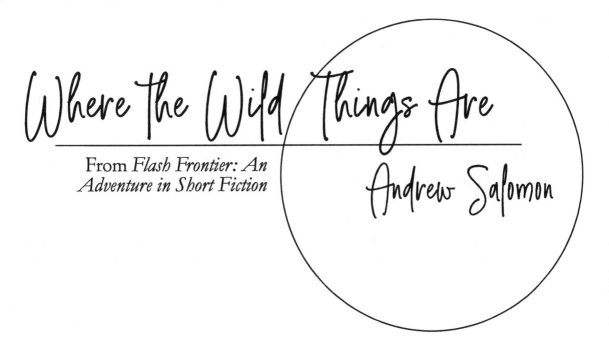

THIS WAS BACK IN ninety-six, a mere two years after democracy. Struggling to find work in archaeology (that's what you get for just assuming there's a job at the end of a degree), I worked as a bartender.

The bar was small and decorated in an affable mismatch of objects: a crystal chandelier; a stuffed springbok head; a huge, mottled antique mirror on one wall. Close to the door hung a framed postcard of Mandela as Superman. Someone stole it. We put up another one and that got stolen as well; a small illustration of the manic optimism and rampant crime that permeated our newly minted democratic state.

It was early evening and almost empty, except for two students sitting at the far end of the bar counter. Brandy and Coke for him, gin and tonic for her. I could tell he was keen on her by how hard he was trying to sound indifferent when he asked where in the States her boyfriend was.

'He's in New York,' she said.

'Oh,' he raised his eyebrows. 'What does he do there?'

'He's an actor, so he works in a bar.'

At that moment a new customer walked in. He was dark and shiny, like polished ebony, with small, child-like teeth and bricklayer's hands.

He ordered a Lion Lager in his Mozambican accent, wrapped his meaty fingers around the cold bottle and took a swig. 'Have you seen one of these?' he asked, turning the label of the bottle towards me. I was unsure what he was getting at – people sometimes think they can try and take the piss just because you're serving them – but his manner and his question seemed sincere.

'I see quite a few of them most nights.'

He shook his head. 'No, have you seen a real one?'

The penny dropped. 'If you mean wild lions then yes, I've seen a few. Mostly on holiday in Botswana and the Kruger Park.'

He looked at me for a few moments and nodded, as if coming to a decision. 'I have seen one too in the Kruger Park. Very close.' He took a bigger swallow of beer, frowned like it tasted bad. 'Me and my brother. We were coming by foot through that place to get here.' He shrugged. 'No passports, no work permits.'

'That can be a dangerous place on foot,' I said.

He looked around, his gaze resting for a moment on the two students, but they were absorbed in their own conversation. 'It was the second day. The bush was thick, and the lion found us.'

'What did you do?'

He ignored my question and leaned across the bar. 'It looked at me.' Then he pointed at the empty space to his right. 'And it took my brother.'

I realised I had been holding my breath and exhaled loudly. 'I'm sorry, man, I–'

He cut me off. 'My brother was screaming, calling for me to help. In the lion's jaws he looked like a child.' He grimaced. 'I did not help him. I just run.' His eyes closed as he lifted the bottle to his lips and tilted his head far back.

I felt I should say something to him, but the two students waved and pointed at their empty glasses. I turned away to pour them another round. When I turned back he was gone, his empty beer bottle on the counter the only testament that he had been there.

Andrew Salomon's short stories have won the PEN Literary Award for African Fiction and the Short.Sharp.Stories Award. His novels have been shortlisted for the Terry Pratchett First Novel Award and the Sanlam Youth Literature Award. *The Chrysalis* was released by Oxford University Press in 2013, and his fantasy thriller *Tokoloshe Song* was published by Random House Umuzi in 2014. *The Equilibrist* was released in 2016 and *Wonderbear* in 2017. Andrew's day job is working as an archaeologist in Cape Town, where he lives with his wife, two young sons, and a pair of rescue dogs of baffling provenance.

Waves

From *Baltimore Review*

Sarah Salway

BECAUSE THE DOCTOR SAID said she could do with a change of scenery, he rented a little blue fisherman's house for them in Cornwall. Because it was out of season they got a good deal but because she'd left behind her friends and family and everything she held dear including the streets she'd walked down so briefly with her pram, she cried for days, and because she was crying so loudly that the house became unbearable, he took to walking along the seafront. Because he didn't want to stand out too much—she'd told him once how locals had hounded D H Lawrence and his wife because Frieda wore red stockings—he began to copy the fishermen he saw, walking with his hands looped behind his back, his eyes out to sea. Because it's difficult to walk without looking where you are going, and because it was sometimes misty and the winds so raw that he wore a scarf half way up his face, he fell in the sea more than once. Luckily, because there were so many fishermen around he was quickly rescued, but because no one could understand why a grown man couldn't keep out of the water, the rumors began that he was a drunk, or wanted to commit suicide, or perhaps he was just fed up with a crying wife. Because wouldn't you be? Because no one else would now talk to them, and because he couldn't now stop looking out to the sea, they began to spend evenings together in their little cliff top garden, her crying and him looking. Because there's only so much time you can bear like this, one night, she turned to him and asked what he was staring at. Because he was a bit of a bore, to be honest, she expected a lecture on the density of stars or how climate change was affecting oceans and ice levels in the Arctic, or even how although grief takes people different ways, maybe it was time for her to listen to everyone and make an effort to move on, and because of this, when he simply said, 'the horizon,' she was touched. Because of this, she followed his gaze too, thought at first that the haze was her tears but then saw it was fog, and realized that this was how he was seeing the world, and that actually she might be seeing clearer than him, and because neither wanted to talk any more they just spent the night looking out, breaking their silence occasionally by calling out new words for it: 'murk', 'vapour,' 'drizzle,' 'murk', and because she had done English Literature at university, while he'd studied Engineering, she carried on longer than him, 'brume,' 'haar' and 'gloaming'. Because she had forgotten the joy of playing, it took her some time to realize she'd stopped crying, and because he was a sore loser, it took him even longer, but because by then, they had both got so cold in the garden, they stayed close in bed that night. And because it was a better day the next morning, they made a sudden decision to go back to London that day. Because he was a creature of habit, he decided for one last walk, his hands looped behind his back. Because the horizon was clear, there was nothing to interest him there so he looked around instead, saw the men nodding at him, realized the fishing was actually more of a tourist attraction and because it wasn't holiday season any more everyone was bored, and that actually, the sight of a man falling in the sea must have been funny. Because of this, he stopped still and shocked himself with something he realized was a laugh. And because it had been so long, for him and for her, the sound of it carried like a seagull all the way to that blue house on the cliff edge, and because, without all the crying, she had done the packing already, she came out to see what was happening. And because the gloaming, the haar, the brume, the murk had gone, she saw him, saw him waving up at her, and because her heart skipped a little bit and she'd thought it was dead, she waved back.

Sarah Salway has published three novels including *The ABCs of Love*, one book of short stories and two poetry collections. Her work has appeared widely, including on railings, in financial newspapers, plant pots, literary magazines and on national radio. As well as being Canterbury Laureate, she has received residential fellowships from Hawthornden Castle and the Virginia Center for the Creative Arts. She currently lives in Kent, England, with her family. Her website is www.sarahsalway.co.uk.

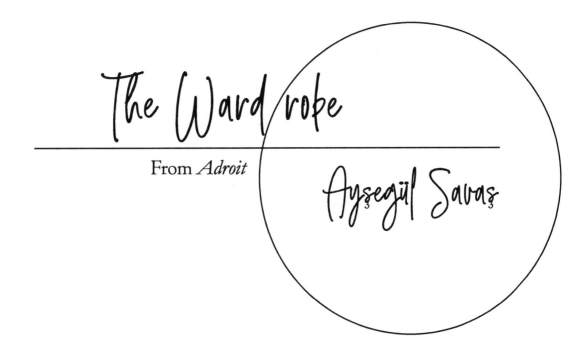

The Wardrobe

From *Adroit*

Ayşegül Savaş

HERE ARE SOME BASICS. The skeleton, if you will.

I can start with warm or cold. That's a classic fork in the path.

Say I go with warm. Then it's brown trousers or canvas, and I build upwards. Green, beige, or mauve. Knitted, cotton, loose. I let them play it out.

If I pick cold, then it's grey or all black. Cold means fitted and starched. And if I've come that far, the wool and the silk, the buttoned or ribbed, all fall into place in minutes.

Other paths are equally simple.

Some days my legs call out, they want to speak! And I reach for a dress to give them the stage.

Other days they're silent. And we go from there.

And the weather, of course. Boots can lead the path to everything else.

But mostly, the weather's inside. A day wearing glasses is always rainy, no matter the clouds. And some days are pure turquoise, even in the dead of winter.

But this day, I was lost in front of my own wardrobe. By the time I came back for a second look, I had tears in my eyes.

Sometimes I get a glimpse of someone in the park, in a museum, at the bakery line, and I go out to assemble all their pieces. It's a pang to see them like that—such strangers in their perfect nests of clothing, looking so much like themselves.

All this makes me feel naked, laying it out piece by piece.

My mother had sets of clothes like costumes. They hung side by side, each one on a hanger with its own set. That was the thing with my mother, she always knew who she was on a given day. All she had to do was pick from left to right, Monday to Friday.

Trouser, shirt, blazer. Skirt, jumper, necklace. Skirt, blouse, scarf.

Monday, Tuesday, Wednesday, Thursday, Friday.

Strict and soft. Tireless but tired.

On weekends, it was jeans and a sweater and that meant young and witty. Mothers in jeans have a way with words.

At one time, I would write down the combinations for each day, to leave no room for confusion. All I had to do was look at the menu first thing in the morning and see what was being served. Sometimes I made a little sketch next to each one. The flare of the skirt, the straightness of a coat. To remind myself what I was thinking when I decided. Never doubt your old selves! Let them speak!

At some point, things used to be simpler. That was the era of the prized items. There were only ten or fifteen of them. Each year had a certain number of days when they would be worn.

The most prized were those long gold earrings, like they come from the dowry of royalty. And sure enough, those earrings ushered in the Queen. Eyeliner, combed wet hair, something dark and velvety to match the reserved smile. The Queen sent waves of charisma all across the room. I knew this the moment I saw the earrings, and I yearned for the Queen for months, before I could bring her home.

Another prized item was the blue suede heels. The librarian. I say that with affection. Yellow cardigan, green socks. You know the type. Flustered but cheerful. I would know on my way to the wardrobe that it was the day of the librarian, and I would hop with joy to greet her.

And the medicine woman, if I had to give her a name. Mismatched, with a whiff of the alchemist about her, or a witch—rings, shawls, and colors of the forest. But she stopped appearing when we caught up to her imaginary age. When old became old.

Characters that were never meant to be in the wardrobe can easily be imagined in there. A touch of the haggard, the humiliated, the ordinary. My rule is this: if an outsider imagines a character that's not in your own wardrobe, then any trace of the character must be wiped away.

My mother used to say of a woman in our neighborhood that she *let herself go*. As if the woman was swept away by an ocean tide. I can't remember what her name was, and I guess that's the point. What this woman should have done was to go in there and take out anything that drooped or swept or sagged. Anything that couldn't hold up to the pull of life.

When I set the rule of wiping away the traces, prized items became abundant.

And what struck me, as I stood staring in my towel, was the beauty of it all. No witchy tatters, bookish sweaters, threadbare shirts. The items from my mother weren't there, either. Sentimentality is one thing, but we're all busy people. The days rush by us.

There was nothing to reproach, nothing lurking in the shadows.

Listen, we don't have all day to take things apart. All I'm saying is it was resplendent. And I ached to know this person, residing a step away.

Ayşegül Savaş is the author of *Walking on the Ceiling*. She lives in Paris and teaches at the Sorbonne.

Warm Flank, Wet Straw

From *NOON*

Christine Schutt

THIS IS AN OLD story, so I will first tell it fast: in a closed off room someone bigger once abused someone smaller with equipment nailed to one wall of the room and pleasure and pain and surprise followed for the bigger person as much as for the smaller.

Here is elaboration of that story: the room with the equipment is built atop what was once a barn that housed some cows, and at the end of the barn behind a wall, a bull. The barn had a cheesy-cow smell with the old girls shifting in their stalls in the draw-down and sharp-squirt tin-plink of milk. Cold hour, warm flank, wet straw.

One day the bull was gone and the cows, and the barn, emptied, was left to fall. The wet bark-like barn boards were slow to dry, and we forgot about the barn and the cows and the bull, and the boards turned to bones that, when the land was purchased, were shoveled away and a new larger box put in its place for arts and crafts and dance, so little girls, faint as spring, might pip around the room as ballerinas. A magical teacher was hired and came with confetti and equipment she nailed to one wall: chains, arm grips, stuff that looked like ski straps, all of which, she explained on parents' night, as part of the exercise routine.

And the chains were pulled on like water-ski ropes—and the little girls leaning over the wake.

Oh, you know the rest of this story: the seduction of the little girls who grew to like being bound and yanked by straps and chains. They liked being strapped to the wall, which is how the teacher left them before she spirited herself away. This version of the old story is tired but true: when found the girls cried to be bound up again.

Christine Schutt is the author of three novels and three collections of stories. Finalist for both a National Book Award (*Florida*) and Pulitzer Prize (*All Souls*), she is also the recipient of Guggenheim and NYFA fellowships. Her most recent book, *Pure Hollywood*, was a New York Times Notable Book for 2018.

Passengers

From *Gulf Coast: A Journal of Literature and Fine Arts*

Leslie Contreras Schwartz

MY GRANDMOTHER, MARISOL, TAUGHT me to respect storms. Hurricanes deserved respect more than fear. Fear freezes you, Moni, her nickname for me, she'd say. But that was in Guanajuato, where the rules seemed different somehow. When I arrived in Houston ten years ago, I knew this place was a different world. Everything so perfectly symmetrical, from the food in the grocery store, to the houses and their yards and their carefully placed perennials. I was used to wild gardens, hardy gardens, one made from dry soil and a handful of manure, bursting with life and color. I was used to streets and alleys with no names, the urgent feeling of so many bodies pressed up against each other in the market. I was used to the storms that brought flooding and a wildness that was not surprising to us, who lived in such proximity to each other and the open world in so many ways.

But now Houston, this more sanitized city, although wild in its mix of people and its own ways, is my home. I was thinking of the differences as I watched the hurricane clouds install itself closer and closer, little by little. "Are you a guest or an invader?" I asked myself as Flor and I stared out the window at the rain pour itself angrily, inching up the staircase outside our apartment. I looked at Flor by my side, her small head in tight braids that I'd done this morning, and remembered that to many, we, too, are invaders, not guests in this country. I felt then a sibling to this storm.

Isn't it this – this fury of wind and let-down river, that the gringos, and all human beings, are afraid of? We are just the symbols they've chosen to mean death, me, a house cleaner and Flor, a slight five-year-old learning how to read and write.

The sky cracked and cracked some more, sending Flor and me to hide in the closet for several nights from tornadoes. When we came out the fourth and last time, we stepped into a foot of water in our apartment. The water kept rising. The sky had come for us. We could not just sit tight until it was done.

I could respect this axe in its attempt to splinter us, its cruel rotten water, rising and rising. I can respect it because as I put my daughter in a laundry basket, prepared myself to swim until I found a place to hide, I knew that this kind of foe comes indiscriminately: the young, the old, the Mexicans, the "aliens," gringos, the drunk, the homeless, and yes, even those rich people whose houses I cleaned.

As I swam, shouting over the rain to Flor, who was cold and wet, that we would be okay, we saw all of our neighbors were on the balconies or going into the water with their families, their children too in laundry baskets, bins, containers, or holding onto makeshift rafts.

Not a single passenger escapes, and our boxes in which we are ferried from this life to the next, that is our only choosing. Which boxes.

My daughter and I escaped, as if well tucked in another box, a box made of flood and wildness, a dangerous embrace, that looked at all humans with the same regard. This is the kind of death song I respect, that sky showing itself, reminding me that here the world of people can cave with the same fall, the same dance. I saw my neighbor, a viejita who always gave us a dirty look in the laundry room like we might contaminate her clothes with our dark skin, our human smell.

I swam to the lady in her white cotton robe, her silver hair out of its usual perfect curled shell, and held out my hand. Her hair was matted to the sides of her face in tight curls as she looked at me, her translucent blue eyes. It was if we had just met, and in many ways, we did.

Leslie Contreras Schwartz is a multi-genre writer from Houston. Her work has recently appeared or is forthcoming in *Iowa Review, Pleiades, The Missouri Review, The Collagist, PANK, Verse Daily,* and *Catapult,* among others. Her new collection of poems, *Nightbloom & Cenote* (St. Julian Press, May 2018), was a semi-finalist for the 2017 Tupelo Press Dorset Prize, judged by Ilya Kaminsky. Her fiction will be included in *Houston Noir,* edited by Gwendolyn Zepeda (Akashic Press, May 2019). She is currently a poetry editor at *Four Way Review* and is a graduate of The Program for Writers at Warren Wilson College.

The moon by Train

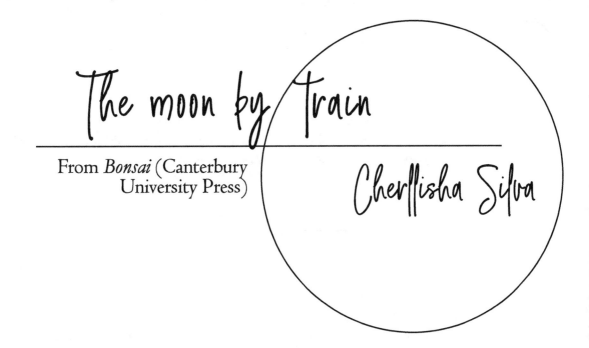

From *Bonsai* (Canterbury University Press)

Cherllisha Silva

1967. KATHIE'S TWELFTH WINTER. She travels overnight, six hundred and eighty-two kilometres nearer ice with her mother and Teenie, fourteen in dog years, ninety-eight had he been born human. With smiles and pats, they encourage him to sit beside a metal cage, above carriage wheels. Kathie worries. Isn't Teenie exposed? He manages a tiny wag of stump of tail but his irises are black moons afloat across their whites. Head drooping, he follows, sits on straw. The locomotive accelerates, whistle blows and Kathie remembers other friends, the ones she leaves behind.

The train rockets through darkness punctured with golden rectangles – suburban planets – where families watch TV, warmed by fries and mugs of steaming cocoa. Here, heaters aren't working, Kathie doesn't sleep – is unprepared for outer space.

Stopped. Eyes cupped, peering through glass – a sign, 'National Park,'– is pinned to mountains of pitch. She follows a point of light, bobbing closer, notices ash – no, snowflakes – seen for the first time, flitting on gusts of air, thinks of Teenie, black on black, this longest, coldest night of the year.

Morning. Her father meets them, rolls rotund Teenie out. He plumps to ground, stiff, lifts and drags his body along platforms of a new city. The house is sparse. They warm sausage and water, feed and wrap their doggie in hotties, moving blankets and Kathie's whole-child-body hug. They sleep.

Two winters, two houses later, Apollo 11 lands. Human beings first walk on the moon. A high-

school first year, Kathie surfaces, at home, as usual, calling — but no arthritic wag, no bared teeth, no Teenie rendition of a human grin. Mum turns from dicing dinner, fixes Kathie's gaze with hers, nervous. 'The vet put him to sleep today.' Mum revealing only her sad back, says, 'If you'd known, he would've known.' Kathie remembers. Black irises. Bright moons.

Cherllisha Silva lives everywhere over Aotearoa New Zealand from mountain to coast, forest to sand, north to south, following the land's beauty and warmth. She was born in the north of the North Island, usually residing in the south of the North. She has poems and stories published in newspapers, anthologies and journals, and broadcast on Radio N Z, in Aotearoa, Australia and now, the U S. She also composes with a camera and loves to boogie. "The moon by train" was first published in *Bonsai: best small stories* from Aotearoa New Zealand, Canterbury University Press, 2018.

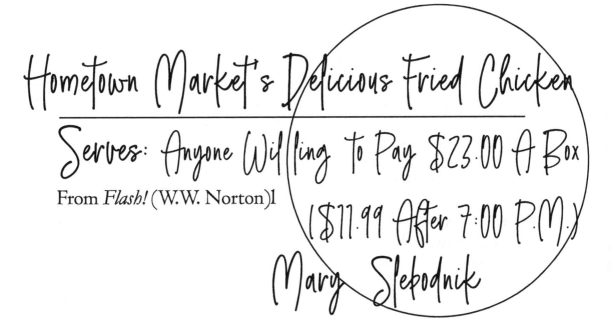

Hometown Market's Delicious Fried Chicken

Serves: Anyone Willing To Pay $23.00 A Box ($11.99 After 7:00 P.M.)

From *Flash!* (W.W. Norton)1

Mary Slebodnik

1. TIE THE APRON. STRETCH your fingers into the plastic gloves. Go to the cooler, that dark cell filled with raw meat in the back of the grocery store, and pull the chicken out of the cardboard boxes. Count the wings, breasts, and thigh—shapes you have memorized—and drop them into the green bucket. The cold chicken blood numbs your fingers through the gloves. Distract yourself by humming along to the chorus of the song playing over the intercom: "If I Had a Million Dollars."

2. Haul the bucket to the sink and wash each piece of chicken. Roll the chicken around in the silver tub of seasoned flour and begin daydreaming about your Great American Novel, but become distracted by what you would do with a million dollars instead. You find yourself wanting to sit somewhere French with a typewriter while wearing a smoking jacket.

3. Turn on that monster, the fryer: a big vat of boiling vegetable oil. Make sure it's hot. The last time you cooked, you put the chicken in too early, and the breading got all slippery and slimy, the pieces hanging in lukewarm oil, suspended--chicken in purgatory. Be kind to the chicken. Give it no hope of survival.

4. Drop the chicken piece-by-piece into the fryer. (Of course, you will need to have lowered the wire basket into the grease first. If you did not do this step, grab a set of tongs from under the deli counter and fish the chicken out before it burns on the hot coils. That's what happens when chicken has the freedom to do whatever it wants.)

5. Notice that you didn't put on the apron referred to in step one. Your belly has a certain

prominence and somehow you can never keep it out of the flour. Put on the apron now so Jake the Adorable Stockboy won't see your gut covered in bleached wheat. He calls you Fitzgerald because he knows your literary ambitions. Wave to him when he makes his 9:00 a.m. appearance with the milk stacked on a pushcart.

6. Set the timer for the chicken.

7. Stir the chicken halfway through its cooking-time with a giant metal spatula to keep the pieces from sticking together. This will be around the time Jake comes over to flirt with you. Ask him what he would do with a million dollars.

8. When Jake says he would buy a boat, explain that a million dollars would buy far more than a boat. Do not betray your disappointment when he says he'll buy a "big boat."

9. When you realize you forgot to set the timer (like last time), take the chicken out and poke it with a thermometer. If you can poke through the breading without too much trouble, put the burnt chicken in the case and sell as much as you can before your manager comes back. If you have to unduly exert yourself to stab through the breading, throw the chicken away. Cover it in the wastebasket with paper towels. Pretend it never happened. Do steps 1-4 again.

10. When a customer calls, ask her, "What would *you* do with a million dollars?" When she says, "Oh, no! I just wanted the deli people," reassure her and jot down her order.

11. Go to the cooler with two green buckets so you can accommodate the caller's request for 39 skinless chicken breasts for her family reunion. Tear off the skin, and toss the chicken into the flour.

12. Don't want more. Don't ever want more.

Mary Slebodnik earned her MFA from Florida International University in 2017. She has previously been published in John Dufresne's instructional book, *Flash!: Writing the Very Short Story* (2018). She teaches high school English in South Florida and frequently visits her hometown in rural Ohio.

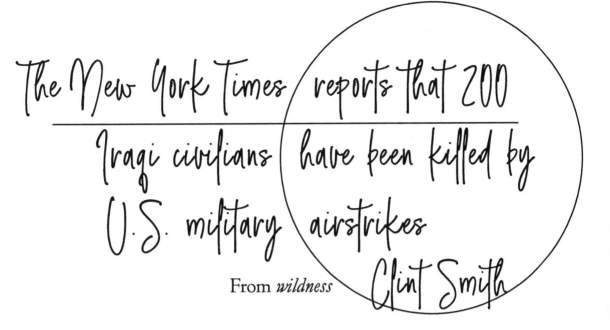

The New York Times reports that 200 Iraqi civilians have been killed by U.S. military airstrikes

From *wildness* — Clint Smith

after Hanif Abdurraqib

& THE MAN ON THE television calls it *unfortunate yet inevitable collateral damage* & i wonder what it is that turns mourning into a metonym   or a proclamation of conjecture & i read his bio & see that he has a wife   & i can't imagine he would call it inevitable if her body were pulled from the quiet implosion of scattered rubble   & i see that he has a son & i can't imagine he would call the boy who bears his name collateral in someone else's war & i see that he has a daughter   & i think of what it might mean for someone to render her final breath an inescapable reality of global politics   & i understand what he means i know he means that war is callous & unforgiving   that a militant can surround himself with a dozen women & children so that the pilot must decide between a target & the soft ache of his own heart's detonation   i do not misunderstand the cruelty of war   but i regret the way we talk about its casualties   how their lives become tacit admonitions how the tyranny of a border made out of thin air means that bombs are only dropped on one side of it   but i too have felt the empathy corrode inside the most cavernous parts of me   have taken the quarters from my pocket & used them to cover my collusion   who among us has not used spare change to ornament our contrition   laid a garland of rations atop the bodies of names we do not know & i'm not sure what it means for us   not to be the one to fire the bullet   but to behave as if the bullet always belonged in that chest & not our own

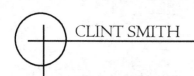

Clint Smith is a doctoral candidate at Harvard University. He is a recipient of fellowships from the Art For Justice Fund, Cave Canem, and the National Science Foundation. His writing has been published in *The New Yorker*, *The Atlantic*, *Poetry Magazine*, *The Paris Review*, the *Harvard Educational Review* and elsewhere. His first full-length collection of poetry, *Counting Descent*, was published in 2016. It won the 2017 Literary Award for Best Poetry Book from the Black Caucus of the American Library Association and was a finalist for an NAACP Image Award. His debut nonfiction book, *How the Word Is Passed*, is forthcoming from Little, Brown.

The Bad Thing

From *Connotation Press*

Nancy Stohlman

ONCE A BAD THINIG happened, and the people were horrified and cried, played the details over and over like a particularly painful heartbreak. And someone decided that a memorial should be built and everyone should wear red and once a year everyone wore red and remembered the bad thing and it seemed right.

The next time a bad thing happened people decided it was only fitting to designate another color—white this time—and people wore white and some people wore red and white together to show how the two bad things were connected and that also seemed right.

But the bad things kept happening. Soon the primary colors were gone—then the secondary colors. The newest tragedies had to come up with creative coloring like teal or lavender and soon it expanded beyond colors—people in mourning for a specific tragedy could either wear the color or buy a bracelet made of that color and some people had 10-15 bracelets going up their arm until it was pointed out that the bracelets weren't produced in an environmentally friendly manner and then people got rid of all the bracelets and tried to go back to the colors, but even the colors didn't work now, because every color was affiliated with a tragedy and if you were wearing, say, lime green pants, but you didn't know which bad thing was being mourned in lime green, then you might be called a poser and accused of trivializing other people's suffering.

And still the bad things increased until there were several bad things every week, and new symbols had to be devised to express your horror: praying hands and beating hearts and hugging arms you could send electronically or made into magnetic bumpers stickers for cars or bicycles and you could also swap your electronic picture frame to one specially made to announce your devastation at the new bad thing, but sometimes another bad thing would happen on that same day and you would not know if you should keep the original picture frame to mourn the first bad thing or if you should update to mourn the most recent bad thing and those who updated would be called insensitive by the ones who had not yet finished mourning the first bad thing.

It got to the point where the bad things had to compete with the other bad things, and a thing that would have been pretty bad back in the days of the primary colors was now almost ignored. And people abandoned the picture frames but they didn't know which symbol to use, now, which led them to create new symbols, like baking cakes in the shapes of tragedies that needed to be mourned and sometimes they traveled to the locations of the bad things just to feel the awfulness more acutely and they became jumpy like children in volatile households who are trying to read the signs and see the next bad thing approaching and so sometimes they would see regular things as bad things and jump at the sight of prayer hands or beating hearts or hugging arms until they became numb and the bad things kept happening but they were out of colors and out of ideas and so, eventually, they did nothing.

Nancy Stohlman's books include *Madam Velvet's Cabaret of Oddities*, *The Vixen Scream and Other Bible Stories*, *The Monster Opera*, and *Fast Forward: The Mix Tape*, a finalist for a Colorado Book Award. She is the creator and curator of The Fbomb Flash Fiction Reading Series, the creator of FlashNano in November, and her work has been published in over 100 journals and anthologies including the W.W. Norton Reader *New Micro: Exceptionally Short Fiction*. She leads flash fiction workshops and retreats worldwide and teaches at the University of Colorado Boulder. Find out more about her at www.nancystohlman.com

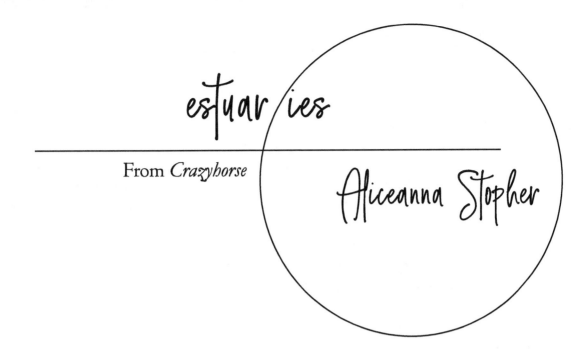

estuaries

From *Crazyhorse*

Aliceanna Stopher

AT THE START OF that summer we were a tangle of limbs, locked arm in bare arm, freckled and radiant, our sandals slapping sidewalk in a fearsome beat, the very thrum of our collective girlhood. We were the girls in the wide-brimmed hats and oversized plastic sunglasses we'd lifted from crowded flea market stalls. We were remorseless and took what was ours with the seriousness, the severity, of the war-hardened daughters of Genghis Khan, of the pirate queens imprisoned on our bookshelves, growing dust in our stubborn insistence we'd outgrown them.

Everything that summer belonged to us. The patches of dead grass, the everywhere smell of honeysuckle, the roving packs of teenage boys on rusty bikes who hollered at us, never even once acknowledging that they were but guests in our kingdom. We took sun tea from its pitcher on our fifth grade math teacher's porch; we stole our older sisters' lipsticks, which never suited us. Ours was the wet of the Georgia heat, the sag of black walnut and oak trees at the mouths of finger creeks inching their ways closer home, toward the sheltered heart of Eulonia, and small Baptist churches that, for all our imagined worldliness, bewitched us the week long with the mournful echo of their Sunday morning songs.

"Lot of fuss over nothin'," we'd say, elbowing each other in the ribs, eyes wide, exaggerated. We knew from the books our older brothers brought home from their farnorth colleges how we should be embarrassed of God, our parents' faith in him, our backwoods parades and Holy Week festivals, those big joyful noises we were convinced could be heard clear to Savannah.

We were coming to know the correct ways to be ashamed of ourselves.

Still, we'd walk past those tall white churches, their cemeteries, with held breath and break loose running, eyes set on the next corner, chests on fire, and our laughter afterwards always sounded hollow, even to us.

"Trouble," our mothers called us. "What are you girls doing out all day but making spectacles of yourselves?"

"Hell, woman," our fathers would say, "let them be young."

We tried to get paid washing cars or cutting grass. We went door to door. We knocked with four sets of fists. We wanted money for no reason other than we felt we deserved it. There wasn't anything we wanted to buy, anywhere to go. There wasn't much we wanted at all before you told us about the baby.

Your jaw set hard when you said you wouldn't be starting ninth grade with us come August. Your chin refused to shake but your puffed-out cheeks jiggled like ambrosia salad, you said "By spring, I'll be a mama," and just like that we were four separate girls with naked knees and scuffed elbows and dirt beneath our fingernails. You said, "I want to call her after you" and I wouldn't have known you were talking to me if the others hadn't already begun to walk ahead of us, away.

Aliceanna Stopher's story "estuaries" is the winner of the 2018 *Crazyhorse* CrazyShorts! prize. She is an MFA fiction candidate at Colorado State University where she teaches undergraduate creative writing and works as an Associate Editor for the *Colorado Review*. Her short fiction may be found, or is forthcoming, in *Gulf Coast*, *Crazyhorse*, *The Normal School*, *New South*, and elsewhere. She lives offline with her partner and their daughter, and online at aliceannastopher.com

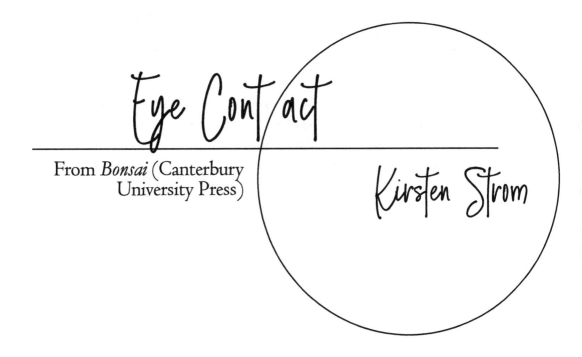

Eye Contact

From *Bonsai* (Canterbury University Press)

Kirsten Strom

M is for magnetic

M IS FOR MAGNETIC. Have you noticed the finite time strangers make eye contact? One-point-one milliseconds.

I tested it once. I stretched it to three seconds. He didn't look away. He was a crumpled blond with surf-blue eyes, untangling from a Western-bound window-seat sleep. I sat alone across the emptying carriage. He wasn't supposed to keep looking.

The electric train hummed, gutless. Too quiet. The white walls glared. He made me feel like a poster-board screwed high in Aotea Square, two-dimensional behind glass. I hunched into my sleeves and watched for Sunnyvale.

I would rather be loved for my soul.

O is for open

O is for open. A pair of Pasifka boys, black-haired and walnut-skinned, laughed and jostled each other, chasing the rubbish truck down Sunnyside Road. It had just rained, and there was an unearthly glow to the trees, less scrape and more swish to the pavement. The scent of wet earth lingered. The long-haired one spied me and yelled, 'Hello!' with a grin. They scrabbled to clear a spilled box. His enthusiasm surprised me. He shifted his construction orange coat and lifted a box with lean arms. I could hear him singing, 'Soleeeee,' as the truck flew them round the bend.

Kirsten Strom is a young writer, composer and conductor. Born in New Zealand, she spent much of her childhood overseas but ended up in the same little West Auckland house her parents built. She conducts school and community ensembles and her pieces have been performed internationally, aired on radio and played by national orchestras. Her writing captures the everyday moments that make up our lives.

The Night of the Mononoke

From *Haibun Today*

Charles D. Tarlton

I am the metaphor
for every human being
who thinks as I do
     - Kawazu Tobikomu

FADE IN:

EXT. HOUSE IN A CLEARING - NIGHT - CALIFORNIA, 1942

A SMALL WHITE CLAPBOARD house surrounded by orange groves and big Eucalyptus trees.

The dark figure of SHOKI-SAN stands partially in the shadows. He speaks now into the camera, but afterwards there will only be his voice.

                 SHOKI-SAN
          this story is true
          a demon got blood onto
          his gory fingers
          rage in his eyes, nights of fun
          at someone else's expense

CAMERA approaches the house and through the windows.

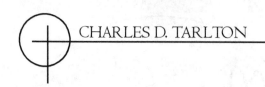

INT. KITCHEN - NIGHT

In the kitchen, the MOTHER, a small Japanese woman, cooks dinner, looking into pots, tasting, stirring.

She sings softly along with the gentle music from a radio.

INT. LIVING ROOM - NIGHT

In the living room, the FATHER sits at the end of a sofa under a lamp reading a Japanese newspaper.

The radio on the table beside him plays soft Japanese music, a little louder now, closer up.

Two small children lie on the floor reading and listening to the radio.

> SHOKI-SAN (O.S.)
> the demon queller
> watches from out of the dark
> this peaceable home
> about to fall into fire
> demons come out of the night

EXT. ORANGE GROVE - NIGHT

Two dark stake-bed trucks without headlights come bumping up the dirt road and stop abruptly at the edge of the clearing in front of the house.

The trucks are filled with men, but it is hard to make them out in the dark. The men climb out of the trucks.

Voices grumbling and cursing. Truck doors slamming.

CAMERA back to the windows looking in.

The Japanese family inside the house stop everything suddenly and listen.

The two children stand up and go anxiously to their FATHER who abruptly puts his paper down and stands.

The MOTHER comes in from the kitchen and the four of them stand perfectly still, apprehensive and listening.

> SHOKI-SAN (O.S.)
> their last minute runs
> away, the present horror
> settles at the end
> of its flight, a hawk with death
> in its beak and bloody talons

DISSOLVE TO:

EXT. HOUSE IN A CLEARING - DAY

Two boys, CHARLES and MICKEY, stand in front of the house, taking it in.

It is the same house, but a dilapidated ruin now. Its windows are broken out and the house is surrounded by tall weeds.

The boys nod at each other and go in through the broken screen door.

> SHOKI-SAN (O.S.)
> lost minutes and hours
> have dried up and blown away
> all the sounds are gone
> only the terrible fear
> still sticks to everything

INT. HOUSE - DAY

The living room is unrecognizable from before. No sofa, no radio, no tables or chairs, nothing but refuse.

The broken remains of the bookcase lie scattered across the floor, bits of broken China everywhere, old newspapers, and tin cans.

                         MICKEY
                Well, no one lives here,
                that's for sure.
                    (pause)
                I think I'll take a look
                around.

Mickey goes off into another room. He calls back.

                         MICKEY (O.S.)
                Nothing back here, either.

                         CHARLES
                Who do you think lived
                here?

                         MICKEY (O.S.)
                Who knows?

Charles kicks through the rubble in the living room, stops, pushes aside the remnants of the broken bookcase, and reaches down.

With both hands he lifts up a big, red book. He carries the book over to the window ledge and opens it.

                         CHARLES
                Mickey, come here. Look
                at this!

Mickey comes back into the room.

                         MICKEY
                    (excited)
                What? What'd you find?

                         CHARLES
                A dictionary, a Japanese

dictionary!
(pause, pointing to an
open page)
See?

MICKEY
(disappointed)
Who cares?
(turns and leaves the room)
Call me if you find anything
really interesting.

(O.S.) Faint Japanese music as before.

Charles stands at the window, concentrating on flipping through the pages of the dictionary.

Shoki-san steps out of the shadow of the trees and speaks to the camera.

SHOKI-SAN
hard words now stark as
barbwire fences; what's written
he can't yet sound out
caressing the black scratchings
something must surely be wrong

FADE OUT.

Charles D. Tarlton has been writing tanka prose and flash fiction since 2006. He has published poetry and flash fiction in *KYSO Flash, Haibun Today, Contemporary Haibun Online, Atlas Poetica, Rattle, Blackbox Manifold, Ilanot Review, Ink, Sweat, and Tears, Ekphrastic Review,* and others. Muse-Pie Press nominated three of his poems from *Shot Glass Journal* Issue #6 for the

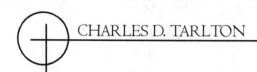

CHARLES D. TARLTON

2013 *Pushcart Prize* and his ekphrastic tanka prose, "The Miletus Torso" was nominated for the *Best of the Net* anthology (2018). A print collection of his ekphrastic poems, *Touching Fire*, will be published as a book early in 2019 by KYSO/FLASH publishers.

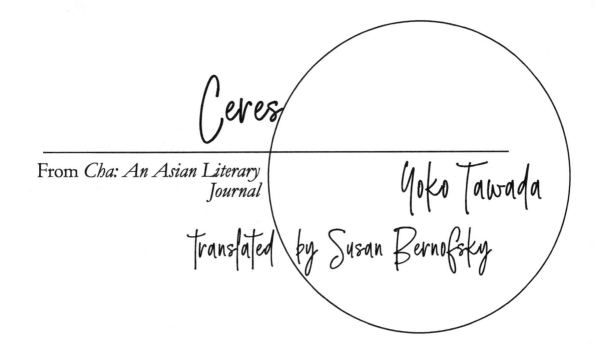

Ceres

From *Cha: An Asian Literary Journal*

Yoko Tawada

Translated by Susan Bernofsky

CERES FORGOT TO BRING her twin sister into the world with her. The forgotten girl got lost somewhere between the other side and this one. Perhaps her mother had closed up the escape hatch as soon as the first bit came out. She must have thought a single daughter was enough. Two daughters are one too many. Mother and daughter, after all, are already two women. Three women would produce a love triangle. Wishing to avoid this, Ceres's mother arranged for the second girl to disappear. And so Ceres entered this world as half a set of twins.

Ceres, too, had a daughter. She became a mother without the least forethought. She was nomadic by nature, no roof ever sheltered her for long. Now she lived with a fellow who was studying at university and had a roomy apartment. Now she fell in love with a singer and followed her about everywhere. One day, she met a man in a bar. He told her about his wife, who slept twelve hours a day. At the time, Ceres was able to sleep only five or six hours a night. During the day, she felt like an inside-out glove. Surely it would be lovely to sleep for twelve hours straight. She would be able to process the impressions absorbed during an hour spent awake during an hour of sleep. When you spend less time asleep than awake, you lose your balance. What happens to the surplus daytime hours?

"Your wife leads a symmetrical life," Ceres said.

A few weeks later, she told the man, whom she now was seeing on a regular basis: "I'm going to try to sleep for twelve hours, too."

He felt a certain discomfort. A few days later, his discomfort had grown. Then he left.

For six months, Ceres attended dance school in the *Eidelstedt* district, where she was living. Every third morning, she gargled in the bathroom mirror and hurried off to class. There a young teacher awaited her. Every time Ceres moved, the teacher said "No." Ceres groaned, but her groans sounded hedonistic. She wanted to be negated by a woman. One day things went too

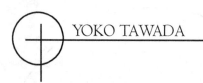

far.

"Your legs look positively agricultural," the young teacher said to her in the dance school office. Ceres slapped the teacher's face; at once, the teacher burst into tears. Ceres wept as well.

Just a day later, she made the acquaintance of a choreographer. She brought him home with her, and he stayed for three days. He lived in another city and was on the road looking for dancers for his next project. He stayed with her to save the expense of a hotel room.

"I'm sorry, but I can't with women," he explained at 12:30 a.m.

"But I can. I can with women," Ceres replied happily. The next morning Ceres gargled loudly in the mirror. The choreographer gargled, too, but in a much deeper register.

"I wouldn't have believed it, but it really appears to be true that I find the intelligence of others erotic," Ceres explained at a marriage bureau and was offered a quiet, talented scholar. Ceres wanted only one thing from him: a daughter.

Ceres's daughter was also named Ceres. No name could have suited her better than this one. Ceres's daughter Ceres left the house. Night fell, and she didn't return home. She'd just wanted to stop by a friend's house and go for an ice cream with her. She'd skipped out of the house clutching a coin in her hand. Ceres telephoned her daughter's friend, but the friend said that Ceres hadn't been there. At midnight, Ceres called the police. But even the police didn't succeed in finding little Ceres.

Ceres went to the museum to look for her daughter. Several of the portraits of the royal family contained little girls. They had wrinkled foreheads and brooding eyes. In fact, they appeared to be neither gayer nor more innocent than the adults, they had merely been trimmed down to size. But the names of these girls were nowhere to be found. No wonder a lost girl cannot be found again. One ought to try leaving a little girl at the museum, Ceres thought. Maybe she will grow up in a picture. What will she look like as an adult? Will it be possible to find her again?

Ceres wandered from picture to picture, inspecting every bit of female nudity, and she became more and more furious. Why did all the painters lie? One painter called his picture "Hera," but you could see at once that the woman he'd painted was his wife. Why didn't he just go ahead and entitle the picture "My Spouse"? What a stupid pretense, using Greek names like that.

Cornois is rewriting her story. In the first version, the plot was completely different: the main character, Ceres, hired a man to abduct her daughter. Ceres's daughter was also named Ceres, and Ceres didn't want to have Ceres around any longer. After all, what woman could love another woman who has the same name as she does? It's dangerous to have a name, for a name must be shared with many other people.

When the daughter had been eliminated, the main character regretted what she'd done.

She'd only wanted to destroy the name of her daughter, she didn't want the daughter herself to vanish. Ceres wept, struck herself in the face until she bled and spat out shreds of words. Forgetting that she herself had hired the man, she told the police the name of the abductor.

Hello, my name is Ceres. I'm disguising myself as Ceres the daughter to pay a visit to mother Ceres. How are things? It's been ages! I couldn't visit you before: I'd been abducted and locked up. Many years have passed since then. I'm so terribly sorry. I had myself abducted on purpose, to get away from home.

After a few drinks, most projects strike me as absurd. Always eating together with another person: a gastronomic project. Buying a house and installing a television, a stereo system and a bookshelf: a multimedia project. Someone who has no children can still produce one by the fall: a biological project. You might also acquire a female dog and a cat. What progeny, what planning. Then you'll also need a car to transport the heavy cans of food.

Even in a highly occupied individual such as Ceres, there was still an unused corner, unburdened and free of furniture, dusty and forgotten. While Ceres went on speaking without respite, arranging her life, I sat down in this corner. Hello there. I spoke to her, my voice was soft, but it landed in the one silent moment of her life. Ceres stopped short and listened.

Hello there, I'm a counterfeit daughter. It isn't good to cling unduly to one's flesh-and-blood daughter. You paid a lot for her, but still you can't keep her, for every daughter must abandon her blood mother in order to survive. In her place, you should receive guests from far-off lands. Concern yourself with another woman.

Ceres cooks me barley porridge, she cooks me rice pudding, she cooks me. Ceres doesn't want me to speak too much. If I do, it immediately makes her feel she's doing something illegitimate. But when we cook grain together in silence, when we knead the dough and bake bread, we have no secrets. Perhaps it is good not to say a word, to knead dough together for hours, then there is no more I, no more she, no more mother, no more dead, only the kneading of four hands.

Yoko Tawada was born in Tokyo in 1960, moved to Hamburg when she was twenty-two, and then to Berlin in 2006. She writes in both Japanese and German, and has published several books—stories, novels, poems, plays, essays—in both languages. She has received numerous awards for her writing including the Akutagawa Prize, the Adelbert von Chamisso Prize, the Tanizaki Prize, the Kleist Prize, and the Goethe Medal. New Directions publishes her story collections *Where Europe Begins* (with a Preface by Wim Wenders) and *Facing the Bridge*, as well her novels *The Naked Eye*, *The Bridegroom Was a Dog*, *Memoirs of a Polar Bear*, and *The Emissary*.

Susan Bernofsky directs the program in literary translation at Columbia University. A Guggenheim fellow, she has translated classic works by Robert Walser, Franz Kafka, and Hermann Hesse. Her translation of Jenny Erpenbeck's novel *The End of Days* (2014) won the Independent Foreign Fiction Prize, The Schlegel-Tieck Translation Prize, the Ungar Award for Literary Translation, and the Oxford-Weidenfeld Translation Prize. Her translation of Yoko Tawada's novel *Memoirs of a Polar Bear* (2016) won the inaugural Warwick Prize for Women in Translation.

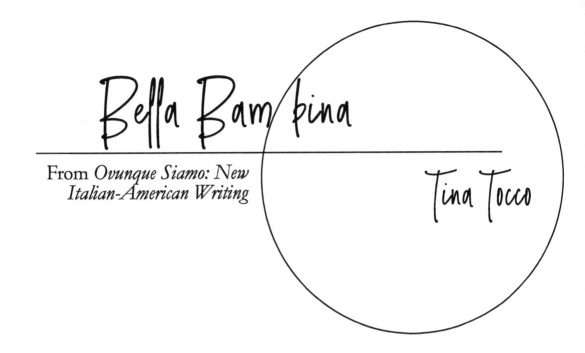

Bella Bambina

From *Ovunque Siamo: New Italian-American Writing*

Tina Tocco

WHEN MY FATHER FOUND out about me, he hired a waiter/actor to record a new message on his burner phone. On the same day, he switched from Gmail to Yahoo! and started paying cash for things. His bills went in the girlfriend's name, and she wrote the rent checks for the new apartment that didn't have a lease.

This is what Nonna tells me and has been telling me. It is what Sister Rosemary says, too, when she comes on Fridays for tea, right before she makes the sign of the cross over my whole body. Sister Rosemary and Nonna have been friends since Immaculate Conception Elementary, and their hearts and minds are still one in Christ. She sees my father in me, she says. Deep. She lights the candles closest to the altar when I come to mind. Sister Rosemary pinches my cheeks — *"Ah! Bella bambina!"* — too tight. She scoots me away with a slap on the rear that makes even Nonna flinch.

Nights when Mom works, which is mostly, Nonna grips my headboard so she cankneel alongside me. She tells me to pray for Mom, whose boss does not pay her every week. And for Nonno, who went up to *Paradiso* long before my soul came down. And for my father, who needs to be cleansed through suffering, because *puzzones* like that should get everything they deserve.

Nights when Mom works, which is mostly, she sits against my ribs when her shift is through. She smells of oil. Delicious fried things. She strokes me in the place where Monsignor Jack leaves the smudge on Ash Wednesday. She does not speak. She murmurs. Our Father. Hail Mary. Salve Regina. Twice, sometimes.

She flattens a hand to my chest. I hold my breath so she thinks I am asleep. When my lungs give up, I release, inhaling the overnight shift. I open my eyes as her hand,knuckles

prickled with blisters, works along my ribs, the ruffles of my nightgown. She looks into me. Deep. *"Bella bambina,"* Mom whispers, her smile held in the blush of the streetlight. Behind her, over my desk chair, she has laid out my plaid jumper and rosary in case she is asleep when I wake.

I weave my fingers through her hair, wet with steam. It has been pinned up for more hours than I have been awake. I breathe in, and she slips her curls from my hand, says I was made for other things. That I will burst out, always ready for the new and exciting. The most beautiful spirits cannot be bound, Mom says. They must breathe. These walls are not thick enough to keep me. Oh, she says, I am my father's girl.

Tina Tocco's microfiction has appeared in *New Ohio Review, Crab Creek Review, River Styx, Roanoke Review, Harpur Palate, Portland Review, Potomac Review, Passages North,* and other journals. A New Stories from the Midwest nominee, Tina was a finalist in CALYX's Flash Fiction Contest and an honorable mention in the *River Styx* Schlafly Beer Micro-Brew Micro-Fiction Contest. She has contributed to multiple anthologies, including *Wild Dreams: The Best of Italian Americana,* and is the author of the children's poetry collection *The Hungry Snowman and Other Poems.* Tina earned her MFA from Manhattanville College, where she was editor-in-chief of *Inkwell.*

The Menstrual Cycle of a Grieving Woman

From *Cleaver*

Jennifer Todhunter

I LIE ON THE couch wide awake, cramps gouging my uterus. In my stupor, I picture the trappings of a baby girl, her translucent skin, her nail-less fingers, her snake-coiled legs. She has Jake's smile, I think, the way the edges of her lips twist up, the way her left cheek dimples. I wonder how her laugh sounds, if it comes from her belly like his.

I name the cramps Rita. She is unrelenting. I see her name in the dirt on the windows, in the grime on the floor of this house that is ours. I trace the letters with my pinky finger, wonder how her tiny fingers compare to mine, how tightly she could grip them. She is here, she is there, she is everywhere. *Why won't you join me?* she asks. *Don't you want me?* I picture cuddling up beside her, the softness of her hair, the freshness of her scent. *I want you,* I whisper from my cave of blankets on the couch. *I want you, I want you, I want you.*

I call my sister. We haven't spoken since I told her about the accident. She says my voicemail is full, that she's been worried. Her two children play in the background; their soft, small voices split me in half. My sister says she isn't able to come out before Jake's funeral next week, starts droning on about her unbreakable obligations, and I tell her it's all right, it's all right, but start crying anyway.

 I say, *I'm sorry, I'm sorry, I don't know what's wrong with me,* and hang up the phone, but the tears won't stop for the rest of the day. I cry through Jake's drawer of t-shirts, through his bag of toiletries, through his box of ticket stubs under the bed. It's like PMS, but infinitely worse. It's like wishing you were dead, but you're not.

I wake up with my period. Every trip to the bathroom reminds me there is no tangible piece left of Jake. No daughter. No son. I won't recognize the curve of his features, the quirk of his mannerisms in our offspring.

Jake's funeral is a sea of hats and jackets, the rain falling in sheets outside. I greet everyone as they arrive, listen to their anecdotes about Jake, accept their hugs, their kisses from cheek to cheek. By the time everyone is seated, my tampon is soaked through, blood pooling onto my nylons. I excuse myself to the washroom, sink to the floor and sob. My sister finds me, helps clean me up, hugs me like she used to when we stayed up late watching Friday night horror flicks. *I don't know what's going on*, I choke out mangled words, *it's never been this heavy before*
. Later, when I'm alone with Jake's casket, I am struck by how young he looks. How young we both look. How his locker was next to mine when I got my first period.

My doctor refuses to schedule a hysterectomy. *You are only thirty-two*, she says. *It is the grief, it will pass.* She tells me to spend some time thinking about my decision, prescribes sleeping pills instead. I start with one, then two, then three. Then I dump the bottle and flush, sit on the toilet and bleed. It's like my uterus is mocking me.

My next-door neighbor leaves a chicken pot pie on the doorstep and a note offering her condolences. *We are so sorry*, everyone keeps saying, *we are so incredibly sorry*, and I want to ask what they are sorry for. Nobody can apologize away an errant deer on a clear night, a mis-twisted steering wheel, a severed aorta.
 I eat half the pot pie directly from its aluminum container. It is the first proper meal I've eaten since the police knocked on my door. I am thick and bloated, my stomach distended. I rub my paunch with my palm and close my eyes. This is as close to pregnant as I will ever be.

Jennifer Todhunter's stories have appeared in *SmokeLong Quarterly*, *Necessary Fiction*, *CHEAP POP*, and elsewhere. She was named to *Wigleaf's* Top 50 Very Short Fictions 2018, and is the Editor-in-Chief of *Pidgeonholes*. Find her at www.foxbane.ca or @JenTod_.

The Serpent's Daughter

From *Paper Darts*

Jennifer Tseng

EVERY HUMAN BEING, LIKE every machine, was created to do something. Trains carry people over land, under sea; a fan moves air; an iron presses cloth; a mug holds tea. Likewise, a nursing mother makes milk, a doctor sews skin, a tailor sews clothes, a spy watches people, a philosopher thinks, a judge makes decisions, and Sister Mah prays. She prays all day the way some people hum while they knit or chew gum while they're taking your order.

We ate in a restaurant once. In the town where our post office box was. It was called Billie Jean's. They cooked the food we asked for. In exchange we gave them money—something I rarely saw. We had very little. As Sister Mah put the light green portrait of Andrew Jackson on the table, I saw her lips quiver with what I read as regret. She'd never eaten at Billie Jean's; I'd begged her to take me. She didn't know the food would be awful. She probably suspected as much but wanted to grant me the exotic, albeit terrible-tasting, pleasure of eating in a restaurant. We bowed our heads and prayed before we ate. As soon as Mah was done eating, she started mumbling her regular prayers again, while I looked wistfully at the dessert menu. I thought: This person belongs in a convent and I don't.

This person was created to pray and I wasn't.

"Mah," I say, interrupting her murmurs. If I want to say anything, I interrupt. "Can I ask you something?" Sometimes she crosses herself then looks up at me with our round green eyes. I feel at once grateful for her attention and stricken by the triviality of what I'm about to say. Though we're just resting in our room on a Sunday, I feel I should have something bigger or better prepared. Something more worthy of her attention. "Where does the Serpent live?" I've found that using her name for him increases the chances she'll answer my question. I feel like a traitor calling him that but I do it anyway.

"Orange Grove," she says. I imagine their yellow house sitting in the middle of an orange grove, its windows open, its rooms smelling of oranges. I see him sitting at a picnic table on a patio, slicing an orange into eight pieces. Eight is the Chinese lucky number. I like to think of him making eights for good luck. Cutting his meat into eight pieces, taking eight steps down the hall, picking eight oranges at a time off the orange tree. There really is an orange tree in the backyard. She told me that once and I wrote it down under Things I Know About Ba. It's a small but essential section of my notebook. I know there is just one tree. Still, I like to picture a grove of eight for good luck. We need luck, he and I, to find each other.

When I look at her to ask my next question, I see she is murmuring again. Her attention, like the tiny stained-glass window in the chapel's cupola, has closed.

"What does he look like?" I ask.

"I don't know. I haven't seen him in seventeen years."

I sigh loudly. "Mah, you know what I mean! What *did* he look like?"

"You know I don't like to talk about the Serpent."

She opens her desk drawer. For a moment I think she's going to take out the picture of him and show it to me but she takes out a rosary instead. It's her way of ending the conversation.

Before she can begin the Apostles' Creed, I sit on her lap and the rosary slips out of her hand onto the floor. In a flash, I pounce on the sparkling blue spheres and hold them up over my head.

"Simone!" My mother yells my name, momentarily forgetting herself, forgetting the Sisters are within earshot.

"Just tell me what he looks like and I'll remember. I promise I'll never ask you again."

"Jesus Christ, you're worse than the devil himself."

"What does he look like?" I ask again.

She stares out the window with her green eyes at the flowers. "He looked like you with brown skin. He looks like you. Is that what you want to hear?" But no one ever knows I'm Chinese! I want to yell back. Instead, I throw the rosary onto her desk and run down the hall, down the back stairs, out the back door, and into the woods.

"Do you have a picture," I say. To ask would be bearing false witness because I've seen it before, mixed in with her things like a foreign stamp or a lost playing card. A black and white photograph, out of place but mixed in, a part belonging to a whole that exists elsewhere. When she goes to town in the truck, I go through her things. That's when I see it. Now, a week later, she doesn't say yes or no, doesn't stop murmuring, but she hands it to me. I gasp like a child in the dark in front of a Christmas tree.

"Keep it in your drawer," she says. "I don't ever want to see it again. Do you hear me?"

I slide my desk drawer open and put the Serpent inside. Without looking at him. Without even a glance. I shut the drawer quickly to demonstrate my obedience and to keep her from changing her mind. The slim metal drawer is like a safe surrounding the picture, a barrier she will have to breach if she wants him back. If there were a lock on the drawer I would use it, but there isn't. It doesn't matter. She has given me everything. Eyes, nose, mouth, skin. The empty space in her desk where, for years, she kept the picture. The woods with its trail and its waterfall. Beyond that, the stream and its bridge.

Jennifer Tseng is an award-winning poet and fiction writer. She teaches for OSU Cascades' Low Residency MFA Program & the Fine Arts Work Center's online writing program, 24PearlSt.

Being the Murdered Babysitter

From *Passages North*

Cathy Ulrich

THE THING ABOUT BEING the murdered babysitter is you set the plot in motion.

Your geometry homework will still be on the Harrisons' coffee table, a boy's name written on the grocery-bag cover, traced again and again with black pen.

Mrs. Harrison came home tipsy, she'll say tipsy, husband's arms supporting her, giggling like a girl, tangled hair catching on her wedding ring. She won't remember if you were still there when they returned, won't remember if you needed a ride from Mr. Harrison or if you said you'd walk, sometimes you did that, just a couple blocks away, quiet neighborhood, safe.

It was our anniversary, Mrs. Harrison will say. We were celebrating.

The kids loved her, she'll say.

You drew them pictures of horses that they pinned to their walls, taught them how to swear in Japanese.

After your death, the Harrison children will say kuso, kuso, ride ghost horses through the house. Mrs. Harrison will think she hears the beating of hooves, touch Mr. Harrison's forearm, do you hear that?

It's just the children, he'll say.

Mr. Harrison will be interrogated for hours, interrogated, Mrs. Harrison will say, left hand twitching, like a criminal.

He'll say he gave you a ride. He'll say he let you off at home.

The police will push Styrofoam cups of steaming coffee across the table to him. The police will talk to him like equals, like friends. One will have a wife in the PTA at his children's school.

Did you wait to see if she got inside?

Mr. Harrison will say yes, will say I think so, will finally say I don't remember.

I had a glass of wine, he'll say. Maybe two.

He'll say: I probably shouldn't have been driving.

When the police talk to your parents, your mother will say: My baby. She'll say my baby, my baby, my baby. The youngest of your four older brothers will sit on a bench at the station beside her. He'll blink and blink and chew on a stick of gum from your mother's purse. He'll stay seated on the bench when the police come out with Mr. Harrison, when your mother throws herself at him like they do on television, beat her hands against his chest, my baby.

Mr. Harrison won't be able to look at your mother, won't be able to step away from her tiny, flailing fists. Mr. Harrison will try to say I'm sorry, I'm sorry, but his mouth will only open and close without a sound.

Mrs. Harrison will do the laundry after your death, run the linens through the wash again, again, again.

Do these smell musty to you? she'll ask Mr. Harrison.

Mr. Harrison will say they don't smell like anything at all.

I'll wash them one more time, Mrs. Harrison will say, just in case.

She'll fold the sheets in the youngest child's bedroom, keep an eye on the drawings of horses pinned to the wall. She'll think how alive they seem, as if the paper is only barely holding them back. She'll remember how much her children loved horses after you started babysitting, how the youngest told her the names of the ones in the drawings: Charley Chase, Marion Davies, Max Linder. She'll think the names are familiar, think maybe they were people once, long ago.

The youngest child will come back to her room, find Mrs. Harrison still there, folding and refolding sheets.

These horses, Mrs. Harrison will say. Are they real horses?

Mrs. Harrison will swear she can hear hoofbeats, will say to her youngest: You hear it too?

Mrs. Harrison will think of the name written on your geometry book, the dedication inherent in the tracing.

She must have done it every day, she'll say to her book club, goblet of red wine in her hand.

She must have been, Mrs. Harrison will say, so in love.

Mrs. Harrison will hear the beating of hooves, Mrs. Harrison will be beset by phantom horses, will insist on taking down every one of your drawings from her youngest's room, over the child's protests, march them out to the garbage.

It's not horses, Mr. Harrison will say after rescuing the drawings in the evening, smoothing them out, laying them on the youngest child's bed.

What is it, then, Mrs. Harrison will say, and her husband will put his hand to her chest, and she will feel his warmth, feel her own racing heart, the way her pulse is pounding in her ears.

Cathy Ulrich, a Montana resident, is the editor and founder of the flash fiction journal *Milk Candy Review*. Her work has been published in various journals, including *Wigleaf, Black Warrior Review, Pithead Chapel* and *Passages North*. This story is part of her "Murdered Ladies" series, which she is working on along with her "Astronaut Love Stories" and "Japan" series of flash fictions.

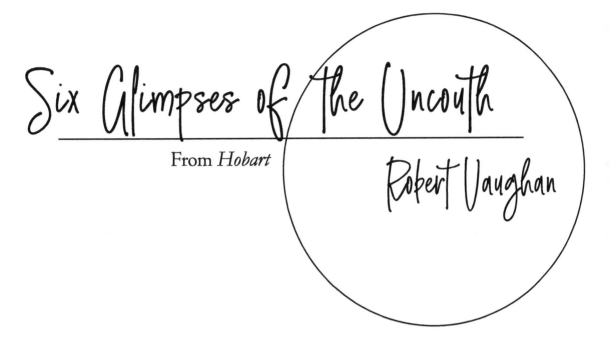

Six Glimpses of the Uncouth

From *Hobart*

Robert Vaughan

Street: 1:34 a.m.

HIS RAINCOAT WAS SPLATTERED with light spots of splayed dirt. The books behind him in the broken shop window were scattered and scarce. It was much later I recalled both his hands stayed in his pockets the entire time we made out. He was groping me through the jacket. Hands like clubs. It was diverse and hazy, like the winter was shedding.

House: 3:40 a.m.

Back at his place, he made me watch these home movies of some unknown person's life. At first I kept wondering why, who is this, what are we doing? But then I felt privileged, like it was something exotic. A peacock. Then that made me excited. The wilderness stretched out forever; just you and me. And a prescription to keep the hounds at bay.

Statues: Monday

That week he asked me to meet him on the corner of 12th and Lafayette. On the steps of the huge statue of Gilgamesh. He brought Jean Genet's play, "The Maids," and when we read it aloud, he used more than ten different voices. I was amazed, like the first time you realize the tooth fairy is just another lie. Or that big girls don't cry.

Dancing Queen: Valentine's Day

We all ran around the back yard playing a home-made game, crazy valentine. And you acted like

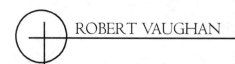

nothing left. We all ran all around. Susie had hers off completely, Danny poured beer all over us, Fern screamed so loud she spit. The back yard, running around. "Crazy Valentine." And you lit my hair on fire. Poof, that acrid smell. It was really fun.

Iraq: 1987

After you left for another war, I went looking for him or for traces of him, like a correspondent, like a common genie looking for its self. I wore a uniform of the northern people so I would blend in with Susie, April and Fern. You went AWOL when I ripped my shirt off because of the spilled beer, Fern lent me her shawl. And we couldn't find you.

Garage: 12:34 today

Another day at work. Phone call, meet me at the garage. I did. Scary because it had been decades, another lifetime. Then you walked in, raincoat still a mess. Talking gibberish and mumbling this and that. Pacing like a panda behind bars. We went walking and cast a pall over the shed skins of the misfortunate. What did I do to make you do the things you did.

Robert Vaughan is the author of five books: *Microtones* (Cervena Barva Press); *Diptychs+ Triptychs + Lipsticks + Dipshits* (Deadly Chaps); *Addicts & Basements* (CCM), *RIFT*, co-authored with Kathy Fish (Unknown Press) and *FUNHOUSE* (Unknown Press). His blog: www.robert-vaughan.com.

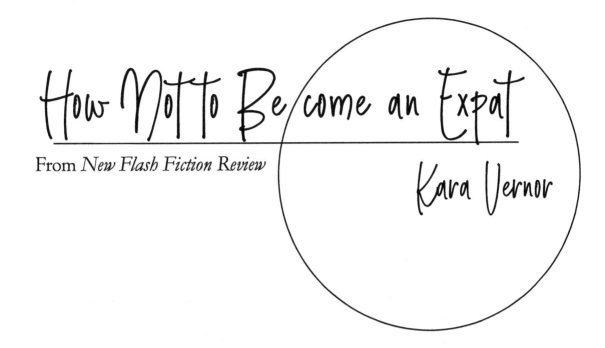

How Not to Become an Expat

From *New Flash Fiction Review*

Kara Vernor

for Annik

FLY TO COSTA RICA on a one-way ticket. Don't think about the reasons you're leaving, not now as your city shrinks beneath you. Now, you are a free bird.

Find a room in a house run by a local guy and stay drunk for a month. Have sex with local guy, and make out in the bathrooms of lesbian discos with women you can't talk to. Learn to merengue. Smoke all the time.

Find a part-time job teaching English and make a monthly budget. When the balance comes to negative two seventy-eight, check your credit card limits. Swear off math.

Notice the flyer in the window of the supermercado announcing, "Assistant Wanted 12 Hours/Wk– Native English Speakers Only." Rejoice! You are qualified. Arrive to the interview in what is now your interview dress, the only dress you stuffed into your backpack.

Sense the quiet of the house, a stranger world than the already strange world you bussed through to get there. Sense it's not a good idea to say, "Dinah won't you blow?" after she tells you her name. Be young. She prefers near girls or a gay men. Smile and ignore the chunks of food stuck in her teeth. Don't ask why the husband has his own wing.

When the husband drives you back to your place, don't tell him to drop you at the white house. Beige? he'll insist. You mean the beige one?

On your first day of work and every day after, change into chancletas immediately after closing the front door behind you. Scrub your hands and fingernails and display them for her to inspect. Wipe your chancletaed feet on the damp hand towels that lie before every threshold so germs won't transfer from one room to the next. Mind which *side of the knife* has sliced the skin of the papaya and use *the other side of the knife* for the flesh. Do not address her on her left. That side of her aura was damaged as she exited her mother's vagina. Not that she remembers it—That would be absurd, she'll say—but a medium she consulted saw it all. Stick to the assigned route when you walk to the restaurant to pick up her food. When you glance over your shoulder, pretend not to notice her husband ducking behind a parked taxi. When Dinah defecates with the bathroom door open, narrating her progress aloud—*just a little bit more to go, come on*—keep dusting the Kuna molas that pave the walls of her cool tomb of a living room.

Don't ask why she doesn't leave her house. Don't ask if she is under the care of a mental health professional. Don't hint that the world inside is unlike the world outside. Remember you are the world outside, at least for now.

After a few months, do not spike her daily Pepsi with LSD. Do not shove her out her front door to revel in her flailing. Quit now while you still can on good terms, the terms of the young and resource-less. When she calls you a month later to see if you need work, count the cash you've tucked under your foam mattress on the floor and be tempted. For a second.

Remember her living room, the frame after frame of vibrant textiles, each a different hand-stitched maze, the walls they hang on a white grout between these neural maps, the wrapping mural of her brain, the only brain of reference. This is what it is to deny. This is what it is to hide away.

Have a couple more nights on the town. Fuck one more stranger. Forgive yourself for not learning Spanish. Buy your ticket home.

Kara Vernor's fiction has appeared in *Ninth Letter, Vol. 1 Brookly, Fanzine, The Los Angeles Review,* and elsewhere. She has been the recipient of an Elizabeth George Foundation scholarship, and her writing has been included in *Wigleaf's* Top 50 Very Short Fictions, *All of Me: Love, Anger and the Female Body,* and *Golden State 2017: Best New Writing from California.* Her fiction chapbook, *Because I Wanted to Write You a Pop Song,* is available from Split Lip Press.

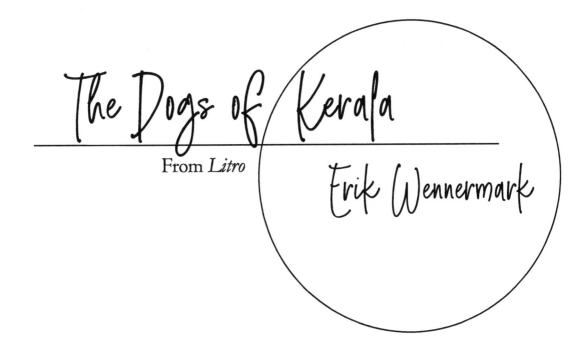

The Dogs of Kerala

From *Litro*

Erik Wennermark

THE DOGS OF KERALA walk on walls like stalking gargoyles, eyes reddened by dust, yellow-cornered, ridden with disease. In the dirt, a puppy young-in-health runs between my legs; he bites playfully and his tooth snags in the fabric of my trousers. He is startled, afraid; he does not know to relax or be pulled deeper.

There is howling outside the window – shrieking, fighting, snarling – the scene lit by a harvest moon, orange the color of a swami's robes. The dogs wake me at half two with my alarm set for a quarter to five. I need to kindle the lantern, bring the offering, a drink for the guru. At the end we take what God has left behind. I drift back to sleep for a few precious hours.

Two astride the dogs trot the mazy paths fronting the Varkala cliffs. They run in circles going nowhere. Paw prints left behind in the early morning sand glisten in the rising sun. Tracks of paws washed away by the rising tide. We meditate on impermanence while men smoke and women work or talk.

The man next door screams in the night. He stamps when the dogs approach, curses. He is a loud man, filled with sea wind. The dogs see through his bluster, but run all the same. The howls return, like suffering. Perhaps they never leave, just subside beneath waves of exhaustion or bliss. The fisherman's catch is poor again.

A dog pokes her head through the front gate. She steps in unsure, someone hisses, she looks, decides, turns and trundles away. There are cats too: three kittens appear for a few days, mewing and crying, skinny and lice-ridden, begging to be scratched and fed. One got into my room, twice, hid under the bed, out of reach my grasping hand. But a kitten can't stop moving for long; a kitten can be waited out. The kittens disappear. If it's the dogs, crushed by a spinning tyre, drowned in the deep ocean, I don't know.

In the naming ceremony Guruji christens me swan. They are finicky creatures,

swimming in circles. When they get too close to one another they erupt in screams and honks, flap their wings. They quickly forget and swim again. I hold anger in my hand like a hot coal, wounded fingers grasp fire to throw at the enemy.

Do the screaming dogs nurse resentment? Do the same dogs fight each night? Do the dogs call each other adversary, know their foes strengths and weaknesses? Do they hate? Animals don't remember such things we are told: names of offenders, lists of grievances. Each day, each minute is new. I am not so sure.

The dogs of Kerala exist and eat what they can and multiply when they can. The dogs of Kerala howl at the moon and wind, while we lay sleepless, preparing to rise, waiting. Hanging on the edge of perilous knowledge.

Erik Wennermark writes various prose in Tokyo, Japan. His works include the Falun Gong inspired novella *The True Story of Yu Fen*, short story collection *Evil Men*, and essays on topics such as the politics of Hong Kong independence and the death rattle of an Indian guru.

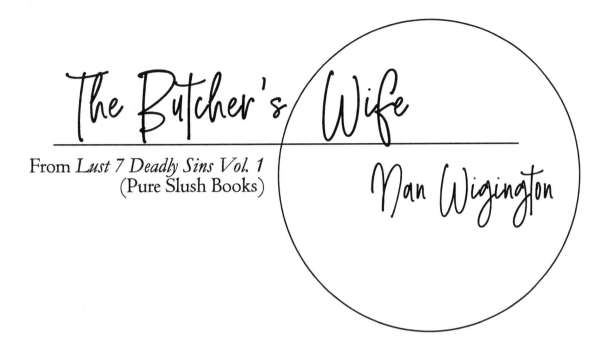

The Butcher's Wife

From *Lust 7 Deadly Sins Vol. 1*
(Pure Slush Books)

Nan Wigington

SHE WROTE WHEN SHE thought he wasn't looking. Notes about the business. On the brown paper she wrapped the bloody bits in, little red blotches swelling beneath black letters. He believed she had taken an interest in the business and this was her way of loving him and remembering butchery. He wasn't sorry that he had married a younger woman. She was strong, could carry on.

Once he saw her write, "The carcass can be chilled or hot boned."

Another time – "Secondary butchering is the trimming of primal cuts."

At night, after flank steaks and potatoes in their little apartment above the little shop, she would serve him tea and he would try to tell her all his secrets.

"Every carcass is different," he would say, "You want to see muscle on the bone. The color of the fat, too, is important. Yellow means grass fed. White is grain."

But the old butcher got too sleepy too soon. His lessons were short, lacked purpose and passion. Barely five sentences and he would rise, peck his wife on the cheek, and go to bed. He worried that he'd never tell her enough. Sometimes he had nightmares. How she might botch a job, cut off his hand, wrap it in brown paper. Sometimes he saw suet with his kidney still attached. One night he thought he woke up to laughter from the other room – hers and another man's. They seemed excited by the carnage.

"Just because I want to cut him up doesn't mean I don't love the old animal," she said clearly. But wasn't it just part of the nightmare? She was a good woman. How could he marry someone so secretive and callous?

The next morning, he smiled as she flirted with the customers, one boy in particular, dressed like a rich man's son.

"I can give you whatever you want," she was saying.

He knew she was only drumming up business, selling more meat to a boy who had enough already. The butcher smiled. An odd wave of pride and lust pushed him toward the pair. He held her from behind, feeling her sinew and muscle, and added –

"We can kill the beast and cut it to your specifications."

"I'm sure you can," the young man said as he accepted an additional brown paper package from the butcher's wife.

That night, they both went to bed directly after tea. The butcher tried to make love, but he began to worry about the young man. Had he been a voice in the old man's nightmare? How often had he come to the shop? How many packages had he already received? How many notes had she written to him? Which were about butchery and which were about love? Nothing on the old man seemed to work. He fell away from his wife in a sad, jealous heap. But she wouldn't give up.

She asked, "So how do you kill the beast?" Then licked her lips.

"You take a bolt gun stunner," he said, lifting his right thumb and index finger. "You touch it to a special place –" He aimed low, then touched high – the middle of her forehead right above her eyes. "Then bam. That's it. You hoist him up, bleed him, take off the hide."

"And split him?" she said as she mounted her husband's hips.

"Yes," he whispered.

The butcher's wife touched the center of his forehead, touched each of his breasts, and said, "Bam. Bam. Bam." His body felt strong and whole again. The love was so good, the butcher felt as blissful as a beast gone to slaughter.

Nan Wigington works as a paraeducator in an autism center classroom. Her flash fiction has appeared in *Pithead Chapel*, *100 Word Story*, *Occulum*, *Envy 7 Deadly Sins Vol. 6*, and *Lust 7 Deadly Sins Vol. 1*. She was honored to receive an editorial mentorship in 2017 from Gordon Square Review. Both Nan and her husband once considered themselves vegetarians. They live with their dog in Denver, Colorado.

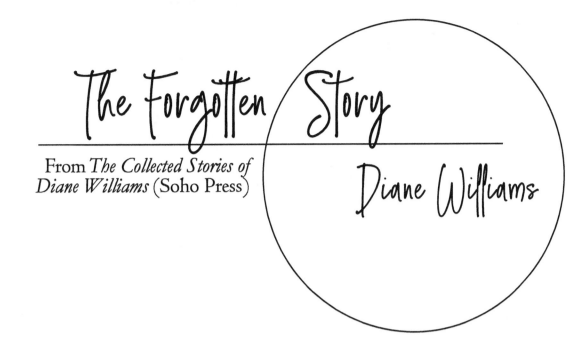

The Forgotten Story

From *The Collected Stories of Diane Williams* (Soho Press)

Diane Williams

PLEASE LET ME SPEAK --- I used to want to, but I was still unready at the banquet to air my views, nor was I going to provide any explanation in an area of significance.

Although, I told myself that I would, and then I scheduled something else. I ate the food --- pulpous and semisolid and I still have some level of pride. I was wearing my new Swiss vintage wristwatch with its good sword hands.

Now more than ever --- I got not much further than at the point of arrival, when I said, "Where is the restroom? Is elevator service available?" and "Could I use the bathroom now?"

I had taken the tiny single-serve butter packs that were provided and the tiny half-and-half tubs and made of them a colonnade that then tipped and leaned itself intact against my water goblet.

One should be able, in conversation to recall, just so, an attitude or an impressive deed in one's life, slot it in, watch it climb.

"Do you know this lady?" --- a woman I didn't know pointed at me.

"Yes, ma'am. She's my wife," the man across from me said.

"Why aren't we listening to this nice woman?" the interlocutor continued, "For instance, what does she think about Trey Gowdy?"

My little tower fell down. There was laughter and then a shadow the size and shape of an unclad foot, whose toes were wagging, showed up behind the head of the man, so that I was not left with a positive feeling.

I looked at my empty restaurant plate. It had a green-stripe around its border and a logo with an eagle and the date nearby it.

Oh, listen, I didn't say a word. A waiter brought bread that I took between my hands,

broke into bits, scattered about on the plate. I regained my senses and made a small province with the crumbs, or country.

The Collected Stories of Diane Williams was published by Soho Press in 2018. She is the founder and editor of the literary annual, *NOON.* She lives in New York City.

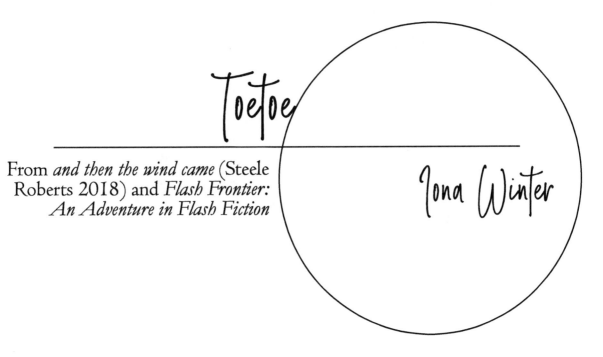

Toetoe

Iona Winter

From *and then the wind came* (Steele Roberts 2018) and *Flash Frontier: An Adventure in Flash Fiction*

OVER THE READ FROM us men in wheelchairs beg for bus money, while their socks dangle limply in the breeze. Our pockets are always empty but we check them anyway, the poor subsidising the poor, while the rich amble by in designer shoes swinging distended bags crammed with so many unnecessary things.

Up here in the city, pōrangi people go to sleep in shop doorways during the day. Yesterday one of them screamed, 'Let me out, for God's sake, let me out!'

Together we watched the woman's arms wave toetoe-like, as if in a breeze, and her wild eyes looked the same as ours used to at kapa haka practice whenever we tried to get our pūkana on.

We said 'aroha' under our breaths as we walked past and, by instinct, flinched when other people laid latex-gloved-hands on her body – as if a hungry swarm.

Inhaling a cigarette and our musty clothes, I prayed for silence, to welcome back all the fractured pieces of me; like listening to a band blindfolded, my other senses come alive. *Nights in White Satin* was playing on a radio somewhere, interwoven with police sirens.

'Cos I love you, yes I love you, oh oh how I love you…

My man pulled me into his shoulder and whispered, "Maybe she is one of those people who can see how lost we've become."

And then we laughed, to make light of our own dark places without doorways to shelter in.

Iona Winter (Waitaha/Pākehā) lives in Ōtepoti Dunedin, Aotearoa New Zealand. Published and anthologised in Aotearoa and internationally, she writes in hybrid forms that explore the spaces between poetry and prose. Her debut collection *and then the wind came* was published in 2018 (Steele Roberts). Shortlisted in 2018 with the Bath Novella-in-Flash Award, Iona has read her work at the Edinburgh International Book Festival, and won the Headland Frontier Prize in 2016. Her flash can be found in *Bonsai, Reflex Fiction, Bath Flash Fiction, Ora Nui, Meniscus,* and *Flash Frontier.*

I'm Exaggerating

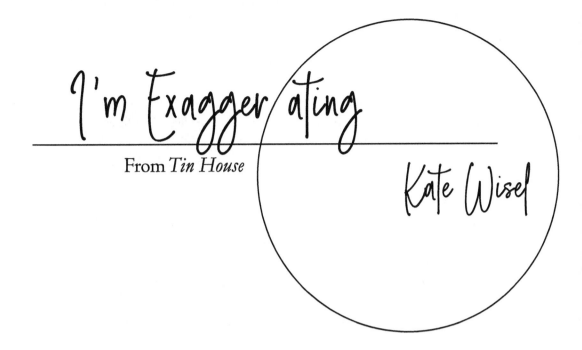

From *Tin House*

Kate Wisel

SERENA WORE A NAVY two-piece suit, sensible flats, twisted-up hair, a buttoned cuff over the wrist—read the faded *blah blah blah* script. Her first flight was to Wichita, and she had asked Niko if he knew what Wichita looked like from the sky. She wanted to hurt him. For him to picture her cloud-height, off the ground, sixteen hundred miles to the middle, untouchable.

She scooped ice and twisted bottle caps. Balanced her palms on headrests during dips. The aisle a tightrope. It rattled: the overheads, the ice, her fingers. Sometimes the pilot and the co-pilot looked like the cops who rapped on her door the month before. In the cockpit, their hands on the gears against the bright, complicated look of the control panel. The backs of their heads against the bright, complicated look of the sky. She cracked the front door, chain off the bolt, swollen eye. Her smile a cross, index finger against her lip. Niko was passed out in boxers, in the bedroom, in a deep sleep. The cops pushed through, ignored her.

"I made a mistake," she said. She paced, the blood in her hair graffiti orange and stiff. Blood on the white table, sprays of droplets from huffs where her mucus went loose under the break, her wrists twisted back.

"I'm exaggerating!" she told the cops, then recognized it as something he would tell her. Right in her ear like a basketball coach fighting the side-line.

"Get up," Niko would say. "You're faking all of this."

Wichita was not what she thought. Little Rock, Providence. Nowhere she'd been, or belonged, but all familiar. She had a day off in Spokane. Bumpy wheels of luggage by her heel, she roamed down Division St., smokestacks spilling filth up towards an ocean-colored mountain. Janis Joplin on a brick wall, fingers outstretched. Towards the river, the smell of spoiled milk and a sign: *near nature, near perfect.* Pine trees that could see inside homes and for miles.

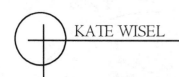

Back on the plane she found passengers to their rows. Locked in the Clorox-blue of the bathroom, she fingered her new insignia, a wing pin she wore like a crucifix and to sleep. And on the dark seat, facing backward, going forward, she thought of what to do. This she thought of terminally. What was down there. What wasn't. There was no losing of a baby or liters of liquor in desk drawers.

Maybe there was a lost baby; to be exact is to lie.
She had enough money to run up a credit card. There was a lease, the stain of their signatures, one under the other. Hers under his, as if he could hold her down with ink.

Somewhere above Lake Superior she heard an infant's cry. It was a salt-water gargle, as disturbing and rangy as a vocal warm up. She walked down the aisle, nearing the sound, and found a mother dozing on the seat. She lifted the infant from the mother's sleeping arms. Her tee-shirt was splotched with milk at the nipples, her slump vaguely sexual like she'd been slipped a mickey.

Serena strode the aisle with the infant in her arms, its wail an emergency. It filled the cabin with an engine-like force, though those fat-ringed thighs kicking against her stomach went nowhere. She watched as a business man's eye's popped open. She gazed at them, felt his shock upon waking. Mid-air. Mid-shriek. She palmed the little one's wet head, the mask of a soft wet scalp under her eyes. The seam of her lips by an ear the size of a bottle cap.

She whispered, "Hey there."
She whispered, "Don't be quiet."
She whispered, "Keep screaming."

Kate Wisel is the author of *Driving in Cars with Homeless Men*, which won the 2019 Drue Heinz Literature Award. Her fiction and nonfiction have appeared in publications that include *Gulf Coast*, *Tin House online*, *The Forge*, *Redivider* as winner of the Beacon Street Prize, and elsewhere. She is currently the Carol Houck Fiction Fellow at the University of Wisconsin-Madison.

The Earth is All Stones

From *Blue Five Notebook*

Marjory Woodfield

The Edge of the World and Acacia Valley

Leave Riyadh by turning right at the King Khalid Eye Specialist Hospital. (24° 41.751'N, 46° 38.126'E)

WE CLIMB TO WHERE cliffs drop. I photograph a sand gecko on the escarpment edge. Find the swirling shell of a sea snail embedded in rock. *Turritellidae.* Jurassic era. Overlook ancient caravan routes. Endless desert haze. Brush of sand.

The earth is all stones. There are camels in the distance. Ahmed and Hasan spread a carpet. Swirls of red and blue, with tasseled ends. We drink coffee from a Bedouin pot, dallah. Burnt gold with a long crescent spout. The coffee is black and smells of cardamom and cloves. Qahwa.

When Ahmed pours he stands, holding the dallah high in his left hand. It curves through the air in a graceful arc, filling the small handleless cups in his other hand. Hasan passes us dates. Sukkary, Ajwa, Madjoul. They walk a few paces away. Stand and face Makkah. Afternoon salah.

Raghbah

Take the new Makkah Road West down the escarpment. (24°33.162'N, 46°14.179'E)

'The old mud town was established in 1669. You cannot miss it, because the watchtower is visible from the road. Turn left when you spot the tower, and drive into the village from any place you see fit. It is one of the famous ruins of Najd. The tower has six parts of different heights. Small windows for light and ventilation. At the top the diameter is less than a metre. If Raghbah is on your itinerary, you should not miss a climb to the top of the tower.'

I. Tumbling houses. Straggle of goats and darkling beetle. A blue door hangs askew, swings open, asking in no one. You say to take my abaya off before climbing. The spiral staircase narrows with each step. At the top we stand shoulder to shoulder and sense the tower swaying in the wind.

2. Mess of mud bricks. There was too much rain Salwa said, and the tower fell, but perhaps one day they will build it again.

3. Across the road, he hangs clothes on a line between two whitewashed walls. Wind catches the edge of his jalabiya. A good day for drying.

The King's Forest

From Exit 13 on the North Ring Road take the well-posted tarmac road to Rawdhat Kuraym. (25°22.709'N, 47° 12.266'E)

We drive in convoy. Stop beside a roadside market. There is everything here for picnics. Neatly stacked firewood and fire pits. Large canisters of water, fruit, snacks. Chairs and rugs, a line-up of plastic toys. Two young men want to sell us a soccer ball. Yes, we do play, but no, we don't want one today. Instead we buy a kite, rainbow colours, five riyals after bargaining. Ourania speaks Arabic, gets the best price.

At the King's Forest I look for tall trees. There is no Kahikatea canopy here, just a smattering of scrubby acacia. We gather wild flowers. Buttery mimosa, orange aloe and spires of milkweed. In the distance, Al Dahna sand dunes are stark red against the King's green meadows. We picnic. Samara flies her kite. Later, when she gets home, it is broken, the structure too flimsy to last.

Ourania gives us plastic bags, tells us to shovel in handfuls of sand. She will use it in her garden. Later Amir will get cross and shout because the sand has gone everywhere. Ourania says that's just what sand does and shouldn't he know that anyway, because after all he's from Sudan. She props up her wildflowers in the sand. Let's the hose run. Dreams bright colours. The next day when I pass her house they are drooping.

Marjory Woodfield is a New Zealand teacher and writer who has lived in the Middle East. Her work appears in a range of publications, both print and online. These include the BBC, *Takahē*, *Star 82*, *Flash Frontier*, *Blue Five Notebook*, *Cargo Literary*, *Raven Chronicles*. She is a Bath Ad Hoc Fiction winner, was long listed for the Alpine Fellowship (Venice), and won the Dunedin UNESCO City of Literature 2018 Robert Burns Poetry Competition.

A Thousand Eyes

From *PANK*

Tara Isabel Zambrano

RAKESH RUNS HIS FINGERS on my midriff, warns about the humidity at this time of the year in Guwahati. Adjusting the pleats of my sari, I think about his mother. "As a newlywed, you should visit Kamakhya where Goddess Sati used to retire in secret to satisfy her amour with her husband, Lord Shiva," she said, her mouth drawn into a thin line, her chin drooping. I can tell she was beautiful once.

Goat scat shines on the hilly road. On the side, wildflowers entwine with weeds. We walk past the panels with sculptured goddesses, the pallu of my sari covering my nose, my anklets jingling, my thoughts absconding to the afternoon before the nuptials when I saw Rakesh's father with my neighbor, a widow of nearly ten years, in the back room: his hand caressing her back, his lips softly biting on her neck. Moans and whispers. Space filled with abandon. I felt hot behind my ears. I felt mysteriously hungry. For the rest of the day I couldn't decide if I felt outraged at Rakesh's father or lusted after Rakesh.

The sun burns behind the clouds, a subdued flame. A dull pain rises in the right side of my abdomen, as if something is released. I scan a dark indent at the horizon: Wonder if it'll rain again, if the monsoon will leave us alone. After a while, the endless, relentless rain reeks, doesn't feel clean anymore.

The courtyard is streaked with animal blood. Offerings to the goddess include flower garlands, sweets and animal sacrifices. Sati is also famous as the bleeding goddess. She supposedly menstruates in the month of June and the Brahmaputra River near this temple turns red. In reality, the priests drop vermilion into the water to glorify Sati's fertility and fulfill the tradition.

Barefoot, the scat is pressed under our heels and stuck between our toes, some of it warm. A man, with a goat on a leash, turns a finger clockwise in his ear as he leads it downstairs to the sacrificing platform. My eyes are anchored to the animal's pleading eyes. A line forms and slithers towards the passage in the shape of a womb. At the entrance the stone wall glistens as if engraved with a thousand eyes.

Rakesh holds my hand, looks at my feet. I study his sweat stained collar, his arms and his strong wrists. The air is weighed down by ringing bells. "I'll give you a bath," he whispers, his breath a flame under my earlobe. I wonder how long since his parents touched each other: if absence of fucking makes you stiff as a corpse, if lack of passion is mistaken for being closer to God. I wonder if this is the place to think of sex. If not here, then where?

Ahead of us, a pregnant woman tucks her hair behind her ears. A carving of another Goddess overlooks us. Garlands between her breasts, thick thighs, her skin grey, rubbed with time. A draft comes from inside the temple, warm as a tongue. The animal downstairs makes a sound, distinct like death.

I lift my saree that billows around my ankles. Chants drone on above us, the passage gets narrower and darker as if we are about to be crowned, as if we are about to be born.

When the line stops moving, I put my hand in Rakesh's side pocket, caress the fabric of his khakis. He places his hand over mine: his head slightly bent, his curly hair pointed at me. He resembles his father but clean-shaved, guilt-free. I want to tell him what I saw and felt: part rapture, part shame. In his brown eyes, I want to see my whole self and know if we'll ever have what Sati and Shiva had or if we'll drift away and I'll become compromising like his mother. If years will come out of us like colorful birds in the sky or if they'll hang like roots of a banyan tree, limp. If one of us goes first, how will the other live?

Inside the cave, a sheet of stone slopes downwards from two sides, meet in a uterus-shape depression. The Goddess is not a sculpture but a stone kept moist from an underground perennial spring. The man, who came with the goat, makes his offering. A musty, sharp smell settles inside me. The pregnant lady bows, picks a flower lying next to the Goddess and touches it on her forehead.

I close my eyes, fold my hands. And images crack open like an egg: Sati's mouth ringed with blood, the goat's head on a newborn, Rakesh opening and closing my legs: penetrating me in a hundred different positions. Bodies resting in dirt or washed off to the seas, corroded to salt. Bodies returned to stillness before they are done being dead, before they turn into pristine wombs and hearts, ready to be broken in again.

Tara Isabel Zambrano moved from India to the United States two decades ago. She works as a semiconductor chip designer. Tara is Assistant Flash Friction Editor at *Newfound.org*. In the recent past, Tara has served as a hospice volunteer. She also holds an instrument rating for single engine aircraft. Her work has won the first prize in the *Southampton Review* Short Short Fiction Contest 2019, been a Finalist in *Bat City Review* 2018 Short Prose Contest and *Mid-American Review* Fineline 2018 Contest, and has been selected for *The Best Micro Fiction* 2019. Her stories have been previously nominated for *Best of the Net*, *The Best Small Fictions* and *The Pushcart*. Tara lives in Texas with her husband and two kids.

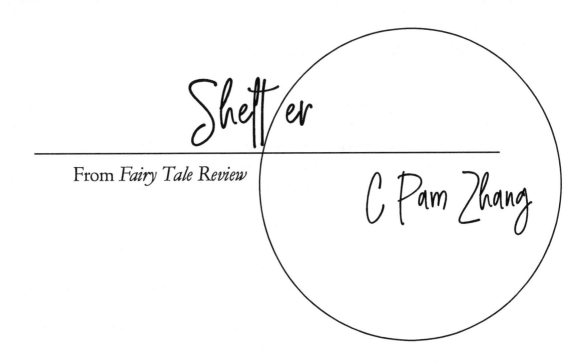

Shelter

From *Fairy Tale Review*

C Pam Zhang

WE RAISED BONE TO our mothers' houses. Joints lashed fast with sinew, pale ribs curved to beams like long strange teeth. We made a game of construction, bared our tiny canines and giggled.

Girls, our fathers called out in warning.

We desisted.

Back we went to stirring the pots for our mothers' glues. Each lifted its own head of steam, its own scent: vanilla, aloe, bread. My mother's vapor mingled and ran with my sweat. She smelled of eggs and skin musky from her morning run.

As the sun rose, play became work. Soon our shoulders ached from bending bone to shape. Outside the circle our fathers murmured encouragement, hands fluttering in their laps as if they could help us. When they slipped into siesta, we cheated. We pressed our cheeks to the bones and hummed our mothers' lullabies—we'd be good girls, we'd clean our rooms and floss our teeth, we'd remember them. The bones relented and softened.

When they stirred awake, our fathers sensed echoes of song in the air.

Girls? they asked uneasily.

We pretended not to hear them.

On this day they couldn't cross the line of ashes, couldn't shake us for answers. Building was our task alone. We stacked and tied faster than any man; the blueprint was in our blood, fizzing behind our closed eyes. *Faster*, it urged. *Stronger. Taller.*

At some point a femur clattered down and rang a girl's head like a bell. One clear tone that ached behind the breastbone, rattled between the jaw and the snail's shell of the ear. Our fathers sucked their breaths as the girl smiled, unhurt. Her teeth a cipher in the sun. One by one they smiled back, afraid to admit their fear. We knew our mothers would never harm us.

Dark fell and we dipped into the pots where our mothers' flesh had boiled down to their sticky glues. We stretched roofs from our mothers' skins, painted ceilings with our mothers' blood. From time to time a drop fell on a lifted forehead. These marked girls would become the most valued wives, the most fiercely protective mothers.

Near the end of the night, our fathers pressed closer to see our work. Mine approached in a bristle of words.

Daughter, he said, *did you know that human bone is ten times stronger than steel, gram for gram? Did you know it conducts heat better than copper pipe? That its medicinal properties lower blood pressure, promote thyroid health, and decrease the likelihood of dementia?*

I lowered my eyes, which my father took for deference. But it was shame. I was too old for fairy tales.

In truth, human bone can prove fragile. But my mother laughed loud all her life and ran five miles each morning until the day she died, drank the yolk of two raw eggs. *Daughter,* she said as I watched the slip of her muscled throat, *you see how strong I've become?* I loved her then: her faint mustache, the whorls her calluses left in dough. She went to her slaughter laughing like a hyena, so loud we clapped our hands to our ears, missing the point at which her laughter turned to screams. Some mothers went weaker, their bones softer, their houses crooked and their daughters left shivering at night in fear of their own motherhoods to come. But my mother said, *Don't cry.* Said, *It's not how many years they give you. It's what you choose to give.*

Tonight we'll sit in vigil as flesh and blood and bone reknit into a house overhead. Alone, we'll memorize the new architectures of our mothers' bodies, the hatchings of bone as intricate as the wrinkles that once framed their eyes. Tomorrow we'll invite our fathers and brothers in. They'll duck to enter, shamed by their weakness, but we'll greet them smiling, with soft voices and warm towels and meals cooked with our mothers' spices, knowing that from this day forward, we must be strong enough to shelter. That inside our bones are steel.

C Pam Zhang's debut novel *How Much of these Hills is Gold* comes out in 2020 from Riverhead Books in the US and Virago Press in the UK. Her short fiction appears in *American Short Fiction, Kenyon Review, McSweeney's Quarterly,* and elsewhere. Born in Beijing and an artifact of many American cities, she now lives in San Francisco.

Spotlighted Journals

Best Small Fictions (**Michelle Elvy**): Let's begin with the journal's name – a combination of Africa and Reader. How does this fit your vision for the journal, for African readers and writers?

AFREADA (**Nancy Amidora**): When I decided to run with my idea for *AFREADA*, I started by looking at the magazines and journals that already existed. I noticed that the best kind of literary storytelling in Africa has historically been circulated amongst a small group of writers and intellectual elites, and the natural result of this is that a limited amount of attention was paid to the look and feel of these websites. These magazines were focusing on the writer, the quality of the written words, and not the experience of the reader. They weren't considering the visual effects of a cover image, or the impact of font styles, but as a reader, I wanted to read stories on pages that looked beautiful and thoughtfully designed. So I decided to create this experience with *AFREADA*. Our name is a recognition that readers are the backbone of the publishing industry, so we insist on making them a core part of our publication.

BSF: Where did the idea for *AFREADA* begin – and has it turned out as you expected?

AFREADA: The journal began with a profound love for multimedia storytelling in Africa. I studied Law at university, and then went on to do a Masters at the African Leadership Centre. Everything up until that point indicated that I would go on to pursue a corporate career, but I've always been a reader, a love which was solidified when I received Chimamanda Ngozi Adichie's *Half of a Yellow Sun* for Christmas when I was 14 years old.

I went through a season of reading short story collections and I found myself enjoying the fast-paced nature of them. I particularly loved the ability for me to effortlessly travel to different spaces and times, and meet new characters, in the time it took me to travel from my home to my office. At the same time I was coming across exceptional short stories on people's personal blogs and realised the value of a 5- to 10-minute short story which could easily be accessed from phones or an alternative mobile device.

AFREADA, founded in December 2015, sources stories from writers across Africa and the diaspora, then we edit them, source content images, and promote the final product on a central platform. We began as a digital publication with an exclusive focus on fictional short stories, and have since published in excess of 200 stories from Kenya to Nigeria, Madagascar, Rwanda and beyond. Since launching, we have managed to attract a truly global community of enthusiastic and engaged readers from across the world. We exist for the writers who can't find readers, the readers who can't find writers, and everybody in between. I'd certainly say that we are pleased with our accomplishments so far, but we still have a very very long way to go!

BSF: Who is *AFREADA*'s audience?

AFREADA: *AFREADA*'s tagline is "stories from home" and with this tagline we are making a bold statement about who our target audience is. We share stories from Africa and the diaspora so naturally our stories come from across the world and attract an equally global audience, which we are immensely grateful for, but our aim will always be to serve readers who look at Africa, and think of home.

BSF: The description of the journal reads: *Imagine travelling across Africa in a single day. No visa applications, no airports. Just awe-inspiring short stories. We are bringing words and worlds together. Cape Town to Cairo. Lagos to Lusaka.* As big and diverse as the continent is, this implies a breakdown of borders, both geographically and metaphorically. Can you speak more to this vision?

AFREADA: My Nigerian heritage is something that fills me with immense pride but, above all, I am pan-African. I have a profound sense of love and respect for the wider continent of Africa. There are so many commonalities across the rich diversity of the continent and I realised that fostering a greater sense of unity and understanding amongst people from different communities can only be done through effective storytelling. It was best said by Zimbabwean writer, Irene Sabatini: "If you want to know a country, read its writers." In the same spirit, we want our readers to travel through stories. When we publish fictional stories about weddings in Kenya or stories about bustling markets in Tanzania, we are in fact engaging in a profound and

transformative cultural exchange and this will continue to be one of our core values.

BSF: The selections from *AFREADA* in *BSF* 2019 include "A Pinch of Saffron" by Ally Baharoon, "Miss Freda Pays a Visit" by Zoe Gadegbeku and "Locked Doors, Lead Melodies" by Amarachi 'Amie' Ike – three very diverse stories in tone, content and writing style. Can you discuss why these works stand out for you, as the editor of the magazine?

AFREADA: I am a reader, first and foremost, and I am drawn to stories that stir my imagination. When I read, I don't want to see words or punctuation, I want to see vivid pictures and hear lively conversations. Now this may sound idealistic, but it's a feeling that led me to fall in love with stories many years ago, so it's a feeling that I seek in every submission I read. The ability to skilfully craft a sentence is impressive, but in an editor's view, the story a writer is trying to tell will always be more important. What all three of these writers have in common is that they managed to skilfully craft truly exceptional stories. "A Pinch of Saffron" had me craving coconut candy, "Miss Freda Pays a Visit" left me feeling cold and a little scared, and "Locked Doors, Lead Melodies" positioned me right at the heart of a bustling market. These are very different stories, but equally powerful in their ability to capture the minds of their readers.

BSF: What comes next for *AFREADA*? What do you envision for 2020 and beyond?

AFREADA: We have a lot planned for the coming years, most of which will be announced later this year. But what I can say is that we will be exploring multimedia publishing more broadly, as a means of adopting a more holistic approach to storytelling and attracting a wider audience. It's really exciting times for storytelling, particularly on the Continent as there a number of new initiatives that are enabling Africans to tell their own stories, on their own terms. We're extremely privileged to be a part of this movement and we're looking forward to an exciting and exhilarating future!

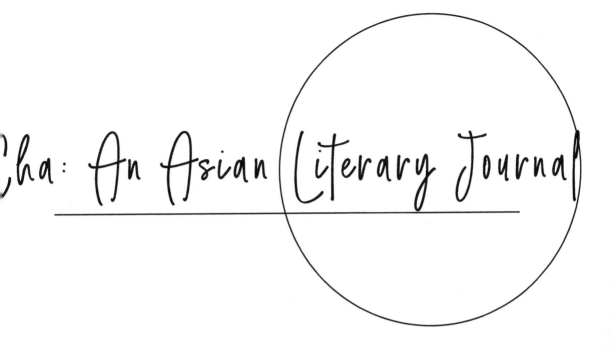

Best Small Fictions (Michelle Elvy): What's in a name? Please share with our readers more about the naming of *Asian Cha.*

Cha (Tammy Lai-Ming Ho): *Cha* means tea, which remains a quintessentially Asian drink. Its near ubiquity on much of the continent certainly speaks to its fundamental position in the region's social and cultural life. *Cha* has clearly become a unique element of many Asian cultures. On this matter, there is no more eloquent source than Okakura Kakuzo's classic commentary on the central role of tea in Japanese life, *The Book of Tea* (1906). But one need not scour high-minded philosophical tracks to understand tea's central position in Asia—a few minutes spent on the ground on the continent would suffice. Try taking a train ride in India without a hawker offering you a cup of *chai* or visiting a Korean household without being offered some *cha*, hot or cold. *Cha* may have Chinese roots, but in myriad local variations, it has gone well beyond this heritage. It is a taste of these variations that we hope to capture in our journal.

BSF: The journal's website states *Asian Cha* is '*the first Hong Kong-based international English-language free-access online literary journal.*' Tell us a bit about your submissions, and also your intended audience.

Cha: The submissions we receive reveal not only the great depth of Asian experience, but also a consistently deep pool of talent and vision. When we started Cha in 2007, we were sure that there was a lot of great writing from and about Asia out there, and all we had to do was start a home page and it would come flooding into our email boxes. We had no idea.

BSF: Can you tell us about *Cha*'s early days – and how the contents of the journal have changed over the years?

Cha: When we started *Cha* in 2007, we felt there was a comfortable space for our endeavour on the internet, especially as the number of resources for writers in Asia was quite limited. Unlike the crowded marketplace of online publishing in other countries, English internet publishing in Asia was underdeveloped. We were confident that we were in a good place to start such a project. For us, this offered the great opportunity of entering a market not as crowded as in North America or in the United Kingdom. Currently there are still only a handful of Asian online journals. We do not expect (nor hope) that this will continue. As Asia expands its economic and cultural influence, we are certain that interest in English Asian literature will increase.

BSF: How does being part of Hong Kong impact your own creative work, be it as a writer or editor?

Cha: I wrote almost exclusively in Chinese until university and it was mostly just silly scribbling. When I was an undergraduate student at the University of Hong Kong, I spent a great deal of time in the library. One day, I picked up a copy of *Ambit* off a nearby shelf and started reading. I was especially drawn to the poetry by living poets and shortly afterwards I began trying to write creatively in English. I showed my first poems to one of my professors and received positive feedback, which encouraged me to continue writing. I was also fortunate enough to be published in *Yuan Yang*, the university literary journal, and *Asia Literary Review* around that time. I have been writing ever since. The city of Hong Kong has inspired me greatly. Its rhythm, places, people, stories, grievances and hopes. Growing up in Hong Kong also means that the city contains almost all of my childhood memories (I spent some time on the mainland when I was two years old), which I write about in my poems as well. In recent years, I feel a stronger urge to record in poetry what is happening in the city and the changes we are witnessing due to the increasing influence of Beijing.

BSF: *Asian Cha* is a literary journal but also a programme that reaches into the community – through your writing workshops and your reading series. Can you tell us more about these endeavours?

Cha: In 2017, when the journal turned ten years old, I wanted us to do different things and do them more systematically, in addition to publishing four regular issues a year. Apart from starting to publish issues focusing on specific Asian places, we also now run the Cha Writing Workshop Series, which aims to provide workshops (poetry, prose, language skills) for school students and underprivileged groups in Hong Kong. The workshop leaders are all *Cha* contributors, who are also respected and dedicated educators in the city. Also, since November 2017, I have been organising the Cha Reading Series, which takes the online journal out into the community. The series features discussions and readings on a variety of topics at various locations around the city. A typical *Cha* reading usually features two to four speakers, while I act as the moderator. Our audiences are generally a mixture of students, scholars, writers and literary-minded members of the public. Most of our readings involve reading of selected texts, discussion and Q&As.

BSF: This year, you will celebrate your twelfth anniversary with the December issue. Please tell us more about how you expect to celebrate twelve years of *Cha!*

Cha: To start, I am hoping we will be able to publish the issue on time. Because of my other obligations and academic research, I am finding it increasingly difficult to sit down and work on *Cha* for long stretches. Compiling submissions, reading them, discussing these works with my co-editors and guest editors, and, later, editing the accepted pieces and putting them online—all this takes a tremendous amount of time. If we do manage to publish the issue in December, I'd like to party with those contributors who are in Hong Kong!

BSF: What comes next for *Asian Cha?* What do you envision for 2020 and beyond?

Cha: I want us to continue to build a local reading and writing community and connect this to the rest of Asia and the world. Looking ahead, if we can get more financial support, I'd like us to expand both the Cha Writing Workshop Series and the Cha Reading Series. And I have been discussing with my co-editors the possibility of starting a boutique publication house called the Cha Press, mainly to publish attractive and affordable books written by *Cha* contributors to further promote their work—maybe one day this dream will materialise.

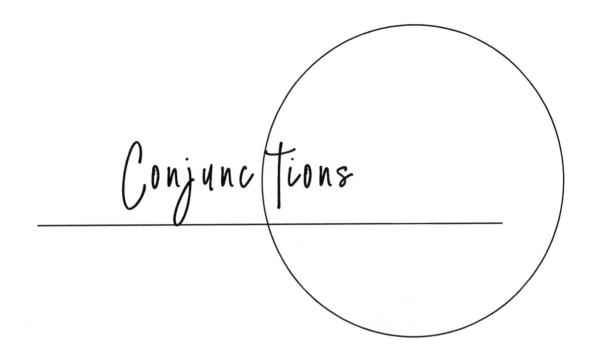

Conjunctions

Best Small Fictions (Jen Michalski): Three works from *Conjunctions* appear in *BSF* 2019: "The Malingerers" by Kristine Ong Muslim (one of the ten spotlighted stories), "Film: Nox Transfer" by Karla Kelsey and "Why Brother Stayed Away" by Ann Beattie. All of these examine perceived reality and deploy innovative structuring to complement the themes of memory, identity and perception. What spoke to you about these pieces, as the editors?

Conjunctions (Nicole Nyhan): These three contributions struck us for very different reasons, but it's fair to say that their examinations of perceived reality, or the subjective narrative terrain presented in each, is something that particularly intrigued us as editors. In "The Malingerers" the underworld is accessed via a photobooth—a fantastical conceit to be sure, but one which provides for an examination of great quandaries, from identity permanence to collective delusions to a philosophical critique of narcissim (and many old gods, for that matter). In "Film: NOX Transfer" images purportedly culled from a film reel are repeatedly reimagined and distorted, much in the way one might psychologically respond to trauma. "Why Brother Stayed Away" is a more realist tale, but it subverts the conventional narrative by presenting a riddle that leads readers to abandon initial assumptions about the central characters, thereby exposing the subjective, and limited, nature of the story. "The Malingerers" is compelling because the story is somehow both deadly serious and serious fun, in addition to being expertly composed.

BSF: When did *Conjunctions* begin publishing flash -- or, as you call it, short-form fiction?

Conjunctions: We have been publishing short fiction ever since the journal was first launched by Bradford Morrow in the early 1980s (he remains the editor today). *Conjunctions* published authors like Lydia Davis and Diane Williams early in their careers, but we never really considered their work with this terminology in mind. Then and now, we tend not to delineate between "flash fiction" and other forms of short fiction. Other boundaries are perhaps more interesting to examine: how to categorize an essay written in verse, for instance. Our contributors tend to experiment with formal and genre boundaries, often transgressing both, so distinctions on the basis of length alone are less important to us.

BSF: What do you look for in short-form fiction? What would you like to see more of, in terms of submissions?

Conjunctions: As with all the writing that we publish, we look for short fiction that is innovative, fully realized, thoughtfully constructed, and rendered with a distinct voice. Authors of short fiction have the uniquely daunting task of raising narrative stakes and capturing readers' attention using only a few sentences or pages. This does put increased pressure on the narrative to be carefully crafted. So, as in poetry, how do you make every word count? One must be economical in their use of language, but also extremely thoughtful about what they're trying to communicate. It's tough to say exactly what we are looking for, since we're always hoping to be surprised!

BSF: Are there any pieces in *Conjunctions* you think of as the most representative of the journal's mission?

Conjunctions: *Conjunctions* has endured over many years, which means that exemplary contributions, insofar as they relate to our mission, are inextricably tied to the time in which they were published. In a way, everything we publish is representative of the journal's mission: to create a space where authors can freely experiment with and develop new literary forms. We are proud to publish writers who challenge preconceived conventions and push their respective forms into new territories.

BSF: Which journals do you recommend for emerging flash writers to read, and why?

Conjunctions: Writers should be reading whatever journals they can get their hands on and identify the publications that resonate with their own work, not just in terms of preferred form, but also in relation to voice, subject matter, style, etc. You never know where you might discover the next brilliant work of short fiction, so keeping an open mind is important. Many, if not most great writers begin as voracious readers and spend a great deal of time reading work unlike anything they would create themselves. One of our taglines is "Read dangerously," but we might also add "Read omnivorously."

BSF: Among your contributing editors are esteemed writers Diane Ackerman, Brian Evenson, Rick Moody, and Peter Straub, to name a few. What is the role of contributing editors in fostering a journal's mission?

Conjunctions: Diane Ackerman and Fred Moten are *Conjunctions'* newest contributing editors, and we're thrilled to have them on board. The contributing editors send their own work for publication, of course, but they also keep us updated on what they're reading and help to enrich our publications by bringing in writers from their own networks. They also sometimes contribute to the development of new issue themes and occasionally help to coedit issues for which they have special expertise.

BSF: What percentage of your submissions comes from the slush pile, and what percentage are solicited, if any?

Conjunctions: We strive to include in each issue at least one author for whom the contribution marks their debut literary publication, and we've successfully done so in all of our most recent issues. Roughly 1/3 of the contributors to our 2018 print collections were from writers new to our pages. Our unsolicited manuscript pile is a treasure trove for us, and we read everything—and I mean everything—that comes our way. The unsolicited manuscripts are in some sense our lifeblood, our main avenue for the discovery of new and emerging voices.

BSF: Where do you think short-form fiction is headed? Where would you like it to go?

Conjunctions: Short fiction, like all forms of the written word, is in a constant state of evolution. It is impossible to predict the future of fiction, and that unpredictability is a good thing—at the very least, it means there is always potential for something new and unexpected to emerge. Surely the platforms may change over time, which may or may not significantly impact the fictional form itself (witness the sudden rise of hypertext stories in the 1990s, a technique perhaps less widely used today). Technology may shape the way that we read and write to some degree, and new technologies do provide opportunities for innovation that were never before possible, but as recent reports on e-book vs. print sales have shown (and contrary to many publishers' fears), the printed word is far from obsolete.

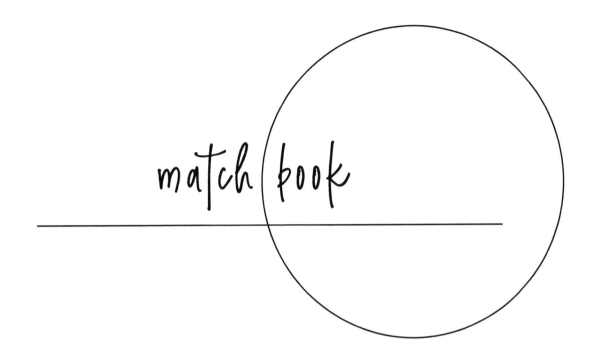

Best Small Fictions (Tyrese Coleman): Please tell us the history of *matchbook*. How and why did you start the journal?

matchbook (Brian Mihok): My friend Edward Mullany and I were intrigued by the potential of online journals back in 2009. The main drawback of publishing online, it seemed, was the flip side of its strength: the costs were much lower than print, but as a result, the amount of work published was overwhelming. Keeping up felt like an impossible task. We imagined a journal that would attempt to slow down the online torrent to something dependable and more manageable: one new piece of flash prose every other Monday. The author's note both gave writers an opportunity to say something about the published work and further distinguish us in what was already in 2009 a crowded field.

BSF: How has this streamlined approach to content help sustain your popularity and the quality of the work you publish? Does it provide the online version an element of exclusivity that one might get from a print with page length requirements?

matchbook (BM): If you read a piece the day we publish it, we'd like you to read it again the following week. Let it sit with you. Turn it over. Come back to it. We publish work that surprises us each time we read it, and by the time we publish it, we've read it sometimes upward of a dozen times. That sets a high bar for submissions, but it also means each piece we accept earns its spotlight on the site.

BSF: Congratulations on the three stories selected for inclusion in the anthology: "James Monti" by Marcelle Heath, "My Father's Girlfriend" by Lenora Desar, and "The Joke" by K.C. Mead-Brewer. What hooked you the most about these pieces and how do they fit *matchbook*'s literary aesthetic?

matchbook (**R. B. Pillay**): A joke, at its basic level, is a setup and a punchline. The punchline should both surprise you but also feel inevitable. K.C. Mead-Brewer's "The Joke" is funny from the very beginning, which is part of what grabbed us, but the story takes a turn about halfway through from being a variation on a familiar feeling to something incredibly, wonderfully unfamiliar but also somehow inevitable.

In contrast, Leonora Desar's "My Father's Girlfriend" is more like a sinkhole that opens underneath your feet without warning. Everything is simultaneously recognizable and terrifyingly alien. And just when you think you're starting to get the lay of the land, the land turns into a bird and flies across the room.

Marcelle Heath is one of two authors (the other being J. Bradley) we've published four times. Every time, she surprises us. The opening line of "James Monti" is basically perfect, and somehow, the story only gets better from there.

I'm not sure if *matchbook* has a literary aesthetic beyond the Venn diagram of the stories Brian likes and the stories I like, but one element all these pieces have in common is the care of craft. With each of these stories, as soon as you start reading them, you feel confident that the author knows what they're on about, and you can relax and enjoy the ride.

BSF: What is it about small fictions or flash fiction that captures you the most? Why does your journal highlight flash fiction out of all other forms of fiction writing?

matchbook (**RM**): In practical terms, very short prose was a good match for our own online attention span. Aesthetically, it can be an astounding reading experience. We loved very short writing in 2009 and we still love it in 2019. Writing this short can have the scope of a novel with the attention to detail of a poem. It's a unique form that continues to excite us.

BSF: What do you hope for the future of *matchbook*?

matchbook (**RBP**): We're currently working on a website redesign that we hope to unveil for our ten-year anniversary, and we've been talking about the possibility/feasibility of increasing our payments. In the long term, provided we remain energized by the work of editing and producing

matchbook, we'd love for it to be a place writers and readers can return to find work that is innovative and challenges expectations in another five, ten, maybe even twenty years.

New Flash Fiction Review

Best Small Fictions (Nathan Leslie): You founded *New Flash Fiction Review* in 2014. It seems as if flash fiction has really grown in stature over the past several years. Are you surprised by the success of flash fiction in general?

New Flash Fiction Review (Meg Pokrass): Yes! Blown away by what is happening. The form has come in to its time! There are hundreds, maybe thousands of literary journals that publish flash in 2019. What used to be an obscure literary niche is now a form that is taught in university writing programs and published in magazines like *The New Yorker*. Demand for quality flash fiction is growing so quickly. One could never have ever imagined this even three years ago.

BSF: Are you surprised by the success of NFFR?

NFFR: I'm delighted by our progress in the last two years, since I have moved to England. I made some important improvements, and they've paid off. I hired editors: Al Kratz, Steven John and Claire Polders (webmaster). Santino Prinzi helped us for quite a while; he injected the magazine with new energy and introduced us to some great British writers. Having this dedicated editorial help has given us the boost we've needed. And then bringing in guest editors such as the great Josh Russell and other illustrious guest editors like *Sudden Fiction*'s Robert Shapard, and Nin Andrews. Our Special Features Editor, Steven John, has brought us an amazing gift in stunning microfiction triptychs and artwork he selects to accompany them. There are our ongoing New Micro interviews, created by interviewers such as Tommy Dean, Steven John and Sandra Arnold. In 2018 we created The Anton Chekhov Award for Very Short

Fiction. Angela Readman was the winner of this inaugural contest.

BSF: Talk a bit about the aesthetics of *New Flash Fiction Review,* if there is such a thing. Is there a signature style or approach that you think works best for flash fiction?

NFFR: Simplicity felt right to me. Letting the work glow on its own, not trying to manipulate the readers' experience. Minimalism because it matches the form. Not saying anything with the look and feel, creating a bare, open field in which stories can be seen. I decided on an image very early, a group of sheep standing in the fog near a charismatic tree. It became our logo, and readers seemed to love it. I was drawn to the the sheeps' faces, as if they all had stories they wished they could tell. The quiet sincerity of their expressions.

BSF: This year's *Best Small Fictions* includes three outstanding stories from *New Flash Fiction Review:* Kara Vernor's "How Not to Become an Expat," "Insurance" by Elaine Chiew and "Shop Girl" by Dionne Irving Bremyer. What about these particular small fictions makes them so effective?

NFFR: I love what Margaret Atwood says about the very nature of stories, which is true for each of these winning pieces: "There's the story, then there's the real story, then there's the story of how the story came to be told. Then there's what you leave out of the story. Which is part of the story too."

With all three of these pieces there is an intricate world of unspoken emotional complexity which becomes clear to the reader as the story behind the story unfolds. All of them benefit from multiple readings. It is as if a novel lives in each of these. That the heft of the subject matter is far greater than the compressed glimpses we are shown. There is a strong feeling of a longer-standing narrative arc. The reader feels lucky and grateful to have glimpsed its prismatic glow.

Because *BSF* 2019 is spotlighting "Shop Girl" by Dionne Irving Bremyer, here are some words from our guest editor, Josh Russell, about this very special piece:

"Shop Girl" is an amazing meditation on family, place and work—and therefore it can be at once super-specific (those details!) and still speak to each of us, no matter where we're from, who raised us, or how we've labored.

BSF: Both "Insurance" and "Shop Girl" utilize the second person. Do you find that this point of view is especially effective for flash fiction?

NFFR: Second person stories can be ideal for flash fiction if used well. This allows the "teller" to speak directly to the reader, succinctly engaging their emotional participation. For example, Dionne Irving Bremyer's "Shop Girl" uses second person in such a way that the reader can't escape the claustrophobia of the child's early work experience. We see it, feel it, smell it. It feels personal.

"Insurance" by Elaine Chiew brings us into the story in a similar way; inescapably, we are thrust into the main character's vulnerable world, enhanced by being addressed directly. We, the reader, have somehow become one with the narrator. We're *partners in crime*, for better or worse! Second person perspective is often considered a bad choice because it can make a reader feel uncomfortable and uneasy. And this is precisely why these two stories benefit from this skilful use of second person POV.

BSF: Are there any other trends in flash fiction that you would like to talk about?

NFFR: I believe flash fiction stories are lessening in word count. We still define flash fiction as "stories under 1,000 words." But I've certainly noticed that most of the submissions we receive are in the 300- to 640-word range. As far as trends in flash, I feel as if writers are taking terrific risks, doing more experimental writing. With flash fiction, there are simply no rules. Writers reinvent the form every time they write it. It's so exciting to see such a bounty of creativity and brilliance now that flash fiction is being published widely.

Editor Biographies

Rilla Askew is the author of four novels, a book of stories, and a collection of creative nonfiction, *Most American: Notes from a Wounded Place*. She's a PEN/Faulkner finalist, recipient of the Western Heritage Award, Oklahoma Book Award, and a 2009 Arts and Letters Award from the American Academy of Arts and Letters. Her novel about the Tulsa Race Massacre, *Fire in Beulah*, received the American Book Award in 2002. Askew's essays and short fiction have appeared in *Tin House*, *World Literature Today*, *Nimrod*, *Prize Stories: The O. Henry Awards*, and elsewhere. She teaches creative writing at the University of Oklahoma.

Nathan Leslie's ten books of fiction include *Three Men*, *Root and Shoot* and *The Tall Tale of Tommy Twice*. Nathan's poetry, fiction, essays and reviews have appeared in hundreds of literary magazines including *Boulevard*, *Shenandoah* and *North American Review*. Previously Nathan was series editor for *Best of the Web* anthology 2008 and 2009 and he edited fiction for *Pedestal Magazine*. He was also interviews editor at *Prick of the Spindle*. Nathan's latest work of fiction, *Hurry Up and Relax*, was just published by Washington Writer's Publishing House after winning its 2019 prize for fiction. He is the founder and host of the monthly Reston Readings Series and he teaches in Northern Virginia. Find Nathan on Facebook and Twitter as well as at Nathanleslie.net.

Michelle Elvy is a writer, editor and manuscript assessor. Her online editing work includes *52|250: A Year of Flash*, *Blue Five Notebook* and *Flash Frontier: An Adventure in Short Fiction*. In 2018, she co-edited *Bonsai: Best small stories from Aotearoa New Zealand*. She was also an associate editor for *Flash Fiction International*. Her poetry, fiction, travel writing, creative nonfiction and reviews have been widely published and anthologized. Her new collection, the *everrumble*, is a small novel in small forms, launched by Ad Hoc Fiction at the UK Flash Fiction Festival in June 2019. Find Michelle at michelleelvy.com.

CPSIA information can be obtained
at www.ICGtesting.com
Printed in the USA
LVHW100906281019
635535LV00011B/271/P

9 780999 750162